THE
FLIRTATION
TARA SUE ME

HEADLINE
ETERNAL

Published by arrangement with Berkley,
An imprint of Penguin Random House LLC

First published in Great Britain in 2017
by HEADLINE ETERNAL
An imprint of HEADLINE PUBLISHING GROUP

1

Cataloguing in Publication Data is available from the British Library

ISBN 978 1 4722 4272 3

Typeset in Perpetua Std by Jouve (UK), Milton Keynes

Printed and bound in Great Britain by CPI Group (UK) Ltd, Croydon, CR0 4YY

Headline's policy is to use papers that are natural, renewable and recyclable
products and made from wood grown in well-managed forests and other
controlled sources. The logging and manufacturing processes are expected
to conform to the environmental regulations of the country of origin.

HEADLINE PUBLISHING GROUP
An Hachette UK Company
Carmelite House
50 Victoria Embankment
London EC4Y 0DZ

www.headlineeternal.com
www.headline.co.uk
www.hachette.co.uk

*To those who know what they want
and do what's necessary to get it*

Acknowledgments

As I'm writing this, it hits me that it's been over eight years since I finished *The Submissive*, and all I can think is WOW. Eight years ago, I never thought I'd be in the position I'm in now. Writing full-time seemed like an unattainable dream. My deepest thanks to all of you for making it happen.

Chapter One

It was never a good thing when Nathaniel West showed up at your office unannounced. Simon Neal had been a Dom for more than ten years with his New York BDSM club, and he'd heard of Nathaniel showing up five times at a club member's office. Not one of the members had ever returned.

Simon tried to think reasonably. Nathaniel wasn't very active in the club anymore, and since Simon ran a temp agency, maybe he needed a temp, or he might have just been in the neighborhood and decided to stop by. There was no reason to think he was stopping by on club business.

As soon as Simon opened the door and saw Nathaniel's expression, though, it was clear the man had not stopped by for a friendly chat.

Wondering again what the hell was going on, Simon waved the other Dom inside. "Nathaniel, good to see you. Come in and have a seat."

"Thank you," Nathaniel said, and proceeded to sit in a chair across from Simon's desk.

"Is Abby in town with you?" Simon asked, taking his seat.

He hoped never to have to play poker with Nathaniel, as the man had the ability to wipe all trace of emotion off his face. It was a bit unnerving, especially when he turned that blank face toward you, like he was doing now.

"She is," Nathaniel said. "But we are both in town just for the day."

"I'm glad you stopped by. I haven't seen you since Luke DeVaan's party."

Luke, a mutual friend, had thrown a party at his BDSM club a few weeks ago for the launch of his book, *The Muse*. Nathaniel and Abby had been at the club that night. Simon's gut clenched as he remembered who had been with them. Lynne Ryder.

He tightened his fingers into a fist. He wouldn't think about Lynne right now. He wouldn't think about Lynne ever. That chapter in his life was closed, and he wasn't going to reopen it.

Nathaniel watched him with eyes that Simon knew missed nothing. He wondered what Nathaniel was watching him so intently for.

"I'm not sure you're aware, but Abby and I hired Lynne several months ago as our nanny," Nathaniel said.

Simon's breath came out in a whoosh. "No, I didn't know." *Holy shit, Lynne works for Nathaniel and Abby.* "I'd heard she'd left the city, but I had no idea. She's your nanny?" And why was Nathaniel here? He'd said she'd been with them for months, so obviously, he wasn't stopping by to tell him they'd hired her. "Wait a minute. Is something wrong? Is she okay?"

"I can assure you she's fine. Or at least she was when I left her with Abby twenty minutes ago."

Relief flooded Simon's body. "If I may be direct, what brings you by? I know you didn't stop by to tell me you hired my ex as your nanny. But I get the distinct impression this isn't a social call, either."

Nathaniel gave him a curt nod of his head. "You're right. It's not. You see, Lynne wants to go back to school to get her teaching certificate, and a summer program opened at Columbia that could get her closer to that goal. As it turns out, Abby's blog at the news station is on hiatus for the summer, freeing up Lynne to attend the program."

Lynne was going to be back in Manhattan. Damn, but he was a bastard for how excited that made him.

You're to stay away from her. She's not for you.

No matter how truthful the voice of reason was, it still hurt like hell to hear it echo inside his head.

Simon cleared his throat. "I assume she'll be moving back to the city?"

"She'll be staying in our penthouse. It's safe, near the campus, and will offer her the peace and quiet she needs to study."

Simon nodded—he was still trying to figure out why Nathaniel was telling him this. Surely, he could have accomplished the same thing via a phone call.

"In the few months she's been with us," Nathaniel continued, "Lynne has become part of our family. The children and Abby adore her, and I view her as my little sister."

With those words, Simon knew immediately why Nathaniel had decided to stop by his office.

"Nathaniel, I—"

Nathaniel held up a hand. "Let me finish. In the last few weeks, Lynne has expressed a renewed interest in BDSM. She's told us she's going to take it slow. She doesn't even want to pursue membership at the club." Nathaniel's voice dropped, and he leaned forward. "She's under my protection, and you know what that means."

Yes, he did. He sure as hell knew.

Nathaniel's eyes flashed with warning. "You are to stay away from her. I don't know what happened between the two of you, but if I find out you've disregarded my request or that you've hurt her in any way . . ."

He didn't have to say the rest. No one crossed Nathaniel West. Not if they were smart.

"I understand," Simon said. He didn't need anyone to tell him that he wasn't the right man, or Dom, for Lynne. Wasn't it obvious that he'd figured that out ages ago? Why the hell did Nathaniel think he'd ended things with her in the first place?

Nathaniel nodded. "I'm sure you do. I like you, Simon. More than that, I hold you in the highest regard. You are one of the few people I've allowed into my playroom and to observe my Abby. But let there be no doubt about it; I will have your balls on a silver platter if you harm Lynne. Mentally, physically, or emotionally."

Yes, he understood completely, and it pissed him off that Nathaniel felt the need to threaten him over something he had no intention of doing. But he liked and respected Nathaniel, too, so he kept his growing anger to himself and stood up.

"I assure you my interest in Lynne ended some time ago. You have nothing to worry about. Unfortunately, I have a meeting at the top of the hour, so I'm going to have to cut this short."

Simon walked to the door and waited for Nathaniel to stand. Nathaniel looked as though he was going to say something further as he walked out, but at the last minute he seemed to have

changed his mind. Simon closed the door behind him, determined not to even think about Lynne.

"I think that's everything." Abby closed the closet door after
hanging up the last of Lynne's clothes. She looked at her watch.
"Nathaniel should be back soon. We're going to have a quick
dinner after we leave here and then pick the kids up from his
aunt Linda."

Lynne nodded, already missing Henry and Elizabeth. She'd
been with the West kids almost every day for the last six months,
so it had been hard to say good-bye to them earlier. Nathaniel and
Abby had dropped them off at his aunt's house so Abby could help
Lynne get settled while Nathaniel left for a mysterious meeting.

Abby had raised an eyebrow when he said he'd be back, but
beyond that she hadn't questioned him. But Lynne was certain
he'd whispered, "Later," to her when he'd hugged and kissed her
before leaving.

She had the strangest feeling the meeting had to do with her,
but that was silly, wasn't it? What could he possibly have a meeting about that concerned her?

"It's going to be so odd staying here without you guys," Lynne
said. Since she was their nanny, she had her own room at the
penthouse, but they'd never spent a lot of time in it. Both Nathaniel and Abby preferred their Hamptons estate when visiting
New York.

Abby hugged her. "You'll get used to it, and when the summer's over, you'll probably beg to come back here. Alone. For
peace and quiet."

They walked into the living room, and Lynne looked around.

The room was spacious with floor-to-ceiling windows that over-looked the city. Everything about the space screamed wealth, and because of that, she felt hopelessly out of place. She didn't tell Abby that she would never get used to it.

Her new laptop was on the coffee table, and Abby had taken care of stocking the kitchen with her favorite foods. "So you don't have to worry about shopping your first day." Abby was like that, always thinking of others and how she could help.

Lynne knew she was beyond fortunate to work for such a kind and generous family. They had done so much for her, and she loved their kids.

"Are you okay?" Abby asked, her brow wrinkling as she looked at Lynne.

"Just nerves at doing something different, you know?"

Abby nodded, but Lynne knew she didn't fully buy her excuse. Lynne was saved from any further questions by Nathaniel entering. Abby's head shot up, a million questions in her eyes, but her husband only nodded.

"Did you ladies get everything taken care of you needed to?" he asked.

"Almost," Abby said, sliding up to her husband and snaking an arm around him. "I haven't given her the 'no wild parties' speech yet."

Lynne snorted and Nathaniel smiled. "I'm thinking we can skip that. Lynne would never throw a wild party."

"Of course not," Lynne agreed. "Any party I throw will be completely civilized. We'd travel to the estate before going wild."

Nathaniel and Abby could both laugh because they knew she didn't even know enough people to throw a proper wild party.

"If you have everything settled, we're going to head out for dinner," Nathaniel said, slipping his arm around Abby. "We'll get out of your hair so you can settle in."

"I think that's everything." Abby's eyes grew teary as she looked around the penthouse. "Oh my God, I suddenly know what it's going to be like when Henry and Elizabeth go to college." She turned to her husband. "Promise me we'll keep them at home forever. They can attend college online."

Nathaniel brushed one of her tears away with his thumb. "We have a long time left to worry about that, and you might change your mind during the teenage years."

They all three said their good-byes while Abby insisted that would never happen. Ever. Nathaniel finally steered her out the door, but before Lynne could fully get a sense of the quietness that would be her normal background for the summer, she heard Abby nearly yell, "You did what?" right before the elevator chimed its arrival.

Lynne gave a little laugh, imagining the scene that was probably unfolding in the elevator. Whatever Nathaniel had done, Abby apparently didn't like it and would give her husband an earful. Lynne loved watching the two of them, because even though they lived as Dominant and submissive a lot of the time, they somehow managed to dispel every preconceived idea she'd had about the D/s lifestyle.

She appreciated how open they were and how, though they never did anything blatant in front of their children, they never felt the need to hide or keep anything from her. Of course, they never went so far as to have sex with her in the room, but there had been plenty of times when she observed how Abby would kneel at her husband's feet while he stroked her hair. Not to mention the times Nathaniel would look at her with *that look* and say, "That's one."

But most of all, she remembered the looks that would pass between husband and wife, the unspoken communication of a Dominant and his submissive. The look of a passion so fierce, anyone standing nearby could feel its heat. It stunned her how much a raised eyebrow or the simple touch of one fingertip to a collarbone could say, how much love was conveyed in a look. It shook her to know that Nathaniel and Abby had been married for as many years as they had and they still felt that way.

She shivered, remembering. But it was more than remembering. It was also longing. Longing to look at someone that way. To have someone look at her that way. And it was despair. Because she feared she'd never have an intimacy that deep.

The downside to Abby stocking her pantry and refrigerator, helping her unpack, and, for all intents and purposes, making sure she had nothing to do was that she had nothing to do. Lynne had thought moving into the penthouse on Saturday would give her plenty of time to adjust and settle, since classes didn't start until Wednesday. Unfortunately, now that she had arrived, she feared all she'd done was give herself plenty of time to be bored.

The penthouse was way too quiet for her taste. She was used to two young and energetic children. Normally her days were far from quiet. She debated turning the TV on, but she didn't feel like watching anything. She could go for a walk, but the thought of being back in the push-and-shove crowd of Manhattan didn't appeal to her either.

Her eyes fell on the built-in bookcases on the other side of the living room. Before marrying Nathaniel, Abby had been a librarian, and though Nathaniel had tried several times to get her hooked on an e-reader, Abby continually told him she preferred print books.

Lynne walked over to one set of the large and completely

filled bookshelves. Knowing Abby the way she did, she had a fairly good idea of what she'd find, and she smiled when she saw that she was right. Abby had a fondness for romance novels. All types from the looks of it. Historical, contemporary, and everything in between, including what appeared to be an alien romance. Lynne decided to skip over that one, though, from the cover, it seemed as if the alien hero had quite the six-pack.

Her fingers danced along the spine of what looked like a BDSM novel. Could she read it, or would the story hit too close to home? Would she be able to read it objectively, or would thoughts of Simon keep her from enjoying the characters?

Simon.

Dammit. Her hand dropped from the book. Her first and only attempt at the BDSM lifestyle had involved a relationship with Simon. Two years ago, she'd just been hired at a law firm and, after a conversation with another employee who'd caught her reading a BDSM romance during a break, joined an online lifestyle forum. Simon had reached out and taken her under his wing, so to speak. Now, of course, she knew he'd viewed it as his responsibility. At the time she'd been flattered and continued to chat online with him.

They'd taken things super slow, and it was months before they'd met in person. She'd really been getting into the submissive role, and Simon had been such a kind and understanding guide. He'd never pushed her beyond what she could handle, and he'd been patient as she'd tentatively explored that side of her sexuality.

Maybe that's why he'd left her, three months after their first face-to-face meeting, because she'd been too tentative. Simon was an experienced Dominant, and naturally he'd want a submissive who didn't have to be taught everything. Except . . .

She told herself to stop this unhelpful train of thought. She'd had this exact conversation in her head every other day, it seemed. Every other day and it never did any good and she never came close to figuring out why Simon had broken up with her.

The day it happened, he'd told her he was ending things with her because he didn't think she was truly submissive. At the time, she'd been too caught off guard to question him. Completely floored, she'd nodded and hadn't thought to protest, but now, if she could get that time back, she'd have asked him how he'd come to that conclusion.

For a long time after that painful day, she had shoved the submissive part of her to the side, fearing he was right and then deciding he must be. He was very experienced, after all, and surely he knew a submissive when he saw one.

But she'd eventually learned that shoving things to the side didn't really get rid of them. They just stayed there, waiting for her to come back to them. Living with Nathaniel and Abby had helped her see she was submissive. Once she'd accepted that, it seemed only natural to tell them she was ready to get back in the lifestyle.

So why, then, had she told Nathaniel she didn't want him to recommend her for membership at his New York club when he'd asked her?

Because she knew Simon was part of the club and she didn't want to see him playing with a woman he had deemed submissive enough. Watch his strong hands, hands that had felt so good on her skin, touching another woman. She didn't want to see him give someone else what he wouldn't give her.

She left the bookcase, knowing she didn't want a made-up romance, and went to her laptop. On the other hand, the online world was perfect. And real.

She logged on to a few sites she hadn't been on in more than a year. The more she read, the more she wondered why she had stayed away for so long. Being back in that world, even online, felt peaceful. It was almost as if she'd found a part of herself she hadn't realized had been missing.

Later that night she'd ditched the laptop for the BDSM novel. Always a fast reader, she tore through it, only to find out it ended with a cliff-hanger and the second book in the series was nowhere to be found. She sent Abby a text, and Abby replied, saying the rest of the series was with her in Delaware. Abby promised to drop them in the mail the next day.

With a sigh, she undressed and got ready to take a shower in the spalike bathroom. Her mind was filled with images from the book, but she put herself and Simon in place of the hero and heroine. As she undressed, she imagined him watching and, when she finished, ran her hands over her body, pretending they were his. But pretend hands were never as good as the real thing, and she gave up quickly.

She brushed her hair and couldn't help but fiddle with her brush. It was flat and square and perfect for administering a spanking. She reached back and ran the bristle side over her butt cheeks. Would he spank her with that side?

Flipping it over, she ran the wooden base along her thighs and slipped it between them. Would he spank her there?

Curious, she spread her legs wider and gave herself a slap with it. *Ow.* But it didn't sting that much, and she knew it probably wasn't the same as someone doing it to her. Sort of like the pretend hands.

Unfortunately, there wasn't anyone around to spank her, so she'd have to do it to herself.

She closed her eyes and tried to imagine a situation where Simon was spanking her. What would she have done for him to spank her? He had only spanked her once when they were together, and that had been for fun. Would he do it harder if it were a real punishment?

That one time he'd spanked her, he'd used his hand, and while it had felt good, she couldn't help but wish he'd done it harder. Looking back now, she realized she should have told him, but at the time she was embarrassed. Who actually said to someone, "Sorry, but could you spank me harder?"

It was frustrating as hell, because no matter how hard or how many times she spanked herself with the brush, it just wasn't good enough. Unsatisfied, she put the brush away and stepped into the shower, knowing her vibrator would leave her unsatisfied tonight and not for the first time.

"Master Neal," Luke DeVaan said from his place at the front desk of his BDSM club. "Haven't seen you here lately. Glad you decided to stop by."

Simon plastered a fake grin on his face. He hadn't planned to stop by the club, but following Nathaniel's visit, he had felt compelled to come. Needed the release he knew he'd find. "I decided it's been far too long since I allowed myself the release that follows a hard scene."

Luke didn't pass any kind of judgment or look at him like he was a freak. That was the comforting welcome of this club. Here, he fit in.

Luke pulled up a screen on his computer. "There are several single subs here tonight who would likely be a good match for you."

Simon cringed. *A good match for you.* But of course Luke would know what he was, and being a responsible club owner, he would want to ensure any submissive who agreed to play with Simon knew anything pertinent about him as well.

"Thanks," Simon said. "But I think I'm going to observe for a while."

Simon bade Luke good-bye and stepped into the comforting familiarity of sex and leather. His body relaxed as he breathed in the air tinged with arousal and need.

Yes, he'd made the right choice in coming tonight. He needed this. It'd been far too long. His gaze swept across the room, taking in who was present and who was available. He recognized a few subs. Most of them he'd never seriously consider playing with, but there were a few he'd taken before.

He took a seat at the bar and ordered the one drink he was allowed per night. He'd planned to use the time at the bar to scope out a willing partner, but every woman he looked at reminded him of Lynne.

Lynne. Fuck. She was here in New York. So close and yet farther away than she'd been when she was in Delaware. Nathaniel said she wasn't interested in membership at the club, but what if she changed her mind? What if she showed up?

He'd stay away from her—that was what he knew he should do.

But another part of him, a more honest part, knew he wouldn't be able to. She'd look up at him with those wide, innocent eyes that had first caught his attention when they'd met in person after chatting online for two months. Just one look and he'd been a goner. And he knew it'd be the same way if she showed up in his life again.

He needed to get her out of his system. And fast.

Standing, he nodded at a nearby submissive who'd been watching him since he walked in. He knew her. Knew she could take

him. At his nod, she approached him and dropped to her knees
before him, her head bowed.

"Are you free tonight, girl?" he asked.

"Yes, Sir," she replied.

"Are you willing to submit to me tonight?"

"Yes, Sir."

She'd been with him before; she knew how he was, what he
liked, what he needed. But he had to make sure.

"I'm going to hurt you."

Her only response was a breathy "Yes, please, Sir."

Chapter Two

On Sunday Lynne was merely bored, but by Monday she knew she had to get out of the penthouse or she'd go crazy. What she needed, she decided, was new lingerie. Lingerie always made everything better.

As far as addictions went, she thought her obsession with lingerie was relatively harmless. She limited how much she spent, though it did help that the Wests paid her well. And she usually tried to buy when the designers were having a sale. No one else knew about her addiction, because her love life was nonexistent.

Late Monday morning, she called for a cab and made her way to what had been her favorite shop for upscale lingerie when she lived in the city. She felt like a kid at Christmas, thinking about what she'd look for. Knowing she had sexy things on underneath her clothes always made her feel more confident and secure. For her first week of school, she thought a simple bra and panty set would work.

Once she made it into the store, she waved hello to the sales associate on the floor, smiling brightly when the woman scurried over to her.

"Lynne! I thought you had fallen off the face of the earth. Where have you been?" She leaned closer and whispered, "You missed our annual clearance sale. That's not like you."

"I know. It killed me to miss it. I'm living in Delaware now, but I'm here in the city for the summer."

"Delaware?" The saleslady looked at her in shock. "Why?"

"Job. The law firm I was working at let a lot of people go." She shrugged. "I was one of them. But I have a great job now, and I love it. Delaware has been nice."

"As long as you're happy." She pointed toward the back of the store. "Got some new corsets you should check out."

"I'll go look." She adored corsets. Maybe she should get a corset and forget the bra and panties. Either way, it didn't hurt to look. She walked to the corset display, surprised to find another customer already there. Not wanting to disturb her, she scooted behind her to look at the corsets to her left.

"Lynne?"

She stiffened and turned in surprise. "Anna Beth?"

The tall woman with dark hair stood with one hand on her hip. "Look what the cat dragged in. It *is* you."

Lynne gritted her teeth. She supposed she should have felt a fondness toward Anna Beth. After all, Anna Beth was the one who'd given her the final push to actually attempt the BDSM lifestyle. But Lynne didn't. The woman was a total bitch.

Anna Beth's look was cruel. "You still reading those ridiculous books, or did you become woman enough to handle a real Dom?"

Lynne would never forget the day Anna Beth had caught her

reading a BDSM romance in the employee break room. She'd shaken her head and said reading about it was fine, but living it was so much better. She then went on to brag about hot Dom after hot scene after hot sex, shutting up only when the break room was invaded by a senior partner. Later that afternoon, Anna Beth had left a card on Lynne's desk with the name and address of the club she frequented.

There had been no way in hell Lynne would want to go to Anna Beth's club. Instead, she had gone home and joined an on-line BDSM group. From there she'd met Simon. She supposed she had Anna Beth to thank, and she hated feeling like she was indebted to her.

"Actually," Lynne said, "I broke up with my Dom. I've moved to Delaware and didn't want to do a long-distance thing."

It wasn't the truth, but she wasn't about to say Simon didn't think she was submissive, and besides, Anna Beth would never know any different.

"Delaware?" Anna Beth's nose wrinkled. "Why the hell would you move from New York City to Delaware?"

"The firm let me go, remember? I had to go where I could find work."

"Too bad you don't work in IT like I do. Two words: job security." She cocked her head to the side. "So, why are you here today?"

"I'm taking classes this summer."

Anna Beth's eyes rolled. "Not here in the city, doofus. Here in this store."

Why was she still standing there, letting Anna Beth talk to her like she was? Because she was too damn nice—that's why. "I'm just looking."

"Me too. I'm looking for something my Dom will like."

The bitch had a Dom. Lynne almost felt sorry for him. "That's nice."

Apparently, that was all the encouragement Anna Beth needed. "We haven't been together long. We've played together a few times, but Saturday he came in and sat at the bar, like he was looking for someone. Then he looked at me and said, 'Come here, girl' in this sexy-as-fuck voice." She stopped talking for a minute and fanned herself.

Lynne really didn't need or want the play-by-play. "Good for you. I'm glad you found someone." *And may the Lord have mercy on his soul.*

Anna Beth nodded. "Rumor is he's hung up on his last girl-friend, who must've been a real bitch, but after that scene? Let's just say it's time for him to forget her, and I'm the one who's going to see to it that he does."

Lynne had no doubt she could do it. She remembered her as stubborn as all get out in the office, never taking no for an answer. Glancing at the black lace corset in the other woman's hands, she didn't think any man alive would stand a chance against Anna Beth. Putting them both together was a deadly combination. "I'm sure you'll have him on his knees in that corset."

But Anna Beth shook her head. "I'm not about to have him on his knees. That defeats the purpose. As long as I'm on my knees, that's all I care about."

Lynne didn't bother to tell her it was a figure of speech. Instead, she decided she'd been friendly enough and could leave without seeming rude. "Good luck with that. I hope it works out. See you around."

Anna Beth's eyes lit up. "The thing is, he's a sadist."

She paused as if waiting for Lynne to show some sign of

shock, but it didn't come as a surprise to Lynne. She'd been around the Wests, as well as their friends, long enough that she knew BDSM was practiced in many different ways.

She'd heard Nathaniel once talk about a submissive he'd played with before he met Abby. That relationship hadn't lasted long, he'd said, because the woman had needed more pain than he felt comfortable giving. Lynne respected him for that, though she always wondered about the sub. What exactly were her limits? How far did she want to go?

And sometimes, in the dark of night, she wanted to taste that world.

"Nice," Lynne said.

"It's beyond nice. It's incredible." Anna Beth's eyes grew dreamy as she talked about the scene. "He was so careful. First, he used a flogger, and from there, he went to a whip. Damn. Just thinking about it makes me horny as hell. Of course, it hurt, too, but that made it so much better. Because the pleasure that came after was like nothing I've ever experienced."

Lynne believed her. It was easy to tell from her blissed-out smile that she was telling the truth. Seeing Anna Beth so happy and content made Lynne just the tiniest bit jealous. But she stuffed that inside, refusing to let it take hold. One look at Anna Beth, though, made it clear she wouldn't have noticed anyway. She was too lost in her memories or, by the way she fingered the corset, her future plans. She snapped back to the present and looked irritated that she'd said so much.

"Not that I expect you to understand. I mean, seriously, you're basically still a newbie. A sadist would eat you for breakfast." Anna Beth laughed and turned to leave. "See ya!"

After Anna Beth left with her purchases, Lynne wandered

around the store, not as excited as she'd been before. She didn't want to look at the corsets, and the bra and panty sets now seemed boring. She blinked back tears. Shopping for lingerie was stupid anyway. No one would ever see it on her. What did it matter?

She couldn't hold back the memories of the few times she'd undressed for Simon. The way his sharp eyes had traveled up and down her body, taking her all in. At the time she'd felt as if he were memorizing her. Had he? Did he ever think back to their time together . . . and if he did, would he remember how she'd stripped for him?

No matter how many times she told herself it was time to move on, she found she couldn't. She'd tried pursuing a vanilla relationship after Simon, and halfway into the date, she'd known it wouldn't work. Though she knew numerous people in BDSM circles who would have jumped at the chance to set her up with someone, her heart wasn't in it if it wasn't Simon. Instead, she'd settled for neither kink nor vanilla. Anytime she felt lonely, she'd remember how it had all started.

They had chatted online for two months before she'd agreed to meet him in person. Even then, she'd met him in a public place and had a friend go with her. Most people she'd mentioned her meeting to had told her she was out of her mind to meet a guy she knew only from the Internet.

At times before they first met, she'd thought she might be crazy to have said yes. She only had to watch the news to hear all about how easy it could be to open yourself up to danger. But she didn't feel in any danger with Simon, Ever. He had a calming presence about him that immediately set her at ease.

The day they'd met in person, finally, he'd asked her to dinner, and though her friend had gone with them, she'd ended up leaving before the entrées arrived. Simon had been kind, and later, when they'd progressed to where they'd talked about BDSM, he was patient and gentle.

Which was why it had come as such a surprise when he'd broken up with her.

She often thought back to their time together, trying desperately to figure out what she'd done wrong. He'd known from the beginning that she had no experience as a submissive. They had even gone to Nathaniel and Abby's Hamptons estate to watch a scene. She had been mesmerized by the two of them. And when it was over, Nathaniel had carried Abby out of the room and Simon had taken her out to their pool and they'd talked.

It was that day that she'd finally begun to understand and accept that she was a submissive at her core. She'd told Simon the same thing and he'd looked so happy.

Yet it wasn't but a few months later that he'd left.

"Lynne?"

She looked up. The saleslady was watching her with worried eyes. "Are you okay? Do you need help finding something?"

Lynne looked around. Somehow, she'd made it to the pajama section. Strange. While she loved pretty undergarments, she'd never bought fancy pajamas before.

Suddenly, she knew exactly what she was going to buy. It was time for something new. Time for her to leave the past behind and move forward. It was time for a new Lynne. And New Lynne wore naughty pajamas to bed.

She turned and smiled at the saleslady. "Actually, you *can* help me find something."

Simon answered the phone on the second ring without looking to see who it was. "Hello."

"Master Neal," a familiar voice answered.

"Master DeVaan?" Simon asked with a frown. Luke calling him was almost as unexpected as Nathaniel coming by. At least this time he knew the conversation wouldn't be about Lynne.

"Sorry to bother you at work, but there's a situation at the club I wanted to make you aware of."

"Okay." Simon tried to imagine what could possibly need his attention. After all, his visit almost a week before had been his first in months.

"Last Saturday night, you ran a scene with a sub by the name of Anna Beth?"

He had. It wasn't the first time he'd played with Anna Beth. She knew what to expect, and she always kept things uncomplicated. The club members knew he wasn't looking for a long-term relationship.

"Yes," he said, answering Luke. "Is something wrong with her?" He hadn't hurt her, had he? He'd been so careful, cutting the scene short when he'd noticed she wasn't into it, and he'd extended her aftercare. But what if he'd missed or overlooked something? Had he hurt her and not known it? Had he let the scene go too far before he'd stopped?

That's why you shouldn't go to the clubs, you freak. You're going to really hurt someone one of these days.

"No," Luke said, putting his mind at ease. "Nothing of the sort. In fact, quite the opposite."

"How's that?"

"She's been at the club looking for you every night this week."

"She what?" That didn't even sound like Anna Beth.

Luke gave a snort. "I'm not sure what you did, but whatever it was, she wants more. A lot more. She asked the front-desk staff for your phone number."

"Dammit."

"They didn't give it to her, of course, and they let me know immediately, but either way, I wanted to let you know."

Simon ran his hand through his hair with a sigh. He shouldn't have gone to the club last Saturday night. For damn sure, he shouldn't have played with Anna Beth. He should have sat at the bar and observed like he'd told Luke he was going to.

"Thank you," he said. "I appreciate it." He just wasn't sure what he was going to do with the information.

"I'll take care of her from this end," Luke said. "I hope it won't keep you away."

"No, of course not," Simon said, but in his head, he was thinking, *There is no way I'm going back there.*

"Good," Luke said. "I was hoping you'd say that."

"It'll take more than Anna Beth to keep me away."

"I also wanted to know if you'd be interested in doing a demo at an upcoming BDSM conference I'm working on."

Simon bit back the groan that threatened to come out of his mouth. He had the strangest feeling he'd just been played.

"What type of demo?" Simon asked.

"Single tail."

"Do I get to pick which type?"

"Of course," Luke assured him. "I'm putting together a few sessions of advanced techniques and figured anyone who had a submissive that into them after the scene you did needs to be the one to lead the demo."

"I'm going to take that as a compliment."

"As well you should," Luke said. "And you can pick your own submissive, too. Hell, make a weekend of it and stay for the entire thing. It runs Friday afternoon through Saturday night. Most people don't leave until Sunday."

At least he had time to find someone. He thanked Luke, told him he'd be in touch, and said good-bye. Now, where the hell was he going to find a submissive?

Lynne turned on her laptop. She was going to act courageously again. She'd done it before and met Simon, so why shouldn't she use the Internet a second time to find someone different?

Because she was New Lynne, she decided she needed a new username. The old one had too many ties to Old Lynne. And Simon. She picked SassySubGirl, because in her mind, New Lynne was a little sassy.

But New Lynne wasn't that far removed from Old Lynne, because she went to the same online boards. She told herself it wasn't so she could look for Simon, even though his name was the first she searched for. She smiled when she saw it because it hadn't changed. SirSimon looked to be a well-respected member.

Judging from his posts, he wasn't with anyone. His writing was informative with a touch of humor sprinkled in for good measure.

God, she missed him.

She drummed her fingers on the table. She needed a plan. He'd left her because he didn't think she was a submissive. What if she could prove she was? Maybe if he could see that she was serious about it, he'd take her back.

She wanted to send him a message, but she didn't think it'd be a good idea to approach him right away without any activity under her username. She needed to be patient and approach him in a few days.

The first thing she did was post a few comments on the threads he'd recently been part of. She had her location set to New York and wondered if he'd notice. Then she kicked herself. Why would he? There were a ton of people from New York.

She turned her laptop off when she finished posting. Classes started the next day, and she had a few things to get together.

The next afternoon she returned to the penthouse happy. The classes so far were just what she'd hoped for, and everyone was so friendly. Any misgivings she'd had were gone. She called Abby quickly to tell her and to once again thank her for everything she and Nathaniel had done, but her voice mail picked up so she left a message.

She had some homework to start, but at the moment she was too hyped up to sit still long enough to do it. Instead, she pulled out her laptop to check and see if she had any messages from her online postings. She'd purposely set her profile up in such a way that she didn't get an e-mail whenever someone replied.

There were several replies to her and quite a few private messages. But her attention was drawn to one. From him. Her fingers trembled as she clicked on it to open.

SassySubGirl,

Welcome to the boards. I hope you find what you're looking for. I noticed you're in the New York area and wanted to invite you to the NY State board. I included a link below.

Best,
SirSimon

She leaned back in her seat. Wow. She really hadn't expected to hear from him that fast. Granted, it was only a welcome e-mail and probably a form one at that. More than likely, he sent the same thing out to everyone who joined from the area. But still.

It was communication from Simon. And it was more than she'd had since they'd broken up. She debated whether to respond, finally deciding he was the one who had made the first move; she was only throwing the ball back to his side of the court.

She hurriedly typed out her reply.

SirSimon,

Thank you for the kind welcome and I appreciate your invite to the NY board. I'll check it out. I'm assuming you are from the area? I'm new in town.

Best,
SSG

She hit the SEND button before she could have second thoughts and decide to delete the e-mail. She felt a little guilty at the "new in the area" line, but she justified it by telling herself that she lived in Delaware and was only in the city for the summer. It wasn't an out-and-out lie.

Though she wasn't sure Simon would agree.

How long would it take for him to reply? What if he didn't reply? What if he replied and told her to leave him alone?

She turned the computer off with a sigh. She'd drive herself crazy with the *what-ifs* if she didn't stop. He'd write back or he wouldn't. It was out of her hands, either way.

The penthouse was too quiet. She got up and turned some

music on, but it didn't sound the same as Henry and Elizabeth running around asking her what they were going to play next. It hit her then that if she became a teacher, all her days would be like this. Once she got home from school, there would be nothing to greet her except an empty house.

She wasn't getting any younger, and she wasn't dating anyone seriously. Hell, she wasn't dating anyone casually. Maybe she should have taken Nathaniel and Abby up on their offer to get her into their New York club.

But no, it was more than the dating she longed for. She wanted a connection with someone, a person she could call when the best thing ever happened or who would be there for her when her world came falling down.

She turned the music off and went into the kitchen to make something for dinner. Cooking for one sucked, too. At least most of the time she was able to eat the leftovers for lunch. If you looked at it that way, cooking for one was a good thing.

But deep down, she knew better.

Later that night, she turned her computer back on. She told herself not to expect anything. It had only been a couple of hours, and he probably hadn't had time to reply to her e-mail. It wasn't until she opened her e-mail and saw a message waiting from him that she realized she would have been horribly disappointed if he hadn't replied.

It was short, just a few lines.

SSG,

Welcome to the city. If you're into the local scene, I can recommend a few places for you.

Let me know,
SirSimon

Her reply was likewise brief.

SirSimon,

Thank you for the offer, but I'm really not a club kind of a girl. I would like to say I'm looking for something a bit more private, but that seems very forward for me to say in an e-mail.

—SSG

He didn't reply for several minutes and she thought he might have been done for the night. She was just getting ready to turn off the laptop when a message came through.

Message me

He'd added his private e-mail address so she could reach him privately and not have to go through the messaging system of the online site. Her hands trembled, fingers poised over the top of the keyboard, wondering what to type.

She opened the message window using the account she'd created with her assumed name and typed in his address. Basic. Basic was good.

—Hello.

—Is that you, SSG?

—Yes.

—Thank you for messaging me. Why don't you tell me exactly what you're looking for?

She hesitated. This was so similar to the discourse they had gone through the first time they had met. She couldn't help but wonder if he did this frequently. Was it possible he went from girl to girl, finding a new online partner whenever he got tired of the old one?

She didn't want to think that of Simon; despite the shock of his sudden dismissal of her when they were dating, she wanted to think she was different. Her fingers flew over the keyboard.

I'm not 100 percent sure what I'm looking for. I don't want to do anything public, because of my profession. I understand the confidentiality aspect of play, but I can't do it in public.

There was a pause, and then his words filled the screen.

I don't play very much in public either, but I would never try to set up anything with you privately. And I suggest you don't meet anyone privately that you meet online.

She rolled her eyes. Did he think she was stupid?

I'm twenty-five. I'm well aware of how to handle myself online.

There was a pause before his reply came back.

Just doing my part to ensure you're safe.

Dammit, she hadn't meant to insult him.

Forgive me, Sir. I just didn't like the implication that I don't know what I'm doing, or that I'm not smart enough to check someone or something out before jumping into it.

Let's start over. I'm SirSimon. No need to call me "Sir" at this time. I believe a Dom has to earn that title.

She smiled. This was the Simon she knew.

I'm SSG. And thank you.

There was another moment's pause. And she feared he was going to ask her name.

Pleased to meet you, SSG. Tell me about yourself.

She breathed a sigh of relief, pleased that she wouldn't have to reveal any secrets yet.

I'm in school, working toward getting a teaching certificate. What do you do?

I manage an employment agency. Mostly temps.

How long have you been in the lifestyle?

About fifteen years. You?

Not very long. That's another reason I didn't want to go public. I know a friend who met someone online and they played that way for a while.

Is that what you're looking for?

She paused, not sure how to answer that. What was she looking for? What did she want to get out of this? Finally she typed:

I'm not sure. I think it's a good place to start.

Simon looked at the blinking cursor on his computer screen. What was he doing? Why was he talking to this newbie? Was this enough of a distraction? Another online relationship?

He told himself that was a foolish line of thought. He wasn't trying to start a relationship. He was being nice to a new person in the area who happened to share a common interest with him.

He drummed his fingers on the desk, unable to keep his mind from wandering to Lynne. He had met her online, and the relationship had proceeded from there. For whatever reason, after her, he had never gone back to online dating or used the Internet as a way to meet potential subs. Maybe it was time he tried again.

I think you're right, SSG. I think you're right. I would like to continue our conversation, but unfortunately, I have an early meeting in the morning, so I have to log off for tonight.

I understand. Have to get ready for class tomorrow.

He suddenly didn't want to let her go without making sure they could talk some more.

Chat again tomorrow night at 7:30?

He couldn't help but smile at her reply:

Yes. Thank you.

He stood up and stretched. He hadn't lied about the early-morning meeting, but he knew it would be worthless to go to bed at this time. His conversation with the sub known as SSG had made him rethink things. But he wanted to bounce ideas off somebody first.

He dialed a familiar number.

Luke answered on the first ring. "Hello?"

"DeVaan, it's Simon."

"Simon, what's happening?"

"Can I ask you something? What are your thoughts on online relationships?"

There was a shuffling sound from the other end of the phone. "Hold on. Let me get you off speaker."

Simon held back his groan and hoped only Meagan had been listening in. "Next time tell me I'm on speaker, why don't you?"

"Sorry, man." There was more shuffling, and this time Simon heard a female giggle. "Had my hands full, if you know what I mean."

Meagan, Luke's submissive, was obviously spending the night at his place. "I can call back tomorrow at a better time for you."

"No. Hold on." There were a few whispers, but nothing Simon could make out. "Now, tell me what's going on."

Simon questioned whether he should've called Luke in the first place. He felt a little silly now, especially since it had interrupted whatever the two of them were doing.

"I wanted to know your thoughts on online relationships."

"I don't have a lot of experience, personally," Luke said. "Several members of the club have, though."

"Let me rephrase. What do you think of somebody like me having an online relationship?"

"When you say someone like you, you mean . . . ?"

Simon took a deep breath. "A sadist. That's what I mean."

"I mean no disrespect," Luke said. "But how exactly do you practice that online?"

"I wouldn't be in this case. It would just be more like taking the edge off." He thought back to Lynne. "I've done it once before. We ended up meeting, but nothing really happened along those lines." He didn't add that he had been the one to break things off.

"And you think you'll have a different outcome the second time?"

"I don't think I'm going to get anywhere by doing nothing. And let's face it: the club scene hasn't really worked for me lately."

"In that case, give it a try. You could start with small things and work your way up. Who knows? You might find someone who's willing to meet you and take some pain at the same time."

Simon laughed. "My perfect sub is out there just waiting for me to take the reins?"

"Yes, and to beat her with them."

They both chuckled and hung up. Simon went back to his

computer, feeling encouraged, and typed out an e-mail message to SSG. If she wanted to play online, he'd see how serious she was. He proofed the e-mail and set it up to send automatically at six the next morning.

Chapter Three

Lynne chewed her cereal while reading Simon's e-mail. It had really been a fluke that she'd checked it at all before she went to class. But for whatever reason, she hadn't been able to sleep well and had eventually gotten up much earlier than she usually did.

Thank goodness for flukes, she decided, as she read through it one more time.

SSG,

I've been thinking about what you said and examining my own goals at the same time. I think you made a valid point last evening when you said trying something online was a good place to start.

I don't do a lot of this. In fact, I've done it only once before. But if you'd like to try, I will as well. I don't want

*to start anything too strict or overbearing. We don't
know each other well enough for that yet.*

*That said, I would like to get to know you better. If you
are not comfortable with a phone call, perhaps we can
continue with the instant messaging. Please send me an
e-mail and let me know which you would prefer. Also, if
you're free tonight, let me know that as well.*

*Best,
SirSimon*

She hadn't dreamed it. Simon had e-mailed her and wanted
to try something online. Tonight. Suddenly, the next twelve
hours couldn't pass fast enough. She typed back a quick reply to
let him know that she would be free.

All day, the e-mail kept coming to mind and she had a hard
time concentrating in class. She told herself not to be distracted;
she was in the city to learn and to get her teaching certificate. And
yet he was always there, in the back of her mind. Waiting.

She made it home at three o'clock in the afternoon. In what
she thought was a Herculean effort, she would not allow herself
to log in to her e-mail until she finished all her schoolwork. Fortunately, there wasn't much to do. Unfortunately, it was only
five thirty by the time she finished. Unable to wait any longer,
she turned on her laptop to check her e-mail. She was only
mildly disappointed to see that she did not have a response from
Simon, since she didn't really expect there to be anything.

She busied herself making dinner and then spent an inordi-
nate amount of time cleaning the kitchen. It was stupid, as the
kitchen was spotless to begin with. And even if it wasn't, the
Wests had a cleaning crew coming by weekly.

She looked at the clock when she finished. Six thirty.

Unable to stay away from her laptop any longer, she glanced over the recent posts on the online BDSM forum. She saw someone who might have been Anna Beth and made note of the username. She wondered if her Dom had liked the corset.

Unable to think of anything else to do, she decided to exercise. Jumping jacks. Stretches. And those god-awful yoga poses Abby had shown her once.

Finally. Finally. It was time.

She hurried over to the place on the couch where she had set up her laptop. Earlier in the day, she told Simon that she preferred to chat online instead of on the phone. She wasn't sure she could disguise her voice enough so that he wouldn't recognize it.

Was she being dishonest? Yes. She knew she was, and she knew Simon wouldn't like it if he ever discovered the truth. In the short time they had been together, he'd repeatedly stressed how important honesty was between partners in a BDSM relationship. She told herself she wasn't being *that* dishonest. But deep inside she knew she was wrong to lie to him.

But that wasn't going to stop her.

At eight o'clock exactly, her laptop chimed with an incoming message.

Hello, SSG.

It occurs to me that I should call you something more meaningful. Unless you like to be called SSG.

It didn't escape her attention that he was talking as if she were there. He had not asked her if she was present. Nor had he asked

for any sort of confirmation that she was, in fact, at the computer. It only proved what she knew. When Simon issued commands, he expected them to be followed.

She thought quickly, not wanting him to think she hadn't
been ready and prepared for his message.

**Hello, Sir. SSG does sound a bit too clinical. You may
call me Faye.**

It was the first thing she thought of. Her middle name.
She didn't think she had told him her middle name when they
were dating. There was always a chance he knew somehow, but
hopefully he would chalk it up to a coincidence. She also decided to add the "Sir," believing this new step warranted the
title, as it showed her trust in him. If he didn't think so, he'd
tell her.

Thank you, Faye.

It was ludicrous that she felt so happy at pleasing him. Especially since it wasn't even a name she went by. The fake name
wasn't a rare thing, though. A lot of people played with assumed
names. The practice was actually encouraged. But even so, she
knew Simon would expect her to tell him who she was since
they had a history. Maybe she would. One day.

But that day wasn't today.

He wrote again.

**I thought tonight we'd just get to know each other a bit.
How does that sound?**

It sounded like a perfectly reasonable thing to do, and if it had been anyone else, she would have jumped in with both feet. Even knowing him the way she did, the thought of getting to know him better thrilled her.

Yet she wasn't as thrilled about him finding out about her. For the entire conversation, she'd be worried something would strike a chord with him and he'd put two and two together and realize it was her. The only other option was to lie, and that was an even worse idea.

She knew there was nothing to do but agree.

Sounds great, Sir.

His reply came quickly.

I'm aware I'm an unknown. If I ask you anything you don't feel comfortable with, just tell me. You don't have to answer.

And that was her out. If he asked her a question and she felt the answer would give away who she was, she would tell him she didn't feel comfortable discussing that topic.

With a sigh of relief, she replied.

Thank you, Sir.

His first question made her smile.

If you weren't talking with me right now, what would you normally be doing?

It definitely wasn't the question she'd expected. Far from it. She glanced at the quiet television. Should she tell him?

What the hell? Honesty it was.

You know those reality TV talent shows?

The singing ones?

Yes. I'm secretly addicted to those.

And one's on right now?

Yes.

Turn it on. BRB

She turned the TV on and waited for him to come back.

Okay, I'm back. So tell me who in their right mind told this guy up now he could sing?

She laughed, and by the time the show went off the air two hours later, she couldn't remember a time she had had so much fun watching TV. Simon had a snarky side she hadn't known about. They said their good-byes and good nights, and Simon said he'd e-mail her soon.

She left her laptop open while she got ready for bed, and she was surprised to find an e-mail waiting for her after she showered. Just seeing his name with an unread message made her feel aroused and tingly.

She flushed as she read the message.

Faye,

I had such a great time chatting with you tonight. I really enjoyed getting to know you better. I know we both want to take this slow, but I thought if you'd like to continue, we could add a few things along the way. Not too much and not too quickly.

If you agree, your orgasms now belong to me. You will not play with yourself or come without permission. I know we're only communicating via the Internet right now, but believe me when I say that I'll know if you're telling the truth.

Yours,
SirSimon

She bit the inside of her lip. After chatting with him, she'd planned to spend some quality time with her vibrator once she finished her shower. The thing was, she still could. Simon wouldn't know she'd read his e-mail tonight. For all he knew, she'd turned her laptop off and wouldn't read it until tomorrow morning.

If she played it that way, she could still have a marathon vibrator session tonight. It would be so easy. . . .

Her shoulders slumped.

She couldn't do it. She had never been a good liar, and though she wasn't sure what he meant by "I'll know if you're telling the truth," she believed him. Either she'd feel so guilty, she'd con-

fess, or he'd use his supersonic Dom sense to pull the confession
out of her. She'd lived with Nathaniel and Abby long enough not
to discredit the existence of supersonic Dom sense.

Not only that, but being around the Wests had proven that
things Did Not Go Well for submissives who disobeyed or lied
to their Doms. The truth of the situation was, she'd told herself
she wanted to experience another BDSM relationship. She'd sought
one out. A Dom controlling a submissive's orgasms was fairly
standard and something she'd expected.

But dammit all. Why did it have to start tonight?

"Why didn't I turn the computer off before I took a shower?"
she asked the empty penthouse.

She stared at the screen as if Simon were going to send another message, saying, "Kidding! Just seeing if you were paying
attention." No such message appeared, though, and after five
minutes, she typed back a reply.

SirSimon,

*I can't remember the last time TV was so much fun.
Thank you for sharing your evening with me.*

My orgasms are now yours.

—Faye

It felt all kinds of awkward signing her name as Faye. Looked
weird on the screen, too. She checked her regular account to
see if anyone had sent something to that account. Just when she
was getting ready to turn the laptop off for the night, once and
for all, an instant message popped up.

Your response pleased me. You may make yourself come once tonight.

Her response to him was swift.

Thank you, Sir.

She decided that sometimes it paid to be the good girl who couldn't lie.

Chapter Four

After two weeks of playing online games with Faye, Simon was more sexually frustrated than he'd ever thought possible. He blamed himself. He'd always believed that he shouldn't give his submissive an order that he couldn't obey himself.

Since telling Faye that her orgasms belonged to him and allowing her that one night to come, he hadn't given her permission again. Because he was a damn sadist, he decided the same would apply to him. He had no idea two weeks could seem so long.

Things were moving along great with Faye. They chatted by computer almost every day and he'd been pleased to discover that while she appeared sweet on the surface, she had a sarcastic streak that matched his. Things had progressed to the point where he'd really like to meet her in person to see if they were compatible off-line as well as online.

He would have to tread sofly and with care before they took such a step. Asking to meet a woman who only knew of him what he'd told her online was a huge step. He knew he wasn't a deranged maniac, but that didn't mean there weren't plenty of predators on the Internet who were.

Before he asked her to meet in person, it might be better to push her a bit more online. So far he'd been pleasantly surprised that she didn't whine or pout about the lack of anything sexual between them. Perhaps it was time he rewarded her behavior and added a touch of something physical.

Or as physical as you could get while communicating via a computer. A webcam would be a nice place to start.

He sent her a quick e-mail asking if she had the ability to do a video chat.

Three hours later, he was packing up to head home and he still hadn't heard from her. That wasn't typical. Normally she'd reply almost immediately. He hoped he hadn't turned her off by suggesting a webcam. Surely, she didn't think they were just going to get by on e-mails and web chats?

He wouldn't push, though. Setting up a video chat with an almost perfect stranger would certainly give most women pause. At least it should. If she didn't reply before their scheduled eight p.m. chat time, they could discuss it then. If he needed to pull back, he would. No matter how blue his balls were.

By the time he made it back to his apartment, he'd accepted the fact that the video chat wasn't going to happen. Not that night anyway. He'd convinced himself to such a degree that he didn't check his e-mail until six thirty. He almost dropped his phone when he saw she'd replied.

SirSimon,

Please forgive the tardiness of this reply. I wanted to ensure I had the capabilities to do a video chat and to

make sure I knew how to work it (new computer). I can
get everything to work except the audio output. The
input works fine, so I can hear you, but you won't be able
to hear me. I hope that won't be an issue. I can get it
looked at and hopefully fixed, but not in time for tonight.

Best,
Faye

Well, damn. He smiled. He hadn't been expecting that. It was always nice when someone surprised him in a good way. No, the audio situation wasn't optimal, but she would be able to hear him so they could work around it for now. It would be similar to him commanding silence from a submissive or gagging her.

He hurriedly went about getting something together for dinner, while at the same time planning what he was going to do in a few hours. He'd just sat down to eat when his phone rang. He looked at the display. Luke.

"Hello?" he answered with a frown. He couldn't think of a reason why Luke would be calling him.

"Master Neal," Luke said, "I'm so sorry to interrupt your evening, but I have a situation. You know I wouldn't bother you otherwise."

Club business. That couldn't be a good sign. "What's the issue?"

Luke sighed. "Anna Beth."

Of fucking course it was Anna Beth. He cursed the day he'd decided to go to the club and played with her. "What now?"

"One of the staff has information that she's been going around telling the subs you've played with before that the two of you are together, but you can't go public because of her job. She's threatening anyone who expresses any interest in you."

"What the fuck?" Surely Luke was making this up. "I don't even go to the club that often."

"I know, but the fact is, she's causing trouble and dragging you into it. I don't believe her, but some people are accepting what she's telling them." Luke took a deep breath. "I can deal with her myself, but it'd send a stronger message if you could come down and be part of it as well."

Simon closed his eyes, knowing what the answer would be but having to ask the question anyway. "When?"

"She's coming tonight at eight."

It had to be eight. Of course it had to be. "I had plans, Luke."

"I understand. I'll take care of it."

But he shouldn't have to. Yes, he was the club's owner and manager, but Anna Beth was a problem because of Simon. "I'll be there," he said, forcing each word out.

"I truly appreciate it."

"Yeah, no big deal." Except it was. He hung up after telling Luke he'd be at the club by seven forty-five, and then he wrote Faye.

Faye,

I am so sorry. I've had an urgent issue arise that I have to take care of tonight. We're going to have to reschedule. Tomorrow night, same time?

Apologies,
SirSimon

In less than two minutes he had his answer.

I'd love to take care of any issue you have that's come
up, but I have the feeling my help isn't needed in this
instance. Maybe next time . . .

—Faye

He chuckled at her sense of humor and again bemoaned the
fact that he was going to have to spend his time taking care of
Anna Beth instead of experiencing what had the promise of
being a very enjoyable video chat with Faye. He'd have to make
it up to her at some point in the future.

However, even with the promise of a future video chat in the
back of his mind, Simon arrived at Luke's club in a foul mood.
It was a Thursday night and the crowd was heavier than a normal weeknight. In some ways that was a good thing; it meant
there would be more witnesses. On the other hand, the very
fact that there would be more witnesses meant that Anna Beth
would be even more upset. Not that he cared; he would have
nothing to do with Anna Beth after tonight.

Not for the first time, he went back over the last scene they'd
had together. He'd started out slowly. He'd played with her before, but it had been a long time and he'd wanted to get a feel
for what she could handle before he did anything too extreme.
It'd quickly become obvious, to him at least, that Anna Beth
was not a masochist.

Yes, she'd begged him for more. She'd said she wanted it
harder, but he had enough experience to know when he was
being lied to. Worse yet was the way her body flinched. It wasn't
a movement of acceptance and need for the pain he gave, but
rather a shrinking away.

It'd made him feel even worse than when he'd started in the lifestyle. He decided then and there the situation was too fucked-up for words. Unfortunately, Anna Beth wouldn't use her safe word, so he'd decided to end things with the whip. He went light on her. Too light, really. And he made sure she got off. But that was it. He'd walked out of the room they'd been in and realized it was the first time he'd ever played that he didn't get hard during the scene.

And now the chit was telling people they were exclusive?

What the ever-loving fuck?

He nodded to the doorman.

"Good evening, Master Neal," the man, whose name Simon couldn't remember, said. "Master DeVaan is expecting you. He said to tell you he'd be waiting at the bar."

"Thank you."

Normally, after he arrived at the club, he would stop by the locker room. But this was no normal night and he had no reason to stop there. He pushed open the double doors leading to the main area of the club.

As expected, there were a good number of people in attendance, but he didn't stop to talk with any of them. He wanted to get this over with as soon as possible. He looked over the crowd at the bar until he spotted Luke.

The club owner had his back toward him, and at the moment, his attention was focused on the lovely blond woman at his side. Simon recognized Meagan Bishop, who was not only Luke's sub missive, but also the newest morning news anchor for the local television station. Their heads were close together and they appeared to be discussing something intently.

They didn't move apart when he walked up to them, and it wasn't until he cleared his throat that they stopped whispering.

"Sorry for interrupting," he said when the two finally looked his way.

"Master Neal." Luke slid off the barstool. "Thank you for coming. I apologize again that you had to change your plans."

"Nothing that won't keep," he said.

"Meagan was just telling me about a conversation she overheard in the ladies' locker room." He nodded toward her. "Tell him what you told me, sweetheart."

Meagan was frowning, which wasn't like her at all. Not only that, but something lurked behind her expression that gave Simon the chills. "I was in the shower area, but no one knew I was back there because I wasn't exactly showering." She cut her eyes to her Dom.

"She was cleaning the tile floor," Luke explained. "When she gets stressed, she stress-cleans. She also turns into a brat. The shower needed cleaning and I needed her to stop being a brat. Win-win."

Meagan didn't look like she so much agreed with the win-win part. "Anyway, I was out of sight, but I could still hear the conversations in the dressing rooms. One of the unattached subs, Gennie, started talking. Said you were part of an online group and that lately you've been out of pocket more than normal because you found an online play partner."

He gritted his teeth. Now they had a bigger problem than just Anna Beth. Seemed as if Gennie needed a refresher course in basic confidentiality. He glanced at Luke.

"I'll deal with Gennie," Luke said with a wave of his hand. "There's more."

"Turns out, she was talking with Anna Beth," Meagan continued. "And Anna Beth told Gennie that if she found out who the whore was you were seeing behind her back, she'd hurt her."

Simon was at a loss for words. None of what Meagan said made any sense. Why would Anna Beth insist they had a relationship? And what the hell was she doing threatening a woman she didn't even know when there was nothing at all between her and him?

"That right there is enough to get her kicked out of the club," Luke said. "I don't allow any type of threat made of that sort, joking or not."

"I don't think she was joking, Sir," Meagan said, worry still etched across her features.

Luke put his arm around her. "It's okay. I'll take care of it."

"But what about . . . ?" She glanced first to Simon and then back to Luke. "Should someone tell her?"

"I'll leave it up to you," Luke told Simon. "With whatever you decide to tell your other partner or partners. It's probably only talk, but I'd hate to make that assumption and be wrong."

What Simon didn't want to do was tell Faye to watch her back. Seriously, if he didn't know what she looked like, how would anyone else find her? But like Luke had said, the possibility of something happening if he didn't tell her was more than he could imagine.

"I think she's safe, but I'll let her know the threat has been made," Simon said. Damn, he hoped she didn't run away after he told her. Odd as their relationship was, he enjoyed the time they spent chatting together. "What's the plan for Anna Beth?"

Luke was rubbing Meagan's back. "She thinks you two are in a relationship? I say break up with her. Here. In public, so there's no doubt."

"She sounds a bit unstable," Simon said. "You don't think that will set her off?"

"I think she'll handle it okay since you're the one she's ob-

sessed with," Luke said. "From what I gather, she's all about making you happy."

"Obviously not, or she wouldn't threaten the woman I am
with."

"After you break up with her, I'll be here with some backup
and we'll escort her out," Luke said. "I'll talk with her. If I think
she was exaggerating for dramatics, I'll send her through the
retraining program. If I think she was serious, I'll let her know
she's no longer welcome and that if she comes back or threatens
anyone in the group, we won't hesitate to call the police."

"Here she comes, Sir," Meagan whispered.

Simon looked over at the women's locker room and, sure
enough, Anna Beth had just trotted out and was making a beeline toward him.

This was not going to be pretty.

Lynne knew it was crazy, but she kept her laptop out and ready
on the off chance Simon was able to finish whatever it was that
had come up for him and was able to chat. She'd spent so much
of the day stressing out about how to do the video conference
and not reveal who she was, it was sort of a letdown now that it
wasn't going to happen.

She'd found a mask to cover her face. It was a no-frills black
number that covered what she thought were her most telling
features. The eye holes were small enough that she didn't think
anyone viewing her from a webcam could tell much about them.
There was nothing remarkable about her nose, but the mask
covered it as well. The only part of her face left uncovered was
her mouth.

She'd made up the part about her audio output not working.

She hated to add in another lie, but she couldn't think of a way to change her voice on such short notice. It was only a little lie in the big scheme of things. And the only other option would have been to tell him she didn't want to do it, and she was too curious about what he had planned for the video chat to tell him that.

And what was her reward? Some emergency had popped up and he'd had to reschedule. She'd been so worked up about what she hoped he had planned, she'd let loose and joked with him. Now, though, she had an entire evening of nothing planned.

If she really tried, she probably would have been able to convince herself that she'd brought it on herself for lying about the audio. Served her right. She'd always been told that there were consequences for lying.

However, she'd do the same thing again, if given the chance. More than that, she knew she would keep up the pretense of the audio output not working. Consequences be damned.

The *ping* of an e-mail made her jump.

Simon!

She grabbed her laptop and headed to the couch to read. Her smile withered when she saw it wasn't Simon, but Anna Beth, and it disappeared completely as she read the e-mail.

Lynne,

I know we aren't close, but you're one of the few people I know in "real life" who's into kink. It's been crazy at work, and then shit has been going down at the club. You would not believe what happened tonight. I'm still furious.

I'm telling you in case you decide to revisit a club—be careful who you confide in. The place I was going to always seemed to be on the straight and narrow (or at least as straight and narrow as a BDSM club can be! LOL).

Someone at my club has been telling vicious lies about me. Straight-up LIES. Not only that, but when I showed up, the Dom I told you about? He said he wasn't going to play with me anymore. In front of EVERYONE. It was so humiliating.

Ridiculous, right?

I don't know who would do such a thing to me. Maybe someone who wants my Dom?

I don't know.

I don't know anything.

I don't even know why I'm telling you all this.

—Anna Beth

P.S. I mentioned running into you to Lori—remember her? She had this old picture she asked me to send. Good times, right?

Lynne sat and stared at the screen for several long seconds, trying to process what she'd read. It was a serious matter to be kicked out of a club. And to have it done in such a manner? That made her think there might have been some credibility to what was being said. But she couldn't tell that to Anna Beth.

Actually, she decided, it was late, she was tired, and it appeared Simon's issue or whatever was still ongoing, and he wasn't going to be able to chat. She closed her laptop. Plenty of time tomorrow to worry about the hot mess that was Anna Beth.

She clicked on the picture and smiled at Old Lynne at a party, three years ago. Though why Lori wanted her to have it, she didn't know.

She changed into her pajamas, got into bed, and picked up her e-reader to read a few more chapters in her current BDSM romance novel. As she read, her hand drifted to the hem of her gown.

It would have been so easy to let her fingers keep going and to grant her body the relief it craved. But she stopped, her fingers curling into a fist. She had more self-control than that. She'd held up over the past two weeks. Surely, she could handle a few more days. With a heavy sigh, she put her e-reader on the nightstand and turned out the light. Maybe, if she was lucky, she would have a sex dream.

As it turned out, it was longer than a few days before they had a chance to get together again. The day after he had to cancel their evening appointment, he was called out of town. His regretful tone was evident through the e-mail he sent. He explained that as manager of the temp agency, he'd been asked to step in and visit a major client that was having personnel issues.

Lynne told him it was fine—she actually had exams to study for. As fun as it was to be spending time with Simon again, she couldn't forget that her first priority was to study. She looked at the few days that Simon was away as a chance to buckle down and focus on her coursework.

The other thing she did was reply to Anna Beth. She kept it

simple but straightforward, thanking her for the picture, telling her that she was sorry to hear that Anna Beth had had such a rough time at the club, and yes, it was uncalled for and totally unacceptable for someone to spread lies. She almost added that she hoped the club's management found out what happened soon, but changed her mind. For one, she wasn't certain Anna Beth was telling the complete truth, and if she wasn't, Lynne didn't want her to think she somehow condoned anything she had done.

She contemplated telling Simon about it, but didn't want him to think she had whack jobs as friends. Eventually, she decided to keep the e-mail to herself, thinking maybe she'd talk to Abby about it in the future.

Finally, six days after they were supposed to have their video chat, she received a message from Simon right before she headed to bed.

Faye,

I'm finally back. Missed chatting with you. Reschedule video chat for tomorrow at 8 p.m.?

—SirSimon

Lynne was both excited and nervous. She was still going to say that her audio output wasn't working. Maybe make it sound like it was more expensive to fix than she felt she could spend. She replied, telling him that eight p.m. the next night was perfect and she was looking forward to finally connecting.

As she turned her computer off, her blood suddenly ran cold.

Had Simon ever been to Nathaniel and Abby's penthouse? Holy shit. How had she not thought of that before? She didn't know, and she couldn't very well ask Abby. She glanced around the living room. There were so many pictures displayed, of the kids, the entire family, and Nathaniel and Abby alone. She could make sure the pictures weren't seen, but if Simon had ever been in the penthouse, there was no doubt he'd recognize it.

She carried the laptop to her bedroom and looked around. This room was nondescript enough. It could have been a bedroom anywhere, and there was no reason to believe Simon had ever been in the Wests' guest room.

She messed around with the setup until she found a spot she liked. The entire time she was thinking that it was really a good thing Simon had gotten called away last time. If he hadn't and she hadn't realized what she just did . . .

She didn't even want to think about it.

With a smile of satisfaction, she went to bed, hoping to dream about Simon and all the dirty things they could do together on video the next night.

Simon looked at his date with Faye as a reward for the hellish week he'd had trying to fix the issues at the Miami company that had kept him occupied all week. He'd never cared much for traveling, at least not by himself. Traveling with a submissive? That he could handle.

The trip to Miami wouldn't have been as bad or seemed as long if he'd been able to chat with Faye. But before he left, she'd told him that she had some special projects due for school that week and they would take up a lot of her time in the evenings. Though it was difficult not to send her a message, he respected she was working and working hard. Simon appreciated her work ethic. But enough was enough. They'd both been working hard. It was time to play a bit.

The day of the planned video chat, he was able to keep himself busy, and for that he was grateful. Time went by a lot quicker when he had something to keep his mind occupied. Even still, his plans for the evening were never far from his mind. He just wasn't able to let himself dwell on them for long.

By the time eight p.m. came around, he was ready to play, tease, and torment Faye. She hadn't been able to get her audio output fixed yet, and while that was disappointing, it wouldn't ruin the session.

He logged in and was immediately met with the picture of a woman kneeling in a large bedroom. After chatting with her online so many times, he'd wondered what she looked like. With a sigh, he realized he still wasn't going to know because she wore a mask.

He snorted and then smiled. It was absolutely brilliant. He actually wished he'd thought of it. Tease her a bit. But no, all she had to do was look up and she'd see him.

Since her head was down, he decided to just watch her for a few minutes. She knelt with perfect form. He had told her not to be naked, knowing they hadn't reached that level in their relationship yet. But even so, he could still appreciate her lithe body and graceful curves.

Her hair was pulled back into a ponytail, and it looked to be a light brown. He wished he was in the room with her so he could run his fingers through the strands and feel how soft they were.

The room itself spoke to a certain wealth, which surprised him. The way she'd set up the computer's camera, he could see out a window. The room appeared to be on a high floor, judging by the tops of buildings he could see through the window. And for Manhattan, it was a very large bedroom.

She had told him she was twenty-five, and even with her mask on, he remembered she was several years younger than his thirty-three. How had she achieved so much at such a young age? He had a sudden urge to confirm she wasn't married. That's all he needed—to have an angry husband burst into the bedroom.

He hoped to God he hadn't gotten involved with a married woman.

Or maybe her parents were wealthy.

He wasn't going to let her social status impact the way he saw her. If she was well-off, what did it matter to him?

Except he found it difficult to believe she couldn't afford to get her computer fixed.

"Faye," he finally said, "you look perfect. And I have to say, that's an amazing view you have there."

Her position had relaxed when he praised her, but at the mention of the view, she tensed up. Interesting. There was definitely something there. He'd look into it later. For the moment, he wanted to play.

"I like the mask, too. Adds a bit of mystery." And, as he'd hoped, at his words of praise, her body once more relaxed. "Look at the camera, Faye."

She hesitated. It was only for a split second, but it was noticeable. Then she lifted her head and looked into the camera. He couldn't see her eyes because they were obscured by the mask, as was most of her face.

Yet he had the most peculiar feeling of familiarity. He couldn't put his finger on what exactly it was or where he might have seen Faye before. But it was there and it shocked him.

As the silence grew longer and longer, Faye's chin lifted a notch. That was it. There was something about the way she held her head that struck him as something he should be able to identify. Damned if he knew what it was, though.

She had probably visited a club he frequented. That was the only thing he could think of. She didn't appear to be studying him closely, but then again, he had his picture online on the boards they were part of.

"Stand up for me, Faye," he said, wanting to see all of her.

She moved gracefully to her feet, so gracefully, he was almost certain she'd had some sort of dance lessons. He couldn't help himself from asking, "Are you a dancer?"

She shook her head, and the uncomfortable tension in her body returned briefly. Very interesting. For some reason she was not fond of him guessing and observing details about her life. At least those that she didn't freely share.

He should have left it at that. So she had secrets? Didn't they all have things they didn't want others to know? He hadn't exactly been straightforward about his particular needs either.

Because he couldn't yet. Besides, for whatever reason, she intrigued him more than he'd anticipated. This woman who lived in a multimillion-dollar apartment and yet couldn't afford to get her computer fixed, who obviously needed the release that came with being a sex submissive, yet kept her identity a closely guarded secret.

Suddenly, it hit him. She was probably the daughter of an elected official. That had to be it. Now that he thought about it, it made perfect sense.

Damn, but this could become a nightmare.

The last thing he needed to do was to get involved with a politician's daughter. Let word get out that someone in those powerful circles was involved with a sadist? No, thank you.

The only problem was, he didn't think he cared. He was taken with her.

And he wanted more.

"You're very lovely, Faye," he said. "If you're comfortable, take your shirt off."

He hadn't planned on asking her to strip, but with the thought that she could be related to a powerful political figure came the realization that their time might be limited. He wasn't going to waste one minute.

She didn't hesitate with following his command. As soon as the words left his mouth, she unbuttoned the pajama shirt she had on and pushed it over her shoulders.

She anticipated I'd have her take her shirt off.

The thought hit him as soon as her shirt landed on the floor. She'd anticipated he'd have her strip, and she'd prepared by wearing a shirt that buttoned as opposed to one she had to pull over her head, which could dislodge the mask. That knowledge turned him on.

"Did you wear that shirt hoping I would ask you to take it off?" he asked. She didn't have a bra on underneath. There was nothing but Faye. And she was gorgeous.

She nodded, and not for the first time, he wished he could have heard her say, "Yes, Sir."

She had to get that computer fixed. Either that or they had to meet in person.

He clenched his fist. No. Not yet. It was too soon. If he brought up meeting her now, he'd scare her. He needed to take things slow and fully earn her trust.

"Very nice," he said. "That pleases me. Once we log off, you may bring yourself to climax."

She nodded, both in acknowledgment and thanks, he assumed.

"Now I want to see the rest of you," he said. No, he hadn't

planned on having her strip, but now that he'd started, he'd be damned if he'd go halfway. "Keep your eyes on me."

There was that tilt to her head again. The one he thought he should have been able to place. But it made sense. If she was a politician's daughter or related to a public figure, he might have seen her on television, or perhaps she shared mannerisms with her famous relative. That would explain why she seemed so familiar and yet he couldn't place her.

She slowly pushed her tiny shorts down, and he was pleasantly surprised to see that she didn't have any underwear on either. He stifled a groan. The sight of her standing in that bedroom, naked. Oh, the things he could do to her.

"Very nice, Faye."

He thought he saw a hint of flush under the mask.

"I don't want to push you too much on our first video call, so I'll let you get back to your evening." He paused, thinking. "Actually, I'm going to give you a bit of homework. I want you to write a fantasy before you make yourself come and send it to me before you go to bed."

She gave a quick nod and mouthed a *Yes, Sir*.

"Good night, Faye. Talk soon."

Lynne fell on the bed as soon as Simon disconnected. While not as stressful as she'd thought it might be, it had been stressful enough. She lifted her head to see what was visible outside her window. She hadn't even thought about the window giving her away.

She was fairly certain he wouldn't be able to tell anything other than she lived on a high floor. Though, frankly, that was enough.

She grabbed a nearby blanket and wrapped it around her

shoulders while she thought back over the session. It had been hot as hell to strip for him. She knew he'd been affected as well. More than once, she'd heard a low groan she was almost certain he didn't think she heard.

The only thing missing was now she wanted to be in his arms. That was the downside to doing everything online. She missed the touch of another person. Most importantly, she missed his touch.

She remembered the day they'd gone to Nathaniel and Abby's. After the scene was finished, Nathaniel had taken Abby into their bedroom for aftercare, and Simon had taken her to the Wests' indoor pool.

If she closed her eyes, she could almost feel it. The warmth of the room. The slight humidity that seemed so out of place for the time of year. But mostly, she remembered Simon. He'd pulled her into his lap, and they'd sat and talked about the scene they'd just witnessed.

Then, ever so slowly, his hand had inched down her body to the waist of her jeans. With a coarse voice, he'd told her to unbutton them, and when she had, his knowledgeable fingers had slipped inside.

She could probably come again just remembering.

And she might try, but not yet. First she had to write a fantasy. Funny, as she remembered that day, she also recalled having lunch afterward with Nathaniel and Abby. They had been talking, and Abby must have said or done something, because the next thing she knew, Nathaniel had commanded his wife to tell them all about the fantasy she was thinking of.

Lynne thought she'd be embarrassed, listening to a woman she barely knew talk about her sexual fantasy. But Abby didn't seem to mind, and neither did Nathaniel or Simon, so she acted like it was no big deal as well.

And what a fantasy it had been. Abby was a complete exhibitionist, and her fantasy involved playing in front of people. It had definitely been hot. Lynne remembered how aroused she'd gotten, sitting at the table, listening to her describe how the scene played out. Her own fantasies, however, were much more private.

Though she knew some people in the BDSM world enjoyed public playing, the idea never did much for her. She always envisioned herself as a private player.

Would she play in public with Simon? She hadn't thought about that. He was a very experienced Dom, and she assumed he played in public. They had exchanged checklists back when they were dating. Where had she put his checklist? She didn't think she'd thrown it away.

She stood up, the blanket falling from her shoulders. She wanted that checklist. She needed that checklist. A quick search of the papers she'd brought only served to confirm what she'd thought. She didn't have it with her, which meant it had to be in Delaware.

How could she get it without alerting the Wests that she was involved with Simon?

Her fingers drummed on the bookshelf. She'd think of something. Until then, she had a fantasy to write.

Lynne scrolled through the private New York message boards on Sunday while she ate dinner. She had chatted online with a few of the members and found everyone both interesting and informative. Most of them were also members of Luke DeVaan's club, which was the one club she didn't want to join because it was also Simon's, as well as Nathaniel and Abby's.

She'd thought about going to one of the other clubs but hadn't taken any steps to do so. Before she went to one of them, it would be a good idea for her to find someone who was already a member so she could have a reference.

She took a bite of her salad while deciding which of her contacts she should ask about going along to visit a club. She was just getting ready to send a message to a woman she'd chatted with several times when a new message from Simon to the group popped up.

All interest in messaging the other member fell away as she read Simon's post.

All,

I'm in need of a submissive to partner with during an upcoming single-tail demo session. Possibly involves weekend stay.

Message me for details.

—SirSimon

Lynne was hit with an overwhelming urge to do the demo with him. She knew there were plenty of persuasive reasons not to do the demo. Could she even do it and keep her identity a secret? Plus, she'd never had a single tail used on her. It was ridiculous to even think about offering to do the demo.

And yet she couldn't stop herself.

SirSimon,

I would be willing to do the demo with you. As long as I can keep my mask on. Please let me know the details.

Best,

Faye

She sent the message quickly so she wouldn't change her mind. Once it left her in-box, she logged out, not wanting to see evidence of what she'd just done.

Shit. She was an idiot. What had she been thinking?

She didn't have to think too hard to understand what had made her send the message and volunteer: She didn't want Simon playing with anyone except her. It was idiotic and childish and several other adjectives, but the truth was the truth. Just because it was idiotic or childish didn't make it any less true.

Even though she'd logged out of the boards, Lynne hadn't turned off the laptop, so when the private message came through, she was alerted with a chime.

She knew it had to be Simon. She didn't communicate via private messages with anyone else. Part of her dreaded reading the message for fear he'd ask what the hell she was thinking.

But she knew the curiosity would eventually win out. To counteract it and hopefully prove to herself that she had at least a shred of self-control, she wouldn't let herself read his message until she finished dinner.

It was the quickest she'd ever eaten.

When she finished, she told herself she now had to clean the kitchen. Five minutes later, the kitchen was more or less cleaned, so she took her laptop and curled up on the couch to read.

Are you sure? I thought about asking if you would be interested, but I know you mentioned you didn't like to play in public. If you'd like to help me, I'll take you up on it. I'm okay with you wearing a mask.

Her first thought was *OMG, he's okay with it*, quickly followed by *Holy shit, now what?*

First things first though.

Yes, Sir. I'm sure.

He wrote back almost immediately.

Great! Will e-mail details.

She logged in to her in-box to wait for Simon's e-mail and noticed a new message from Abby. Lynne smiled as she read it.

Abby talked about how the kids were doing and added that they all missed her and looked forward to her coming back in the fall. She told her about how Elizabeth decided to play school in order to show Henry what a teacher did. Lynne giggled as she read Abby's account of Henry telling his sister to "Sit down. Not Lynne."

Abby ended by telling her that they were planning to come to the city the next Friday because they had meetings on Saturday. The kids would be staying with Nathaniel's aunt but, if it wouldn't be a bother, could she and Nathaniel stay in the penthouse Friday night?

Lynne nearly laughed with the ridiculousness of it. Abby was asking if it was all right for them to stay in their own penthouse?

She sent back a quick reply telling her that they could come whenever they wanted, that she looked forward to seeing them next weekend, and to give the kids hugs for her.

Once she'd sent the e-mail off, she noticed Simon had sent the information. A quick look told her he'd included more than only the information; he'd also added his checklist.

She took a deep breath, exhaled loudly, and began to read. When she finished, she read it again. The entire time, one thought kept repeating in her head: What had she gotten herself into?

Chapter Five

"You want me to *what?*" Nathaniel hadn't snorted coffee out of his nose the way she thought he might, but only because he'd already swallowed before she asked her question.

Thinking back, it probably wasn't the best subject to bring up over Saturday morning breakfast. Especially since he and Abby were meeting with several potential donors for his non-profit in a few hours. And though she probably thought she was being helpful, Lynne didn't think Abby standing in the doorway saying, "Just listen to her, Nathaniel," was helping her case.

Lynne took a deep breath. "I want you to use a single tail on me. I want to know how it feels. And I'm asking you because out of all the Doms I know, I trust you the most."

"That's what I thought you asked." Nathaniel turned his cool blue eyes her way. "No."

"But——" she started.

"No," he repeated.

"Nathaniel . . ." Abby said from the doorway, wearing a frown on her face and shaking her head.

He pointed at his wife, which stopped her from walking farther into the room. "The answer is no. It is not open for discussion, and before you decide to argue with me, I'll remind you I don't have a problem using a single tail on you."

Abby didn't flinch. Instead, she put her hands on her hips and gave him an evil look. "You can be such a fucking hardheaded ass at times."

Nathaniel silently stood up and made his way to his wife. He looked beyond angry as he invaded her space, but Lynne had to give Abby credit; she stood her ground.

"Did you just curse at me, Abigail?" he asked in that low and dangerous voice of his.

Abby didn't back down, but Lynne saw her swallow hard as her husband towered over her. She noted Abby was wearing her submissive collar. Definitely not the time to call her husband an ass. Especially since she was in the room. Her stomach ached, because she knew Abby had done it for her. Lynne just wished she'd gone about it a different way.

"Yes, Master," Abby said, "I did, and I'm not sorry because it's true."

Nathaniel stood still, watching her for several long seconds. It was only when Abby dropped her gaze that he spoke. "I appreciate your honesty, but it's not enough to spare your ass a chastisement you won't forget. You disrespected me, and you did it in front of Lynne. Go wait in the playroom while I contact our prospective donors and let them know we'll be delayed."

Nathaniel and Abby had only recently had the playroom added to the penthouse. Lynne knew because they'd traveled to the city a few times during construction. Most of the time, when they came to the city, she'd remained in Wilmington because Nathaniel's family had wanted to watch the kids. But there had been a weekend she came to the city with the Wests because the rest of the family had had the flu.

She recalled Abby mentioning the playroom was soundproof, and Lynne had never been happier than she was at the moment. Whatever was happening between Nathaniel and Abby, she didn't have to listen to it.

But it was somewhat of an awkward position to be in. She couldn't picture herself hanging out in the kitchen or living room while the two of them were locked away. She finally decided to go to her room to study. Besides, she wanted to see if Simon had sent her a message.

Her in-box was empty, so she settled in to her favorite reading chair and studied for an upcoming exam.

She was so engrossed in the material, she jumped when Nathaniel cleared his throat.

"Sorry," he said. "Didn't mean to scare you."

"It's okay," she said. He didn't look like a scary Dom anymore, standing there in her doorway. He was back to the Nathaniel West she knew. The one who gave piggyback rides to his son and played princess teatime with his daughter.

"Abby's in the shower," he said. "Can I talk to you for a minute?"

"Sure." She stood up so they could walk into the living room. She'd been his employee long enough to know he would never cross the threshold to her room while she was in it alone. She'd thought he was crazy at first but had come to realize it was just one of his boundaries, and she actually grew to appreciate the gesture. It made her feel even safer with him.

He sat down on one of the couches, and she took a seat in a

nearby chair. As she would've expected, he got straight to the point.

"Why the sudden interest in single tails?" he asked.

She almost told him to forget about it, that she wasn't interested anymore. But she couldn't bring herself to lie to him. Besides that, he would see right through her. She took a deep breath and looked him straight in the eye.

"I've met someone online. He's doing a demo, and I asked him if I could help," she said.

"And you've never met him? In person?"

"No." She wondered if she should tell him it was Simon. Would knowing make it better or worse? "But there's no need to worry. I've checked his references and talked with others who have played with him before."

"I don't like the sound of this. At all." He was frowning. "There's so much that could go wrong."

She knew all too well. And though she might be able to ease his mind by telling him who the Dom was, something told her not to.

"How about this?" she asked, as an idea came to her mind. "I can't tell you his name because that would break confidentiality. But I can tell you that he's a member at Luke's club. He's been vetted there."

It was then that Nathaniel studied her. Really studied her. She didn't know how Abby dealt with it. After just a few seconds under that intense stare, she was ready to spill all her secrets and make up a few, too.

"That means I probably know him." Nathaniel's voice was very calm and even, but she had a feeling he was anything but.

"That's why I don't want to give you his name." She hoped

she sounded firm, and she forced herself to look in his eyes. "Confidentiality."

Yes, working for Nathaniel, she had learned a lot about him. His love for his family, his integrity in business, and, along with those, the fierce belief that their lifestyle remained confidential. And she knew that what he requested of others, he also gave.

He leaned back in his seat, obviously not happy with the way the conversation was going. He slapped his hands on his upper thighs. "Unfortunately, I can't argue with that."

She breathed a sigh of relief.

"However," he said, "you do need somebody to work with you before you do a demo. And I don't feel comfortable doing that."

She dropped her eyes. Dammit. Now what was she going to do?

"I happen to have a good friend who is somewhat of an expert with single tails. You may have met him. Daniel Covington?"

Yes, she knew Daniel. She knew his submissive, Julie, better, though. She hadn't been aware that Daniel was an expert with the single tail. She liked him. He was a lot more easygoing than Nathaniel, and Julie was really sweet, too. Lynne thought she could work with Daniel.

"Yes, I know him and Julie."

"The only thing is," Nathaniel said, and Lynne had the suspicious feeling she had just been backed into a corner, "I know Julie just about as well as I know Daniel, and while I don't think she'll mind if he practices his single-tail skills on you, I'm fairly certain she would want to be there in the room watching during the scene."

She thought that was okay. It would actually be better, she

thought, for Julie to be in the room. Maybe it would take away any awkwardness.

"I wouldn't have a problem with that," she told Nathaniel.

"Good. She had a friend who was injured once in a bullwhip scene. She's trying to overcome her fear, but Daniel is going very slowly. Right now he's only letting her watch."

Sasha. That was the friend, Lynne thought. She had met her not too long ago. And though she was injured, it didn't seem to have had a lasting effect on her. She was now wearing the collar of one of the Delaware members.

Nathaniel stood up. "If it's okay with you, then, I'll give Daniel a call and set something up. I'm not sure if you want them to come here, or if you should travel back to Delaware."

"I'm open to whatever Daniel would like to do."

He nodded. "I'll call you and let you know what he says."

As it turned out, Nathaniel and Abby ended up staying until Sunday night. They'd planned to head back to Delaware on Saturday afternoon, but apparently, the kids were having so much fun with their cousins, they extended the weekend.

Since they were staying longer, Nathaniel scheduled a business dinner with several of his executives for Saturday night. As soon as she heard his plans, Lynne turned to Abby.

"Are you doing anything?" she asked. "Because if not, I have a few things I want to talk to you about. Girl things," she added with a quick look at Nathaniel.

Abby covered her shock nicely, she thought. "Oh? Okay. Sure." She exchanged a look with Nathaniel. Lynne ducked her head and tried not to be jealous, but man, she wanted to have a relationship like that, where you could communicate without saying a word. When a lifted eyebrow and a slight upward curve of a lip said more than words ever could.

"And 'girl things' means it's time for me to leave," Nathaniel said. He kissed Abby, whispered something in her ear, and nodded toward Lynne. "Have a good evening."

Abby waited until he left before she started her inquisition. "Tell me everything. I want his name, what he looks like, how you met him. Everything."

Though she was smiling when she asked, Lynne knew Abby was completely serious about getting all the details. She stood up.

"Wine first," Lynne said, making her way to the kitchen.

"Of course." Abby followed. "What was I thinking?"

"Clearly, you weren't."

Once they each had a glass, they went back into the living room. Lynne sat on the couch and tucked her legs underneath her. "Before I tell you anything, I have to know, how much of what I tell you will you tell Nathaniel?"

Abby took a sip of wine, sitting beside her. "I don't have to tell him anything if I don't want to. But if you're doing something dangerous or illegal, I'll tell him, for your sake."

Lynne nodded. She would expect nothing less. "I promise it's nothing illegal and the only danger is to my heart."

Abby looked a bit worried. "Who is it, Lynne? Because I have a feeling it's not a stranger."

Lynne could no longer keep her secret. It was time to share. "Simon."

Abby went completely pale and didn't say anything for several long seconds. Or at least Lynne thought they were only seconds. It felt like hours, but surely it hadn't been that long.

"Holy fucking shit," Abby finally said.

Lynne didn't think she could breathe, much less speak. Out of all the ways she imagined Abby reacting, that wasn't one. She'd thought maybe she'd be shocked, but only slightly. More than anything, she thought Abby would be happy.

Abby had seen her upset when Simon had first broken up with her. Hell, they had gone to Luke's book debut party at the club not too long ago and Simon had been there. Abby had been the one to come to her that night when they had gotten home to make sure she was okay.

It had been to Abby that she'd first mentioned rejoining the BDSM community. Looking back, Lynne could see her desire to get into it for what it was. An attempt to get back into the lifestyle, yes, but more than that, a longing for Simon.

Not only did Abby's reaction shock her, but it hurt.

She pulled her knees up to her chest and hugged them tight. "I don't know what the big deal is. You know I still have feelings for him."

"Has Simon said anything about Nathaniel?" Abby finally asked.

The question stumped her until she realized that of course Simon wouldn't have said anything about Nathaniel. "No." She shook her head. "He doesn't know it's me."

Abby's eyes narrowed. "I think you need to explain to me what exactly is happening."

Lynne took a deep breath and gave her a quick rundown of the last few weeks. By the time she'd finished, Abby had a look of total horror on her face.

"What?" Lynne finally asked.

"This is a mess and a half."

Lynne knew she was in a bit of a pickle, but surely it wasn't as bad as Abby was making it out to be.

Abby drained the remainder of her wine. "I should have poured us something stronger."

"I don't know what the big deal is." Lynne shrugged, trying to play it off like it was nothing. Maybe if she could get Abby to agree it was okay, she could start to believe it herself. "I mean, I get that I should have been up front about who I am, but if he gets to know Faye, what's it going to matter that her name is really Lynne?"

"It'll matter when Nathaniel finds out. He went to Simon's the weekend you moved in and told him you were off-limits. That if he so much as thought about contacting you, he'd have him kicked out of Luke's."

"He did what?" Lynne remembered how Nathaniel had disappeared in the middle of moving her in. She'd wondered where he'd gone. Wondered what could have been so important that he had to go right then and couldn't wait another minute. She didn't give Abby a chance to reply to her first question before asking her second. "Why?"

"Why?" Abby rolled her eyes in what was the first halfway humorous thing she'd done in almost an hour. "You have lived in his house for almost a year, right? I mean, you get that he has the most asinine and broad definition of *protection* known to man. And I mean that in the most loving way possible. His behavior can be infuriating."

"But why would he care about me and Simon? I'm his nanny."

Abby made a *tsk* noise and patted her knee. "Oh, honey, you really don't know him, do you? Yes, you are his nanny. You live in his house and take care of his children. You're family, whether you like it or not. And as part of his family, you get to be on the receiving end of his innate determination to protect you."

Lynne still didn't get it.

Abby must have sensed her confusion. "Nathaniel saw how upset you were when Simon broke things off with you. As your protector, he will do anything in his power to keep you from experiencing that again. And if that meant threatening Simon, that's what he'll do."

The enormity of what Nathaniel had done was starting to sink in. "Shit. And here I thought my biggest problem was going to be a slightly pissed Simon." Now she was going to have to deal with Nathaniel as well.

"Have you given any thought to telling Simon who you really are?"

"Yes. That's one of the reasons I wanted to talk to you tonight. I was thinking about telling him before we did the demo, but now . . ." She bit her lip. "Now I think I'll leave my mask on. He told me I could, and there's really no reason to tell him."

"I disagree."

Lynne turned her head sharply to look at her. "Why?"

"Look, I'll be the first to admit that Nathaniel was a bit forward in his warning Simon away from you. Trust me when I tell you that I gave him an earful about what I thought when he told me. But keeping your identity from the man acting as your Dom? That's never a good idea. It's not going to end well, Lynne."

Lynne couldn't put a finger on the expression Abby gave her at first, but then she realized what it was—pity—and her body grew cold with fear. "Oh my God, you're going to tell Nathaniel, aren't you?"

Abby sighed. "I should. I really should. If for nothing else than I won't be able to sit for a month if he finds out I knew and didn't tell him. But I gave you my word I'd only involve him if what you were doing was dangerous. And while I think it's not smart, it's nothing that's going to put you in harm's way. At least not physically. So, no, I won't tell him, but I strongly recommend you think about telling him and also come up with a plan for how to handle this."

Come up with a plan. Yes. Lynne knew she could do that. She'd come up with a plan to tell Simon who she was *after* the demo weekend.

"I'm not going to like whatever thought you just had, am I?" Abby asked, a bit of her normal humor back in her voice.

"Probably not," Lynne agreed, and then quickly changed the subject.

The West family left the next afternoon. Nathaniel's aunt brought the kids to the penthouse that morning, and Lynne was delighted she was able to spend some time with Henry and Elizabeth. She hadn't realized how much she'd missed them until they'd left and she was once more alone.

She didn't like the quiet. The weekend had been so much fun, spending time with everyone and feeling like she was part of a family again. It was stupid, since they weren't her family. Her parents lived not too far from Wilmington, and she saw them often enough. Maybe it was that Nathaniel and Abby were such an integral part of her kinky family.

The thought of a kinky family made her smile. And even more than that, before Nathaniel had returned home the night before, Abby had taken her aside and showed her where the playroom key was. "Just in case you want to look around. You know, familiarize yourself again with things."

Since her classwork was all caught up and she didn't have any upcoming exams, that's what she decided to do. She took the key and let herself into the locked room.

It was small. Smaller than she had envisioned it. But then again, the penthouse hadn't been built with the intent of adding a BDSM play space. Abby and Nathaniel had renovated a closet and an extra bathroom into the room where she now stood.

Small, yes. But still large enough for two people. She ran her hand absentmindedly across a padded wooden and leather bench. She could picture Simon in this space. Maybe after she confessed who she was, she'd invite him over.

Or maybe that's how she'd tell him.

She'd ask him if he wanted to come to her place, and once she gave him the address, he'd know. She bit her lip as she imagined it. Maybe she'd just tell him the building and she could meet him downstairs. If he knew it was her, he might not show up. Especially considering what Abby told her Nathaniel had said to him.

Damn, she'd gotten herself into a fine mess. But looking around the room, she was filled with a deep longing, and she knew if she could get back with Simon as his submissive, everything would be worth it.

Nathaniel called Lynne a few days later to tell her that Daniel could work with her on Saturday and that Luke had offered his club, late Saturday morning, before it opened to members. It sounded perfect, and she told him yes, not believing her good luck until she hung up.

It struck her that there was no way it was a coincidence that the session would take place at Luke's club. Sure, that's where Nathaniel was a member, but it was also where the man she'd admitted she'd been seeing was a member. Other than the play-room in the penthouse, both the Delaware house and the Hamptons estate had private play spaces. Not only that, but she was almost positive Daniel had his own room as well.

So, why hold the session at Luke's?

She fingered the numbers on her phone, tempted to call Nathaniel back and say that wouldn't work. But if she did that, he'd want to know why, and she couldn't come up with a reason to tell him other than "I think you're up to something."

She could just imagine his response if she told him that. No doubt he would say, "Yes, I am, and what are you going to do about it?"

Nothing. There was nothing she could do about it. The best thing she could do was to go along with him and to be hyper-aware of any snooping he did to try to find out Simon's identity.

As it turned out, though, Nathaniel didn't even show up at the club. She spent all week thinking up ways to keep him from finding out about Simon, and when she walked into the club, only Daniel and Julie were present.

"Hey, Lynne," Julie said, coming up and giving her a hug. "How's your summer going?"

"Busy. I'm in class most of the day." Lynne had always liked Daniel's submissive. She was friendly and funny, one of those people who made you smile by just being near.

"That's what Abby said." Julie leaned close and whispered, "Though it sounds like you're not all work and no play."

Lynne felt her face heat. "True enough."

Daniel walked up to them. He was incredibly handsome,

with dirty blond hair, blue eyes, and a smile that made everyone feel welcome. "Hello, Lynne."

"Hello, Master Covington," Lynne said. "Thank you so much for agreeing to work with me this morning."

"Oh, it's no trouble," he said, his eyes dancing with mischief. "It's been entirely too long since I've been able to take a whip to someone."

Julie punched him on the shoulder. "Stop. You'll scare her."

"I'm fine," Lynne said, but a twinge of fear had indeed started to worm its way around in her belly.

"He doesn't get to use a single tail very often because it's been a hard limit for me." Julie took her by the arm and they started walking toward the play area. "I've only recently asked him to use one on me, and we're taking it slow. Today's the second scene I've witnessed since . . . well, for a long time."

"Master West said he was the best." It felt weird calling him that, but she knew that the house rules stated she call him that and not "Nathaniel" or "Mr. West."

"He is," Julie said. "Though I'm a bit biased. I think he's good at everything."

Julie's love and respect for her Dominant were obvious not only in her words, but also in the way she looked at him. A look that was reciprocated every time Daniel's gaze made its way to Julie. Lynne couldn't help but feel a little jealous. Who wouldn't want a man to treat her that way?

They entered the main room of the club, and Daniel motioned for them to sit down on one of the couches set up near the equipment. Julie sat by his side, and Lynne found a spot on the love seat across from him.

"I have a few things to go over before we start." At Lynne's nod, he continued. "Do you have any medical issues I should know about?"

"No, Sir."

"What's your safe word?"

"Red."

"I'll be using a flogger on you before the single tail. Do you have any concerns or issues with that?"

"No, Sir." She was more excited than anything.

"Are you okay being topless?"

"Yes, Sir."

"From what I've gathered from Nathaniel, you've never been in a single-tail scene?" Daniel asked.

"No." Her eyes drifted over to where the play space waited.

"What types of floggers have you experienced?" he asked.

Lynne shifted uncomfortably in her seat. He would ask that. She'd known he would, but still, she was hesitant to tell him. "I've never had anyone use a flogger on me."

Daniel frowned. Surely Nathaniel had told him how relatively inexperienced she was. Or maybe not, judging from Daniel's expression. It really wasn't Nathaniel's place to tell him, because when it came down to it, the only person who really knew about her experience level was Lynne herself.

She forced herself to look at him. "I have only a little bit of BDSM experience."

Daniel's lips had tightened into a line. "And you think a single tail is the best way to get more experience?"

"No." Lynne shook her head. "The Dom I'm with is doing a demo with the single tail and I want to do the demo with him."

"And this Dom thinks it's acceptable to jump from nothing to a bullwhip?"

Dammit. She couldn't exactly explain that Simon didn't know.

If she told Daniel that, she had no doubt he'd refuse to move forward. From the corner of her eye, she saw Luke's office door open, and she knew he'd be joining them in a matter of seconds. She needed this conversation over by the time he made it to them.

"We've discussed, at length, our plans and steps going forward. This is what I want." It wasn't a lie. Not really. It was just a creative way to avoid the question.

Daniel nodded in understanding, but he clearly wasn't happy.

"Hello, Master Covington," Luke said, walking up to them, and for the first time, Lynne noticed he wasn't alone. Anna Beth was at his side. Her eyes were wide and her mouth went slack when she recognized Lynne, but almost immediately, she schooled her features into indifference. "This is a submissive from the club who is going through a retraining. I asked her to come in to observe, but she's not allowed to speak."

It was Lynne's turn to stand in disbelief. Anna Beth was a member of Luke's club? How did she not know that? That meant the Dom she wanted and the sub who supposedly told the lies about her were also members here.

Along with Simon.

Daniel nodded tersely. "If you could have her go with Julie and sit beside her." He gave Anna Beth a look of warning that spoke more than any words he could have said.

Luke motioned with his hand for Anna Beth to go to Julie's side.

Daniel turned his attention back to Lynne. "I'll give you ten minutes to get ready. Meet me over by the St. Andrew's Cross closest to the bar."

"Yes, Sir," Lynne said, and hurried off to the locker room to change. She didn't have a lot of fetish wear, but she had a few items. For today, she changed into a short skirt and a tight tank top that showed off her midriff. She'd debated wearing high heels, but had eventually decided not to, thinking that she'd rather be barefoot for her first encounter with a single tail.

She took a brief glimpse at herself in the mirror and nodded in satisfaction at what she saw. With a deep breath, she promised not to pay any attention to Anna Beth. This was an important step for her, and she was excited to see what it was going to feel like.

Daniel waited for her by the cross, and her eyes drifted up to a nearby clock to make sure she wasn't late. Daniel smiled. "I'm horribly punctual. You're not late."

She swallowed her fear, slid to her knees before him, and bowed her head.

"I know this is new for you," he said. "I need you to promise me you'll use your safe word if anything becomes too much."

"Yes, Sir."

"Stand up for me and take your shirt off."

This was it. Arousal and anticipation pounded through her veins. She slowly rose to her feet and, keeping her eyes straight ahead, drew the shirt over her head and dropped it to the floor.

"Very nice, Lynne," Daniel said. "Go face the cross."

She was thankful she didn't have to look at anyone to accomplish that task. This way she could concentrate on what she was doing and not on who was watching. In her mind, she made Daniel Simon and imagined that they were the only two people in the room.

With efficient fingers, Daniel secured her wrists and ankles to the cross. She closed her eyes and relaxed as much as possible.

"Everything feel okay?" Daniel asked. "Not too tight?"

She pulled experimentally against the bonds. Nope, she wasn't going anywhere. "Everything feels good, Sir."

"Thank you, Lynne."

She was willing to bet he wasn't so formal with Julie. But that was fine. She had zero interest in pursuing any kind of relationship after this with Daniel.

"I'm going to start out slow," he said, and she exhaled, willing her body to go slack.

The first falls of the flogger surprised her. She'd prepared herself for them to hurt. But they didn't. Instead, it was the strangest sort of caress. He probably wasn't putting a lot of power behind his swing, and her body relaxed further.

He kept up the light strokes for quite some time. She wasn't sure how long it was, but she grew accustomed to the rhythmic thuds falling, and at one point, she sighed because it felt so good. Her eyelids grew heavy, and it was as if she melted into the wooden cross.

"Still okay?" Daniel asked.

"Mmm . . . Yes, Sir." She forced herself to answer his question before she slipped back into that dreamlike state where everything was so pleasurable.

She might have heard Daniel chuckle from behind her. She wasn't sure, and the uncertainty didn't bother her. Gradually, the strokes grew heavier, but she hardly noticed the change in sensation. In fact, it was as if she wasn't standing in a kink club; she was racing down the corridors of her mind, looking this way and that. But no, she wasn't racing; she was floating and it was the most magical feeling she'd ever experienced.

There was a break, and she almost told him not to stop, but the next thing that hit her skin had a bite. She sucked in a breath, and a peculiar warmth spread throughout her body. The bite came again, and she laughed.

"Lynne?" Daniel asked.

"Don't stop, Sir."

He didn't, but she found she couldn't help herself, and each time the whip made contact with her back, she giggled. She tried to stop, but the more she attempted to hold it in, the harder the giggles came. It didn't make any sense. There wasn't anything funny about the scene, and the whip actually hurt. Or at least it hurt more than the flogger did.

She was afraid Daniel might get the wrong impression, that he might think she was being disrespectful. The first time she laughed, he did hesitate before continuing, but he didn't seem to mind or care after that.

Much too soon, he stopped.

"No," she said, surprising herself. "Don't stop, Sir. I won't laugh anymore."

But instead of starting again, a blanket fell around her shoulders and she was released from the cross. "I'm not stopping because of the giggles," Daniel assured her, "though I've never had that type of response before. I'm stopping because I don't want to push you too far your first time."

"Will you do it again?" she asked.

Now it was Daniel's turn to laugh. "I think you might have a streak of masochist in you."

He took her by the elbow and guided her to the bench where Julie sat. As they approached, Luke tapped Anna Beth on the shoulder and motioned for her to follow him. They were halfway to Luke's office before Daniel had Lynne situated on the couch between him and Julie.

Daniel kept one hand on her shoulder while he talked with her. "Everything okay? You feel all right? Any questions?"

She'd expected to be in pain when it was over, so she was

surprised to find that she was not. "I feel a little weightless, and warm. Is that normal after a session with the single tail?"

"You're probably still feeling the effects of subspace." Daniel looked over her head and gave some sort of signal to Julie. "I'm going to put cream on your back. There are no open wounds, just some marks that will disappear in a day or two. You don't need to do anything special. Just be aware of it and take some medicine if it hurts."

Julie handed him the tube of cream, and Daniel had Lynne face away from him so he could take care of her back. His hands were knowledgeable and sure, but in her heart she longed for them to be Simon's hands. She closed her eyes and tried to pretend he was there with her, but it didn't work.

When he was finished, he had her put her shirt back on. After she was dressed, Luke came out of his office without Anna Beth and sat across from them. He passed her two extra-strength ibuprofens and a bottle of water. She swallowed the pills and drank half the water. She'd had no idea she was so thirsty.

"Everything okay?" Luke asked.

"Yes," Lynne said. "It was so different from what I had expected. Not nearly as painful, and I'm sore, but everything has a pleasant sensation."

"I'll call you tomorrow," Daniel said. "Just to check on you. And I'll have Julie talk to you as well."

"That's not necessary," Lynne said. "There's no need for you and Julie to go out of your way."

"It is necessary, and we're not going out of our way." The way Daniel spoke let her know in no uncertain terms that it was not up for discussion.

Lynne nodded. "There is one thing I was wondering."

"What's that?" Daniel asked.

"Why do you think I giggled so much? I never heard of that! Is that normal?"

Daniel exchanged looks with Luke, and Luke was the one who answered.

"First, throw away any definition you have of normal. Second, it's not common, but it happens. Some people react differently to pain than others. Some people cry, and a few of them laugh. That doesn't make it wrong. Understand?"

No, she didn't totally understand, but she knew that normal was different for everybody. She just wished her normal were more in line with everybody else's normal.

"I would suggest alerting the Dom you're playing with about your tendency to giggle," Daniel said. "Again, not because it's wrong, but because it's different. And you don't want him to be caught off guard."

It all made sense when they said it, but Lynne still felt like the biggest freak there was. Suddenly, she wasn't warm and weightless anymore. She was cold and alone. A tear escaped from her eye.

"Master," Julie said, with a nod toward her.

"And she crashes fast, too," Daniel said, scooping her up in his arms right as the dam burst.

Later that afternoon, Lynne went for a long walk, just to clear her head and to allow herself time to think. She couldn't believe she'd cried all over Daniel like she had. He assured her it was fine and completely understandable, but she still felt utterly foolish. What would Simon think if she cried after her demo with him? She tried to decide which was worse, laughing during the scene or sobbing hysterically after?

Maybe Simon had been right all along about her not being a submissive.

Daniel had repeatedly told her it didn't mean any such thing. When she'd finally stopped crying, she'd been mortified, but he'd taken it all in stride and asked her to join him and Julie for lunch. She'd almost said no, but Luke had given her a look and Julie had taken her hand and begged her to join them.

Lynne had ended up giving in and had a delightful lunch with the fun-loving couple. They were both so down-to-earth and funny. She didn't feel like a third wheel at all, and by the time they finished and she had returned home, she'd felt much better.

Daniel had mentioned that a bit of exercise would also help keep the symptoms of subdrop down. He'd told her that was what she'd been experiencing when she'd cried and it was a common reaction to the endorphin drop after a scene.

As a whole, she didn't exercise all that much. When she was in Delaware, the kids kept her busy, and in the city, she usually walked. But she thought she needed to walk farther than she normally did, so once she stepped out of the penthouse building, she headed away from school, toward an area of the city she didn't often frequent.

Once there, she wandered around, feeling almost like a tourist taking in all the shops and cafés that had been added since her last visit. She'd just passed an ice-cream shop and was debating on whether she wanted to get a cup or a cone when she saw a new jigsaw puzzle store.

All thoughts of ice cream left her mind. She'd loved jigsaw puzzles in college. They'd provided an outlet for stress relief. In fact, she'd enjoyed them so much, she couldn't remember when she'd stopped doing them. Probably when she took the job at the law firm. The long hours and almost nonexistent weekends hadn't allowed her to have much time for hobbies.

But now . . . She stepped inside and felt the same feeling she did when she walked into a bookstore. So many options to pick from. She knew she was taking a puzzle back to the penthouse; she just didn't know which one.

Fifteen minutes later, she'd narrowed it down to two: a ten-thousand-piece New York City scene or an eight-thousand-piece puzzle of a painting that featured a medieval peasant couple. Deciding she would rather have the couple, she put the city-scape box back and started toward the register when the shop door opened and she stopped in her tracks.

Simon. Simon was here in the jigsaw puzzle store.

He didn't see her right away. He was all smiles as he walked up to the counter to speak to the sales associate. It was clear from their conversation that he was a frequent customer.

She didn't know how long she stood there, frozen, trying to decide if she wanted to withdraw deeper into the store or to place the puzzle on a nearby shelf and try to leave without being seen. Or if she wanted to stay right where she was so she could look at the all-male deliciousness that was Simon.

"Can I help you?"

A sales associate she hadn't been aware of came up behind her. At the same time, both Simon and the guy he was speaking with looked her way.

"Ma'am?" the person behind her said.

Simon turned a bit pale, and his eyes grew wide in recognition. "Lynne?"

"Simon . . . uh, hi," she said, feeling like the temperature had risen twenty degrees in the last thirty seconds. She lifted the box she was holding. "Just looking at puzzles."

The corner of his mouth twitched upward in the slightest hint of a smile. "I see that. I didn't know you enjoyed puzzles. And not the simple ones from the looks of it."

"Oh, yes." She nodded. "The harder, the better. I like it hard." *Fuck.* "I mean, I like them hard. The puzzles. Not anything else." *That didn't sound right.* "Except some things." She realized she was staring at his crotch. "I . . . uh . . ."

Even the sales associates were stunned into silence. She set the box on a nearby table. "I'll just, uh . . . yeah." She ran out the door as fast as she could and headed straight for the ice-cream shop.

Dammit, she thought, wiping the tears that threatened to fall. She should have gotten ice cream like she'd planned to in the first place and never gone into the new store. Now she didn't have a puzzle and she'd made herself look like an idiot in front of Simon and his friend, the sales guy. Plus, she could now never go back into that store again.

The chime on the door rang out as the door opened, and she shifted lower into the booth she was sitting at. If only she'd thought to bring a book. Then she could pretend to be reading. Or taking notes. Or doing anything other than sitting in an ice-cream shop, trying not to cry.

Maybe whoever it was would order and leave.

"Lynne?"

But no. It had to be Simon.

She didn't look up. "Just leave me alone. I've embarrassed myself enough for one century. Please don't make it worse."

"Lynne."

The way he said her name, the way it washed over her body, left chills in its wake. She couldn't help it. She lifted her head, and the sight of him took her breath away. She'd forgotten how his very presence invaded her space, like he was filling her up completely. Until that moment, she hadn't realized how much she'd missed it. And all too soon, she knew he'd leave and she'd once more be without his strong presence.

"Hello, Simon."

Chapter Six

Simon knew he shouldn't follow Lynne out of one store and into another. Even if it weren't for Nathaniel's warning sounding loud in his head, he knew better. He'd been so shocked to see her standing there in the jigsaw store, he hadn't known what to say, and then she'd gotten all flustered. And he'd felt bad because it was his doing.

Sitting in the booth by herself, she looked so miserable and alone, he wanted nothing more than to sit by her side, gather her in his arms, and tell her everything was going to be all right.

But she wouldn't allow that, and he couldn't afford to do it. Instead, he did the next best thing. He pulled the bag out from behind his back and placed it on the table.

"You forgot something," he said.

She sniffled. "I didn't forget it. I never paid for it."

"You were going to. That is, I assume you were. So I went

ahead and did it for you." He didn't add that he'd been impressed with the level of difficulty of the puzzle she'd chosen.

"Thank you." She took out her purse. "What do I owe you?"

"Nothing. My treat." He couldn't believe she thought he would let her pay for it.

"I can't let you do that. It's too much."

"Let me do this one thing for you."

She nibbled on her bottom lip, and he clenched his fist, because he remembered her doing that when they were together before and it was damn near the sexiest thing he'd ever seen.

"I don't know," she said. "It doesn't feel right."

"In that case, why don't you make it up to me by inviting me over and cooking me dinner?" He didn't know where that had come from. It was very high-handed and forward, but he discovered he wasn't at all sorry he'd said it. For some reason, seeing her again brought to mind all the reasons why he'd wanted to be with her in the first place, and he couldn't remember why he'd broken things off. Or maybe they just didn't seem all that important at the moment.

Her head shot up. "What?"

"I could help you with the puzzle."

Except she might not want his help. Hell, she might not want him, period. Or to have anything to do with him. He wasn't sure why he wanted to be with her so badly, as it wasn't a good idea. He knew that she would say no and he'd go home. Back to his quiet apartment with the lovely view. The evening would drag by. Even more so because the only things he'd looked forward to lately were his online chats, but he didn't have one scheduled with Faye.

"Okay," she said, so quietly he wasn't sure he'd heard her.

"Yes?" he asked, just to make sure.

She wiped her nose and pulled herself together. "Yes. I'm at Nathaniel and Abby's penthouse. You can come over tonight for dinner if that works. Seven?"

"That would work wonderfully." He tapped the top of the box. "I'll leave this with you, and after we eat, I'll show you my mad puzzle skills."

That actually got a half laugh out of her. "No, I don't think so. After we eat, I'll show you a thing or two about putting a puzzle together."

"Deal." He stood, silently watching her for a second longer than necessary, and then, before he did something he knew he'd regret, he told her he'd see her later, and left the shop.

As he walked outside, he asked himself what the hell he was thinking. Why would he practically throw himself at Lynne when nothing good could come from it? He knew he was no good for her, Nathaniel had already threatened him, and he had a kinda, sorta, maybe relationship with Faye.

The best thing he could do was turn around, go back into the shop, and tell Lynne he was sorry, but dinner and puzzles were a bad idea. But to do that would upset her and he couldn't take that risk. No, the best thing he could do was to go to the penthouse for dinner, be a friend, not think about the sexy way her teeth bit ever so lightly into her lip, and tell Faye he'd had dinner with an old friend. Yes, that was the plan and he was sticking to it.

As it turned out, his plan lasted for about ten minutes after Lynne let him inside the penthouse. He'd brought a bottle of wine over and followed her into the kitchen when she went to get two glasses and the corkscrew.

Everything would have been fine except they both reached

for the corkscrew at the same time, and when their hands touched, they both let go of it. Lynne flushed that lovely pink shade he appreciated and bent down to pick it up. Unfortunately, she accidentally kicked it and it rolled under the island in the middle of the kitchen.

Simon watched in stunned silence as she crawled across the floor to get it. Not because her ass looked so fine, though it did, but because her shirt hitched upward, revealing bullwhip marks across her back.

She was completely unaware as she grabbed the corkscrew and hopped up with a joyous "Got it!"

Her smile turned into a frown when she saw his expression. "Simon? What's wrong?"

He was being ridiculous. He knew it. And yet he still couldn't stop it. Something inside him morphed into a possessive caveman who thought if anyone was going to take a bullwhip to that delectable flesh, it should have been him.

And though he knew he was being ridiculous, and he knew it wasn't any of his business, he couldn't stop himself from asking, "Who did that to your back?"

Her face went so pale, for a moment he thought she was going to pass out on him. But no sooner had he blinked than she drew herself up and her cheeks flushed pink. "What's it to you?"

"What?" He took a step back. This confrontational Lynne was different and unexpected. And hot.

"I said, what's it to you? You made the assumption I wasn't a submissive. Well, guess what. You were wrong. And that means if I have to find someone else to give me what I need, it's none of your business."

"I know. I'm sorry. It's just, I wasn't expecting that." And that was the understatement of the year. He gave her a small smile. "Forgive me?"

She appeared calmer, but only a little.

"Apology accepted." She turned back to the countertop. "Besides, the Dom I was with today said he thought I might be a masochist. You probably couldn't give me what I need anyway."

He caught himself before he dropped the wineglass he held. "You're a masochist?" It couldn't possibly be true. Not Lynne. No way.

She peeked over her shoulder and looked uncertain for the first time. "I don't know. Maybe?"

He shouldn't be the one she had this conversation with. There was no way he could even pretend to be neutral. Fucking hell. What if she was and he'd let her go? But no, he couldn't allow himself to think that way.

"I suggest you talk with Abby," he finally said. "She's not a masochist, but I'm sure she could put you in contact with a few people who are."

Lynne nodded.

"Can I see your back?" he asked. "Just out of curiosity."

And because he wanted to make sure the Dom she was with knew what he was doing. He told himself it was just part of who he was, that he would do the same with any submissive he knew. And he might, but he'd have been fooling himself to think that it didn't go further than that with Lynne.

"Umm." She looked like she was going to say no. "Sure. Just a second."

She put the wine bottle down and turned toward him. The flush still slightly stained her cheeks, and she looked adorably unsure. "Here in the kitchen?"

"This will be fine."

She faced the countertop, away from him, and took the shirt up and off. Instead of letting it drop to the floor, she held it tight in her fist and bent, just a bit at the waist. Her hands rested on the marble.

He was surprised at the obvious expertise exhibited by the Dom she'd played with. The marks were even and well placed. He traced one line with his fingertip, and under his touch, she sucked in a breath.

He shouldn't have touched her. Just the feel of her soft skin made him want her. He wanted her so badly, everything else fell away. All the reasons why he shouldn't be with her. All the reasons he'd recited to himself in the weeks following their split. Nothing. They were gone. The only thing left was Lynne, and she was under his touch for the moment, no matter how briefly.

She sighed, a dreamy, earthy sound that had him tracing another whip line just to see if he could get her to repeat that sigh. When he did, he lowered his head, desperate to taste her, to entice more sounds of pleasure.

Her phone rang, and she shot up, almost hitting him in the chin. "That's Nathaniel and Abby's ringtone."

Nathaniel. Shit.

"He doesn't have a hidden camera in here, does he?" He asked it like a joke, but he was halfway serious, too.

"Not that I know of." She grabbed her phone and answered. "Hello?"

Simon took the opportunity to get himself under control and open the wine, but he kept an ear tuned to the one part of the phone conversation he could hear.

"Yes, everything went great." Lynne had taken the phone to the opposite end of the kitchen and stood looking out a window.

"I know I should have called sooner. I had a bit of subdrop, so we went out to eat and then I took a walk when I got back here. Yes, I'm much better, but can you have Abby call me when she gets home?"

He wasn't surprised at all that Nathaniel knew she was playing with someone, though it would have been nice if he could have told him that when he'd stopped by Simon's office to give his stay-away-from-Lynne speech.

"I invited a friend over," she said. "We're going to have dinner and then work on a jigsaw puzzle."

When she started talking to Elizabeth and Henry, Simon let his eyes drift to the window. He tilted his head and looked closer at the buildings. It was almost the same view Faye had from her bedroom window. He couldn't say with any certainty that they were the same buildings, but the look was similar. His heart raced. Did Faye live in this building, too? What were the odds?

No, that would have been way too much of a coincidence. She probably lived in a nearby building, but there was little to no chance it was the same one the Wests lived in. She was close, though. That's why the view out the window looked familiar. He'd have to pay closer attention next time he chatted with Faye.

Tomorrow night.

"Thanks, Nathaniel." Lynne had turned back and was watching him. "No, I don't think that's necessary. I think I'll be fine now." She laughed at something he said. "Already heard about that? Yes, I'll be sure to tell him."

She hung up and cocked her head. "Did you see something interesting out the window?"

"No." He took one last look at the skyline and focused his attention back on Lynne. "I just saw a similar view the other day, and I was wondering about how close the other building was."

A strange expression crossed her face, but it was gone before he could get a good enough look to identify it. In its place was the sweet smile he'd always associated with Lynne.

"Excuse me for a minute," she said, and didn't even wait before scampering down the hall. He heard a door close and assumed she'd gone to the bathroom. Several minutes later, she returned, her cheeks a bit flushed. "Sorry about that."

"Quite all right. Everything okay?"

"Yes. Ready to eat? I made Italian." She didn't explain further, but went straight to the cabinets to get plates out. He wondered if she remembered Italian was his favorite.

"I'll get the wine."

Lynne didn't take the plates to the dining room. Instead she carried everything over to an intimate dining nook beside the kitchen.

"I love eating here," she said. "I hope you don't mind. The view is fantastic. Besides, I think the dining room is too stuffy."

Once he saw the space, he had to agree. It was surrounded by floor-to-ceiling windows and offered an amazing view of the city. "This is something else," he said, putting the wine on the table. "If I had a view like this, I'd spend all my time in this spot."

"I know, right?" Lynne waved toward the outside. "From up here, it looks so peaceful. Busy, but peaceful."

Freed from the expectations of a date, Simon found himself enjoying the dinner with Lynne. She'd grown up in the time since they'd been together. Granted, she'd never been childlike, but there was a certain maturity about her that hadn't been present before.

She didn't appear ill at ease or awkward, which he'd feared, especially considering their accidental meeting in the jigsaw puzzle store. Gone was that woman. Here, in this penthouse, she appeared settled and secure in who she was. And damn, she could cook.

He set his fork down. "That was the best lasagna I've ever had. Thank you for cooking for me."

Her cheeks blushed the slightest bit of pink, and she ducked her head at his praise. Lovely. "Thank you," she said.

"Any way we can bring the puzzle to this table?" He started clearing their places to make room.

"Only if you pour more wine."

He cleared the table and got the wine while she put the dishes in the dishwasher and retrieved the puzzle. Moments later, they were back at the table, and she opened the box.

"So tell me, Simon." Her eyes danced when she was playful. He loved that about her. "Do you do the outside first or the inside?"

"Outside first. Once you have the edges, you're set."

"Would you call that edging?" she asked.

At her mention of the word "edging," his mind formed a perfect image of her on her back and him above her, thrusting into her with just enough power to make her moan, but not nearly enough to bring her to release.

"What would you know about edging?" he asked, his voice rough, even to his own ears.

"Sometimes at night, I play with myself. See how long I can stay on the edge without coming." She spoke as if she were mentioning the weather or the lack of parking in the city. *She's tipsy. Has to be the wine.* He could think of no other reason for her to be so uninhibited.

"Is that right?" he asked, almost afraid to speak for fear she'd stop talking. "How long can you go before you come?"

She looked mildly surprised, as if she couldn't believe she'd spoken her thoughts out loud. "I don't come."

"You don't?"

"No." She shook her head. "The Dom I'm with won't allow it."

The Dom who had whipped her back so expertly. Of course, he would also have claimed ownership of her orgasms. He tried not to show how her words affected him. "I take it you've been a good submissive?"

"Yes, Sir," she whispered, and her eyes grew dark.

He clenched his fists. *Fuck.* What those two words did to him when they came out of her mouth. "Dammit, Lynne."

He stood completely still, knowing if he didn't, he would walk the five steps to her, take her into his arms, crush his lips to hers, and damn the consequences that would follow.

The Lynne he'd known before would stutter through an apology, flush a few shades of pink, and not look him in the eyes for the rest of the evening. But as he'd ascertained earlier, this was a new Lynne, and the new Lynne didn't seem to be embarrassed by sharing what was on her mind.

She gave him a sultry smile that told him she knew exactly what her words did to him, and in a smooth and graceful motion, she slid into the chair and sat down.

"Now I'm going to show you how to put a puzzle together," she said as if he weren't standing there with an erection so hard and uncomfortable he might just bust his jeans wide open.

He took a deep breath and sat down, but in his mind, he wasn't putting a puzzle together with Lynne; he was taking apart the puzzle that was Lynne.

Lynne groaned and leaned back against the door as soon as she closed it behind Simon. What the hell had she been thinking acting the way she did? It had to be the wine. She wasn't used to drinking, and they'd gone through the entire bottle he'd brought over.

Not to mention, the view from the window was something that had never crossed her mind. Not in five hundred years would she have thought about Simon looking out the window. She'd have to add that to her list of things to worry about the next time she had a video chat with him. And how the hell had she forgotten to close the bedroom door? Thank goodness he'd brought up the view, because it had been that comment that had triggered her to go make sure he couldn't accidentally come across Faye's room.

In a moment of weakness, and because she couldn't stand the idea of not seeing him again, she'd asked him if he wanted to come by later in the week to work on some more of the puzzle. He'd hesitated so long, she expected him to say no. But all at once his face broke out into a rare smile and he told her to name the date and time and he'd be there.

Now she was really in a mess. Tomorrow night she would be Faye and video chat with Simon, and the next night she would be Lynne and would work on a puzzle with him. If she'd only waited, maybe she'd have found her way back to him without becoming Faye. But it was too late to think like that now.

The fact was, she didn't want to give up Faye. Simon was doing the demo with Faye, and even though he'd been surprised by her actions a few times tonight, she had no doubt that he would never do a demo with Lynne.

For now she would have to keep up her split personality.

Her phone rang, and she jogged over to the table they'd been doing the puzzle on, expecting to see Simon's name, but instead found an unknown number.

"Hello?" she said.

"Lynne. Girl, what the fuck are you doing?"

It took her a second to recognize the voice. Anna Beth. Ugh. "Hey, Anna Beth. How are you?" She tried to make her voice as friendly as possible. "Quite a surprise seeing you at Luke's today."

"Shut up, bitch. I know what you're doing."

Lynne's heart pounded. How did Anna Beth know? "What?"

"Luke DeVaan thought he was so smart keeping me in his office while he talked to you after that scene. Well, the joke's on him."

"I don't know what you're talking about."

Anna Beth's laughter sent chills down Lynne's spine. "Sure, you don't. Just remember, I'm the one the firm came to when they needed someone to hack into something off the record."

Lynne didn't have a chance to ask her what she was talking about because Anna Beth hung up. Not even stopping to think twice, she punched in the number Daniel had given her and alerted him that Anna Beth had possibly hacked into Luke's computer and could he let Luke know?

Her strange and wonderful day became even more strange but a lot less wonderful as first Nathaniel called and then Luke. By the time she finally crawled into bed, she couldn't shake the feeling Anna Beth was still sitting somewhere, laughing at her.

"What do I do to liars?" Simon asked.

Lynne knelt on the floor, knowing what he wanted her to say but unable to speak the words. She shook her head.

Simon grabbed her chin and made her look at him. "Tell me what I do to bad girls who lie." When she still didn't answer, he tightened his hold on her. "Now. Unless you want me to do this in front of the club."

She couldn't have that. Bad enough everyone knew she was being punished. Damned if she'd have him do it where they could watch.

"You punish them," she said, but of course, it wasn't enough.

"You have one more chance. Tell me where and how. Tell me what I'm getting ready to do to you."

She swallowed. "You're going to fuck my ass."

"That's right. Bad girls get their ass stretched by a big cock and then get fucked hard and can't come." He let go of her chin. "Go get the lube and prepare me."

She began to rise, but he pushed on her shoulders. "Bad girls don't get to use their feet."

She crawled, secretly enjoying the fact that he was staring at her ass. He stood watching her when she turned around, and she was mesmerized by the sight of him stroking his cock.

"That's right," he said, his eyes never leaving her. "Watch as I get my cock ready to punish your ass. See how hard I am just thinking about it? Now get over here and get it nice and slick so I can push it inside that tiny hole of yours."

But when she got ready to squeeze the lube into her hands, he took the tube from her. "Changed my mind. Go bend over the bench. I'll take care of this."

This time she didn't even think about trying to walk. She crawled over to the bench and positioned herself the way she knew he wanted her. Behind her came the sounds of flesh on flesh as he stroked the lube over his cock. She closed her eyes and counted. By the time she got to fifteen, he was behind her.

"I used lube, but make no mistake about it. This is a punishment, and it's supposed to hurt. You'll take your fucking in stillness and silence or else I'll repeat this punishment every day for a week. Understand?"

"Yes, Sir." She gulped and grabbed on to the edge of the bench, willing herself to remain still.

He was hot against her backside, and she took a deep breath as he began pushing into her. He was so big and she felt so full and, like always, there was a stretching pain as he worked his way inside.

She bit the inside of her cheek because she knew she shouldn't be turned on by what he was doing. It was a punishment and it hurt. She told herself a normal person wouldn't be turned on. But she'd come to terms long ago with the knowledge that she wasn't normal, and so it wasn't all that unexpected when she felt her arousal grow. She knew she was in trouble, and it was only made worse because Simon was a sadistic Master who knew all too well how she'd react.

"Naughty girl," he said, thrusting into her harder, chuckling as the first twitches of her orgasm rippled through her body. "Pain slut likes for her ass to be pounded. I'm going to have to be more creative when I discipline you for coming during your punishment."

And, God help her, she thought as her release claimed her, she was looking forward to it.

Her eyes flew open and she panted in the darkness as the last traces of the dream fell away. Dammit. She wondered what Simon's punishment would be for coming in her sleep.

The ringing of her phone woke her the next morning. She fumbled around on her nightstand to grab it, hoping to get to it before it stopped.

"Hello?" she said, without checking to see who it was.

"Lynne?" Luke asked. "Sorry to call so early. I've been thinking, and I had to give you a call."

"Is something wrong?"

"I'm not sure. That's why I wanted to talk to you."

Lynne braced herself for the worst, knowing she wasn't going to like whatever Luke had called to tell her. "Go ahead, tell me."

"You called last night concerned about Anna Beth hacking into my computer."

She did not like where this was going, especially since her stomach had started to hurt. It always did that right before something bad happened. "Yes."

"It does appear that somebody hacked into the computer. That's what my computer security expert's telling me. And he brought up an interesting point. Have you checked your computer to see if it's been hacked?"

She froze. She had not. She had not even thought about it, and now she felt stupid for not doing so. "Oh no."

"I'm sorry to be the bearer of bad news, but I wanted to alert you as soon as possible."

"Thank you." They were the only two words she could form at the moment. She had to get to her computer. "I'm going to check now. Thank you. Bye."

Luke started to say something else, but she didn't have any more time to talk to him. She hung up without listening to what he said and made her way on shaky legs to her computer. She turned it on but realized she had no way of knowing how to check to see if it had been hacked. And the last thing she would do was ask a stranger. There was no way she was going to give anybody access to her private life through her computer. The only thing she could do was wait.

Unfortunately, she was not a patient person. Her mind came up with too many things that could have gone wrong. If, in fact, Anna Beth had hacked into her computer, she had access to everything. She would know that Lynne was lying to Simon, as well as her assumed name. And since Anna Beth was a member at Luke's club, along with Simon, Lynne was certain she would tell somebody.

She thought about confronting the woman. But what if Anna

Beth had not hacked into her computer? All she would be doing was giving her more ammunition to use against her. No, she could not confront Anna Beth. All she could do was wait.

She fixed her breakfast while trying to decide what to do, if anything, about Anna Beth. The sad fact was if Anna Beth had hacked into her computer, she already knew everything and there was nothing left to do. Lynne could only hope that Anna Beth had ruined her reputation so completely that no one would believe anything she said.

She was feeling better when her laptop dinged with an incoming message. She almost didn't check for fear that it was Anna Beth. But curiosity got the better of her and she went to see who it was. Her heart leaped into her throat when she saw that it was from Simon. Surely Anna Beth hadn't figured everything out and already e-mailed Simon.

She wasn't sure what to think after reading his message.

Faye,

I'm sorry to do this, but some things came up and I have to cancel tonight. I promise to make it up to you. Would you like to get together before the demo for a practice run-through? The conference location has asked if we'd like a practice time the day before. That would mean an overnight trip. It's up to you, but I promise to be a perfect gentleman if you say yes. Mostly.

—SirSimon

Lynne knew it was stupid, but she couldn't help analyzing every word in his message. Was he canceling because he had heard from Anna Beth? If he had heard from her, would this be the way he would react? She didn't think so. Besides, he asked her if she wanted to practice before the demo, and she didn't think he would do that if he knew of her deception.

Though part of her hoped that he was canceling on Faye because he couldn't keep Lynne out of his mind.

Either way, she had to decide if she wanted to do a practice run-through for the demo, which also meant an overnight trip. If she did decide to go, she would have to do something about her voice. Her mind was running through the possibilities even as she replied to Simon.

> **SirSimon,**
>
> **I completely understand that something has come up. As much as I'd prefer an evening with you, I will make do with my fantasies tonight. Speaking of which, I don't know why I'm telling you this, but I came in my sleep last night.**
>
> **Yes, a practice run-through before the demo would be a great idea, and I don't mind it being an overnight.**
>
> **Yours,**
> **Faye**

She glanced at the clock and realized that if she didn't hurry, she would be late. Without waiting for Simon to reply, she shut her computer down and got ready for school.

Something had seemed out of sorts at school. She'd noticed it the first day but had never been able to put her finger on exactly what it was. That day at lunch, she realized what it was. There was no one in her classes she felt close enough with to consider a friend. At least not the kind you would hang out with or invite to your place for dinner.

And she surely did not have any submissive friends in the city, though she wished she did. She could only imagine how nice it would be to have someone in the lifestyle whom she knew and trusted nearby. She took a few minutes to look around at her fellow classmates during lunch. Could any of them be submissive? Or maybe dominant?

It was silly to even think she could guess just by looking at somebody. After all, what did a submissive look like?

With a sigh, she threw her trash away and decided to go to the library to study. But if she'd been hoping to find peace at the library, that wasn't to be. As soon as she found a quiet corner and sat down, she turned on her laptop to find an e-mail from Simon. Something told her not to open it, not just yet, but she couldn't stop herself.

Faye,

Normally, I'd tell you that you can't help what you do while you're asleep, but I have a bit of a sadistic side and it's been under wraps for longer than it likes, so I'm going to let it out to play. As punishment for coming, you are to do the following:

—Take your panties off. Now. If you're in public, you may go to the restroom to do so, but I want them off within five minutes of you reading this e-mail.

—You are not allowed to wear them anymore until I say you can.

—Write out what you can remember of your sex dream (I'm assuming you had a sex dream if you came in your sleep). Send it to me.

—Since I'm not there to do this, you will have to do it yourself. Sometime tonight, you will strip naked, take a hairbrush, and get on your bed. Once there, you will spread your legs wide and spank that naughty pussy with your hairbrush. You will give yourself fifteen hard strokes. I want that pussy sore and red, understand?

Let me know if you have any questions.

—SirSimon

Holy fucking shit. Was he serious? And what did it say about her that his e-mail turned her on so much? She glanced around to see if anyone was watching her, but of course they weren't.

Unable to even think about studying, she gathered her stuff together and headed to the bathroom.

Two nights later, she was kneeling naked in her bedroom, waiting for Simon to call into the video chat. This time, she'd drawn the curtains over the window so there would be no chance of him trying to pinpoint her location. Even so, she was the slightest bit apprehensive.

Tonight would be the first time he saw Faye after seeing her as Lynne. She didn't think there was any way he would know they were the same people, but like most Doms she knew, he was extremely observant. With that in mind, anything was possible.

"Very nice, Faye."

His voice brought her out of her mental wanderings. She'd told him that the sound on her computer still wasn't fixed, so he wasn't expecting her to answer. Instead she gave a quick nod of her head.

"Since you can't talk, at least not to where I can hear, you'll have to listen." The roughness of his voice turned her on. She couldn't help but question if he spoke like that as a result of her nakedness or because of what he had planned for tonight.

She nodded, so he'd know she'd heard.

"I want you to go get the hairbrush you used earlier in the week and show me how you punished that naughty pussy."

Her head snapped up. He wanted her to what?

From what she could see on her laptop, he was staring straight at her and he had a wicked grin on his face. "You heard me. Now go."

She nodded and started to stand.

"Negative, Faye," he said. "I read your dream. I know what gets you off. Crawl to get the hairbrush."

Her breath left her body in a big swoosh and her heart pounded so hard, she heard it in her ears. Hot damn. This was really happening.

"Now, Faye."

She nodded and, as quickly as possible, crawled to the bathroom to get the hairbrush. It didn't escape her attention that technically he wouldn't know if she stood up once she made it outside of the camera's view. But she didn't want to. She wanted to crawl the whole way and pretend that Simon was watching and getting turned on by the way her ass moved.

She had to admit, she liked this side of Simon. It was a side he'd never shown her when they were dating, and she wondered why. It didn't seem possible that the guy who'd just commanded her to crawl to get a hairbrush was the same man who not more than two days ago sat at her table and worked on a puzzle with her.

She crawled back to her bedroom to see Simon was waiting for her.

"Up on the bed, naughty girl," he said. "Show me how you spanked yourself."

When she'd set the laptop up earlier, she'd made sure that the bed was in range of the camera. Even still, as she climbed on top, she checked the display to ensure Simon could see. Once she was in the middle of the bed, slightly propped up with pillows, she let her knees fall to either side.

She glanced to the laptop, and the expression on Simon's face was so intense, she half expected that he would leap through the screen. It was that intensity, she believed, that gave her confidence and helped ease any insecurities she had.

Feeling brazen and bold, she spread her legs farther apart and was rewarded with a groan from Simon. Empowered, she took the brush and lightly tapped her inner thighs. It was what she'd done earlier in the week. It warmed her skin while making her anticipation and arousal grow.

"Very nice, Faye," Simon said. "If I had you in bed, positioned for punishment, that's the way I'd start, too."

She closed her eyes and pretended he was in the room administering the spanking. She put more power behind the strokes, knowing he wouldn't go easy on her.

"That's right," he said, obviously seeing what she was doing. "Spank those thighs."

She continued until the ache between her legs grew to where she couldn't stand another second without friction of some sort. Even then, she teased herself with a light smack on her clit.

"Fuck, yes," Simon said. "Spank your pussy. Hard."

She brought the hairbrush down again, and it felt so good, her hips lifted off the bed and she gave a gasp of pleasure.

That caught Simon's attention. "Damn, this isn't a punishment for you at all, is it?"

She shook her head.

"Did you orgasm the night you spanked yourself?"

She shook her head again.

"Like I said before, you don't have control over yourself in a dream, so it's not really something I'd punish you for." He paused and appeared to be thinking. "I'm going to change it up. I want you to make yourself come by spanking alone. Think you can do it?"

Oh, hell, yes, she could. Once a day and twice on Sunday. She smiled and nodded at the camera.

"Get to it, then," he said. "Let me see you come."

It wasn't going to take much, she thought. Between the way she'd tormented herself as well as Simon watching and saying those deliciously dirty words, she was halfway there already.

She tried to make it last, to stretch out the pleasure that came from anticipation, the stinging pain of the brush only making the promise of what was coming better. She went back to light swats, and only on every third or fourth one would she give herself the hard spank she craved.

But she wasn't used to prolonging her orgasm, no matter what she'd told Simon when he came over for dinner. All too soon, the peak of her release was upon her, and she held her breath, desperate to hold on.

"One last hard one," Simon said, obviously seeing how hard she was trying to hold back. "And let go. I want to see you come."

She whimpered in obedience and brought the brush down

for the final time. Her pussy clenching around nothing as her orgasm hit. Her hips lifted, greedy and wanting more. She needed him inside her. Video play was fun, but it was nowhere near as satisfying as having a man with her. In person.

Holy shit, if she could come like that when it was only her, how much more intense would her release be if it was actually Simon holding the brush? She squeezed her legs together, trying to find some sort of relief, no matter how minimal.

"Better watch it," Simon warned. "You're only allowed the one tonight."

She forced herself to be still and to wait patiently for him to give further instruction.

"Sit up, Faye."

She slowly made her way into a sitting position, but thought better of it and moved to her knees on the bed.

"Good girl." Simon's voice still had an edge to it, and she realized it was probably because he hadn't come.

Another reason why it was so much better to be with him in person as opposed to a video. If he was here in the room, she was willing to bet he'd be fucking her mouth at this very second.

"I think that might have been the hottest thing I've ever witnessed," Simon said. "The only thing that could make it hotter would be if I were able to finish off with my dick buried deep inside you."

He sighed, and she knew he was lamenting the fact that they didn't have that type of relationship. At least, she assumed that was what he thought. Either way, she felt a bit down all of a sudden. Simon must have felt the same, because he didn't speak much more, telling her he'd be in contact soon and to look at her calendar for possible days to get together before the demo, before saying good-bye and disconnecting.

Lynne didn't move right away. It hit her how unfair she was being to Simon. The more time that went by with him knowing her as both Faye and Lynne, the guiltier and guiltier she felt. She should do the right thing and confess. It had seemed like a harmless idea at the time, but she didn't want to be Faye anymore. She wanted to be Lynne.

And now, after he'd come over for dinner, it actually seemed possible that she could have him as Lynne. But first she had to get rid of Faye.

The easiest thing to do would be to have Faye move away or somehow break up with Simon. She could do that and he'd never know she was both women. The only kink in her plan was the upcoming demo. If Faye moved away now, what were the odds that Simon would ask Lynne to take her place?

Slim to none.

Which meant she was going to have to be Faye just a little while longer.

Chapter Seven

It was a strange position for Simon to be in, and he could have kicked himself for allowing it to happen. Though, truthfully, he wasn't sure how it could have been avoided. He ran his fingers through his hair. He wanted two women.

He wanted Lynne, and he wanted Faye.

It was almost ironic that after playing casually with partners for so many years, when he finally felt like he might be ready to think about settling down, he couldn't decide on which woman he desired more. The problem was they both appealed to him and he wanted both of them.

Would it be better to end it with one of them now as opposed to later? He'd only talked with Lynne a handful of times, but already he was intrigued enough that he'd have to get to know her all over again. From what he'd seen so far, it would be something to look forward to.

But Faye . . .

She was a sexy mystery, and he'd like nothing better than to peel back the layers of her masks one at a time, little by little, to expose every inch of her. Add to that the way she'd orgasmed from spanking herself? Yeah, he didn't want to let that go either.

The demo was coming up with Faye and with it the overnight trip. It wouldn't make any sense to decide one way or the other with that in front of them. Maybe they would do the demo and it'd be obvious that there was no chemistry. Or it could be that the opposite happened. It could go so well that Faye ruined him for all other women.

Either way, he shouldn't make a decision before playing with Faye.

After the demo with Faye, maybe he'd ask Lynne to come over to his place one Sunday afternoon to work on a puzzle. Sunday would be good. Hopefully, she'd have finished all her schoolwork.

He'd thought about inviting her to go with him to the club afterward, but he'd decided he wasn't ready to make their relationship public just yet. Not to mention, Nathaniel had told him Lynne didn't want to be a member there.

He couldn't help but wonder which camp Lynne would be in. Would she like being exposed in front of others? Old Lynne? No way. But New Lynne?

The possibilities were endless.

He was driving himself crazy, trying to work things out in his head, and he jumped at the distraction when his phone rang.

He didn't recognize the number. "Hello?"

"Hey, Simon."

It took him a few seconds to pick up on the voice.

"Anna Beth?" he asked. "Is that you?" What the fuck was she doing calling him, and how had she gotten his number?

She giggled.

"I'm two seconds from hanging up on you," he warned.

"Now, now, now," she cooed. "You don't want to do that. Not when I have information you need on those two women you like."

Anna Beth knew about Faye and Lynne? How was that possible? Faye made sense because they posted on public boards, but how could she know about Lynne? Everyone who knew them thought they were yesterday's news. The only person who might think differently was the sales guy at the puzzle store.

"I don't know what the hell you're talking about," he said.

"Faye and Lynne. Lynne and Faye," she sang.

Enough was enough. "Leave me alone, Anna Beth. And leave Faye and Lynne alone, too," he ground out. "You go anywhere near them, I'm calling the police."

He hung up.

But if she'd wanted to shake him up, she'd achieved her goal. The call bothered him more than he wanted to admit because it just wouldn't leave him alone. What was she talking about, and what information could she possibly have? More than that, he hated that he couldn't think about either woman without thinking he was missing something.

Lynne drove to the secluded resort in Pennsylvania. She had a bad feeling about the weekend despite her excitement to see Simon again. So bad, in fact, she'd been up most of the night, trying to come up with a plan for the weekend. She wasn't all that happy with what she came up with, but it was the best she could do on such short notice.

There was no way she could go all weekend with a mask on. She knew that. On the other hand, she was afraid if she told

Simon who she was before the weekend started, he wouldn't take her to the conference. Her plan, therefore, was to practice with her mask on and then take it off and reveal who she was before the demo.

It wasn't a foolproof plan—hell, she didn't even think it was a very good plan. Unfortunately, it was the only plan she had. At least she was driving herself, as it would've been horribly awkward to be in the car for two hours wearing a mask. As it was, she planned to put the mask on right before she got to the conference site.

The other concern she had was her voice. She had racked her brain, trying to think of a way to disguise it, and had come up empty. She did the next best thing. She wrote a quick note, explaining that she had lost her voice. She assured Simon in the note that she wasn't sick and she wasn't contagious. She told him she thought it was allergies.

She couldn't shake the feeling, however, that everything was getting ready to blow up in her face. That no matter what she did, it wasn't going to be enough and Simon was going to be pissed as hell when he found out.

She drummed her fingers on the steering wheel, willing the miles to pass faster, but at the same time hoping she never got there. Her phone rang, and she put it on speaker, tickled to have something to keep her mind off the impending conference.

"Hello?" she asked.

"Hey, Lynne." It was Abby.

Lynne had called her earlier in the day, but had to leave a message. "Hey, Abby."

"What's going on?" Abby asked.

"We have a long weekend break this weekend," Lynne explained. "I'm going to a BDSM conference. With Simon."

There was silence on the other end of the phone. She really hoped she wasn't on speaker and Nathaniel hadn't just heard that.

"Does he know who you are?" Abby finally asked.

"I'm telling him this weekend. Probably tonight, after we practice."

Abby gave a sigh of relief. "Thank goodness. It's about time. But why after you practice?"

"Yeah, I know it's time. If I can just get through the next few hours, I think we'll be okay. And I want to do the practice first because I'm afraid if he knows it's Lynne and not Faye, he'll go easy on me."

"Simon is a good guy. I'm sure he'll understand why you did what you did."

Lynne couldn't help but think that Abby was only saying that to make her feel better. She still feared Simon's response once he found out the truth.

"I know he is," Lynne said. "I just wonder how much he'll be willing to accept, you know?"

"Don't sell him short. He may surprise you."

Or he might react the exact way she thought he was going to. But she kept that to herself. They chatted a bit more about the kids, her classes, and their plans for when school ended. Though Lynne felt momentarily better, as soon as Abby disconnected, she was right back to where she was before the phone call.

An hour later, she pulled into the parking lot of the conference site, mask firmly in place before she prepared to exit the vehicle. Abby had mentioned that she and Nathaniel had been to this place twice. Lynne drove past a large stone building to the overnight facilities toward the back.

She wasn't sure about the sleeping arrangements, and she almost went to the front desk. But she realized she had never given Simon her last name. She doubted they would reserve a room under the name Faye with no last name. On a whim she checked her phone and smiled when she saw there was a message from Simon.

Faye,

When you arrive, call me. I'll come down to the lobby to take you to our room.

—Simon

All the breath in her body left with one big whoosh. She guessed that took care of the sleeping arrangements. From the sound of things, she'd be sharing a room with Simon. Definitely a good idea that she was going to tell him the truth tonight. And still, her body trembled at the thought of it.

She typed out a short text to Simon, letting him know that she had arrived and was waiting in the lobby. The woman at the front desk asked if she could help. Lynne shook her head no, not wanting to speak since she wasn't going to talk in front of Simon. Yet at least.

Please let this weekend go well.

Please let this weekend go well.

Please let this weekend go well.

Maybe if she said it enough, it would actually happen.

She didn't have to wait too long for the elevator to *ping* with Simon's arrival. The doors slid open, and he walked out, looking entirely too handsome. How was it he could look so good? Maybe the car ride had revitalized him, but all it'd done to her was drain her. Of course, Simon had probably gotten a full night's sleep the night before.

Plus he wasn't carrying a bunch of guilt like she was. She

firmly believed it was the guilt that made her feel so bad. Partially anyway.

"Hello, Faye," Simon said, holding out his hand.

She took that as a sign that she was not to kneel before him just yet.

He picked up her overnight bag. "Come with me. I've already checked in and got the room ready."

The room where she'd be sleeping with Simon.

He must have seen her reaction to the fact that they were sharing a room. "Don't worry. I requested a suite, so there are two bedrooms."

She smiled and nodded. At her silence, Simon tilted his head. Lynne took that moment to hand him the note she had written. He read it, then looked at her strangely.

"You can't talk?" he asked, and she shook her head. "You can't talk and you insist on wearing a mask. I can't tell if that makes you mysterious and alluring or something else entirely."

She was glad she'd decided to tell him the truth tonight. From his tone, it was clear he wouldn't be too happy if she kept the mask on and didn't talk all weekend. She pushed aside any remaining unease and told herself to focus on what would happen after she told him.

It would only be the two of them, and once she confessed everything, they'd have the entire weekend to catch up. Surely, after they practiced for the demo, he'd see that she, Lynne, was everything he wanted.

No matter what happened, by the time they went to bed tonight, there would be no secrets between them. There was comfort in that. Even if he didn't take it well, she could rest and not feel guilty.

Simon waved at the woman at the front desk and said to Lynne, "Let's go upstairs."

She followed along silently, noticing that a large group had just arrived and was checking in. She was glad Simon had already taken care of everything.

He didn't say anything, not as they walked to the elevators, not while they were in the elevators, and not as they walked down the hall toward the room he'd secured. It wasn't like him to hold back, and suddenly the twinge of unease she'd experienced in the car but managed to ignore became more pronounced.

He took her bag into a large bedroom, and only after he set it down did he address her. "I'm sure you'd like some time to refresh yourself and get settled. I thought we could talk a bit after, but I guess we can't do that with your voice the way it is."

Nope, he was not happy at all. He wasn't exactly mad, but rather, his emotions seemed to lie someplace in the middle. She wanted to tell him she was sorry. That he just had to wait a few more measly hours and everything would make sense.

But she couldn't. Not yet. Not until they'd at least practiced the demo.

The practice demo? What time were they scheduled to do it? And where would it happen? She almost asked him, but stopped herself before she could give herself away with her voice.

Her question must have been obvious, because Simon said, "You'll find our schedule for the rest of today on your nightstand."

Which told her that not only did he have a freakishly creepy way of reading her mind, but he didn't expect her to sleep in his bed. The ball of unease in her belly continued to grow, and as she went into the bedroom to change and get settled, she had the almost overwhelming urge to leave. Simon didn't seem like himself. It couldn't be the mask. She'd told him ages ago she was going to wear it this weekend. Could it be the voice thing?

With a heavy sigh, she sat down on the bed right as she heard Simon leave the room and go out into the hallway.

It wasn't common for Simon to be so unsure about what he should do, and as he would have guessed, he didn't like it one bit. He didn't believe for a second that there was something wrong with Faye's voice. She didn't want him to hear it for some reason.

He'd always claimed to like puzzles, but perhaps he'd better stick with the inanimate kind. The mystery posed by Faye was enough to give him a headache. He had to leave the room because he needed to figure her out and he couldn't do that if she was nearby, watching him through the eyes of that damned mask.

He decided to walk about the complex that was housing the BDSM workshop for the weekend to try to clear his head. Or hopefully, at least start to untangle the mess he found himself in.

What did he know about Faye?

He made a mental list. She lived in an expensive apartment. Maybe somewhere near the Wests. She had a job that made her not want to appear in public, but she didn't have a problem playing in public. She was fine as long as no one could recognize her. And now, today, one more piece—she had a distinctive voice.

When you looked at all those pieces together, she seemed to point toward some sort of public figure. But that could be anyone from a local TV personality, to a politician's daughter, to an actress.

He stopped in his tracks as another thought hit him. If she wanted so badly for him not to know who she really was, why was he going against her wishes? She obviously trusted him. Wasn't that enough? Did it really matter who she was?

But it did, because deep down he wanted her to trust him enough to tell him everything. That was the crux of a successful BDSM relationship, and if she couldn't trust him with something as basic as her identity, how could she possibly trust him when it came to something physical?

He reminded himself they hadn't known each other that long. Trust wasn't a given. It had to be earned. Maybe she'd agreed to this weekend as a way to see how he'd handle himself. If he proved himself trustworthy to her, perhaps by Sunday their relationship would be much stronger than it currently was.

He needed to be patient. And take things slowly. And demonstrate understanding. Because he didn't want to fuck up this thing with Faye. He wanted to prove himself worthy of her trust.

He walked back to the room, prepared to start.

She was in her bedroom with the door closed. He supposed he couldn't blame her. Not with the way he'd acted, storming out the way he had without even saying a word to her in goodbye. He knocked on the door.

"Faye?" he called.

The door opened slowly and she peeked her head out. The way she looked at him with those eyes of hers, so curious and trusting. It reminded him of someone, but who? He tried to picture her on television, but the image wouldn't come. But it did go far in proving that she was a public figure of some sort.

"I . . . uh . . . just wanted to let you know how glad I am that you're here with me this weekend." He hadn't told her that yet, and he could have kicked himself for his lack of manners. No wonder she didn't trust him enough yet.

"Since we have about two hours before we practice, would you like something to eat? I could order something and we could eat on the balcony. I understand it overlooks a courtyard."

She nodded. Damn, it was strange trying to communicate like this.

"Why don't you come into the living room? There are a few menus, and you can point to what you'd like."

She smiled and took his hand when he offered it.

Yes, he decided. This was progress.

Thirty minutes later, they sat on the balcony. She'd ordered some kind of hot tea, and while he'd have preferred a beer, he never drank before a scene, so he'd ordered coffee. Black. Extra strong. On the table between their chairs was a plate with sandwiches. She didn't like onion or tomatoes. It was ridiculous how happy he was to learn tiny details like that about her.

The staff was busy below them setting up various stations for the evening. From what Luke had told him, the courtyard was the place to be after dark. A dance floor was being set up in one corner, and close to it was what appeared to be a well-stocked bar. Impressive since the conference rules limited a person to two alcoholic drinks.

But covering the majority of the courtyard was play space. There were padded benches and St. Andrew's crosses, plus Simon thought he saw what looked like a suspension web being set up in a far corner.

He glanced to his side. Faye sat slightly forward in her chair, as if hoping to get a better look. Her tea sat on the table, forgotten. He looked away so she wouldn't see him staring, but he couldn't help wondering if she'd like to play. Maybe to-night after they practiced or tomorrow night after the demo? He wouldn't mention it to her right now. He'd see how practice went first.

Her gasp caught him off guard, and when he looked at her this time, she'd sat back down in her chair. Was she hiding? Had she seen someone she recognized? He scanned the courtyard, but nothing seemed out of place. If she was a public figure, it wouldn't be out of the ordinary, he supposed, for her to come across people she knew, no matter where she went.

He was starting to see the benefit of the mask.

A quick glance at his watch told him it was about time they started getting ready. Beside him, she was still sitting as far back in her chair as possible.

"Faye?" he said gently, not wanting to spook her. She looked at him, her eyes wide. "Are you okay?" he asked.

She nodded, but he wasn't sure he believed her.

"We probably need to start getting ready to practice. That is, if you still want to." For some reason, it felt necessary to give her an out. "They booked the practice rooms rather tight, so we don't have a lot of spare time."

She took a deep breath and stood up. He suspected he couldn't conceal the look of relief that likely passed across his face. He had been looking forward to finally playing with Faye, in person. But now he had a new goal. She might not let him hear her talk, but he was willing to bet he could work the whip in such a way that she wasn't able to remain quiet.

She wouldn't give him her words, but dammit, he'd have her sighs and moans of pleasure.

As they walked back into the room, he stopped her. "I'm not going to request you be naked until we get in the practice room.

Wear something easy to take off." At her nod, he added, "Meet me in the living room in fifteen minutes."

He went to his own room to prepare. It was only a practice session, but he wanted to give her the full experience. He changed into his leather pants and a black shirt; on his way to the living room, he grabbed his toy bag and slung it over his shoulder.

He stepped into the living room and realized his mistake in telling Faye to put on something easy to take off. The sundress she'd selected was made of some sort of gauzy material that somehow managed to both sway with her movements and cling to her curves. She looked like a walking advertisement for sex. He hated to tell her, but if she'd wanted to stay inconspicuous, wearing that dress wasn't the way to do it.

They walked to the rooms where practice sessions were being held and arrived right as the couple before them was cleaning up. He recognized the Dom and exchanged hellos with him. The woman was unfamiliar.

As they left, he overheard him thank her for filling in. Apparently, the submissive he was supposed to be working with hadn't shown up.

"But I know she's here," he told the substitute.

"I'm available if you need me tomorrow for the demo, Sir," the unknown woman said.

They started walking toward the door and fell out of earshot.

Just as well, Simon figured. He needed to concentrate on Faye and not on other people's missing submissives. At the moment, his submissive for the conference was kneeling in front of the cross and she still had her dress on.

He would have taken it off her himself, but he knew better than to finger the delicate fabric. He'd end up ripping it or snaring it somehow. No, delicate fabrics did not belong in his hands.

"You look very lovely, Faye," he said. "Stand up and strip for me."

She rose gracefully, the movement causing the material to shift slightly. His fingers itched to touch her.

Soon. He balled his fists to control the urge to touch her all over.

She tugged at the dress and slowly pulled it over her head, revealing little by little the smooth expanse of skin underneath. She had been captivating through the computer screen. In person she was stunning.

She lifted her head, and when their eyes met, the look of longing, desire, and excitement took his breath away. At that moment, he hoped his eyes reflected the same to her.

"Go face the cross," he said in a rough voice.

She moved without hesitation, and he couldn't keep his eyes off her ass. In fact, if it weren't for the fact that there was another practice session after theirs, he would have spent more time simply watching her. But, unfortunately, he couldn't take as much time as he would like to.

"Lift your arms up," he said. "Show me that you're willingly putting yourself in my control. That you accept what I'm going to do to you."

She lifted her arms, and he couldn't help but notice they were trembling. The small show of nerves fed the beast within him.

"Oh, Faye," he said, walking slowly toward her. "Do you know how long I've waited to have you like this?"

As he talked, he secured each wrist to padded leather straps above her head. He did the same with her ankles and then he took a step back.

"Holy fuck, Faye," he said. "I don't think I've ever seen anything so hot in my entire life. The sight of you, submitting to me this way. You have no idea what it does to me." He shook his head. Maybe tonight in their room, they could do more, and then he would take his time. He took a bell out of his bag and pressed it into her right hand. "Since your voice is gone, drop this to safeword. Nod if you understand."

She nodded.

He ran a hand down her back, feeling the skin he was getting ready to mark. "I'm only stopping when you drop it."

She sucked in a breath, but nodded.

He took a flogger and began to warm her up, falling into a ritual he hadn't performed in far too long. The mutual give-and-take never failed to turn him on. The dance of submissive and Dominant. Faye felt it, too. He could tell by the way her body swayed and the way she took each stroke he gave.

After warming her up with the flogger for several minutes, he put it to the side and picked up his bullwhip. Sometimes he'd make it crack in the air before using it, but it appeared Faye was already in subspace, and he wanted her to stay there for the moment.

"We don't have the time here," he said. "But after I get you down from there and back in our rooms, I'm going to put you facedown on my bed so I can fuck you while I look at the stripes I'm getting ready to put on you."

She gave a lazy nod.

He studied her as he brought the whip down across her back. Her head fell back and she moaned. The sound was so unexpected, he stopped for a second. Warning bells sounded inside his head, but although it was so familiar, he couldn't figure out why. He whipped her again.

She giggled, and he froze.

Why the hell did it sound familiar? He was torn between bringing the single tail down again and trying to put his finger on exactly where he'd heard that laugh before.

"Finally figured it out, didn't you?" someone whispered from behind him. Another familiar voice.

He spun around. Anna Beth?

She was naked and wore only a victorious grin. "Yes. I'm a bit late. Somehow my practice session got scheduled before yours, and that wouldn't do. I couldn't risk the two of you seeing me before you started."

Their commotion must have ripped Faye out of subspace, because she started pulling at her bonds. Her body jerked at the sound of Anna Beth's voice.

"If you saw me, you would have run away. Isn't that right, Lynne?" Anna Beth spoke with evil sweetness.

"No," the woman he knew as Faye wailed from her position.

"Lynne?" he questioned, but even as his mouth spoke the word, his head recognized the truth.

Holy shit. What have I done?

She dropped the bell and sobbed.

"Serves you right, bitch," Anna Beth spat. "Don't you know not to lie to your Dom?"

A dungeon monitor stepped up beside him. "What's going on?"

Simon didn't know how to answer. Dammit all, this was a mess. He ran a hand through his hair. "You take care of that one." He pointed at Anna Beth. "She disrupted my scene and harassed my sub. See to it that she's punished appropriately. I'll take care of my sub."

My sub. Fuck. The truth was, she wasn't his sub. She was a liar who had played him. Without talking, he stepped around the cross and jerked the mask off Faye. Faye who was really Lynne. She pleaded with tear-filled eyes, but they didn't move him. All he felt was anger.

"I don't know what kind of game you think you're playing,

but I'm going to get you down and then we're going to the room, where we're going to talk." He cupped her chin, hard. "You can talk, can't you?"

"Yes, Sir," she replied miserably.

He unbuckled her, his movements nowhere near as gentle as he'd been when he'd bound her. She sniffled the entire time, but if she thought he was going to fall apart because of a few tears, she was sorely mistaken.

As soon as she was freed, she fell to his feet. "I'm sorry, Sir. I was going to tell you tonight. I promise. I just wanted to do the practice. To prove—"

"Quiet. I didn't give you permission to speak. And stand up. You look ridiculous."

She sniffled again and stood up, reaching for her clothes. Simon snatched them before she could get them.

"Wrong. You don't deserve clothes." He nodded toward the door, dismayed by the number of people watching the train wreck his practice session had become. "Go."

"I get that you don't want me. I'm so sorry. I'll leave—"

He struck her backside once.

"Ow."

"I don't recall giving you permission to talk." He pushed her out the door and into the hall.

"I know, Sir. It's just—"

"Lynne?"

"Yes, Sir?"

"Shut the fuck up," he said, and then instantly regretted doing so. If they were going to have a serious discussion, he needed to prove that he had his temper under control. Yes, he was mad as hell at having been played, but he needed to be in control of his emotions.

He forced himself to take deep breaths, and by the time they made it to the room, he felt calmer. Granted, he was still angry, but all things considered, he was in a much better place.

He pointed to the middle of the floor. "Kneel."

Lynne's head was bowed. She hadn't looked at him since they'd left the practice room. He would let her escape his stare for now.

"Tell me what the hell you were thinking, pretending to be someone else," he said.

Her face flushed. "I wanted to get back into the lifestyle, so I went online. I saw you and I wanted . . ." She took a deep breath. "I wanted to prove to you that I was submissive, Sir. That I could be what you need."

"You think I need a liar?"

She winced as though he'd struck her. It didn't make him happy and it didn't make him proud. Yes, he identified as a sadist, but any pain he dealt out had to be mutually agreed upon.

"You might," she said. "You did play with Anna Beth, Sir."

She had him there.

"True, but I stopped as soon as I saw her for what she is." Her shoulders slumped at his words. "What you've done is played me, acting like a spoiled child who would do anything to get what she wants, no matter the cost. Trust is one of the cornerstones of BDSM. How did you expect to have any sort of relationship when everything between us is built on a lie?"

She lifted her head at that. "I didn't plan on having a relationship. I just wanted to prove myself."

"Which you failed at, because, again, lies and untrustworthiness mean there was no partnership here."

"I'll just get my things and go." She made a move to stand up.

"Don't move," he said. His voice must have been menacing enough because she dropped back to her knees. "You aren't going anywhere because I agreed to do the single-tail demo to-morrow and I'm in need of a sub."

"I'm sure there are plenty of submissives here who would jump at the chance to do the demo with you."

"Probably." He nodded, not missing the flash of jealousy that crossed her face. "But not one of them signed up to do the demo with me, I haven't practiced with any of them, and outside of Anna Beth, I don't know of any of them in need of correction."

He watched as understanding crossed her face. "I didn't think you were demoing the single tail as a punishment, Sir."

"Semantics."

"I could just leave, you know. You can't keep me here against my will."

"Of course not." That she would think he would do something without her consent rekindled his rage. She was trying to goad him, and she would learn real quick that he didn't play those sorts of games. "You're free to leave anytime you want. But you're the one going on and on about how submissive you are. Here's a chance to back it up with more than words. Stay and face the consequences of your actions. Or leave and prove that I was right about you the first time."

Chapter Eight

Lynne swore she could feel the anger radiate off Simon. One glance at him standing there, arms crossed over his chest and the irate expression on his face, was almost enough to send her out the door and into her car. He was mad as hell. But she knew he'd never touch her in anger. Though, apparently, he wasn't above mental play.

"You're trying to manipulate me," she said. "I'm not into playing mind games."

As soon as the words left her mouth, she could tell they were the wrong ones to say. He walked to stand in front of her, and since she was still on her knees, he towered over her.

"Let's get one thing straight," he said. "What we are discussing at the moment is in no way any sort of game for me. I live by a set of rules, and if you play with me, I expect you to do the same. When those rules are broken, there are ramifications. So, are you going to stay and accept my discipline, or should I help you pack?"

"I'll stay," she whispered.

"If you stay, you should know that I'll expect you to be my submissive for the entire weekend and you are to take what I give you."

"But I'll have my safe words, right?"

"Of course. I would never think about playing without safe words. You should know me better."

She started to speak, but he interrupted.

"Of course, I expect you to use them appropriately and not just because you don't feel like doing something."

She didn't understand why he'd want her to be his submissive for the weekend when he was obviously so angry with her and planned to punish her the next day. Lord help her, she was mad to even think about staying. But his words about staying and putting meaning behind her claim to submission made sense.

It was possible that was what he wanted, a chance to see if she was who she said she was. Or maybe he just wanted to use her hard before dumping her like yesterday's trash.

"Why?" she couldn't stop from asking.

"Why what?"

"Why do you want me to be your sub this weekend? Why not just punish me and be done with it?"

"Because I've been jerking off to fantasies of both Faye and Lynne for the past month, and since it turns out you're one and the same, it only makes sense to act out some of those fantasies. Don't you think?"

She didn't know what to think. She wanted Simon, but not like this. Not this angry, almost vindictive man before her.

"Don't tell me you haven't imagined it, too," he said, cutting through to the truth and heart of the matter with one swoop. "Tell me you haven't pictured yourself in the exact position you're in now—on your knees, at my feet and waiting for my command."

"Yes, but . . ." In her fantasies there had always been at least affection between them. Not this simmering stew of unresolved feelings and barely contained anger.

Yet, it was only for the weekend. She should do it and get Simon out of her system once and for all. If he could use her to play out his fantasies, she could do the same thing to him. When it was over and she was back in New York and later, in Wilmington, she could get serious about finding the right man, her one true Dom.

Above her, he waited.

"Are you going to tell Nathaniel?" she asked.

He raised an eyebrow. "Hell to the fucking no. Do I look like I have a death wish? He doesn't know you're here, does he?"

"He knows I'm doing a demo, but not anything else." She debated telling him more, but then decided now was as good a time as any to come completely clean. "Abby knows."

Simon muttered something under his breath and ran a hand over his face. "Abby knows? Fuck, Lynne, why would you tell her?"

"Because she's my boss and a good friend. Plus, she's been a submissive for a long time. I wanted her advice." She bit her lip, hoping the next part was true. "I don't think she'll tell Nathaniel. She's kept it from him this long, and I can't imagine he'd be pleased to know she knew all this time and didn't say anything."

"You're probably right." He cocked his head. "Have you decided, then?"

She took a deep breath. It was time to put away the mask. Time to bare all for him. To be who she knew she was meant to be. "Yes, Sir. I'll stay."

If he was surprised, it didn't show. "That's the first thing you've said that's pleased me all day."

She didn't have time to bask in his praise, because he fisted her hair and pulled her head up.

"Tell me what you saw in the courtyard before we went to practice," he said.

So, he hadn't missed that, had he?

"Anna Beth, Sir."

"I see," he said, but he didn't release her hair. "I suppose you didn't expect her to do what she did."

She wasn't sure if that was a question or a statement, so she remained quiet. Looking back, she probably should have expected her to do something like what she did. Luke had warned her, hadn't he?

The snack she'd shared with Simon before the disastrous practice suddenly threatened to make an appearance. Her computer had been hacked. That was the only possible way Anna Beth would have known not only about her being Faye, but also where she was this weekend and what time she was practicing.

The hand on her chin tightened. "What was that look for?"

"I think Anna Beth hacked into my computer. That's how she knew everything. Master DeVaan had warned me, but . . . Oh my God. She has access to everything."

His expression softened for the first time since he discovered who she was. "I'm sorry, Lynne. I know that's a tough blow. Do you know anyone who works with computer security?"

"I don't know. Maybe Jeff Parks, Dena's husband."

"I know him. Let me give him a call. You stay right here."

"Yes, Sir."

He didn't have to tell her to remain where she was. Between the drive, the practice session, Anna Beth, and Simon, she was exhausted. Even though she was still naked and on her knees, she closed her eyes. Just for a moment, she told herself. It was unclear how long he was gone, but she jerked when she heard him step into the room, and she realized she must have dozed a little bit.

"Were you sleeping?" he asked.

"I think I might have dozed off for a moment, Sir." But she was wide-awake now. Wide-awake and very much aware of the man standing before her.

"I talked to Jeff Parks. He'll look into your computer system when you get home."

Her heart melted a little bit at his kindness. He was horribly upset with her and yet he still wanted to take care of her. That, she decided, spoke more about the man he was than anything else.

He sighed and sat down on the couch nearby. "Oh, Lynne. What am I going to do with you?"

She didn't want to remind him that before talking to Jeff, he'd had lots of ideas. She didn't even risk a peek at him. But she could picture him. He'd be sitting on the couch, elbows propped up on his knees, with his hands covering his face. And it was her fault.

He was miserable and didn't know what to do because of her. But how could she help him? Would he even want her to?

There wasn't much she could offer him. Even more, she wasn't sure he would take what she offered. But she had made a promise to herself to be the new Lynne. That Lynne wasn't going to let a little bit of uncertainty keep her from living.

Moving as gracefully as she could, she slid forward and put her palms on the ground. Ever so slowly, she began to crawl toward the couch. She kept her head down, not wanting to see his reaction yet.

She came to a stop before him and rose to her knees.

"Lynne?" he asked.

"Let me. Please, Sir."

"Look at me," he commanded.

She lifted her head and met his gaze. The anger was still there, but it had been tempered somewhat and was now just a simmer as opposed to the rolling boil it was before. There was also a hint of uncertainty in his expression, and that pained her the most. She didn't want him to be uncertain about her.

"Please," she asked again.

"You know this won't change anything," he said. "I'm not changing my mind about tomorrow night."

"Of course not, Sir." That he would had never crossed her mind. "I want to help you in whatever small way I can. This seemed appropriate at the moment."

She waited while he thought about it, wondering why it was a tough decision. She was offering him the use of her body; that's all it was. She had no hidden agenda. No plan to sway him not to punish her. No plan to distract him. Only to give him some relief.

"Go ahead," he finally said, shifting himself slightly on the couch.

Victory surged through her. When they were together before, he had not allowed her to do this. Part of her couldn't believe he was letting her now. Damned if she was going to question it, though.

She moved closer to him, filling up the remaining space between her and the couch, so she rested between his knees. He made no move to aid her in any way. She undid his pants, happy to see that her hands were not trembling, and lowered his zipper. He wasn't wearing any underwear, and she almost groaned when his cock sprang free.

How many times had she imagined this? Too many to count. And even though it wasn't exactly the way she had envisioned it happening, at least it was happening. Finally.

She licked her lips, wanting to savor and to commit to memory every detail she possibly could. She wrapped her fingers around the base of him, causing him to suck in his breath sharply. He was huge. She'd thought he might be, or at least he had always been in her fantasies, but the reality was so much better.

"You're killing me," he moaned.

She stuck her tongue out and licked his tip, delighting in the way his body shivered under her touch. He tasted a bit salty. She licked him again. The third time she licked him, he grabbed her by the hair.

"Suck it, Lynne. Get me in your mouth now."

His words aroused her in ways she had not expected them to, especially while going down on him. She didn't want to risk another punishment, so even though she would have preferred to stay where she was, tasting him, she opened her mouth and took him inside.

"Yes," he said. "Oh, God, yes."

He felt even larger in her mouth, and she questioned her request to do this in the first place. She'd had no idea he would fill her so completely. But it wasn't just his body; it was everything about him. His smell, his touch, and now, finally, his taste. She feared she would never get enough.

She closed her lips around him fully, urging him to the back of her throat.

"Feels good." He thrust his hips up, claiming more of her mouth.

She'd never done this with a man before, and she didn't think the fruit she'd practiced with counted. She knew she was inexperienced and that she was probably doing something wrong, but every one of his moans and sighs whispered to that insecure part of her, and she felt empowered.

She redoubled her efforts, wanting to take him deeper, desperate for him to use her harder. He answered in kind, reading her actions for the plea they were.

"You like that, don't you?" He had both hands twisted in her hair now, the sharp sting of the pulls on her hair making her want more and more. "You like me fucking your face? I can tell by the way you're desperately trying to get some friction on that little clit of yours. You're such a nasty girl, getting off on sucking cock."

She was a nasty girl who got off on sucking cock, and in that one moment, on her knees before him, she didn't care who knew. After this weekend, she might not ever again get the chance to serve him in this way. So yes, she wanted to shout, she was staying with him for the next few days and she would take whatever he sent her way. She would take it and learn from it and cherish it because it would come from him. And later, when she was alone, she would have this weekend to relive in her fantasies.

She knew no matter how hard she looked, no matter how far she went, no Dom would ever affect her the way Simon did. Truthfully, she didn't want anyone else to.

"I'm getting ready to come," he ground out, pulling her from her thoughts. "I'm going to come down that throat of yours and you're going to swallow it all."

She tensed, not wanting to mess this part up and fearful because she didn't quite know what to expect. He gripped her hair tighter and thrust deep inside her mouth as his release coated her throat. She gulped as quickly as she could, not wanting to miss a single drop, and sighed as he pulled out of her mouth.

Was I good? Did I please him?

She looked up at him, hoping to see something reflected in his expression. His face gave nothing away, and he simply lowered his gaze to his pants in an unspoken command. Moving quickly, she tucked his cock back inside and zipped him up, returning to her knees when she finished.

"Lynne?" he asked, and she was afraid to look up, afraid to meet his gaze, afraid because of what she might find there. Or more importantly, what she would not.

But she had agreed to be his for the weekend and, therefore, to do as he commanded. She looked up. This time, though, her heart jumped up into her throat because she saw pleasure in his eyes.

"Thank you," he said. "That was amazing."

Would he dismiss her now? Send her to her room? Banish her away from him?

He patted the seat beside him. "Come sit with me so we can discuss how the next few days are going to play out."

She wanted to ask him if they hadn't already done that, but he was so much calmer now, more mellow, and she didn't want to ruin it. She scurried up beside him on the couch, tucking her feet underneath her.

Simon took the blanket from the back of the couch and settled it around her shoulders. She cuddled up into it, thankful for the thin covering. It wasn't that she minded being naked in front of him; it just felt odd.

He stood up. "Let me get us some water."

She didn't want him to leave, even for the short amount of time it'd take to get drinks. "I'm fine, Sir. I don't need anything."

"I don't recall asking a question." His voice had grown cool again. "When I'm in need of your opinion, I'll ask you for it."

"Yes, Sir. Sorry, Sir."

He gave a curt nod and crossed the room. She watched as he went down the hall to where the kitchenette was. As she admired how nice his ass looked in the leather pants, the room's phone rang.

That was odd. Who would be calling?

"Want me to get that, Sir?" she called out.

"Go ahead."

She picked up the phone. "Hello?"

"Lynne, thank God." It was Abby. "I've been calling your phone for the last hour and you never picked up. You were supposed to call me as soon as the practice session was over."

Abby. Shit. She'd forgotten she'd told Abby that she would check in.

She glanced at the hallway. Simon hadn't returned yet, and she didn't want to talk with Abby when he was nearby.

"Listen, Abby," Lynne said. "Can I call you back in a little while?"

Abby must've heard something in her voice because she didn't seem eager to let her go. "You sound off. Is something wrong?"

From the back of the room came the sound of ice falling into glasses. Simon would be out soon. "The short of it is, Simon found out. Before I told him, and he didn't take it all that well. But we're working it out. I promise to call you in a little bit."

"Shit," Abby said. "That doesn't sound good at all "

"I promise to tell you all about it when I call you back later."

Abby agreed, and they said good-bye. Lynne had just hung up the phone when Simon strolled into the room.

He handed her a glass of water. "Who was on the phone?"

She took a sip of water and then another, thirstier than she had realized. "Abby. I was supposed to call her as soon as the practice was over. Obviously, I was a bit distracted."

"What did you tell her?"

"The truth. That you had found out without me telling you. That the practice session went fine. And that I would call back later."

He nodded and took a sip of his own drink. "Your unveiling, if you will, has changed the way this weekend will progress. As I mentioned before, you will serve as my submissive the entire weekend."

"Yes, Sir."

"I'm not pleased with your deceit. I feel like you've been stringing me along, playing a little game with me, to see how far you could go."

She wanted to interrupt him, to assure him that she was not stringing him along and that she had not been playing a game with him. But she knew he would not welcome her comments and she would be speaking out of turn. Also, he had used the word "feel." The way he felt was the way he felt. It didn't matter whether she agreed with him not. That was the infuriating thing about feelings. You couldn't argue with them; they just were.

"On the other hand," he said, "I can't say that on some level I'm not relieved you and Faye are the same person."

She laughed at that, and he raised an eyebrow.

"I'm sorry, Sir." She took a sip of water so she wouldn't laugh again. "It's just, I'm glad, too. For a while there, I felt like I was cheating on myself."

He nodded but didn't seem amused. "Be that as it may, the fact remains that there is now a trust issue between us. And I'm not sure how easily that can be rectified."

That sobered her up. He had told her that the blow job wouldn't change anything. On some level, she realized she had held out some hope that he had been wrong. But, of course, nothing was ever that easy. The truth was, she had broken his trust and she was going to have to work to rebuild it.

"I'll do whatever I have to in order to make it up to you, Sir," she said.

He didn't look convinced. She wasn't sure if it was a *wait and see* or a *never gonna happen*. She decided that until he said otherwise, she would take it to mean wait and see. She had to believe there was some sort of hope for them, or else she would never make it through the weekend.

"Tonight," he said, "we're going to eat downstairs in the courtyard and then play it by ear."

She had a feeling he wasn't going to play it by ear. He probably knew already what he was going to do and didn't want to tell her just yet. "Yes, Sir."

"I'm going to go downstairs to work out a few things and to check on Anna Beth. I imagine you want to call Abby back?"

"Yes, Sir."

"I'll be back in thirty minutes. You are to be naked and kneeling on the floor in the bedroom."

Her heart began to race, but she managed to get out a breathy "Yes, Sir."

Five minutes later, Simon had left and she timidly dialed Abby's number. Abby picked up on the first ring.

"There you are," Abby said, before Lynne could get a word in.

Lynne couldn't help but laugh. "I told you I was going to call you back. It hasn't even been fifteen minutes."

"It seems like longer. Now tell me everything."

Lynne started at the beginning. Or at least at the point where everything had started to go wrong. She told her about Anna

Beth, the computer hacking, her plans for this weekend, and how nothing had gone as she'd thought it would.

"Wow," Abby said when she finished.

"I know," Lynne said, closing her eyes. "It's a mess, isn't it?"

"You can say that again."

"I'd rather not." She took a deep breath. "Tell me what I should do, Abby."

"Are you going to listen to me this time? Because I remember giving you advice on this subject before, and you didn't take it."

That hurt. "I know," she whispered.

"I'm not one to say I told you so, and I won't start now. But I will say that things go a whole lot smoother, and easier, when you tell the truth."

Lynne couldn't see Abby ever not telling the truth. "Sometimes it's easier not to."

"No, it only seems easier. Trust me, it is always better to tell the truth from the beginning."

"You sound as if you have personal experience."

"I do. And I have a whole ugly story of how I almost lost the most important and precious thing to me in the world by not being honest."

Lynne was stunned, but she could tell by the tension in Abby's voice that she was telling the truth. "What happened?"

"It's a long story, so I won't go into a lot of detail, but I almost lost Nathaniel."

Lynne couldn't imagine Abby without Nathaniel. They just went together; it was one of those things. You couldn't even think about splitting them up. "When?"

"Ages ago. Before the kids. Before we even thought about kids. Nathaniel and I entered into a relationship with each other and neither of us was honest about our past knowledge of the other person."

Lynne couldn't imagine that, not the way they were now, and she felt like she knew them really well. After all, she lived in their house. "What happened?"

"We split up. For months. And even once we got back together, it took time for us to trust each other."

Lynne chewed her bottom lip. "How much time are we talking?"

"You know? That's the crazy thing. I don't think there was one moment I can pick out and say, 'Oh, yes, that was when I started to trust him again.' Because the change didn't happen in a moment; it was hundreds of little moments, and it was only when I looked back that I saw we had built enough foundation to move forward."

That was what she was missing with Simon. She didn't have hundreds of little moments. She only had handfuls, and handfuls weren't enough to build anything on.

"I need to be patient and truthful," Lynne repeated. "I can do that."

She only hoped it wasn't too late.

Chapter Nine

It took Simon longer than he expected to track down the dungeon master he'd passed Anna Beth off on. He finally found him at the front gate, talking with a security guard.

"Master Neal," he said, addressing Simon, "we ran into some problems with the submissive who interrupted your scene."

He could have groaned. Of course they had. He should have expected as much. "What kind of problems?"

The monitor shifted his weight. "I escorted her to her room so she could get her things. She said she didn't have a car and that she came by cab . . . I . . . ummm . . ."

He didn't have to say it. Simon could tell what happened by the expression on his face. "You left her in the room to pack and you waited outside the door to call a cab."

"Right. I figured I was guarding the door." He shrugged. "That she couldn't get past me."

"How much time passed before you realized she went out the back window?"

The monitor's face turned red. "Longer than I'd like to admit."

"Do you know where she went?"

The other man jerked his thumb toward the security guard. "We were just looking over the security video."

Simon wasn't sure what he could do to help, so he gave them both his card and room number and told them to call him when they found out anything. He walked back to the main building. It was past time for him to meet Lynne back in the room. He ran a hand through his hair. And just what was he going to do about her?

His initial reasons for staying away, namely that she wasn't submissive, didn't hold water anymore. He wasn't even certain he could use the fact that he was a sadist. Plus, after discovering that Lynne and Faye were one and the same, he no longer had to feel guilty about spending time with two different women.

Which left two obstacles. Nathaniel and the trust issue.

He thought he knew Nathaniel well enough to know that if his friend felt he had Lynne's best interest in mind, he wouldn't have a problem with Simon seeing her. Of course, he'd been wrong before. But surely Nathaniel would see reason.

If Simon truly had her best interest in mind, that is.

Did he?

There was still the trust issue to work through, but he was man enough to admit he'd never really gotten over her after they broke up. And now, if there was a chance she could give him what he needed and he could do the same for her, he would be a fool to walk away.

He took the stairs to the room instead of the elevator, giving himself more time to think. He had her for the weekend. She had agreed to be his sub. What was the risk in enjoying the situation for what it was and reassessing Sunday night?

He couldn't think of one, but as he opened the door to the room, he had a feeling he was missing something.

He'd thought since he was later than anticipated returning to the room, Lynne might not be in place. He was surprised to discover he was wrong. He looked through the door of the bedroom he'd claimed as his and saw her waiting in perfect position.

Fuck, he wanted her so bad. He checked his watch. Dinner could wait, and if he decided as the night went on that he wanted to play outside at the party, he really didn't want their first scene together to be public. He should take her now.

His dick agreed.

Though he typically didn't ask his dick's opinion when it came to making decisions, it was nice that all his body parts were in agreement.

He took his time walking into the room. Her spine straightened just a hair when she heard him enter, and he watched her breathing grow heavier. No matter how many times he played, he never grew tired of the way a submissive waited. Anxious. Needy. Yearning. Excited.

To have them so focused on him and his next move was a rush like no other.

For that submissive to be Lynne cranked up the rush by about one hundred percent.

He stood in front of her and took his belt off, making sure he did it slowly enough that she could hear the leather sliding through the loops of his pants. He didn't miss the small shiver that shook her body.

"You know I'm a sadist?" He hadn't told her when they were together the last time, and he didn't want to go any further without being very clear about who he was.

"Yes, Sir."

He let one end of the belt hang so just a part of it was in her line of sight. She sucked in a breath.

Yes.

"Your mind is racing, isn't it?" he asked. "There's the part telling you to stand up and get the hell out of this room. That you're crazy for even thinking about staying here. That no normal person would put themselves willingly into the hands of a sadist."

He didn't need her to answer. He knew he was right by the way she shifted slightly, as if wanting to give in to that advice.

"But the other part of you wants to stay right where you are because even though you know it doesn't make sense, you want nothing more than to be right here, right now, with me. Isn't that right?"

"Yes, Sir," she said, and her response held no fear, only need.

"That part of you is louder than the other part, but if I'm not mistaken, you've been doing all you can to silence it. You've tried telling it no and that it's a bad idea. You probably gave it all the reasons you can think of, and I'm sure some of them are really good reasons. But it's never enough, is it? Deep in your soul, you have a need for this, and giving in and accepting that need is the only thing that's going to shut it up. Am I right?"

"Yes, Sir." Her cheeks were flushed. He'd hit her thoughts exactly, and some part of her was embarrassed. He thought the embarrassment came from her admission of what she needed and not that he'd read her so easily.

"Rest assured, I'll do my very best to give you what you need this weekend. So, for the next forty-eight hours, let's leave the outside world outside. There will be only you and me and what we do together. How does that sound?"

"Really good, Sir." He didn't miss the smile in her voice.

"And, Lynne, look at me." He waited until she lifted her head before continuing. "You are not to feel shame or guilt for any of it. Understand?"

That one was harder for her to agree to. He appreciated that she didn't comply without thinking it through, but he didn't like her hesitation over something so basic in her personality. She was a submissive and she needed to accept that.

"I mean it, Lynne. We'll check out and go home right now if you can't agree to that."

She took a deep breath. "I'll try, Sir."

It would have to do, he decided. As the weekend went on, he would make it a point to check in with her frequently. If he ever caught her feeling embarrassed, he'd simply take her aside and they would talk through it.

"Earlier, I said that I was going to punish you for your deceit during the demo, but I've changed my mind. We're going to go ahead and get that out of the way right now, so we can, hopefully, spend the rest of the day exploring more pleasurable pursuits. Any questions so far?"

"No, Sir."

"Anything you want to talk about that I didn't bring up?"

"No, Sir."

He doubled the belt in his hand. "All right, let's get this over with. I want you to stand up and lean over the back of the couch. I'm going to use the belt, and there is no need for you to count. Tell me your safe word."

"Red."

"Nice and simple. This is a punishment, so it will hurt. And while my expectation is that you will accept what I give you, if it gets to be too much, you will use your safe word without hesitation. If you understand, go get into position."

She slowly rose to her feet and moved to stand behind the couch. He watched her, looking for any signs of distress and not finding any. She presented herself perfectly.

He wasn't looking forward to this. Disciplining a sub was hard. Though he was a sadist, he didn't enjoy inflicting pain for the sake of pain. It was much more enjoyable when both people got something out of it.

He moved behind her and gently caressed her backside. He wasn't sure how many strokes he was going to give her. That was one of the downsides of never having played with her before; he wasn't sure what she could take.

He warmed her up slowly with his hand, spending more time than he normally would because she was so unknown to him. But even then, the strokes weren't painless. He could tell when they really started to hurt because of the way her muscles strained to remained still.

He ran two fingers between her legs and felt the evidence of her arousal. Feeling her excitement made him grow hard. Because this was a discipline session, he wouldn't take her. But he would soon, he promised himself. He definitely would.

Satisfied that he had warmed her skin up enough, he started spanking her with the belt. He didn't go easy on her. He wanted her to have a sore backside so that she would remember what happened when she lied.

He watched her carefully. Silent tears ran down her cheeks, but she didn't utter a sound. Her ass was a deep red, and he knew she'd recall this very moment with just about every move she made.

"Spread your legs more. Give me access to that greedy pussy."

She faltered for a second, no doubt wondering what his plans were. He had just opened his mouth to tell her to do it now when she widened her stance.

"Good girl," he said instead. "Last few strokes."

He brought the belt down on her pussy three times—each one made her jump and squeal. As soon as the last one fell, he dropped the belt and carried her to the bed. He gathered her in his arms, holding her and gently rubbing her back. He knew she'd never been spanked before, and he'd feared she'd pull away from him, but she didn't. In fact, he was happily surprised that she seemed to want to put her arms around him.

He snagged a nearby blanket and covered her with it, not wanting her to get cold. She snuggled deeper into his embrace, and he was glad he'd decided to get that out of the way. Now the entire weekend was before them, promising nothing but decadent pleasure.

He'd forgotten how comforting it was to simply hold a submissive. It'd been far too long since he had. Since their schedule was free for the rest of the day, he decided they'd take it easy for the next hour or so. Lynne might need to talk since it had been her first punishment session.

Or, he thought, tightening his arms around her, she might just need to be held. And he was perfectly okay with that, too.

Because he'd decided that they would rest for the foreseeable future, it took longer than it should have for him to notice Lynne's hands were getting more provocative. He caught her wrist as it traced his jeans.

"What are you doing?" he asked.

"I want you, Sir." Her eyes were dark with lust. "Take me. Please."

Out of all the things he might have expected her to say and all the ways he thought she might react, her asking for sex had never entered his mind as a possibility. His dick, of course, was all for it.

"Now?" he asked.

"Yes, Sir."

He could imagine there were very few men who could turn a request like that down. How could he tell her no? Why would he?

Actually, he could think of a few reasons to refuse her, but at the moment none of them seemed important.

He lifted the blanket from her upper body and dropped a kiss on her shoulder. "I need to care for your backside first."

Maybe the act of tending to her would help keep his libido in check. As it was, it felt like he was losing the tentative grip he had on his control.

"Roll over onto your belly," he said as he got out of bed. What he needed was in the bags he'd brought, but he'd left them in the living room. He made sure Lynne was covered and went to get it.

He'd also left his phone in the living room, and of course it happened to start ringing as soon as he was making his way back to the bedroom. Whoever it was could leave a message. Lynne was his top priority right now.

She was in the same position he'd left her in, but at his entrance, she lifted her head and looked over her shoulder at him. Damn, she was gorgeous.

"Ass hurt?" he asked, even though he knew the answer. He climbed onto the bed, lifted the blanket, and tended to her skin.

"Yes, Sir," she said. "But I like it. Well, not like it, like it. I mean, I don't want to do that again, but yeah. It reminds me of you, and because of that, I like it."

She fisted the sheets, almost as if she needed something to hold on to. "You okay?" he asked. The cream he was putting on her shouldn't be causing her pain, but something was bothering her.

"Yes, Sir," she said.

He kissed her lower back, right above the swell of her backside, and he swore he could feel her body relax at his touch. He caressed her, teased the skin of her back with nibbles and kisses.

Pressing himself along her back, being careful not to put too much pressure on her ass, he dropped his head and whispered in her ear, "I want you to get up on all fours, so I can fuck you while I admire how red I made your ass."

"Sir? I . . . um . . ."

"Yes?"

"Remember when you said earlier not to be embarrassed or ashamed by what I want?"

"Yes." He kept stroking her body, not wanting to let her arousal subside.

"I would like to do something, and, well, it's okay for me to ask, right? I know as a Dom you don't have to do it."

He was struck again at how different she was now compared to when they were together the first time. That Lynne would have never asked for anything. He was so proud of her, he knew he'd give her anything she wanted.

"Tell me," he said. "No more secrets between us. If you have a need or want, you bring it to me."

She took a deep breath. "Do I have to be on all fours?"

That was what she wanted to talk about? Positions? Really?

Instead of explaining why he thought it'd be better for her to be on all fours, he decided to see just how open and forthcoming she was going to be. "How would you like to be?"

"On my back." She wasn't looking at him now. She had her

head turned to the side away from him. That was probably why she was able to talk so freely. He needed to remember that. "I know it'll be maybe a little painful, but I think I'd like it like that. You on top of me, taking me, while at the same time, I feel what you did to my ass not too long ago. The harder you fuck me, the more I'll feel where you spanked me and it'll——"

He cut her off by flipping her over and claiming her mouth with a kiss. Hot fucking damn, if hearing her talk like that wasn't the hottest and sexiest thing he'd ever heard, he didn't know what was. Listening to her had turned a part of him on that had been dormant for entirely too long. Hell, he wasn't even sure it'd ever been turned on. And he was willing to bet she had no idea what her words did to ignite the sadist within him.

Beneath him, she was all softness and sexy curves, her body a treasure map of pleasure that was his for the taking. She wasn't passive in her kiss, either. Oh no, not this new Lynne. She took as well as she gave, and as much as he was tasting her, she tasted him.

He ended the kiss with a bite on her lower lip that made her groan. "I think you've got quite a bit of a masochist in you."

It was his ultimate dream, the one he never thought he could have, and here it was in his arms. Lynne. His Lynne. Looking at him as if he was her dream, too.

It was hard for Lynne to breathe the way Simon was looking at her. His eyes held an intensity she'd never seen before. It was a bit disarming, actually. Like he wanted to devour her and at the same time to shelter and protect her from anything.

"I think you might be right," she said. "And, trust me, that doesn't come as a bigger shock to anyone than it does me."

"Why is that?"

She couldn't believe, given the position they were in, that he wanted to *talk*. She almost thought about asking if he was serious, but being on her back had the exact effect she'd thought it would. Yet the pain from her backside only added to the overwhelming sense of arousal that made her grit her teeth so she wouldn't hump against him, desperate for relief.

But still, she wasn't going to goad him into punishing her again.

"Why is it a shock that I think I might be a masochist?" she asked, repeating his question. "I guess because I always categorized them. Thought that they would look different, act different. I never saw them as someone who could work as a nanny or a schoolteacher."

As soon as the words left her mouth, she realized how foolish they sounded.

"Saying it, I can tell how silly that is. Like your profession dictates your sexual needs or something." She wrinkled her nose. "Or your sexual needs dictate your profession. Either way it doesn't work."

"No, it doesn't. And you are no less and no more of anything because of what you need sexually."

He hadn't moved away in the time they'd been talking, and she was suddenly very much aware of his body towering over her. She could feel him even if she closed her eyes. It went beyond the spanking he'd given her. Some part of him connected with her inner being. She knew deep in her soul that it would never be like that with anyone else.

The mood in the room changed, and Simon must have felt it, too. His eyes grew dark and hungry.

"You have no idea what you do to me," he said.

"Will you show me, Sir?" she asked, teasing him a bit.

"Tell me." He lowered his body just enough that he pressed her a bit further into the bed. Even the slight shifting of his body had her backside moving against the sheets. She was very much aware of all that had happened to her not long before. "When we're positioned like this, is it like you thought it would be?"

He spread her legs apart with his knees, and the soreness from his spanking intensified.

"No, Sir," she said.

"No?"

"It's even better."

That was all it took. He let out a sound that was something between a growl and a grunt, and he came up on his knees. Quicker than she thought possible, his pants were off and a condom was in his hand and he was rolling it on.

"You just shot my plan to go slow and easy straight to hell," he said.

"Oh, thank God," she said, wanting to sit up and touch him, but wanting to obey him more. Since he hadn't given any instruction, she thought it best to wait.

His grin was both predatory and determined. "Have something against slow and easy?"

"No, Sir. Not on principle. But in this case, at this point in time? Yes, I have something against slow and easy."

At odds with his words, his hands grazed the skin of her belly in a way that his light touch made goose bumps pebble up. "Knowing that almost makes me want to go slow and easy just because you don't want me to."

He rolled one of her nipples between this thumb and forefinger, ending with a sharp pinch. She gasped and arched her back, wanting to take more if it was his wish.

"I've wanted you for so long, Sir. I don't care how you take me."

He froze at her words, and she bit her lip. Dammit. She shouldn't have said anything.

"I'm sorry, Lynne."

Now she really knew she shouldn't have said anything. They had gone from hot and heavy to melancholy.

"There's nothing to apologize for, Sir." And since he'd told her he wanted honesty from now on, she added, "I don't mind talking about the past, but I'd really, really like to not talk about it right this second."

He no longer looked melancholy. The desire and lust that had never truly disappeared from his expression had almost totally taken over. "I'm not opposed to delaying our conversation till later. On one condition, that is."

"Anything, Sir."

"Talk like that will get you in trouble with me one day," he said, and though his voice held a bit of a teasing note, she knew he was being serious.

"Almost anything, Sir," she corrected.

"Better." He took her hands and brought them out to her sides so they were perpendicular to her body. "The condition is you have to keep your arms right there and don't move them. If you move them, I stop what I'm doing and you won't come at all this weekend."

She vowed then and there, the room could catch on fire and she wasn't moving her arms. "Yes, Sir."

"You know I'm going to try really hard to entice you to move those arms."

She grabbed on to the sheets. "I expected that, Sir."

He didn't say anything further, but lowered his head to her shoulder and began to kiss his way across and down her body.

He even paid attention to both arms, kissing the bend of each elbow in turn.

She thought it was a pity she couldn't touch him. It was evil and mean of him to deprive her of that privilege. But as he continued his way down, seconds before his mouth found her nipple, it struck her that maybe he'd had her keep her hands to herself because he doubted his control if she touched him.

While she'd expected him to be a thorough lover, she'd vastly underestimated just how thorough that could be. She was positive he didn't skip one inch of her as he licked, kissed, and stroked his way down her body. By the time he finally lifted his head, she had twisted the sheets several times in her fists and was trembling with the strain to keep still.

"I'm impressed," he said, and his voice was so calm and even sounding, she nearly cursed him out.

But she swallowed those words and took a deep breath. "I have to say, Sir," she said, surprised that her voice didn't mimic the tension she felt everywhere else in her body, "you surprise me."

"How so?" He trailed a fingertip around her belly, and she moaned.

"When you told me you were a sadist, this isn't how I expected you to torture me."

He laughed softly and bent his head to bite where his fingers had been. She sucked in a breath as he blew across the wet spot left behind. Her belly shivered in the most delightful way.

"Expecting it to be a bit more like that?" he asked.

"Yes, Sir."

"Lucky for you, I have many, many ways to whip your body into a frenzy." As if to prove his point, he pulled her legs over his shoulders and gave her ass a quick slap.

She yelped—she was still sore from his earlier spanking. But he didn't stop there; he promptly teased her clit, and she almost released her hold on the sheets.

"Dammit." She wrapped more of the cotton around her hands.

"Cursing in bed?" He raised an eyebrow.

"You bring out the bad girl in me, Sir."

"You say that like it's a bad thing."

"Definitely not bad, Sir. I rather like it."

"Do you?" he asked.

The entire time they'd been talking, he'd kept up his teasing fingers along her inner thighs, dipping his finger into her slightly, but never deep enough to give her the relief she desperately wanted.

He was looking at her as if waiting for her to say something. What was it? She couldn't think anymore with those fingers of his doing what they were doing. "I don't remember the question, Sir."

"That's okay," he said. "It wasn't important anyway."

She still had her legs on his shoulders, and she thought she would go crazy as she watched him slowly place himself at her entrance. She thought he would go fast, but once again he surprised her and ever so slowly pushed his way inside.

She arched her back. In the position she was in, she could feel everything. Him filling her up, the soreness of her backside, and when he moved his hands to pinch her nipples, she shuddered.

"You'd better not come without permission." There was no trace of a teasing note left in his voice, and she knew she'd better hold on until he told her differently.

She bit her bottom lip, hoping the pain would help keep her from release. But as she was quickly learning, the pain just seemed to make it more intense.

"Please, Sir."

He didn't answer, but continued to push his way inside. So

slow. He was trying to torture her by pleasure. And he was doing an excellent job at it. He held still for a second, and she took a deep breath, thinking she had taken him all. But just as she was getting ready to breathe a little easier, he thrust the rest of the way in.

She yelped and felt herself start to tighten around him, but she held off. She closed her eyes and concentrated as hard as she could, finally able to hold off the orgasm.

"Such a good girl," he said.

"I'm not sure I can be for much longer, Sir."

He started moving within her slowly, rocking his hips back and forth, as if he had all the time in the world. She supposed they did; after all, they didn't have anywhere else to be tonight.

"You feel so good," he said, and sped up.

She mumbled something, but she wasn't sure what, because at that moment he grabbed hold of her backside and used it for leverage. His fingers dug into her aching flesh. It should have hurt too much, but instead it was just as she'd told him it would be. Between the soreness of her backside and his relentless pounding into her, she felt completely claimed.

"You can move your arms," he ground out in a coarse voice.

It was the sign she'd been waiting for, and she threw her arms around him as if he were the only thing holding her down to earth. "Please, Sir," she begged. "I don't think I can hold off."

"Then come." He tightened his grip on her ass.

That was all it took. She lifted her hips, wanting him to go deeper. He complied, and she shattered around him. He held still until she finished.

She opened her eyes and sucked in a breath. He loomed over her, his body straining, and she realized he hadn't climaxed yet.

"Now it's my turn," he growled.

She could only hold on tight to his arms and nod as he took his pleasure from her body. He was magnificent to watch, all rippled muscle and male strength. She felt another climax approaching, and she looked up to him in question.

"Yes," he said.

She breathed a sigh of relief, and while the orgasm was not as intense as the previous one, it still took her breath away, especially watching Simon giving in to his own release.

He roared with pleasure as it passed. Breathing heavily, he gathered her in his arms and rolled them so she was on top. A minor detail, but one she was thankful for, because now that her body had had a chance to come down from its high, she was aware of every ache and pain.

She winced as she tried to get into a more comfortable position. Simon immediately sensed her need and helped her.

"Let me get you something for the pain," he said.

Frankly, watching Simon walk around the hotel room naked worked just as well as any pain medication, she thought. But when he came back to the bed with two pills, she went ahead and swallowed them, figuring it couldn't hurt.

She drank the water he gave her and giggled when her stomach gurgled.

Simon raised an eyebrow. "Are you hungry?"

"I don't feel hungry, but it seems my belly thinks differently."

"I had planned for us to go down to one of the restaurants on site here, but now I think I'll change our plans." His gaze wandered over her still naked body. She felt completely sated, albeit sore, but thought she probably looked like she was in desperate need of a shower.

Of course, maybe not. From the way he was looking at her, it didn't appear he found her in need of anything. She decided she wasn't going to allow herself to be self-conscious, so even though she felt like pulling the sheet up to her chest, she didn't. In fact, she went one step further and pushed it down to her ankles.

"What do you have in mind?" she asked him.

The corner of his mouth lifted in a slight smile. "I'm thinking we order room service and eat up here."

She wasn't an overly social person. Most of the time she favored an evening at home as opposed to going to a party or any other type of social gathering. That was probably why she did so well as a nanny. She simply didn't care to be surrounded by people.

"We can go down to the party and dance after we eat, if that's what you want," he said.

"Only if you want to, Sir. I'm perfectly content to stay up here, just the two of us."

He nodded. "I wouldn't mind a nice quiet night to ourselves, either. But there are several people who mentioned they wanted to talk to me tonight. I think we'll have to be social for a little while at least."

"I can handle that." She'd heard there would be dancing, and while she rarely had the opportunity to dance, it was something she enjoyed. Looking over at Simon's built-for-sin body, she found it wasn't hard to imagine dancing with him, his arms around her, his hips grinding into hers. An unspoken promise of what he'd be doing when the dance was over.

Damn. She grew aroused just thinking about it.

"In fact, Sir, I might go so far as to say I'd really like to head downstairs after dinner. Especially if you think I might be able to persuade you to dance a little bit?"

She didn't know if he liked to dance or would even want to.

"You might possibly be able to talk me into a dance or two." He grinned. "Though I have to warn you, I have two left feet."

"I don't believe it, Sir."

"It's probably something you have to experience firsthand." He walked to the desk and picked up the room service menu. "Anything in particular you want for dinner?"

She raised an eyebrow.

He snorted. "That I can order from downstairs?"

"In that case, no, not really."

He gave her thigh a slap. "You have thirty minutes, and then I want you back in here."

"Naked?"

"I'll tell you when you can have clothes; until then, assume I want you naked at all times."

She pretended to be outraged, but deep inside she loved it and had a feeling Simon knew it as well. She waited for him to disappear into his bathroom before she hopped out of bed and went into hers to take a shower. She thought about surprising him by saying she thought it was a waste of water for them to take separate showers. But she didn't, deciding she wasn't sure if he'd like that.

Crazy. What normal man wouldn't want to have a willing and naked woman in his shower?

But neither she nor Simon had ever been considered normal.

By the time she made it back to his bedroom, twenty-five minutes later, she'd showered and washed and dried her hair. Simon stood near the nightstand with his back to her, and she took a second to admire his ass, even though he had put a pair of jeans on.

"I really don't think it's fair that I have to be naked and you get clothes, Sir." She crossed her arms and tried to look perturbed.

He turned around and her breath caught. How was it possible for him to look so good in only a pair of jeans? His hair was still damp from his shower, and she wondered if his skin would be as well.

"I thought one of us should be decent when they delivered the food," he said.

As if they'd heard him, someone knocked on the door. Simon flashed her a smile. "Wait here."

Like she was going to give whoever delivered dinner a peep show. When he walked out to answer the door, she went to her knees to wait. It was a small gesture, but one she believed he'd appreciate. It took a bit longer than she'd thought it would for him to come back into the room. She strained her ears, but couldn't hear anything. Finally, she closed her eyes and thought about what his expression would be when he came in and saw her.

She couldn't contain a smile of victory at his gasp when he walked through the door. There were soft footsteps as he approached her.

"Very nice, Lynne," he said, and she delighted in the way his voice sent shivers up and down her spine. Damn, but she loved it when he said her name. "Now, come with me."

She stood and followed him into the living area. He'd been busy. She first noticed the candles scattered around the room. Short pillar candles seemed to be his favorite. There were four on the coffee table alone. Also on the table were three silver-domed trays, a bottle of wine, and a single glass. As they moved closer, she saw there was only one table setting as well. What the fuck? Was one of them not eating?

He led her to the couch and sat down, indicating she should kneel at his feet. She told herself that she wouldn't let thoughts that she shouldn't do any such thing prevent her from doing it. She was kneeling. At a man's feet. And she was naked. *Later.* She would think about it all later. Then maybe she could discuss it with him. She wasn't going to mention anything to him at the moment, at least not about that. She thought she might decide to tell him that she would like something to eat.

Those words died on her lips when he reached for the wine, poured a glass, and held it up to her lips. She took a sip, and was only a little surprised when he didn't drink anything.

"You will eat tonight," he said, stroking her cheek. "But only by my hand."

Having a Dom feed her while she sat at his feet had never played out in her fantasies. She was quite certain that if it had, she wouldn't have thought there to be anything sexy at all about the scenario. Yet, at this moment in time, kneeling at Simon's feet and waiting for him to feed her, it was one of the biggest turn-ons she'd ever experienced.

As he took pieces of bread and held them to her mouth, or bade her part her lips for a taste of shrimp, something deep inside her belly grew warm and wanting. It was the most infuriating thing because he didn't seem bothered at all. Nor did he eat or drink anything. Apparently, it was all for her.

She started to squirm as her clit begged to be touched.

"None of that," Simon said. "Be still."

She bit the inside of her cheek to keep from sighing. It was torture to have him doing something as intimate as feeding her and having to remain still while he did it. He held a block of cheese to her lips, and she took the opportunity to suck one of his fingers into her mouth.

"Such a dirty little girl," he said. "Sucking on fingers like they were someone's cock."

She nodded around his finger. Maybe he'd do something about it now.

"You know, I was going to have you for dessert, but I think I'm full now and I'll save my treat for later."

He was such a bastard. She grumbled around his finger, but he only laughed. "None of that. Why don't you go get dressed and we'll see about dancing? See if I can make you believe I have two left feet."

Two hours later, she believed him. What she didn't believe was how someone as talented as he was in everything else could suck so badly at dancing.

"Sorry," he said, after once again stepping on her toes.

She gritted her teeth, because *damn* that hurt. "I get it now. You're a sadist. You get some perverse pleasure from repeatedly stepping on me."

He gave a short laugh. "Good one. But unfortunately, no. I'm just really bad at dancing, and believe me, stepping on toes is not my kind of kink."

"My feet beg to differ, Sir."

He winced at that. "Perhaps we should sit this one out?"

"I think that's the best idea you've had all day."

He placed his hand at the small of her back, and they weaved their way through the sea of people dancing. Couples and groups of both genders and multiple nationalities gyrated to the rhythmic beat that pulsated through the speakers set up in the courtyard.

There were scattered benches lined around the perimeter of the outside space, and Simon took her to an empty one.

"Sit in my lap," he told her once he sat down.

She thought he'd have her kneel either at his side or in front of him, and she'd actually been looking forward to it. But her disappointment didn't last, because the only place she'd rather sit than at his feet was in his lap.

He gave her a tug, and she tumbled into his lap. "There we go. Much better."

His arms came around her, and her skin heated where he touched her. All it took was that little touch for memories of what they'd done earlier in the day to flood her mind and for her body to crave his hands on her again.

He must have experienced something similar, because his hands didn't leave her body. He placed one hand up high on her thigh, and the other traced invisible lines on her knee.

"This is much better," he said, and because she was in his lap, his breath brushed her skin as he talked. "We can sit here and people-watch."

"I love people watching."

And there was no shortage of people to watch at the moment. From their position in the courtyard, they could see both the dance floor and the play area.

"The problem, Sir, is trying to decide who you want to observe first."

"Very true. I think I've had enough dancing for the moment, so I'll watch the people playing."

That sounded infinitely better than watching people dance. She could see that almost anytime she wanted. Watching people play, however, wasn't something she often had the opportunity to observe. There wasn't a lack of scenes to pick from. From what she could tell, at least with the current activity taking place in the play area, most of the scenes were not extreme or edge play. Though Simon had mentioned that there were private rooms available for rent.

Playing with Simon in private would be fun, but surely they would have plenty of time for that after this weekend. Right? She bit her bottom lip, wondering.

"See that man at the far end?" Simon asked her. "The one with the two female subs?"

The man in question was directing the two women in front of a large web-looking thing. "Suspension?" she asked.

"Yes. He's very good, from what I've heard."

She tried to watch, but suspension wasn't a big turn-on for her, and neither was playing with a female. Her focus kept being drawn to a flogging scene closer to them.

"The gentleman with the flogger is quite good, too," Simon said, and she couldn't miss the smile in his voice.

"Sorry, Sir." She looked back at the suspension scene. "I don't think that's my kink."

"Why?"

"For one, I don't like heights and it looks fucking scary."

He smirked. "All the more reason to do it. Was there a second reason?"

"I don't know if I want to tell you now."

He ran a finger down her arm, and she shivered. "You always have a safe word. No is always an answer."

"I don't want to be in a three-way. Especially with a woman."

He nodded. "Yes, that was on your checklist. Marked as a hard limit. That means it won't happen."

Technically, she supposed it was Faye's checklist, and though she supposed they were one and the same, she appreciated that he didn't bring that up.

"Right," she said. "I forgot that was on there. I should have marked suspension as well."

"The fact that you didn't tells me that deep inside you may want to give it a try. But if I remember correctly, it was marked as a soft limit, and as such, I won't be pushing it this weekend."

His words only relaxed her slightly. She had a feeling there was more he wasn't saying. Maybe that while he wouldn't push the limit this weekend, next weekend was totally up for grabs. There was just enough devilish delight in his eyes to keep her on the edge of uncertainty.

She decided to change the topic of conversation. "That Dom using two floggers at a time is pretty cool."

Simon didn't even look at the Dom she was talking about. "Would that be something you're interested in experiencing?"

"Yes, Sir. Definitely more than suspension."

He muttered an agreement and moved the hand that was on her thigh farther up her leg. "Keep watching the Dom with two floggers. And whatever you do, don't make a sound."

Oh, shit. That didn't sound good. What was he planning to do?

She didn't have to wait long before she found out. He dropped his head and whispered in her ear, "I'm getting so hard with you sitting here in my lap. And watching all these people is giving me all sorts of ideas about what I'd like to do with you."

She would have groaned if he would have allowed it. Damn, but he wasn't going to make this easy. Not that she expected him to.

"I can feel how wet you are through your panties." He palmed her pussy, and the heat from his hand felt so good, she wiggled, trying to get closer. That earned her a sharp slap, right on her clit. "Be still."

She froze in place and pretended to be a stone. That in and of itself would have been difficult enough just sitting on his lap, but when you added in his wandering fingers, she didn't know how much she could take.

"Good girl," he finally said, stilling his hands. "Now I want you to move just enough to slide the panties off."

Here? She looked around. It was stupid to be embarrassed. She'd been naked for the demo practice, and she'd be naked for the demo tomorrow. And hell, it wasn't as if there weren't plenty of naked people in the courtyard this very second.

But somehow the thought of taking her panties off in public made her cheeks heat. Which, again, was stupid. They were just panties. She glanced at Simon, who was watching her with an *I'm waiting* expression. It hit her that this was the reason he hadn't told her not to wear panties. He'd wanted to make her take them off in public.

She'd thought it was odd that he didn't say anything about not wearing them. At the time, she'd decided maybe he was being nice by letting her wear them. Now she knew the truth. He'd known the entire time what he was going to have her do. There was nothing nice about it.

If only she could talk. But he'd told her not to, and she wasn't in a mood to be bratty and disobedient. Which meant there was only one thing for her to do.

She lifted her hips slightly and pushed the panties down and off, wondering the entire time if someone other than Simon was watching, but not looking around to see. Because, damn, what if someone was observing her?

She forced herself to think reasonably. If anyone was watching, they probably thought what she was doing was hot. If the roles were reversed and she was watching a Dom with a sub in his lap and the sub took her panties off, she'd think the scene was hot. Especially if the Dom was as yummy-looking as Simon. She ran her gaze over his body since her eyes were the only part of her that she could move. He'd slipped on a T-shirt before they'd come down, and it stretched across his chest muscles in the most fabulous way. Add in his biceps and, yup, she was done for.

She handed the panties to Simon, but he shook his head. "Put them in your mouth."

What?

She didn't say it out loud, but it must have been written all over her face.

"I don't think I was unclear, Lynne. Put the panties in your mouth."

Funny, when he said he'd be pushing her this weekend, this wasn't what she thought he had meant. She could either do what he requested or safeword. And panties weren't worth safewording over. Keeping her eyes on Simon, she opened her mouth and put the panties inside.

Good God, she wasn't going to look anywhere else. What if people were looking back?

"Wasn't as bad as you thought it was going to be, was it?" he asked.

She couldn't talk with her mouth full of underwear, so she shook her head. Maybe he'd let her take them out now.

But no, he once more started teasing her upper thigh with his fingers, and this time when he reached the top, there was no cloth in his way. She bit down on the material in her mouth, suddenly thankful it was there.

"So wet," he murmured in her ear. "I could unzip my pants and slide right on inside you, couldn't I?"

She nodded, begging him with her eyes. *Please. Yes. Now.*

But that wasn't part of his plan. Oh, no. That would have been way too easy. And if she knew one thing about Simon, it was that he rarely did anything the easy way.

Instead of releasing his cock and giving them what they both wanted, he continued to tease her. He brought her right to the edge. She was so full of tension and strung so tight from withholding her release, she thought she'd combust if he blew the lightest breath on her. Not to mention, she was ever so thankful she had something to bite down on to help keep her from climaxing without permission.

Just as she was getting ready to either say, "Fuck it," and deal with the consequences or safeword, his fingers were gone. She took a shaky breath.

He reached up and took the panties out of her mouth. "You okay?"

Deep breath. "Yes, Sir."

He didn't replace the panties, but stuck them in his pocket. "One more thing tonight and then I'll take you upstairs and do all sorts of wicked and depraved things to your body."

He truly was going to kill her.

If he weren't so hard he feared his dick would be permanently imprinted with his zipper, he'd have laughed at Lynne's look of exasperation. He'd pushed her a bit. Not nearly as far as he wanted or could, but far enough, given her relative inexperience in the kink world. So far, she'd taken everything he'd given her—and she'd taken it surprisingly well.

He watched her process his commands, happy to see that she didn't mindlessly do anything he asked her. She was new to all this, and she took the time to ensure it was not something she had an issue with before she followed through.

He respected that. All too often he'd seen new submissives blindly leap into whatever the Dom they were with wanted without making sure it was also what they wanted. Granted, he held the Dom responsible as well. But it all came down to the sub.

From what he'd seen tonight, Lynne was certainly a sub, but she was no doormat. And because she'd done so well, he intended to reward her once they made it back to their room.

But first . . .

"I want you to dance for me," he told her. "We both know I'm no good at it, and I'm willing to bet neither one of us wants to repeat our earlier attempt. But I don't think you got to dance enough, and I want to watch you without having to worry about stepping on your toes."

She gave a small laugh at his last statement and slid off his lap.

For a minute she looked awkward and uncertain, but he knew she only needed time to adjust and get comfortable.

"Close your eyes," he told her. "It'll make it easier."

She didn't hesitate, but took his advice immediately. Almost as soon as she did, her body relaxed. Very slowly, she started to sway in time with the music. Subtle at first, but then, as she grew more comfortable and confident, her moves became bolder.

Her hips swayed and gyrated. Gradually, she let her arms loosen, and they followed the movement of her torso. Before he knew it and right before his eyes, she turned into a siren. The way she moved, so full of grace and sensuality, completely mesmerized him.

He couldn't take his eyes off the vixen before him. Her dance was both a long tease and the most incredible foreplay he'd ever experienced. He wanted to watch her forever and push her against a wall so he could bury himself deep inside her.

He clenched his hands into fists so he would not disturb her with his touch. Fuck, that one time earlier in the day hadn't been enough to satisfy the need he had for her. Not that he thought it would, but he hadn't expected to need her again quite so badly.

He vaguely wondered how many times and ways he could take her without impacting their stamina to do the demo the next day.

There was no answer forthcoming; he just knew he had to have her. Many times.

"Open your eyes," he told her. "Don't look anywhere except at me."

He'd thought she might be self-conscious, but when she opened her eyes he could tell she was fully into her dance. She didn't once look anywhere except at him. Her eyes had grown dark with lust, and she moved as if her only desire in the world was to dance for him.

"Come closer, but don't touch."

She moved forward, never missing a step and never glancing away from him even though his eyes traveled all over her body. He drank in every detail of the sultry woman before him.

Following his command, she got so close to him, he felt the heat from her body, but she never touched him. Then she totally blew his mind by bending her legs, one on either side of his, and moving in such a way that mimicked her riding him.

Fucking hell, he was adding that to the plan for tonight.

"Tell me, Sir," she said, her eyes still on him and continuing to move in a way guaranteed to make him come in his pants. "I know I can't touch you, but can you touch me?"

He should remind her that he was a Dom and, as such, he could do anything he wanted. Then he should spank her ass for forgetting, but instead he nodded. "Of course I can. However, at this moment, I've decided not to touch you."

She gave a pout, but continued dancing, almost grazing his crotch. *Dammit.* His fingers itched with the need to touch her.

"And if you insist on pouting like a bratty toddler, I'll keep my hands to myself all night."

Her eyes sparkled with mischief. "You can keep your hands to yourself, Sir, as long as you share the other parts."

He couldn't help it; he snorted at her response. How was it he'd never been able to laugh while playing before? And what was it about Lynne that made it possible? Was he stricter with other subs, or was it just her nature and it hadn't been that way for the other women he'd played with? He wasn't sure, but he liked being able to actually *play* during play.

"The other parts?" he asked. "What other parts would that be? I believe I need specifics."

"Your cock, Sir."

He was surprised she'd said it. Even though she hadn't had a problem being vocal earlier in the day, now they were in public. While it was doubtful anyone was listening to their conversation, the possibility always existed that someone could.

He flashed her a grin and, before she could guess his intention, grabbed her by the waist and pulled her down on top of him. She yelped in surprise and he bit her earlobe.

"This cock?" He thrust his hips up, making sure he came into contact with her clit.

"Oh, shit. Yes, Sir." She ground her hips against his covered erection. "That's the one I was talking about."

"It damn well better be. Because you sure as hell aren't getting anyone else's."

She nodded, still trying to find her own pleasure in humping him.

"Stop," he commanded, holding her hips still.

She whined, but froze in place, breathing heavily.

"I think I've people-watched enough for one night," he said, and she nodded in agreement. "I want you to get off my lap and walk in front of me. We're not taking the elevator; we're taking the stairs so I can enjoy watching that ass of yours."

She lowered her eyes and softly spoke two words. "Yes, Sir."

Speaking of her ass, his plans for what they were going to do when they reached the room changed as she walked up the stairs. Oh no, he wasn't finished with that ass just yet.

They made it back to the room and she stood in the middle of the living room floor, waiting.

"Is that how you wait for your Dom?" he asked, crossing his arms.

She let out a squeal and dropped to her knees.

"Very good," he said. "But you're overdressed."

Cursing, she stood up long enough to rip her clothes off and then knelt again, breathing heavily from exertion as well as from anticipation if he had to guess.

"Better," he said. "Next time, let's try to get it right the first time. And next time, I want you in red lipstick; nothing turns me on more than a sub with red lipstick sucking my cock."

She nodded.

"Now." He stepped closer to her, invaded her space, wanting to ensure she thought of nothing other than him and the words he was saying. "You've been teasing me with that ass of yours all night. Not to mention how much I got to see it when I spanked you."

"Oh no," she muttered, probably guessing where he was going.

"Oh, yes. You don't have anal sex marked as a hard limit. Tell me, have you had anal sex before?"

"No, Sir."

He grew harder at the thought of being the first to claim her there. "Have you ever used a plug?"

"Once or twice," she admitted, though she didn't sound like she was happy to be doing so. "I didn't enjoy it, Sir."

He tilted his head. "Did you use one on yourself, or did someone use one on you?"

"I used it on myself, Sir."

"I see." And he did. "However, I really enjoy anal sex and I want it, so that's what we're going to do. I'll go slow and I'll be as gentle as I can, but unless you safeword, my cock's going up your ass. Tonight."

"Yes, Sir." Though she would probably deny it, he could tell by the way she answered, in that breathy voice, that she was more than a little turned on by the thought of what he was going to do.

"Move forward," he said. "Face on the floor, ass in the air."

She muttered something under her breath but moved into position.

"Nice," he said. "Now you're going to stay like that and think about what your ass is getting ready to take while I prepare."

Leaving her in the living room, he went into the bedroom to collect what he needed. She hadn't moved when he returned, though she jerked when he dropped to her side and stroked her backside.

"So jumpy," he mused.

"Sorry, Sir," she quipped. "I'm a bit anxious about that monster cock fitting inside me that way."

"I can handle anxiety." He kept stroking her. "Nerves and feeling a bit scared are okay as well."

"And I'm afraid it's going to hurt."

He massaged both her butt cheeks. "I suppose it will hurt a little to begin with, and there's not much I can do about that. But if you trust me and do what I say, it'll go easier on you. Can you do that?"

"I'll try, Sir."

"That's all I need." He gave her ass a sharp slap. "Now reach back and spread your cheeks so I can prepare them."

"Sir!"

"Is there a problem?"

"That sounds horribly embarrassing, Sir."

"And?"

"And I don't want to."

He rained three hard and fast slaps on her ass. "Did I ask you what you wanted?"

"No, Sir."

He gave her three more. "Do you think I care that you're embarrassed?"

She whimpered, but he didn't miss the wetness starting to appear between her legs. "No, Sir."

"Exactly." He rubbed the skin he'd spanked, making sure she felt it. "What I care about is you following directions. Now reach back and hold yourself open."

This time there was no hesitation.

"Very nice." He reached between her legs and teased her clit, pleased at the ass wiggle she gave him in response. "If you recall what I told you earlier, there is nothing that happens between us to be embarrassed about. When we're together like this, there is no part of you that is to be hidden from me. Nothing about your body. Nothing about your mind. Understand?"

"Yes, Sir."

"Easy to agree to, but much harder to put into practice. Now ask me to prepare your ass for a fucking."

She took a deep breath, and he thought for a minute she'd balk, but she surprised him by saying, "Please, Sir, prepare my ass for fucking."

"With pleasure." He lubed two fingers and pressed one at her back opening, immediately noticing how she tensed up. "You have to relax, Lynne, or this won't work."

She didn't want to relax, so he slipped two fingers of his other hand into her pussy and began a slow pump in and out. The squeak she couldn't hold back encouraged him. She was tight and unsure, but he knew with enough patience he could have her exactly where he wanted her.

Little by little, he worked to get her to focus on the two fingers teasing her G-spot. She rose onto her toes at his continuous movement, but it wasn't until she started pushing back toward him that he knew she was almost there.

"There we go," he murmured low. "That's how you do it."

He slowly started moving his other finger back into her, but this time she didn't tense up.

"Good girl," he said. "Take my finger."

There would be no rushing of this, he told himself. If it took all night, it would take all night, but dammit, he was going to make her love it.

He kept her right on the edge of orgasm, teasing her mercilessly. She rocked her hips and whimpered, but he didn't allow her to have what she craved. Not yet.

"I'm going to add another finger now," he told her, and her only reply was a nod.

Slowly, he eased a second finger into her backside and held still while continuing to hit deep inside her with the other. He smiled at her tormented whimpers. She was close.

"Do you need to come?" he asked.

She shoved her ass back at him. "Yes, Sir."

"Then come for me." He slipped his fingers out of her backside, and she came around the ones he had inside her pussy. Her orgasm passed and he slipped those out as well and lubed up his cock.

Taking a deep breath to ground himself and to remind himself that he needed to go slow, he lined himself up with his cock pressing against her. Under him, she shuddered.

"Are you okay?" he asked.

"Yes, Sir." Her release had left her panting slightly. "I never thought I would say it, but I want it. Please. I'm so empty."

"That's what I like to hear." He eased the tip of his cock inside her, relieved with her moans of pleasure that followed. He reached down and grabbed a fistful of hair. "You like having a cock up your ass?"

"Yes, Sir," she answered, and he was pleased she didn't sound the least bit ashamed or guilty at the admission.

He yanked on her hair. "Ask me to fuck your ass."

"Please, Sir. Fuck my ass."

He kept his hand buried in her hair while he pushed steadily into her. "So damn tight. I love the sight of my cock claiming this virgin ass."

She muttered something, but he couldn't make out what it

was. Based on the way she pushed back toward him, she wanted more, and he gladly gave it to her, pressing forward until she'd taken all of him.

Once he was deep inside her, he held still to allow her time to get used to being filled and to remind himself that her needs came first. He took several deep breaths and pulled her hair tighter. "Good girl, taking my cock. Ready for me to fuck your ass?"

Her body shook with delicious shivers. "Yes, Sir."

He didn't say anything else, but started moving inside her, thrusting slowly at first, and as her whimpers of pleasure grew louder, he moved faster. She was so tight, he gritted his teeth, trying to resist the nearly overwhelming temptation to pound into her unrestrained.

Again, he took several deep breaths to clear his mind. This was Lynne, and she had given him her trust. As much as he enjoyed mind games, he didn't want her hurt in any way.

Feeling calmer, he moved a bit faster, going deeper.

"Please," she begged.

She was lovely in her submission, and he wanted to give her everything he could. He wanted to taunt and tease her and hold her close and protect her with all he had. He wanted to lasso the damn moon and pull it down to earth for her.

Instead, he gave her what he could in that moment. The pleasure of his body. The warmth of his touch. And gentle whispers against her skin.

Fuck, he was screwed.

She should have been tired. It had been a very eventful day, what with the practice demo, Simon finding out the truth, the hot sex, the dancing, and more hot sex. But she wasn't sleepy at all. Some part of her realized she was still running on adrenaline. Surely she would crash and crash hard sooner rather than later. Yet at the moment she couldn't settle enough to go to sleep.

The room was dark, but a slit in the curtain let through just enough moonlight to bathe the air in whispers of silver. She rolled onto her side, trying to move carefully so she didn't disturb Simon, only to find him wide-awake and watching her.

"I thought you were asleep, Sir."

He kissed her lips briefly. "Call me Simon now. And no, though I should be exhausted. It's been a busy day."

"I was just thinking the same thing. I figure we're running on fumes and soon we're going to putter out completely." That sounded like something she'd say to Elizabeth or Henry West. "Or, well, give me a second and I'll think of a more adult analogy."

He chuckled softly. "I can see why you're so good with kids. That sums up every two-year-old in need of a nap I've ever known."

"I'm so close to getting my teaching certificate. If I can take two online courses during the fall semester, that should do it."

"That's great you're so close."

"Yeah, the only thing . . ." She stopped, catching her bottom lip between her teeth to keep from voicing the thoughts that had been turning around in her head lately.

"What's the only thing?" he asked.

She took a deep breath. He was friends with Nathaniel. Maybe it wouldn't hurt to get his opinion. "I hate to put Nathaniel and Abby in a bad spot. I mean, after all they've done for me, to just leave them, with Elizabeth and Henry still so young."

"Wait a minute." He shifted so he could look at her more fully. "Let's look at this a different way. First of all, Elizabeth and Henry are Nathaniel and Abby's kids, not yours. You're under no obligation to work for them until they go to college."

"I know, but still."

"There's no *but still.* You work for the Wests. You're an employee, and you have the right to leave anytime you want to. Although it would be nice for you to give them two weeks' notice. And as for everything they've done for you, they did it of their own free will."

She shook her head. "It can't be that easy."

"Lynne." He lifted her chin so she looked into his eyes. "It is that easy. I've known Nathaniel for a long time, and he would never want to hold you back from doing something you'd want to do just because it'd make life easier for him. Yeah, they'd have to find a new nanny, if they wanted one. And no, you wouldn't get to live in a huge mansion anymore—"

"I don't even care about that."

"I know you don't. But the point I'm trying to make is, if you want to be a teacher, don't let anything hold you back, least of all an obligation that doesn't exist. Life's too short to live it for other people. You only get one life. Live it for you."

Her eyes prickled with tears, not from the words he spoke, but from the passion he voiced them with. She felt one fall as she blinked.

"Hey." He wiped it away with his thumb. "What are the tears for?"

She sniffled. "You. You're being so nice. I lied to you, and here you are, trying to make me feel better about my career choice and—I don't know—how'd you get to be so wonderful?"

"I'm not always so wonderful."

"I've never seen proof of that." She added with a grin, "Not including when you dumped me the last time."

A look of raw pain came over his face. "I was so wrong to run out on you like that, without giving you a valid reason. I was afraid if you found out about what I really needed that you would look at me differently. Like a monster. And I couldn't stand the thought of you looking at me like that. So I took the easy way out."

"And now?" she asked, surprised at where the conversation had turned, but not unhappy about it.

"Now I know that you are strong enough for me. For the truth. And I won't ever hide it from you again."

"See?" She smiled. "Completely wonderful."

"Give me time."

But she knew better. She could give him all the time in the world and he'd never prove himself to be any less wonderful in her eyes.

"Tell me one thing you've done that could possibly prove that," she dared him.

His thumb still rested against her cheekbone where he'd wiped her tear away. "I couldn't stay away from you."

"And that's a bad thing?"

"I don't know. I don't know if I'm good for you or not."

"Who says we have to know that now?" she asked. "As long as we're good right now, isn't that all that matters?"

He leaned his head down and drew her close. "I don't know, but I'm willing to act like it is if you are."

She was still sore from when he'd taken her before bed. Between that and everything else they'd done the day before, there were very few places on her body that didn't remind her with every move that she'd seen more action in the last twenty-four hours than she had the last five years combined.

But none of that mattered as he placed a gentle kiss on her

lips. She couldn't believe how her body reacted to him. Couldn't believe that with just one kiss, he could stoke the fire of need and desire once more within her. Her body craved him, yearned for him, and, whether her brain could make sense of it or not, would let him have her again.

He was hesitant. Never before had he been so tentative with his touch. His fingers lingered gently, and his lips were soft.

"I won't break, you know," she said.

"I'm just very much aware of what I've put your body through. I don't want to hurt you."

She chuckled. "And here this whole time I thought that's what sadists did."

"Yes," he said, with a smile in his voice. "But only in the good ways."

"I promise if you get to be too much or I'm too sore to continue, I'll let you know. But for right now, I want you." She let her hand drift to his waist. "Please, Sir."

He held her tight and rolled them so she was on top of him. "Yes, but this time, you ride me."

She might have been on top, but there was no doubt who was in control. He held her hips tight, allowing only so much leeway. She wanted him hard and fast, but he had other plans.

"Stop fighting me," he said, after she unsuccessfully tried to impale herself on him all at once.

"But, Sir," she whined.

"Patience, Lynne."

She blew a hair out of her face and sighed.

"We do this my way or we go to sleep. Which is it going to be?" he asked.

He was serious about the sleep thing; she saw in his eyes that he'd have no problem whatsoever in doing without more sex tonight.

"Your way, Sir."

"Very nice. Can you say it with a little bit more enthusiasm?"

"I don't think so."

"Well, then, I'll have to see if I can get you to be enthusiastic another way."

She had no doubt that he could, probably with little more than a crook of his finger. But he kept his hands firmly on her hips, easing her down onto him ever so slowly. Her eyes almost rolled to the back of her head, because, dammit all, there was something to be said about going slow and taking your time.

Before it had happened so quickly, she didn't have time to appreciate the feel of him claiming her. Or enjoy the way he filled her up so completely. Inch by inch, he took his time, and when he was finally situated fully inside her, she moaned with bliss.

"Now, that sounded more enthusiastic," he said with a smug grin on his face, though his voice was a bit strained.

"You're going to make me a fan of taking my time," she said.

He didn't answer but, holding her where he wanted her, began to move in a rhythm that was almost enough, yet not quite. She started to complain, but the intense look of his expression told her that wasn't the best idea.

She relaxed her body and let him take control. It was better that way anyhow. He sensed her surrender, and only then did he speed up. Just a little.

"So much better when you follow me, don't you think?" he asked, and then, as if to prove his point, he thrust up into her.

"Yes, Sir," she replied in a half yelp, half moan.

"Patient girls get rewarded." His expression wasn't so much intense as it was downright devious.

"How's that, Sir?" she asked, almost afraid to find out.

"They get fucked."

And with those three words, he held her suspended above him and began pounding into her. All she could do was hold on, enjoy, and let him take what he wanted from her.

"Fuck, you feel so good." He was panting now, his punctuated words a testament to both the strength and control he was exercising as well as what it cost him to do so.

"Oh my God." She nearly came as he hit a new sensitive spot within her. "I'm going to come."

"Yes," he said. She wasn't sure why he allowed her to come so easily, but she wasn't going to argue. Her climax rocked her body, and still he didn't stop, driving into her over and over. A second orgasm hit and was so intense she closed her eyes and opened her mouth in a silent scream.

She didn't remember Simon coming, but he must have because when she opened her eyes, she had collapsed on top of him and he was breathing heavily. It was only then that she noticed the wet spot.

Had he not used a condom, or had it broken?

"Uh, Sir?" she asked.

"Ummm?" He didn't move or open his eyes.

"I think the condom broke." There was no doubt in her mind that that was what had happened; she was all sticky between her legs.

His eyes flew open and he sat up. "Shit."

Now that he was more visible to her, she glanced down and saw nothing. Her heart pounded as she processed everything.

"Dammit." She hopped off the bed. "You didn't use a condom, did you?"

He ran his fingers through his hair. "I can't believe I did that."

"Me either." She stomped to the bathroom to clean up, ignoring his calls for her. He banged on the door, but she'd locked it.

"Lynne!" he yelled through the door.

"Just a minute." She turned on the water and looked at herself in the mirror, not recognizing the woman she saw reflected there.

What was she doing? Is this who she was? Just running around jumping into bed with anyone? Part of her knew she was being ridiculous. Simon was the only man she'd slept with in who knew how long. But the fact that she'd been so out of it that she hadn't realized he didn't use a condom shook her.

She had to put some distance between them so she could regain some control. To that end, she took her time in the bathroom, brushing her hair and cleaning her teeth, and she felt much more calm and collected when she stepped outside.

Simon, though, looked like shit. He sat on the edge of the bed and stood up as she emerged. She noticed he'd slipped on a pair of shorts.

"I'm sorry, Lynne," he said. "I promise I'm clean. I can give you the reports tomorrow. I have them at home."

She shook her head. "It wasn't only your fault. I was there, too. I should have made sure you used one. I've never been that out of it before that I didn't notice."

"Are you on birth control?"

"Yes, thank goodness."

He could only nod. She couldn't get over how scared he looked. Was it the possibility of pregnancy, or something else?

"I'm completely exhausted," she said, and it wasn't a lie. She could tell she was finally coming down off the high she'd been on for most of the day. "I'm going to sleep in the other room."

He didn't argue with her, but let her go after she promised she was okay. She couldn't explain it, but once she crawled under the covers, she started to cry. Not wanting Simon to hear, she buried her head in the pillow until she'd cried herself out. Even then, as tired as she was, it took a long time for her to go to sleep.

Chapter Ten

Simon felt like the world's biggest ass. How the fuck had he forgotten a condom? Even when he was a horny teenager, he'd never forgotten a condom. He'd told her the truth—he was completely clean, and since he'd never had unprotected sex before, that hadn't changed.

He heard her close the door to her bedroom and minutes later thought he heard muffled sobs. It took all his control not to beat her door down. But he was afraid that would make him even more of an ass, so he stayed in bed, wide-awake, until he finally drifted off into a restless sleep.

He woke before she did the next morning, and he couldn't help himself from cracking open her door, just to make sure she was still there and hadn't departed without him knowing in the wee hours of the morning.

Satisfied that she was with him for at least the foreseeable future, he started coffee brewing. She came out of her room about twenty minutes later, looking adorably ruffled in her just-out-of-bed state.

"Morning," she said, making a beeline for the coffee.

"Morning." Guilt had plagued him all night, and seeing her now in the fresh light of day did little to ease that. "Lynne, again, I'm so sorry about last night."

She was turned away from him, pouring coffee, and he couldn't see her face as she replied. "It's okay. It was a mistake, and it could have happened to anyone. I'm sorry I made such a big deal about it."

"It's not okay, and it's never happened to me before." He waited until she turned around before adding, "And you were right to make a big deal of it."

She took a deep breath and smiled. "It's our last full day here and I don't want this to hang over our heads all day. How about we say I forgive you and you promise it won't happen again?"

She was letting him off the hook way too easily, but she had a point about not letting it overshadow their day. "Okay, deal. I promise it won't happen again."

"Ohh, I like it when you see things my way."

He snorted. "Don't get used to it."

"Wouldn't dream of it, Sir." But her expression told a different story altogether.

"Sure you wouldn't. I'm going to order breakfast and then we'll go see if there's a class or demo we want to watch." He didn't want to do too much physically before the demo. Not to mention, she was probably still sore from the day before.

"Okay, I'm going to go take a shower." She gave him a sly look, and then, as if to test his resolve, stripped in the living room and pranced into the bathroom.

Screw it, he decided, following her. If she was too sore, she could safeword.

Lynne took her time getting ready for the demo. Though, to be honest, she wasn't sure why. It wasn't like she was going to be dressed for the majority of the demo time anyway. No, that wasn't it. She knew exactly why she took so much time. She wanted to look good for Simon. She wanted to reflect positively on him. Especially if anyone attending the demo today had heard about the practice yesterday.

She still cringed when she thought about that.

Fortunately, that was in the past and everything pertaining to it had been dealt with. They were going to move forward and focus on the future. A future she now anticipated including Simon.

She stood back from the bathroom mirror and gave herself the once-over. Her hair had been pulled back into a ponytail. That had been the one thing Simon had requested. Her makeup was light and natural, though she did add red lipstick. After hearing him talk last night about what red lipstick did to him, she'd decided she'd be a fool to wear any other color.

Even though she wouldn't have them on long, she selected a tiny lacy bra and panty set. She went with white, simply because he probably expected her to pick black and she wanted to surprise him.

Over that, she slipped on a see through cropped shirt and a tight miniskirt. To complete the look, she wore red *fuck me now and don't make it easy* heels.

"You'll do," she told herself in the mirror. "Not too shabby for a nanny."

Though she certainly didn't look anything like a nanny was supposed to look. Which was a topic she had given some thought to, especially after their talk last night, and would take up later. She pushed that aside for the time being.

All her primping had been worth it for his reaction when she stepped out of the bathroom and Simon saw her for the first time. She wouldn't say his jaw hit the floor, but his mouth did open and close repeatedly, like a fish she'd once had for a pet as a child.

"Lynne." He shook his head. "You look . . . wow . . ."

She was pleased he liked her appearance so much, but decided to tease him. Placing her hands on her waist and cocking her head, she said, "Is that a compliment, Sir, or do I normally look like death warmed over?"

"You always look beautiful," he said. "It's just that today . . . wow."

She decided to let him off the hook. After all, she'd rarely been called beautiful by anyone and she had worked extra hard to impress him. "Thank you."

"And you wore red lipstick," he said.

She refrained from doing the fist pump she wanted to do. "Someone told me it was their favorite."

"Dammit, woman. I don't know if I should beat your ass or fuck your mouth."

"I vote for both, Sir."

He took her by both shoulders and walked her backward to the wall. He pressed her up against it and pushed his hips into hers. "Better watch what you wish for, Lynne. The only reason you aren't over my knee right now this very second is that if I were to spank you properly, we'd be late."

"Does that mean you have time to spank me improperly, Sir?" she teased. "Because that sounds hot and like it might be even better."

He laughed and moved back so she could step away from the wall. "You are so getting it when we get back to this room."

"You say that like it's a bad thing, Sir."

"Let's go," he said, with a swat to her ass.

They made their way down to the lower level where the demo was to be held. It wasn't in the same spot as the practice had been. In fact, it was in a room she'd never been in at all.

The demo before theirs had ended more than an hour before, leaving someone plenty of time to clean up from the previous session and prepare what was needed for theirs. Simon, of course, brought his own bag, but the room was stocked with a St. Andrew's cross as well as safety supplies and a first aid kit.

Because they'd wanted time to prepare before the demo started, they'd arrived early and were the first to show up. Lynne eyed the first aid kit.

"Have you ever had to use a first aid kit during or after a scene, Sir?" she asked.

He'd set his bag on the floor and was inspecting the cross. "Once or twice. Strip down to your underwear."

"Will you tell me about those times?" She removed her clothing and folded it into a neat pile, leaving only her bra and panties on.

"One submissive had an unknown latex allergy," he said. "We were doing a medical role play and I had latex gloves on. Halfway through, a rash popped up on her stomach."

"Itchy."

"Yes, very. Fortunately, we were at a club and there were several doctors and nurses who offered to help. She took some antihistamines and we got her checked out at the hospital. Just to be sure." He snorted. "It was a long-ass time before I did another medical role play. I'll tell you that."

She was getting ready to ask what the second time was when her thoughts were interrupted by her cell phone.

Simon sent her a sharp look. "You brought your cell phone?"

The number said UNKNOWN. "I didn't know there was a rule against it."

"Answer it. Then turn it off. And put it in my bag."

She cringed because he didn't sound pleased. Honestly, she'd forgotten her phone was in her bag. It was actually a good thing it'd rung. This way she could turn it off and there wasn't any chance of it ringing during the demo.

"Hello?" she answered.

"You little bitch," Anna Beth said. "Do you actually think he wants you when he's had me?"

Lynne froze in place and then remembered that no one had been able to locate Anna Beth after the disastrous practice the day before. "What do you want?"

Simon must have heard something in her voice, because he stopped what he was doing and came over to stand in front of her, arms crossed and wearing a frown.

"What do you think I want? I want Simon. I *had* Simon until your newbie ass threw yourself on him and he decided to have pity on you."

"It wasn't like that," Lynne said, and then stopped. Why argue with Anna Beth? It didn't solve anything, and she seemed to thrive on it.

"Give me the phone, Lynne," Simon said. She shook her head.

"It was exactly like that," Anna Beth said. "He called you a pity fuck."

"No, I don't believe you." Lynne looked at the floor, unable to look at Simon any longer. What if Anna Beth was right? Lynne's chest grew tight.

"It doesn't matter if you believe me. Truth is truth. Once he's tired of you, he'll come back to me. Especially if you let him fuck your ass. He's all about the virgin ass. Which is why I haven't let him have mine yet. But I might when I take him back. Just the thought of that massive dick pushing its way inside me. I'll be sure to scream. He likes that, you know. Kinky fucker."

Lynne didn't know how to reply to any of that information. Did Anna Beth know that Lynne had never had anal sex before, or was it only a guess on her part? Either way, there was no way she could know they'd had anal sex last night, was there? And she had to be lying about the pity fuck thing, didn't she?

It wasn't until Simon took the phone from her hand that she realized she'd been staring at it, doing and saying nothing.

He held the phone up to his mouth. "Who is this?" He shook his head. "They hung up. Who was it?"

"Anna Beth."

He cursed under his breath and turned the phone off. "This is why you should have left your phone upstairs. What did she say?"

She took a deep breath and forced herself to look at him. "That you told her I was a pity fuck and she was sure you wouldn't want me after you had my ass."

He swore again, and the tips of his ears grew red. She didn't think she'd ever seen him so angry. "Did anything I did to you yesterday feel like a pity fuck in any way, shape, or form?"

"No, Sir." But having never experienced a pity fuck, that she knew of, how would she know what one felt like?

"And did I give any impression that I didn't want you after last night?"

"No, Sir."

"Then isn't it safe to say Anna Beth is lying through her teeth?"

She shrugged. "I guess so."

He ran his fingers through his hair with an exasperated sigh. "Are you really going to believe her over me?"

"I don't want to. It's just, she's . . ." She crossed her arms over her chest, suddenly feeling very exposed.

"Playing into every doubt you've ever had," he finished for her.

"Yes, Sir," she whispered.

"I don't know how to convince you that there is nothing about you that I don't like." He took a step closer to her. "I regret ever playing with that woman. If I'd never given her the time of day, she wouldn't be trying to tear you down right now. I hate that she's making you feel like you're less than you are."

She sniffled. "It's—"

He pressed a finger to her lips. "Shh, don't say it's okay, because it's not. No one ever has the right to bully you into feeling bad. And that's what she is: a bully."

"Why did you play with her?"

"The first time, we didn't do much, and the second was right after I learned you were back in the area. I knew I couldn't have you, not the way I wanted. I went to the club and she was there. Stupid on my part. I could tell almost immediately that she wouldn't be right for me."

A small spark of hope began to bubble in her chest. "How did you want me?"

"I wanted you the way I took you last night. Raw. Urgent. Hard. Rough." He sighed. "And then I want you soft and tender and open."

She blinked back tears. Damn, but she turned into a crying fool all the time around him. "I find that a little hard to swallow, considering how quickly you broke things off with me last time. Part of me is afraid to let you into my heart because I'm scared you'll break it again and I don't know if I can handle that a second time. Then part of me thinks it doesn't really matter, because I'm already in too deep with you."

"Lynne . . ." He shook his head.

"Tell me you aren't going to hurt me again," she begged. "Promise me."

"I'd be interested in hearing this myself, seeing as how I've already had this conversation with you once before," a familiar voice said from the door.

They both turned, and Lynne gasped at the sight of Nathaniel standing in the doorway, arms crossed and looking like the devil himself. Now she really felt exposed, and she searched frantically for something to cover up with. Shit. She did not want to be standing in her underwear in front of her employer. Though in all honesty, he wasn't looking at her; he was focused on Simon.

"Nathaniel," Simon said. His voice gave no indication of what he was thinking. In fact, she'd never heard him sound so . . . flat.

The two men stood there, silently assessing each other. She wouldn't have been surprised if they started circling each other, showing their teeth, and snarling.

Nathaniel finally broke the silence. "For God's sake, man, cover her up. I'm her employer."

Her face heated once more, and she glanced around the room. Surely there had to be a blanket or something. But she couldn't find one, and Simon appeared in no hurry to obey Nathaniel. Maybe there were blankets in the back of the room. She turned to go look, but Simon held out a hand to stop her.

"Settle, Lynne."

When he said that, she was to kneel at his feet. She chewed on her bottom lip. *Now? In front of Nathaniel?* Nathaniel who still didn't glance her way, but continued to look at Simon as if trying to decide which body part he wanted to relieve Simon of first.

She was caught between two men: her Dom for the weekend and her employer. She wanted to obey them both, and it upset her to know she couldn't. In obeying one, she'd be defying the other. Her mind couldn't decide what to do, but her body reacted instinctively, and she dropped to her knees at Simon's side.

"You've been to this location before," Simon told Nathaniel while he placed a hand on top of her head. The tension left her body. "You must have had some idea of the stage of dress you'd see her in. If it makes you uncomfortable, you can leave. Might be for the best anyway, since you're upsetting her *and* you weren't invited."

Lynne kept her eyes downcast; she did not want to see the look on Nathaniel's face at Simon's refusal.

"Having some idea," Nathaniel said, "is quite a bit different from seeing it flaunted before me. And sorry, but no, I'm not leaving until we talk."

She thought the flaunting remark was low and unnecessary. It wasn't like she got dressed, thinking, *How can I piss my boss off today?*

Simon checked his watch. "One of these days, Lynne, I'll have the opportunity to take a single tail to you and we won't be interrupted. Unfortunately, it looks like today is not that day. I don't think either one of us is in the proper mind-set at the moment to do the demo."

She begrudgingly agreed he was right.

"I'm going to let everyone know the demo is off." Simon held out a hand to her. "Lynne, you can get dressed and wait in the room. And, Nathaniel, I'll meet you outside in the courtyard in ten minutes."

Surprisingly enough, Nathaniel didn't argue, but gave a curt nod and left. Simon pulled her into his arms. "Go back to the room and don't worry. I can handle him." He pulled back and looked into her eyes. "Promise you'll wait there for me?"

She nodded and he gave her a kiss.

"Never forget, you're my good girl," he whispered before pulling away.

She watched him leave before putting her clothes on and making her way back to the room.

Simon found Nathaniel sitting at a table in a shaded corner of the courtyard after he informed the group director that the demo was off. The other man didn't move as he sat down beside him.

"I won't ask how you found out," Simon started. "And while I didn't know the submissive I was talking with online was Lynne until yesterday, I did run into her a few weeks ago and I've seen her a few times since then. I was wrong to keep that from you."

Nathaniel's face was once more void of any emotion. It was freaky as hell how he could do that. Especially since he was so expressive with his wife and kids. "It's not so much that I mind you're with Lynne. What bothers me is I specifically told you she was under my protection. All you had to do was call and tell me you wanted to see her. I would have given you my blessing."

"Your blessing?" Had he heard correctly? "You aren't her father. You aren't even related. She's your employee. You pay her to work for you. Outside of that, she's a grown woman who can do whatever the hell she wants."

"Yes, she is my employee. She's also a young single woman who lives in my house. Add in the fact that she's a submissive and I'm a Dom, you damn well know I'm going to do anything in my power to protect her from . . ."

"Protect her from Doms like me?" Simon finished for him. "That's what you mean, isn't it? If I were a Dom like Luke or Daniel, you wouldn't have an issue with me. Hell, I could be into the twenty-four/seven thing like Cole and you wouldn't mind. But I'm not like them, am I? I'm a sadist, and that's not good enough for her."

Nathaniel leaned back in his chair. "I think you just put an awful lot of words in my mouth that I never said. And you're wrong. I wouldn't want her with Cole either."

"I don't hear you denying that you don't want her with me."

Nathaniel sighed, obviously torn. He scrubbed his face. "Would a sadist be my choice for Lynne? No. I won't lie about that."

"She may have lived under your roof for almost a year, but you have no clue what her needs are. Lynne's a masochist."

He'd rarely seen Nathaniel surprised, but hearing his nanny, the woman he viewed as a little sister, was a masochist? That did it. His look of utter and complete shock didn't last long.

"Well, if that's what she needs? Who am I to argue?" Nathaniel asked, seeming to have rebounded quickly. "Just because something isn't for me doesn't mean it's wrong. I do wish you would have told me when you started seeing her."

"I know and I apologize for that. As soon as I talked to her, I should have told you. If the situation were reversed, I'd be mad at me, too."

"I wouldn't say I'm mad. Disappointed? Yes. But maybe more than anything, surprised as hell about Lynne. And not just the masochist part. Abby told me all about how Lynne kept her true identity from you." Nathaniel laughed. "Did she really convince you her name was Faye and you didn't know it was her?"

Simon could have groaned. He would never live this down. It made him want to spank her again. Or maybe fuck her ass. "How was I to know it was her middle name? I thought she was scared about being recognized in public. I didn't know it was just me she wanted to hide from."

They both had a chuckle over the situation even though Simon wasn't at the point that he thought it was funny yet. But in the midst of laughing, he grew serious at one thought.

"How did you find out?" he asked. "Did Abby tell you?"

Nathaniel frowned. "No. Abby's loyal to a fault, but she also can't lie. She only told me when I asked her directly." He watched Simon carefully as he added, "I actually got an e-mail from an Anna Beth."

Simon fisted his hands. "When?"

"Last night, and I'm glad you brought it up because I want to discuss her with you as well."

"She's a mistake. I played with her twice, and that's two times too many."

"She's also a criminal."

"What?" Whatever he'd been expecting Nathaniel to say, it hadn't been that.

"Alleged, anyway. After I got her e-mail, I called Luke, since she mentioned his club. Come to find out he's had Jeff Parks and his security team look into her. It appears as if she's been siphoning money from the law firm she works at."

"Really?" Simon wasn't sure why that surprised him.

"Yes. We've alerted the authorities, of course. They're following up on their end, but I expect her to be charged and brought in at some point today."

"Hopefully they'll lock her up and throw away the key. She called Lynne right before you got here and upset her horribly. I need to go check on her and make sure she's okay." He stood up and pushed back from the table.

Nathaniel did the same. "Do you think I should——"

He didn't hear what Nathaniel said next because the elevator doors opened and Lynne walked out, carrying a suitcase.

"Lynne?" Simon asked.

Her head jerked up and her red-rimmed eyes told him she'd been crying again. Dammit. Had Anna Beth called her back? He walked to her, wanting nothing more than to take her in his arms and fix whatever had made her upset.

"Don't," she said. "Don't come near me."

Her words were like a punch in the gut. "Lynne?"

"I'm done. Do you hear me? Done. I'm not doing this anymore. She wins." Her whole body shook and he got the impression she hadn't been crying because she was sad or upset, but rather that she was angry.

"Where are you going?" he asked. "You're in no shape to be driving."

"I don't need you to tell me what I can and can't do."

Nathaniel took a step closer to her, but she held out her hand to stop him. "You, too. I can't believe you showed up here. Like I'm a child. Screw you, Nathaniel. I quit."

Though Simon wanted nothing more than to sit her down and try to figure out what the hell was going on, he realized she needed space at the moment. That didn't, however, mean he was letting her get behind the wheel of a car. Simon was getting ready to forcibly take her keys, when one of the staff members stepped into the courtyard.

"Your cab is here," he said, looking at Lynne.

"Thank you," Lynne told him. She turned and glared at Simon. "See? I'm not an idiot. I can take care of myself."

"I never called you an idiot. Let's sit down and discuss what's upset you so much." He felt like he was trying to reason with a wild animal. He was afraid the outcome wouldn't be much different.

"Sorry," she said, though it was clear she wasn't sorry at all. "My cab's here."

"Did Anna Beth call you back?" Simon asked, but she kept walking. Though she did flip him the bird.

But why would she answer her phone? Especially Anna Beth's number? He didn't think she'd pick up an unknown number, either.

"What the hell was that?" Nathaniel asked as they watched her backside retreat. "I've never known her to act like that."

"Something happened." Now Simon needed to figure out just what it was. "I'm going up to the room to see if anything there can shed light on what just happened."

"Mind if I come?"

"No. Let's go."

They took the stairs, walking in silence. Simon was glad Nathaniel didn't try to carry on a conversation; he needed to think. What could have possibly happened from the time he'd left her in the demo room to when she stormed outside? He hoped there was something in the room that offered some kind of clue.

He saw it as soon as he opened the door. On the large-screen television in the living area was a paused image of him and Anna Beth. She was on her knees, sucking him off, and he had her hair fisted in his hand. It appeared to be from the second time they played together. He cursed and crossed the floor, stepping on an opened envelope. It carried his return address and was addressed to Lynne.

Nathaniel picked it up. "If this was Anna Beth, it's a bit low-tech for someone with her skills."

Simon took the remote from the coffee table and turned the television off so he wouldn't have to see that image anymore, though it was already too late; it was burned inside his memory forever. He could only imagine how Lynne had felt seeing it. He'd known Luke had security cameras in his club, so he wasn't surprised the video existed. What made him angry was that it'd been hacked.

"Low-tech or not," he replied, "the damage is done. Anna Beth got what she wanted."

Nathaniel gave him a pointed look. "What about what you want?"

Chapter Eleven

Two weeks later

Lynne splashed water on her face and told herself to stop crying—she was being stupid. Seriously. Who cried because they got their period, right on time, other than women who were trying to get pregnant? No one, that's who.

She didn't even want to have a baby right now. Having a baby was definitely Not. In. Her. Plans. At. All.

So why was she sitting in the penthouse bathroom, sobbing because she got her period?

Someone knocked on the bathroom door.

"Just a minute!" She splashed more water on her face and opened the door. Abby stood waiting for her with the same worried look on her face she'd had every time Lynne saw her for the last two weeks.

Lynne had gotten out of the cab at the penthouse after leaving Simon and Nathaniel, planning to pull her stuff together and check into a hotel, only to find Abby waiting for her. Abby said she was not quitting and that was that and there was to be no arguing. She then pulled out a pint of double chocolate chip fudge ice cream from the freezer and two spoons. Lynne told her she wasn't being fair, but secretly she knew she had the world's greatest boss.

Abby had confessed about telling Nathaniel and tried to apologize. She'd said she didn't want to, but he'd asked her specifically if she knew whom Lynne was playing with. Lynne wouldn't allow her to apologize, telling Abby she would never expect her to lie to her husband for her.

Lynne stepped out of the bathroom, and Abby put her arms around her. "You got your period."

"How'd you know?"

Abby shrugged. "Just a hunch. Come sit down."

Though she had decided to stay on as their nanny, she'd told them it was only through the end of the year. By then she'd be able to teach, and come January, she wanted to have a teaching job and an apartment of her own lined up.

They sat on the couch. It was Saturday. Nathaniel had gone into the office and the kids had spent the night with their cousins. Lynne was thankful Abby didn't have plans; she needed the company.

"I didn't get a chance to talk to you last night when we got in," Abby said. "But have you talked to Simon yet?"

She shook her head. "No. He's sent a few texts, left some voice mails, but I haven't replied. Even those stopped after a few days."

"Did you expect anything else? You left him, remember?"

"So?"

"So. In his mind, he's giving you time. He figures since he never told you to leave or that he didn't want you, and since you haven't replied to any of his attempts to contact you, that he'd leave you alone for a bit."

Lynne eyed her warily. "Did he tell you this?"

"No, and Nathaniel hasn't either. I just know how men think."

"The exact opposite of us?"

Abby laughed, and Lynne had to smile. It felt good. She hadn't done a lot of smiling for the last two weeks.

"Do you still love Simon?" Abby asked.

Lynne squeezed her hands into fists, digging her nails into the palms of her hands so tight, she knew there'd be marks. Did she love Simon? Yes, of course she did. That's why it hurt so much to be separated from him. Why she cried when she found out she wasn't pregnant, even though she didn't want to be pregnant.

She wasn't just in love with Simon; she was stupidly in love with him.

"Yes," she admitted to Abby, and some part of her felt free at the admission.

"Then we need to come up with a plan to get him back."

Lynne wasn't going to call. It hurt, but Simon had come to grips with it. Mostly.

He sighed. Okay, not at all. He hadn't come to grips with it at all.

But it didn't matter that he couldn't accept it. That was the way it was, and no amount of wishing on his part would bring her back. Sometimes he questioned if he'd done the right thing in giving her time. Maybe he should have flooded her in-box with e-mails and her phone with texts. Somehow, though, he didn't think that was the answer either.

No, the only person who could change anything was Lynne, and that wasn't going to happen. He wouldn't even allow himself to ask Nathaniel about her or to check with Luke to see if she'd submitted her application for membership at the club. A clean break was a good break. Or that was what he told himself anyway. During the day it was easier to believe. At night it was downright impossible.

He had followed up with Luke and Nathaniel about Anna Beth, ironically enough. The local authorities found enough evidence to have her arrested, thanks to Jeff and his team. As it turned out, she'd hacked into Lynne's computer, apparently through a bug attached to a photo. Simon, along with Nathaniel and Luke, saw to it that she was denied bail while she awaited trial.

It was a hollow victory.

Of course, lately everything felt hollow. He hadn't realized how much of his free time he'd spent talking to Lynne or planning something to do with her. Now that there was no need to plan anything and since she wasn't talking to him, he often found himself with nothing to do. On the upside, he'd put in a lot of overtime the last two weeks.

By Sunday afternoon, two weeks after she'd left him, he was slowly going crazy. He'd been told by his supervisor not to even think about coming to the office today. He tried working on a puzzle, but doing so brought back memories of Lynne. One of his friends mentioned going to Luke's club, but Simon had shut the man down before he finished asking the question.

He briefly considered getting drunk, but decided it wasn't worth the headache or the hangover. Then he decided just thinking that made him part old fart, part stick-in-the-mud. He fully expected to wake up one morning with nothing better to do than to yell at people to get off his lawn.

The sound of the doorbell brought him out of his misery long enough to sadly laugh that maybe he could tell whoever that was at the door to get off his lawn. Practice, he decided.

He didn't even bother to check who it was. He threw open the door, ready to yell at whoever was unfortunate enough to be standing on the other side, only to freeze at the sight of Lynne.

"Hi," she said.

Hi.

Fucking hi.

Like she hadn't stormed out of his life as fast as she'd breezed in. Like she hadn't ignored him for the last two weeks. Like she hadn't torn him to so many damn pieces he felt like a puzzle that would never get fully assembled.

He wanted to pull her into his arms and kiss her and breathe in the scent of her hair. Hold her until she swore she'd never leave and confessed how much she'd missed him. He wanted to grab her and pull her down the hall to his bedroom and do evil and wicked, wicked things to her body.

Instead, he leaned against the doorframe and said, "What are you doing here?"

Uncertainty clouded her expression, and her lower lip trembled. He could have kicked himself. This was what he'd been wanting for the last two weeks. What he'd been hoping for. What was he thinking with that being the first thing out of his mouth?

"I came to say I'm sorry. I thought about making you a card," she said. "But decided that probably wouldn't be a good idea."

"A card?"

"Yes, I'd put on it 'I'm sorry I acted like an ass. Will you spank mine?'"

He couldn't help it; her answer was so unexpected, he laughed and laughed until his chest hurt. "Come in." He held the door open for her.

She stepped tentatively inside and waited for him to lead the way into the living room. He pointed to a nearby chair. "Have a seat. Can I get you something to eat or drink?"

"No," she said, sitting down. "I'm good. Plus, I'm so nervous right now that if I ate or drank anything, I'd just throw it up, and that would be worse than the spank-me card."

Her hands twisted in her lap. She was looking everywhere except at him. She was obviously nervous as hell and didn't know what to do about it.

"Calm down, Lynne," he said. "I'm not so upset that I'm going to hurt you."

She looked for a minute like she was going to say something sassy, but obviously thought better of it. She was as skittish as a horse, and while he had never been good with animals, he did know nervous submissives. He was convinced he could handle soothing her.

"Take a deep breath." He watched as she followed his instructions. At least that was a good sign. "Another."

By the time she had taken four deep breaths, she had relaxed a bit. Or at least she didn't look as if she was going to run scared and screaming from the room if he said the wrong thing.

"Now, then," he said. "You said you came to apologize, for what exactly?"

Her body tensed, but just a little, nowhere near as bad as it had been. "To begin with, for the way I left." She shook her head. "I know it was wrong to just run off like that, without saying anything or talking about it."

"That was a major disappointment," he said, seeing no reason to lie to her at this point.

"I know." She took a deep breath. "I was able to apologize to Nathaniel, and that was so much easier than coming here. I wondered why for a long time, but recently figured out why that was. Nathaniel was just a job, an employer. You are so much more to me."

"Am I?" he asked. "Up until you left, I was hoping that was the case. But then you left with barely a word to me, and it's been two weeks with no contact between us. So forgive me if I'm being an ass, but why today? What makes today special and not two weeks ago, or last week?"

Whatever it was, she wasn't jumping up and down to tell him. Then it hit him, two weeks. Two weeks since he had last seen her, since they had last had sex. Sex that had been unprotected. He struggled not to show any emotion. Holy fuck. She was pregnant.

She was pregnant and she'd come back to him because she had nowhere else to go and she knew he'd take her in. He would, of course. But even though he wanted her back, he didn't want her in his life this way. With him because she didn't have a choice.

He braced himself for the words. The phrase that would tell him his life would never be the same. Would she grow to hate him? Despite the fact that she was stuck with him because he made the stupid mistake of not using a condom one time?

One time he'd messed up and now he'd screwed up her life forever. She must hate him.

Except, she wasn't looking at him as if she hated him. He wasn't totally sure what the look on her face was, but he was fairly certain it wasn't hate.

"I started my period this morning," she said.

The first thought through his head was *How does she have her period? Pregnant women don't get periods.* Then it hit him.

"You're not here because you're pregnant?" he asked.

She shook her head. "I'm here because I'm not pregnant."

"That doesn't even make sense."

"I suppose I'd be here if things had gone the other way." She looked down at her lap. She was twisting her hands again. "But when I realized I wasn't pregnant, I started to cry and I thought, how stupid is this? I don't want a baby right now. And then it hit me—no, I didn't want a baby. I wanted you. And if I couldn't have you, I at least wanted a part of you."

"Then why did you run off and leave me?"

"When I got back to the room that Saturday and saw the package, I thought you'd had something delivered to me. I didn't understand why you sent me a video to watch, but since there was a DVD player, I thought you wanted me to, so I did, and when I saw . . ."

She didn't have to tell him what she saw; he knew all too well. Hell, he'd lived it. He'd flogged Anna Beth and used a cane. By then he'd known she wasn't into what he needed, so he'd cut the scene short and got her off. The video had ended with a blow job.

"But why get upset when you knew how I felt about her?"

"I don't know. I just remember that at the time it made perfect sense." She locked eyes with him, appearing to beg him to understand. He swallowed. It was too hard to ignore those pleading eyes. She bit her bottom lip. "I don't know if it was Nathaniel showing up or the emotions of the weekend, or what. Suddenly it was all too much to work through. I just had to get out of there."

She'd obviously finished what she'd come by to say. Her mouth snapped shut, and she shifted her gaze back to her lap.

He didn't say anything either. He was too busy trying to process everything she'd said, as well as what she'd left unsaid.

"I guess we've both screwed up things between us," he finally said. "Me, when I gave you that bogus reason for breaking things off with you the first time. And you, just recently when you ran out on us without even trying to talk things through." He took a deep breath. "Maybe we should take it all to mean we aren't meant to be. That the universe is trying to give us an unmistakable sign that we aren't supposed to be with each other."

He didn't go any further with that train of thought, wanting to see instead how she'd react to it.

Her reply was low but unmistakable. "In that case, I hate the universe."

The Delaware submissives had gathered in Abby and Nathaniel's living room. Lynne had feared her presence would be awkward, though why exactly she thought that, she wasn't sure. It actually seemed very silly with the warm reception she was given. It didn't matter that other than Abby, she only knew Sasha and Julie.

She never liked being the center of attention, and though the new person in a group was often everyone's focus, that wasn't the case this time, thanks to Julie.

Since Sasha and Julie co-owned the floral shop they worked at, they'd driven to Abby's together. Though Julie always seemed to be in a good mood, she was unusually buoyant.

"Damn, Julie," one of the submissives Lynne didn't know said. "Would you mind dialing the happy down a notch? Not all of us bathed in confetti and fairy sprinkles this afternoon."

"You can talk until you're blue in the face and it won't do any good," Sasha said, but from her smile, she didn't seem to mind. In fact, she looked like she was in on a secret only the two of them shared. "She's been impossible all day."

"I wouldn't say impossible," Julie said with a mock glare at Sasha. "I'd say high on life." She turned to the other submissive. "And I didn't bathe in confetti and fairy sprinkles this afternoon."

"Yeah." Sasha looked like she was having too much fun at Julie's expense. "I'm not sure what she was doing this afternoon, but it wasn't *bathing*. She came back to the shop after lunch and she had a hickey on the side of her neck. You just can't see it now because her hair's covering it up."

Julie didn't even blush. "Daniel was a bit . . . exuberant."

Abby came into the room, carrying a tray of drinks. With a knowing look in her eye, she walked to where Julie sat and stood in front of her. "Have a drink?"

"Thanks." Julie reached for one.

"Use your left hand."

With those words, everyone's eyes shot to Julie as she slowly raised her hand, revealing the large diamond ring she now wore.

"How'd you know?" Julie asked Abby as the room exploded with congratulations and *Let me sees*.

"I didn't know with any certainty; let's call it a hunch." Abby put the tray down. "I should get some champagne out."

Lynne had never thought she'd be having a champagne toast at a submissive group meeting. She loved the dynamics of the group, though. Everyone was friendly and down-to-earth, and there were a few introverts, just like her.

Once Abby brought out the champagne and everyone toasted Julie, they begged her to tell how Daniel proposed. Julie got a dreamy, faraway look in her eye as she recounted the events of the previous weekend.

Watching Julie talk about her Master and soon-to-be husband, Lynne knew exactly what she wanted. She wanted it all. And she wanted it with Simon. She didn't care what the universe thought.

She told Simon that exact thing when she saw him later that night. He had asked her over earlier in the week. "I mean, you can't let the universe get you down. Even if the universe is against us, I'm willing to bet we can overcome it."

"You think?" They were sitting in his apartment, working on a puzzle. "You and me taking on the world?"

She took a deep breath. It was now or never. "Love conquers all. Or so they say. And I do—I love you, Simon. I think I always have. Even when you broke up with me, I never wanted anyone other than you." She'd been looking at the scattered puzzle pieces on the table, but he was too quiet following her confession. She glanced up, hoping to get some feel on what he was thinking.

He was watching her with wonder and maybe a hint of surprise. It was the wonder that gave her the courage to continue.

"Is it possible, do you think, that you might feel the same about me one day?" she asked.

"I don't think so," he said, his voice void of emotion. "Not one day."

She turned her head, not wanting him to see the hot tears that filled her eyes at his matter-of-fact statement. She tried not to focus on how much her chest hurt and how hollow she felt inside.

She should leave. There was no way she could stay and work on the puzzle now. Sit at a table and pretend everything was okay. It would hurt too much. Hell, it already hurt just being in the same room with him. She pushed back her chair and mumbled something about leaving.

"Lynne," he said, but she refused to look his way. "Lynne, look at me."

She lifted her head.

"Don't go." He reached for her hand. "I said that because one day is already here. It's been here all along."

Her breath caught in her throat. Did that mean . . . ?

"I love you, too, Lynne." He pressed a kiss in the palm of her hand. "I thought once before I was doing the honorable and decent thing by letting you go. I was wrong. The honorable and decent thing is always love."

He stood up and pulled her to her feet, not seeming to mind the tear that escaped and trailed down her cheek. "And with that love, I have a feeling the universe doesn't stand a chance against us."

Chapter Twelve

The bass echo of the song currently playing in Luke's club was so loud the walls vibrated with each beat. It didn't help that the place was unusually crowded for a Tuesday night. There were so many people, Lynne momentarily considered telling Simon she wanted to reschedule. She knew he would accommodate the request. In fact, he'd told her they didn't even have to do the scene.

But she wanted to go ahead with it, and she knew that's what Simon wanted, too, so if there were more people around than normal, oh well, she'd just have to deal with it. Public play wasn't one of her most favorite kinks—she typically enjoyed playing in private—but she told herself to view tonight as an opportunity to stretch herself.

Though she had a feeling the scene itself would be able to do that all on its own.

Tonight—finally, Simon would say—they were going to do

a single-tail scene. And though he had never said so, she had the impression that her ability to handle it would further cement their relationship.

"You ready?" Abby asked.

Yeah, she thought, it was a bit odd to have the Wests in attendance, but Simon told her Nathaniel needed to see them in a scene together for his own peace of mind. She agreed, because after December, she'd be moving back to New York to start student teaching and would rarely, if ever, run into them at the club. Daniel and Julie were also in the club somewhere. Cole and Sasha were not. Though Sasha said she thought she'd be fine, Cole put his foot down and said absolutely not.

Lynne took a deep breath and looked for Simon. He was standing by the St. Andrew's Cross they were going to use, talking to Nathaniel and Luke. His black bag sat ominously by his side on the floor. "I am," she said. "Just waiting for Simon to give me the signal."

The man in question looked up, as if he'd heard them talking about him. She knew he hadn't—it was too loud—but he gave her a wink and held up three fingers. She nodded.

"Three minutes," she told Abby, and the butterflies began to multiply in her belly.

Abby gave her a quick hug. "You're going to do great."

Her mouth was suddenly so dry, she couldn't talk. Giving Abby a smile in reply, she made her way to where Simon waited for her. She was glad he was already there. She feared if he'd had her show up first, the combination of people watching and the St. Andrew's Cross might have been enough to scare her away.

No, some inner part of her insisted. Old Lynne might have turned away, but not New Lynne. New Lynne was strong and tough and sexy. It'd take more than a few people watching and a piece of BDSM equipment to scare off New Lynne. She straightened her back, held her head up, and said good-bye to Old Lynne forever.

She came to a stop before Simon, moving to her knees in one fluid movement. "Sir."

He was not her Master. Not yet anyway. And because of that, he only allowed her to call him Sir. Though she hoped that changed one day.

"Lynne," he said, sliding a hand through her hair. "You look absolutely fabulous tonight."

"Thank you, Sir."

"You're going to show all these people what a good girl you are, aren't you?"

"Yes, Sir." Her hands grabbed her knees. A tap on her shoulder reminded her that was not the way he wanted her hands positioned. She released them and turned them so her palms were up.

"Very nice." His hand tightened in her hair, and she didn't try to stop the moan, knowing that unless he specifically told her to be quiet, he wanted to hear her sounds. He said it was because he liked to know he was affecting her.

She'd imagined he'd say something to the people watching or perhaps tell her again what they were doing, but he did neither. From the way he focused on her with that intense look in his eyes, she got the feeling the people watching didn't exist for him. She decided they wouldn't exist for her either.

"Stand up and strip for me," he commanded.

For me. With those two words, he reinforced what his actions whispered. There were only the two of them. No one else mattered.

For him, she would strip. She wouldn't do it because she was an exhibitionist, because she wasn't. She wouldn't do it because she enjoyed showing off, as that had never been her style. She did it because he asked her, and if he asked for something and it was in her power to get or do, she'd get or do it. Pleasing him had become like a high, and she needed a hit.

She stood, only mildly surprised that she didn't tremble. Looking only at him, she quickly removed her clothes, placing them in a pile on the floor.

He stepped around her in a circle, observing what felt like every inch of her. But he did more than just look; he stroked one arm, then teased a nipple. He came close to whipping her body into a frenzy by barely touching her.

"Do you still want me to use a single tail on you?" he asked.

"Yes, Sir." She was so ready, and her body swayed a bit in anticipation.

"It's going to hurt," he warned her.

"Yes, Sir. I want it like that."

"Should I go easy on you?"

"God, no, Sir. Please." Where had that even come from? Hell no, she didn't want him to go easy on her. If anything, she wanted him to go harder on her. She wanted to prove to him, as well as to herself, that she could take anything he gave her and then some.

"Did I insult you with that question?" he asked.

"No, Sir. You just surprised me."

"Why?"

"I see no reason why you would want or need to go easy on me. That you felt the need to ask me if I thought you should meant you probably thought I'd at least entertained the idea."

"Hell," he said. "I have a lot of work to do if you can speak so eloquently while you're standing naked in front of me."

She felt her face flush, and there was a faint giggling from those people gathered around to watch. "Yes, Sir. And I look forward to you leaving me speechless."

He gave her that easygoing smile that always warmed her heart, but she didn't miss the hint of desire lurking in his eyes. "Go face the cross, you mouthy sub," he said, smacking her backside.

Any lightheartedness she felt at their exchange left as soon as she stood in front of the giant wooden X. No matter how jovial she felt, something about being tied up waiting for someone to whip her sobered her right up.

Again, he surprised her by not addressing the gathering crowd. Of course, she decided, this wasn't a demo, and while it wasn't exactly private, it was a scene just between the two of them.

"Are you okay?" His voice was so soft she was the only one who heard. His fingers brushed across her shoulder blades, easing tension she didn't know was there.

"Yes, Sir. So ready."

One at a time, he took her wrists and bound them above her head. He nudged her feet apart and bound them apart as well. She had a brief moment of panic. He'd never tied all four of her limbs before.

The panic didn't have a chance to grow, not under Simon's watchful eyes. He must have noted her body tense again, because his hands were back on her. This time, he rubbed both shoulders in an impromptu massage. She closed her eyes; it felt so good, and she wondered what was making the humming noise she heard, until she realized it was her and stopped.

"Don't be quiet on my account," Simon said. "I like hearing how I make you feel." Then, as if to prove his point, he proceeded to place kisses along her spine.

He took a step away, and she braced herself for whatever he

had planned. When he brushed her back with the soft tails of two floggers, she decided to give up trying to guess his next move and just enjoy the moment.

He proceeded as if they had all the time in the world, doing nothing for what seemed like forever except running the tails over her body. Little by little it seemed as though her body liquefied under his touch. She was certain the only things holding her upright were the bonds he'd placed her in.

"So beautiful," he whispered. "So soft and accepting."

She didn't answer because he knew he was right just by observing her. The next time he took a step back, she didn't move at all, but remained in her almost Zen-like trance.

He started with two floggers. She was able to tell that much, but he went easy at first, with movements that brought the tails to her with solid impact, though there was a certain softness to his ministrations. It actually felt like a continuation of the massage.

Daniel had been good with the flogger, but nothing she'd ever experienced felt anywhere as good as what Simon was doing now. She thought it was sort of like how she'd heard you should cook a lobster: gradually turning the heat up by doing it so slowly, the lobster didn't understand what was happening to him until it was too late.

It had to be similar. The sound of leather hitting skin exactly matched the strikes she felt and she knew they were no longer soft or gentle. Yet her mind was shouting, "Green, green, green."

"You'll get more when I'm ready to give it, greedy girl," he said. Apparently, it hadn't been only her mind shouting.

"Please, Sir," she added because she wasn't above begging.

"Begging for me to whip you? Are you sure?"

She wasn't sure she'd ever wanted anything more. "Yes, Sir."

"The massage and the sensual flogging were for you, to prepare your body to take what I'm about to give it." When he pressed against her, the rough material of his blue jeans provided the friction she craved. Unfortunately, Simon picked up on that very thing and moved so there was no way for her to get relief. She pulled helplessly on her bonds, but they were secured, and she swallowed her groan, knowing it wouldn't do any good to verbalize how desperately she wanted his jeans, *right there,* on her swollen clit.

"Not just yet," he said. "I'm only getting started, and I'm nowhere near close to letting you climax."

She didn't even try to swallow her groan at that. She'd been almost certain he'd let her come at least once before he used the whip. Moving quicker than she thought possible, he fisted her hair and pulled her head back in a move that turned her on so much she thought for a second she didn't need friction. If he kept that up, she'd come simply from him pulling her hair. "Is that a complaint?" he all but growled. "Because if you were good, I thought I might fuck you after, but if you can't be good . . ."

"I'll be good," she babbled. "I promise. I'll be good."

He nipped her ear with his teeth and she swore she felt it all the way to her clit. "Sir, you're going to make me come," she whined, grateful for the first time that he had tied her legs apart. If he hadn't, she knew beyond a shadow of a doubt that she'd be rubbing them together, well on her way to both orgasm and punishment.

"You like it when I pull your hair?" he asked, jerking it back again.

The pull only magnified her need. "Yes, Sir," she whined.

"Such a wicked girl, aren't you?"

"Only for you, Sir."

He chuckled and let go of her hair. "Good answer."

Her body was on high alert while he moved behind her, but she didn't tense up this time. She wanted him to whip her, needed the feel of the release that would come with it. Fortunately, he didn't make her wait. Without any warning, the whip landed on her butt. The sharp pain diffused into warm pleasure, and she heard herself beg for more.

She felt like she was surrounded by a million flying insects, each one biting her, but the pain and the pleasure merged so well, she couldn't tell which was which. She only knew she wanted more. His strokes increased, and like before, she started to giggle, letting everything inside her bubble up and allowing it to escape with the giggle.

The sound didn't affect Simon at all. He kept landing stroke after stroke: across her butt, along her inner thighs, and almost delicately on her back. He hadn't been lying. It hurt, but it was a different type of pain, and it was turning her on.

Just as suddenly as he'd started, he stopped. She didn't have the opportunity to complain, because he pressed himself up against her. He wrapped his fingers in her hair, and there was nothing gentle about the way he pulled her head back.

"I like to hear your giggle," he said. "It makes the Dom in me pleased. But the sadist in me needs more. He needs to hear you scream. I'm only going to give you five more, but they'll be the hardest yet."

How was it possible to be turned on so much by those words? His lips trailed down the back of her neck, and at the nape, he bit her. She shivered in need. "Yes, Sir. Please."

He ran a hand down her body, pressing slightly on the lines he'd left with the whip. "Such a good girl."

Then get to it already, she wanted to yell, but chose instead to pull on her bonds.

She was unaware he'd moved back into place so quickly, and the sting of the whip on her right butt cheek caught her off guard. She could barely process the pain before its twin landed on the left side and she yelped.

"Getting there," Simon said.

She braced herself for the last three, but they never came. Instead, Simon took a few steps and cupped her pussy.

"Think you can come from my whip alone?" he asked.

Her mind went blank momentarily.

He was going to . . . ? On her . . . ?

She suddenly realized how very, very exposed she was. There was nothing hidden from him, and she was so very vulnerable. "No, Sir. I don't think . . . that is . . . I'm not sure . . ."

"I didn't hear a *red* in there, so unless I do, I owe you three more, and I'm going to see if I can get you to come."

"Yes, Sir." She didn't want to tell him that there was no way on the face of the earth that she could come from a whip. On the other hand, he seemed awfully sure of himself. "It's just if you want to get me off– –"

He still had his hand between her legs, and one of his fingers was getting very, very close. Almost. Almost.

Just a little bit more.

He stepped away. "Trying to tell me how to get you off, girl?"

She could have shouted at him. How could he get her so damn close to release and then leave her like that? But the tail end of the whip stuck her inner thigh, and *ohmygod* it hurt, but it was a beautiful, hazy kind of a hurt that made her see stars, and she wanted it again.

"Please, Sir," she said, and was rewarded with the same thing on the other thigh.

Holy hell, she hadn't ever experienced anything that even

remotely felt like that. She wanted more and she wanted him inside her and she wanted to grind against him so he could get as deep as he could. But mostly she just wanted.

She wasn't exactly sure where the last strike of the tail landed. All she knew was that her release hit her in a wave of white light and a loud squeal, and she knew she'd broken into two million pieces and she just didn't care, because even if she somehow got put back together, she would never feel anything that amazing again. She laughed because the thoughts were spinning around her head in so many different directions and she had no clue what any of them meant.

"Lynne?" Simon was all around her, everywhere, but she couldn't hold her eyes open any longer. "Lynne?"

Two million pieces. "More like Humpty Dumpty."

Out of all the possible outcomes to the scene, Lynne passing out was not one Simon had ever considered. He quickly unbound her, while yelling for someone to get a blanket. He picked her up in his arms, muttering his thanks when someone dropped a blanket around her.

"Follow me." It was Luke.

He led them through the crowd to a row of private rooms. He unlocked one, pushed the door open, and followed Simon in.

"I'll leave you two alone," Luke said as Simon placed Lynne in the middle of the bed and crawled up to curl himself around her and covered them up. "Let me make sure there's water and chocolate in here."

Simon watched him locate both and called to him before he left. "Would you mind bringing my bag in here? There are some things in it I need."

"Sure thing," Luke said. "Do you need anything else?"

"Just make sure we're not disturbed."

"I can do that." Luke's eyebrow lifted. "Out of curiosity, what did she say there at the end?"

"Humpty Dumpty, I think."

Luke nodded. "That's what I thought I heard. Is that her safe word?"

"No. I'm not exactly sure why she was speaking in nursery rhymes."

"Subspace is a curious thing," Luke said, and closed the door behind him.

Simon needed to care for Lynne's back, but at the moment he simply wanted to hold her. He pulled her closer and smelled her hair, enjoying the light floral scent he'd come to associate with her over the last few weeks. Then, because he couldn't help it, he kissed the top of her head and sighed. He tried to live in such a way that he didn't have a lot of regrets. But the one thing he did regret was letting Lynne go the first time. He didn't plan to ever let that happen again.

He wasn't going to let her walk away again like he had at the conference either. Nope, if she tried to run, he was going to follow. Not that he regretted letting her do it then. It was something she had to do to work things out in her head. He didn't begrudge her that time.

But now that they were back together, it wouldn't be happening again. If she had an issue, they would talk about it together.

She gave a little snore in her sleep, and he smiled. Lord, what he'd ever done to deserve her, he wasn't sure, but now that he had her, he never planned to let her go. Realizing he had too much energy to stay in bed, he eased out from beside her but left her on her side so he could see her back.

She was sleeping so deeply, she barely stirred as he cared for her back. He was pleased with the way it looked. There would be enough marks to satisfy her inner masochist, but not anything that would mark her permanently. He placed a kiss on her shoulder blades.

It was his own personal kind of hell. Lynne was in bed, naked, and they were alone. But she was sleeping, and he didn't want to wake her. He had no idea how long she'd be out. She'd never passed out before. At least they had the private room for the night, and she could take her time drifting back to the land of the living.

With her back attended to, he joined her on the bed and pulled her into his arms, finally content to rest beside her.

Surprisingly, she didn't sleep very long. Less than thirty minutes after he got on the bed with her, she began to stir. Of course, doing so meant that she was wiggling around against his dick. He knew she would probably be out of sorts when she woke up, so he told his dick to stand down, that it wasn't time for fun just yet.

"Ow, ow, ow," Lynne mumbled in her half-awake, half-asleep state.

Simon pulled back a bit to give her room and to make sure the ibuprofen and water were nearby. She groaned as she rolled over to look at him, her eyes blinking several times before opening completely.

"Hey," he said, feeling giddy as a teenager on his first date for some reason.

"Hey," she answered back. "Where are we?"

He pushed aside a lock of hair that had fallen in her face. "At Luke's club. One of his private rooms. You passed out after the scene. Do you feel okay?"

"I ache all over and I'm sore everywhere, but interestingly enough, I *feel* fine."

He nodded toward the table. "Even so, go ahead and take two."

She didn't argue, but sat up and took the tablets. "It's coming back to me now."

"The scene?"

"Yes." She took a sip of water. He loved how she was altogether comfortable being naked around him. "You know, there at the end, when you said you were going to make me scream?"

He grinned. "Like I could forget that."

"I didn't know you meant you wanted me to have a screaming orgasm."

"I couldn't tell you everything, now, could I? What would be fun about that? Besides, it's fun to keep you on your toes."

"I couldn't get to my toes. Some mean Dom tied me to a cross so I couldn't move."

"Is that right?" He ran his knuckles across her shoulder, unable to keep his hands to himself anymore, and leaned forward to kiss her gently when she nodded. "But I think we may have to lay off the screaming orgasms."

Her forehead crinkled in that delightful way it did when she didn't understand something. "Why?"

"The screaming orgasm itself is fine. It's when you pass out and call yourself Humpty Dumpty that I have to draw the line."

"Humpty Dumpty?"

"Yes, you called yourself that after the scene. Right before you went out."

"That explains why that rhyme kept repeating in my head."

He brushed her cheekbone. "You sure you're okay?"

"I honestly can't remember a time I felt more okay than I am right now." She looked around the room for the first time. "Private room, you said? How long do we have it?"

"For as long as we want."

"Really?" She dropped a hand between them and slowly let it inch up his leg. "That certainly opens up a lot of possibilities."

He stopped her hand with his own. "Not if you're too sore or tired."

"Do I look too sore or tired?"

He slapped her thigh. "Sassy wench. Who do you think has been holding you while you recuperated from the last time we explored possibilities?"

She bit her bottom lip in mock chastisement and dropped her head, but not before he caught her smile. "Thank you for holding me, Sir. I just wanted to let you know that if you wanted to—*you know*—I'm definitely up for it."

"First, I enjoyed holding you. Second, we're not doing anything until you call it what it is instead of 'you know.' And third, are you trying to tell me what to do?"

"No, never, Sir." At his raised eyebrow, she added, "Okay, but just a little and just so you'd know that I was ready, willing, and able . . ."

"Say it."

"For you to fuck me senseless, Sir," she said, and he loved how her cheeks flushed when she spoke the words.

"That's more like it," he said while devising a plan in his head. He didn't want her in any sort of strenuous position. Not with how she'd reacted after the single-tail scene. In fact, after that scene, the sadist part of him was sated. Now he just wanted her. "But I think since I whipped you senseless not too long ago, maybe we should take it easy?"

"Not to argue, but you didn't whip me senseless, Sir."

"Oh," he said, wondering how she was going to claim that when she'd just woken up.

"Yes, you see, I think it was the orgasm that rendered me senseless." She looked so proud of the fact, he couldn't help but tease her some more.

"In that case, perhaps you shouldn't have any more orgasms."

Her mouth dropped open, and then her lips formed the cutest pout.

"Did I render you speechless?" he asked.

"Yes, Sir. The only reply I have for that is no, no, no, no, no, no. But then I remember you are a sadist, so maybe I shouldn't say that for fear that you'll use it against me. Then I think you probably know my thoughts on that already, because who would want to never have an orgasm again, right? So I'll say——"

"Lynne?"

"Yes, Sir?"

"Shut up so I can kiss you."

She giggled softly but didn't say anything further. She simply looked at him with those deep blue eyes, and her lips parted. He reminded himself not to go at her like a teenage boy high on lust, but to go slow and to remember she was sore and achy.

He gently cupped her face and gave her the lightest of all kisses, pleased at the soft purring sound she made in her throat and how she inched closer to him.

"There we go," he whispered. "Look at you, all obedient and quiet. Such a good girl."

"I wouldn't count on it lasting long, Sir." Her eyes fluttered closed, and she lifted her head, silently asking for another kiss.

He didn't dream of disappointing her. He brought his lips to hers again, but this time his kiss wasn't as soft. And neither was the noise she made in her throat. Yet even though his erection was still incredibly hard, he was content for the moment just to kiss her.

There was something to say about taking your time and simply kissing someone, when you didn't view it as a step on the way to something more but took your time and brought your partner to their knees simply with your mouth.

He deepened the kiss and smiled inside at the little whimper that escaped her. He let his fingers brush the top of her shoulder, and when he brushed the side of her breast with his knuckles, she groaned.

"Please, Sir," she whispered against his lips. "I need you."

"None of that, my impatient girl. We have all night and I'm not rushing anything." Then, to show her he was serious, he moved his hand from her breast and ran it through her hair. "I'm going to take my time pleasuring you."

She didn't object again, but allowed him to position her however he liked. First, he moved her to her back, granting him access to her breasts. He lavished attention on both, sucking the nipple of one into his mouth while pinching the other between his thumb and forefinger.

"Look at you," he said. "Look at how turned on you are by a little pain." He swept his hand low and let it rest between her legs, dipping only the tips of two fingers into her.

She squirmed a bit, but she surprised him by not doing anything to get more of him inside of her.

"So wet and ready for me and my cock, aren't you?" he asked.

"Yes, Sir," she replied, but it mostly came out in moans.

He placed his two fingers at her mouth. "Open. Taste how much you want me."

She sucked his fingers into her mouth, and the feeling was so incredible, he feared he was seconds away from losing his shit.

"That's it," he said. "Get them good and clean. Suck them down like you would my cock."

Holy fuck.

Each time she sucked his finger, it was like a direct pull on his dick, and even though he'd told her they weren't going to rush anything, he wasn't sure he would be able to last much longer.

"Damn, Lynne," he said. "You're bringing me to the edge."

"Only seems fair, Sir, seeing as how you keep me there."

He slapped her thigh. Forget all night. He wanted inside her now. "That's it. On your stomach."

She rolled onto her belly, and he had her lift her butt just a bit. "But keep your legs together," he said. "You won't believe how tight you'll be."

She mumbled something into the pillow that he thought was a curse, and he almost smiled, but then he noticed her body tremble. Normally, he would assume it was because she was excited and eager, but due to how she'd been out of it the last little bit, he wanted to make sure.

"What color are you, Lynne?"

"Green, Sir," she replied without hesitation.

He ran his hands down her back. "Why are you trembling?"

"Because I need you so badly, Sir."

"You're sure?"

"Yes, Sir." Her answer was short and clipped. He got the impression she wanted to say more but was probably afraid he'd stop if she became sassy.

"Let's see if I can fix that," he said, lining himself up.

He eased the tip of his cock inside her, and her hands fisted in the sheets. He didn't thrust into her quickly but took his time, going slow and ensuring she felt every inch of him. His eyes damn near rolled to the back of his head.

"Better?" he asked when he was buried all the way inside her.

She wiggled her ass. "Oh, hell, yes, Sir."

He gave her backside a slap. "I should have brought a plug so I could fuck your ass while I'm enjoying this pussy."

She mumbled something else into the pillow.

"Enough of that," he said, with another slap. "If you're going to say something, say it so I can hear."

"I said, I'd die of pleasure overdose if you did that, Sir."

Based on her reaction to the single tail, she'd probably pass out again. "True. We'd better wait on that until I get you acclimated to the appropriate amount of pleasure."

And speaking of pleasure, he wasn't sure how much longer he could stay inside her without moving. "Tell me, Lynne, do I feel different in this position? Can you feel how deep I am?"

She strung several four-letter words together.

"Is that a yes?" he asked, but he couldn't wait for an answer because his control was shot. He pulled back and then rammed into her. Any prior thoughts he'd had of taking things slow went right out the window when she yelped.

"Fuck, Sir. Harder."

He dropped all pretense of taking all night and started to pound into her the way they both craved. If she wanted him hard and fast, there wasn't any part of his body that was going to object to a good, hard fuck. Maybe they'd try for slow and easy another time. Like next year.

Being with Lynne always seemed to bring out the possessive caveman in him and at no time had that ever been more obvious to him than in that moment. She was his sub. His. And he'd be damned if he'd give her up again. It didn't matter if she was a nanny, or a teacher, or the fucking president of the United States. The world could have the sweet, demure Lynne she showed them. Let them think she was little Miss Innocent with her big blue eyes. He knew her inner, true self. She was a wicked, sexy, dirty girl. She loved sex and she loved it raw and real and nasty. And if there was some pain thrown in, all the better. But more than that, she was all his.

Lynne's breathing finally returned to normal. She was on top of Simon, which was odd because she'd definitely been under him. Or at least she was the last thing she remembered. She cracked one eye open and saw him watching her.

"Did I pass out again?" she asked. That was almost as embarrassing as giggling while she was in subspace. Almost.

"I don't think so," he said. "Unless I did as well. In which case, we're highly dangerous when we fuck and we probably shouldn't do it again."

He said it with a smile, so she was going to assume he was joking. "I think that's quite possibly the worst idea you've ever had."

He snorted. "I thought you'd say that."

The room fell silent, but he was rubbing her shoulder, like he wanted to say something but wasn't sure how to start it. She could almost see the wheels spinning in his head. They matched the way he was stroking her.

"I've learned it's best just to come on out and say it," she eventually said.

"Say what?"

"Whatever it is you're thinking about saying."

"That obvious, am I?"

She pushed up on one elbow and looked down on him with a raised eyebrow. *Really?*

He laughed. "Okay. I guess I am."

And still he wasn't saying anything, but he continued rubbing her shoulder. She'd just about given up when he spoke.

"I wasn't entirely truthful, before," he said.

For the life of her she couldn't imagine what he was referring to. "When?"

"When I broke up with you and I said you weren't a submissive."

"Why did you say that?" She'd always wondered. "It confused me for the longest time."

"There's really no excuse for it. We met online and the attraction was there. But you looked so young and you were so inexperienced. I feared I'd corrupt you if I told you everything I needed in a relationship. Or that I'd change you and you'd end up hating me for it."

"So you thought lying was better?"

He winced. Yup. She'd nailed it. "In my mind, I was only stretching the truth. Saying I didn't think you were a submissive was easier than admitting my own predilections were too intense for most submissives." He squeezed her shoulder. "I'm sorry that my actions led to confusion on your part."

It would be easy to get angry with him. She could allow herself to be wounded and upset. Or she could be thankful they had a second chance and could look with excitement toward the future they were building. Besides . . .

"I think it worked out for the best that way," she said.

He cocked an eyebrow. "How's that?"

"If you'd told me up front what you needed, I probably would have run away. I was too new and scared. But having it happen this way, I've learned on my own, without being influenced by anyone or anything, that I am a submissive. And you have to admit, living with Nathaniel and Abby hasn't hurt either."

A slow grin came across his face. "No, it probably hasn't."

"It's like it all came together the way it did for a reason." She gave his cheek a kiss. "So no dwelling on the past, okay? Only today and the future."

"I can't think of anything better than dwelling on the future with you. In fact." He turned and reached into a bag beside the bed. She remembered he'd had it with him before they'd started the scene. He turned back around and held a small black velvet pouch. "I know you're going to be teaching school, so I didn't want to get anything that would call attention to itself. Lynne, will you wear my collar?"

Her hand flew to her mouth. *His collar?* She'd hoped maybe one day he would offer it, but she hadn't expected it so soon. It wasn't what she normally thought of when she thought of a collar. It was a thin platinum chain with a puzzle-piece charm.

It was quirky and just a little crazy for a BDSM collar. She loved it.

She threw her arms around him. "Yes!"

He pulled her close, and when his lips touched hers, she could see it so clearly: her future with Simon, todays and tomorrows filled with laughter, love, and dirty, dirty sex.

Epilogue

Abby
One month later

I gave Nathaniel a kiss and shooed him out of the house. Dena, Julie, Sasha, and Lynne were over, and we had put a very strict "No Doms Allowed" rule in place. The architect Nathaniel and Luke had hired was coming over to chat about design ideas from a sub's perspective.

I had to admit, I was a bit on edge. Nathaniel just happened to bring up in a very *by the way* kind of tone the night before that it just so happened the architect was Cole Johnson's exslave, Kate.

"It'll be fine," he assured me as I stared at him in disbelief before he left. "Sasha's met her."

"You are such a man," I said. "Sasha may have met her. That doesn't mean she wants to be around her." I wasn't as close to Sasha as Julie, but what woman wanted her significant other's ex in her business?

"You don't give Sasha enough credit."

"Nathaniel." I put my hands on my hips. "How long have we been married?"

"Is this a trick question?"

"No, but it's been a long-ass time, right?"

He nodded.

"And yet even though we've been married a long-ass time and have two kids, and I love you with all of my being, I still don't want to sit down and chat with your exes."

"Cole recommended her."

I rolled my eyes. Honestly. "Cole is also a man."

"Be glad I shot down his idea to have her over with Sasha serving tea." I must have looked horrified because he kissed me softly. "Nothing we can do about it now. Just keep them both away from any sharp objects."

Currently, everyone was gathered in the living room while we waited for Kate to arrive. Far enough away from the kitchen that the knives should be safe. And though we were all trying not to, it was obvious everyone was keeping an eye on Sasha.

"Jesus, would you all chill out?" she finally said. "I am one hundred and ten percent secure in my relationship with Cole, and this is not a big deal. In fact, we actually had Kate over for dinner last night."

"Oh my God." Julie was sitting beside her and punched her arm. "You did not. You guys had dinner with me and Daniel."

"Right, it was the night before."

I didn't believe for a second Kate had had dinner with Cole and Sasha, but Sasha did seem to be taking everything in stride and didn't appear the least bit anxious. In fact, it might have been my imagination, but she had a look on her face that gave the impression she knew something the rest of us didn't.

I didn't have a chance to call her on it, because the doorbell rang. Okay, maybe Sasha was fine, but I was more than a little curious about the woman who'd been Cole's slave for eight years.

For as long as I'd been in the lifestyle, I still had an overactive imagination, and it was a bit anticlimactic when I opened the door to find a very ordinary woman. Granted, she was very attractive, tall and willowy, with pale skin, black hair, and the bluest eyes I'd ever seen.

"Hi," she said. "I'm Kate."

She looked every bit the professional with a leather briefcase and a tailored suit I knew must have been handmade.

"Hello, Kate." I opened the door so she could come in. "I'm Abby. Come on in. Everyone's in the living room."

"Thank you." She stepped inside and looked around. "Beautiful home."

"Thanks."

I led her into the living room and only had to introduce her to Lynne, since she knew everyone else. She said hello to Julie, *ooh*ed and *aah*ed over Dena's infant daughter, and shocked the hell out of me by giving Sasha a hug.

"I knew he'd get his head out of his ass eventually," she said. "And is that his collar . . . ?"

Sasha flushed and fingered the priceless family heirloom Cole had collared her with over the summer. "Yes. It's been in his family for ages."

"I'm so happy for you guys." And by the tone of her voice and the expression on her face, I believed her.

As Kate settled into a nearby chair and started pulling out papers, it struck me that not only was she gorgeous, but she was smart as hell, too. She'd walked into what could have been an awkward situation and immediately defused it. And in doing so, she'd won the respect of every woman present.

She went over her proposed ideas for the club, and we all bounced a few things around. Kate took notes on everything we suggested and offered a few ideas of her own. She told us she'd been to Germany recently and had visited a club there. While drawing up the plans, she had incorporated several ideas.

"You know," I told her. "If you'd like to join a club while you're here, you're more than welcome to join this group. If that's too awkward for you, Nathaniel and I could recommend you for our New York club."

She looked uncertain for the first time since she'd walked into the house. "Thanks, but I'm not in the lifestyle anymore."

"What? Why not?" Sasha asked, voicing what the rest of us were thinking.

"I've decided it's not for me." Her voice sounded certain, but she wouldn't meet anyone's eyes.

"I didn't know you could turn it off like that," Sasha said dryly.

But Kate refused to be goaded into saying more. She crossed her legs, and as she did, I caught a glimpse of red soles on the bottom of her shoes.

"Nice shoes," I said in an attempt to both change the subject and lighten the mood of the room.

Kate grew wistful. "Thanks. They were a gift."

"Wow," Julie said, eyeing the shoes in question. "That's like Christmas, birthday, and anniversary all bundled up together."

"Let's just say the gift was a reminder of a very special time." Kate still had the wistful look, but unless I was mistaken, there was a hint of sadness in her tone as well. Yet just as suddenly as it showed up, it was gone, replaced by a smile. "I think that's everything I needed. You guys have my number if you need me or if you have any questions?"

"I'll make sure they have it," I answered. "We're going to go over some group topics, and I'd invite you to stay, but since you're not in the lifestyle anymore . . ."

Kate was already packing her things up. "No, that's okay. I need to drop by the office."

I walked her out, and we set up a tentative lunch date for the next week. I had been thoroughly impressed with her, though I was a bit perturbed to share that with Nathaniel.

I had no problems sharing it with the other women. Everyone agreed she was perfect for the job. Everyone except Sasha, who was unusually quiet.

Julie picked up on it first. "Tell us what the problem is," she said. "I know that look."

For a few moments I didn't think Sasha would answer. She sat on the couch, her fingers tracing her collar. Finally, she sighed. "If Cole finds out I told you, he'll think I was gossiping, and that won't go over well, but hell, I can't help it." Her eyes danced with mischief. "I know who gave her the shoes."

"Oh?" I said, wondering where this was going.

Sasha nodded. "Yes. Cole's mentor, Fritz Brose, called him a few weeks ago wanting to know Kate's shoe size. Cole thinks they hooked up briefly while she was in Germany."

"Wait a minute," I said, trying to sort out the details. "Cole's mentor and friend, the one who did your collaring ceremony, hooked up with his ex?"

"Cole said he's had a thing for her forever," Sasha added with a smile. "But here's the interesting part—"

"It gets more interesting?" Dena asked. "Because it already sounds like a soap opera."

"Trust me," Sasha said. "Abby, do you remember who the contractor is for the new club?"

I shook my head. "Nathaniel just said it was some . . . Oh my God." I gasped as I remembered. "Some German guy."

"Yup," Sasha said. "And I don't think either Fritz or Kate knows they'll be working together."

Julie giggled. "Damn. What I wouldn't give to be a fly on the wall when that meeting goes down."

Don't miss the second book

in Tara Sue Me's

Lessons from the RACK series,

HEADMASTER

Available in January 2018.

Winnie's Journal

I saw him as soon as he walked into the room. How could I not?
He was by far the hottest man at the party. The way he strolled
in, with that swagger only the most confident of men have. I'm
sure if I had been able to look anywhere except at him, I would
have seen other women similarly obsessed. His dark hair, dark eyes,
and that mouth? Hell, that wasn't even taking into account his
hot-as-hell, fuck-me-all-night body.

But when I had a chance to look around at something else, it
wasn't at other women; it was at Marie, and I know I was in trou-
ble. We'd never wanted the same thing before.

The one thing Mariela could count on to never let her down
was dance—it was one thing she could turn to and lean
on. The one thing guaranteed to make a day better or to take
away all her stress. Through thick and thin, ups and downs, it

had always been her rock. Until today, when the rock crumbled.

She took a deep breath, moved into position, and jumped and turned in a *coupé jeté en tournant.* Finding her technique lacking, she repeated it again and again until, exhausted, she leaned against the barre and let a string of curses fly.

"Bad day?" someone asked from the hallway.

Mariela lifted her head and forced a smile at Andie Lincoln, the RACK Academy's newest chef. "You could say that."

"In that case, I came just in time. Come with me; I need someone to try my icing and tell me if it sucks."

Mariela pushed back from the barre and wiped the sweat from her forehead with a nearby towel. "Isn't that what we have the men for?"

"Yes, well, that and sex. But Fulton always likes everything I make and Lennox just kind of looks at me like I grew a second head and says he doesn't understand why I feel the need to improve upon perfection." She tilted her head. "So now that I think about it, nah, that's not what we have men for. We only have them here for sex."

Mariela laughed, glad that Andie had shown up to drag her away from a disappointing ballet session. "Okay. Let me clean up and I'll be right there."

"Just come like that. No one's here yet."

Mariela looked down at her leotard and tights. Not really dining room appropriate, but then again, the students for the fall session wouldn't arrive for another week. She threw her towel back over the barre. "You're right. What kind of icing are we talking about?"

Andie started chatting about buttercream versus cream

cheese, and to be honest, Mariela zoned out a bit. Cooking and baking were not her things. That's what chefs were for.

Andie pushed open the two wide wooden doors that led into the dining area. "Okay, you go have a seat and I'll bring the samples out to you."

Mariela looked around the area and breathed a sigh of relief at finding there was no one else in the dining area. And by no one else, she meant the headmaster, Lennox MacLure, who, other than Andie and Fulton, was the one other person on the island that housed the academy. The other staff members would be arriving tomorrow.

Unfortunately, she hadn't been sitting for longer than two minutes before Lennox walked through the door. She dropped her head and pretended to be horribly curious about something in her lap.

She expected him to ignore her. After all, that's what he did best. But even with her head down, she could feel him approach her.

"Marie," he said, calling her by the nickname only he used.

She looked up and, like always, he took her breath away. Dark and dashing were the words her best friend, Winnie, had once used to describe him. She had been right. With his black-as-sin hair and gray eyes, he looked like he belonged between the pages of a historical romance, starring as an evil pirate or maybe an unrepentant rake.

"Lennox," she said, cringing because she knew her raspy voice gave her away.

"You are aware the dining hall has a dress code?"

She waited for him to smile and tell her it was a joke, that of course he wasn't going to enforce the dress code when there were only four people on the island. But the smile didn't come, and neither did the "Ha-ha-ha, I'm just joking" line.

"What?" she finally asked.

"The dress code," he snapped. "You're in violation of it."

"Oh my God. You're serious."

"We have rules and regulations for a reason."

"Right, but since there are only four of us here . . ." She trailed off, assuming her intent would be clear.

"You thought you didn't have to follow the rules?"

She couldn't believe he was being such a dick over something so stupid. "Yes," she said, just to goad him. "That's it exactly. I figured since there were only four of us, you wouldn't care if I wore a leotard and tights into the dining room. I mean, seriously, who's it going to bother? Not Fulton or Andie. And you typically don't give me the time of day. I could probably sit on your desk, buck naked, and you wouldn't lift an eyebrow."

"It's my fault, Master MacLure," Andie said, appearing with a tray in her hands. "She wanted to get cleaned up and I told her it didn't matter. Not with there only being the four of us here."

Mariela stood up. "Don't call him 'Master,' Andie. He's not worthy of the title."

She turned and walked out, not waiting for either of them to say anything in response.

Lennox watched Marie walk away with a lump in his throat the entire time. Yes, he was an ass. He shouldn't have said anything to her. But hell, what was a man to do? She'd walked into the dining area in that dance outfit like it was no big deal. Didn't she know what the sight of her in those skintight clothes would do to him?

Hell, why did she think there was a rule that only street clothes could be worn in the dining hall? Technically, the rule stated no fetish wear was allowed in the dining area, but that outfit she had on could in no way be considered street clothing.

Even though she'd left, he could still picture her perfectly in his mind. She was petite, and he liked that about her. Liked that she was small and dainty compared to him. Fuck, it was unbelievable what it did to the Dominant inside him to imagine her tiny body beneath him. How incredible it would feel to take possession of her.

He clenched his fists as the image of her swam before his eyes. The outfit had left nothing to his imagination, and even though he'd seen her naked before, to see her like she'd been today did nothing but mock him.

He pictured it all too clearly. Her lithe body, made strong by her dance routines. The firm muscles of her legs. How would they feel wrapped around him? His fingers itched to run over them, to feel their strength. No, more than that. To master her strength.

For he knew that the rush that came with taking control of a submissive was only multiplied when her submission was coupled with a strength she had willingly laid aside. And he had no doubt that as small as she was, Marie was a powerhouse. To be given her submission would be the sweetest of all gifts.

Yet even though he knew how amazing it would be, he could not allow himself to take it. He strongly suspected she would give it to him. He'd known for a long time that he need only look at her and she'd be on her knees. But it was an offering he could not accept.

He no longer allowed himself to indulge in his Dominant nature. Ever. In fact, he'd buried it so deep and for so long, he wasn't sure he could revive that part of himself. What he did know was that he could not take the chance of finding out. The last time he'd freed that need within him, the results had been fatal. He could not take that risk again. Especially with Marie.

If the end result was she thought him a coldhearted bastard, so be it. He could live with that. What he could not live with was if he killed her the way he'd killed Winnie.

"I feel as though I should apologize again, Sir," Andie said. "But I'm not exactly sure what for."

"Has Andie been causing trouble, again?" Her Dom and one of his Master Professors came up behind her. "Do I need to take her over my knee?"

Lennox smiled as Fulton's arms came around his submissive, even as she swatted at him in mock outrage.

"What's this about 'again'?" she asked. "When have I ever caused trouble?"

Fulton dropped a kiss on the top of her head. "The correct question is when have you not caused trouble?"

Andie crossed her arms. "*Mpph.* I didn't know I caused you so many problems, Sir."

"You're putting words in my mouth, Andie. I didn't say 'problems.' I said 'trouble.'"

"Pretty much the same thing."

"Hey, look," Fulton said, obviously trying to change the subject. "Are those icing samples?"

Andie reached for the tray and held it out to him. "Yes. I was going to have Mariela help me decide which was better."

Fulton grabbed a spoon from the place setting already on the table and took a bite of each one. "Mmm, I don't know. They're both really good to me. Boss?"

Lennox dutifully took another spoon and tasted them. "These

are both excellent, but so is the icing you've been using previously. Why mess with a good thing?"

Andie shook her head and mumbled under her breath while cleaning up the space. She gathered everything together and started for the kitchen without saying anything.

"Andie?" Fulton asked as she walked away.

"Sex," she called over her shoulder. "Just sex and nothing else."

"What was that about?" Lennox asked Fulton as she left through the door that led to the kitchen.

"Damned if I know. I gave up trying to figure women out ages ago. It only gives you a headache." Fulton scratched his head. "But she said 'Sex and nothing else.' That has to be good, right?"

"You would think."

"Wish she'd have left some of that icing. Think I'll go in the kitchen to see if I can get some more."

Lennox snorted. "Good luck with that."

The
Claiming

A Submissive Series Novella

Submitting is just the beginning. . . .

Sasha Blake never thought her emotional wounds would heal—that they were a part of her just like her physical scars. But that was before Cole Johnson's boundless love and overwhelmingly sexy control set her free, unleashing a confident side that she never knew she had. He's more than just her Master; he's her world. And she'll do anything he asks. . . .

Cole's days of restless wandering are done—he's found everything he needs in Sasha. Now it's time to make it official. When his childhood home in England goes up for sale, he realizes the old estate is the perfect place to claim Sasha as his own, and the ideal opportunity to show her just how much she means to him.

As Sasha, Cole, and their closest friends from their Partners in Play community descend on the British countryside for a titillating adult vacation, the submissives and Dominants alike will test their boundaries—and have an adventure none of them will ever forget. . . .

Chapter One

Sasha stretched, sighing in pleasure as Cole's arms tightened around her. He kissed the back of her neck.

"You're still awake?" he asked. "I thought for sure you'd be asleep."

It was a Friday night, and they'd both had a long week. On a typical Friday night, they would not be in bed so early. In fact, at ten thirty p.m., they were usually in the middle of a kinky scene. But tonight, after dinner and a walk outside, they'd both decided to turn in early.

At the time, it had made sense. But suddenly Sasha wasn't so tired anymore. She wiggled her butt against him, delighting in the groan of pleasure he gave in response. "It appears as if I'm not able to go to sleep without sex anymore," she said.

Behind her, Cole chuckled. "Good to know what I'm useful for."

"I didn't mean it like that."

"Seriously, is that why you keep me around? So I can ensure you get a good night's sleep?"

He was teasing her. One of his favorite pastimes. She decided to play along.

"Yes." She turned in his arms so she faced him. "That is *exactly* why I keep you around. That and nothing else."

He had told her recently that he liked her playful side. That he liked it when she joked with him and played around, because he said it proved how comfortable she was with him. And she was, surprisingly enough. Cole made her comfortable. Which was something she would have never imagined months ago. Now, being around him was as easy as breathing.

"Nothing else?" His eyes danced with joy. "Nothing you can think of?"

"Well, you do cook really well. I guess those are two reasons to keep you around."

"Sex—but only to help you sleep—and food. I see."

"But it's really good sex."

He ran his fingers down her arm. "Is that right?"

"Really, really, really good sex."

He leaned closer, and she could almost taste his lips. She closed her eyes.

Cole's phone rang.

"Bloody hell," he said, pulling away. "Who could that be?"

"I don't know, but you should ignore it," she said, but he was already reaching for the phone.

"It's from the UK."

That didn't sound good. She sat up so she could see him better.

"Hello."

He was turned away from her so she couldn't see his reaction to the call. The person on the other end was doing most of the talking. Cole was relatively quiet. She calculated the time difference in her head. It was very early morning in the UK. No, this didn't sound good at all.

"Excellent," Cole told whomever he was speaking to. "Send everything in an e-mail. I'll sign and get back to you within a few hours."

He disconnected and turned back to face her. She breathed a sigh of relief at his smile.

"Everything okay?" she asked anyway.

"Yes." He pulled her to him. "Everything is very much okay. I'm buying my childhood home. I'd heard it might be going up on the market and, because there's such interest in it, I told the agent to ring me as soon as he heard something."

"Really?"

"Yes. In fact, how would you like to go see it?"

"Go to England?" She'd never been to the UK, and the prospect of going with Cole sounded fun.

"Yes." He rested his chin on the top of her head. "I'd like for you to see it. To share with you that part of me."

He had told her a few things about his childhood home. The way he'd described it made it sound like a castle right out of the pages of a romance novel. He'd spoken longingly of the massive grounds and the imposing stone structure that he said had been a happy home right up until his father had left him and his mother for another woman.

But if he bought the house . . .

"Are you going to move to the UK?" She tried not to panic. She knew he'd never do anything like that without talking to her. But still, it was no small thing to buy a house, especially one in a foreign country.

"I'm not going anywhere without you, little one, and I know you're settled here."

It wasn't until her body relaxed that she realized how tense she'd been over the possibility of Cole moving.

And, of course, he'd felt it, too. "Did you really think I'd plan something like that and not tell you?"

"No, Sir. Or at least, the rational part of me knew you wouldn't. The little part of me that keeps thinking being with you is a dream I'm going to wake up out of? That part worried. But just for a second."

"I can assure you this is not a dream."

Though she'd been sleepy when they'd first made it to bed, with the phone call and the ensuing conversation, she was wide-awake. And very aware of the man currently holding her.

"I think I need a bit of reassurance about that, Sir."

His eyes were kind but hungry with lust. "I think I can help with that." He dropped his head and softly brushed his lips across hers. "And I'm going to start with that little part of you that thinks this is a dream. I'm going to pleasure you so much, you'll never want to dream again because sleep only means you're separated from me."

She whimpered low in her throat as he shifted them so she was on her back with him above her. God, she loved him so much. Loved how he was fierce and protective, while never losing the part of him that was her demanding Master.

He dragged his finger along the silk strap of her gown. "New rule," he said against her neck. She shivered at the scruffiness of his cheek. "You're to be naked in bed from now on."

It wasn't that surprising a request. To be honest, the surprising thing was that he hadn't put it into place before now. And she normally ended up naked anyway. But somehow, hearing the command fall from his lips made her want him even more.

"Yes, Sir," she replied, tipping her head back and closing her eyes as his lips traveled from her shoulder across her collarbone to the hollow of her throat.

Normally, when he took her, it was hard and fast. He was a thoughtful lover, but slow wasn't his typical manner. That didn't seem to be the case tonight. Tonight, it appeared he was going to be methodical in his pleasuring of her. She wasn't sure she could handle it; the intensity he brought to the bedroom always left her breathless. How much more would a slow and intentional Cole affect her?

"If sin were a flavor, it'd taste like your skin." He nibbled lower, coming to rest at her breasts.

"If sin were a sound, it'd be that insanely sexy voice of yours."

He ran a lazy finger around her nipple, causing her to suck in a breath. He gave a low and seductive chuckle at her response. "Indeed?"

But she couldn't answer because he picked that minute to roll the tip of her nipple between his fingers and pinch it. Instead she gasped at the sensation.

"You see, I think that sound you just made was sin incarnate." He switched to the other side and repeated his actions, once more drawing a low moan from her. "Yes. That's the one."

She ran her hands down his back. She loved to touch him, but most of the time he directed their sex life, and since she was often bound in one way or another, she didn't normally have the chance.

"No fair, Sir," she teased.

"What's that?" he asked, as his knowledgeable fingers drifted lower, seeking out the places he knew would drive her mad.

"What you do to me. How you affect me. All of it."

His fingers stopped, and she almost whined, but instead she opened her eyes to find him looking down at her intently. "It most certainly is fair," he said, his voice a coarse whisper. "Do you want to know why?"

"Why, Sir?"

"Because it works the exact same way in reverse. Do you have any idea what you do to me?"

She knew parts. The things he'd told her, the few times he'd shared such things. But there were times she still felt the need to pinch herself. It was too hard to believe he was hers. That he was with her and wanted her.

"Not entirely, Sir."

He remained motionless. "Not entirely? Then, Sasha, I haven't been doing my job properly."

"I didn't mean to insinuate—"

"Hush." He placed a finger over her lips. "I know you didn't mean anything malicious with what you said, but I don't ever want you to doubt what you mean to me or how I feel about you. Nod if you understand."

She nodded.

"I have never experienced anything that even comes close to making me feel the way I feel when I'm with you. And I promise you this: I'm going to find a way to prove it to you."

She let his words seep in; he'd spoken them with such passion and intensity, she allowed herself to believe them. "Thank you, Sir."

She saw the warring expression in his eyes and wondered what she'd said to put such a look on his face.

"You have it wrong, little one. I'm the one who should be thanking you." His lips brushed hers, but this time they were reverent. "Thank you for accepting me," he whispered against her mouth. "For taking every part of who I am and not trying to change the parts you don't like."

She wasn't sure who in his past had tried to change him, but it wasn't the first time he'd mentioned something along those lines. Maybe it had been Kate? She'd been his girlfriend for eight years. Though "girlfriend" seemed a bit simplistic for the twenty-four/seven Master/slave relationship she'd shared with Cole.

Sasha made sure he was watching her when she answered. "Why would I want to change part of you? All of your parts make you the man you are. If I take one away because I don't like it, then I'm not really with you. I'm with only a part, and I don't want part of you. I want all of you."

He didn't say anything in reply; he simply dropped his head so he could kiss her again. He loved her with his mouth, worshipping her body with kisses and driving her to the brink of release with nothing more than his lips.

Even when he shifted himself to rest between her knees, he spoke only three words.

"Eyes on me."

She could do nothing other than obey as he slowly entered her. It was overwhelming—the feel of him above her and inside her, combined with the love she saw reflected in his eyes. Her body shuddered as he seated himself fully inside, and she moaned deep in her throat when he didn't move but stayed perfectly still.

Just when she thought she couldn't take any more, he brought his hands to her face and kissed her so deeply and with such passion, she knew if he stopped, she was going to climax before he did anything.

"Please, Sir," she whispered. "I'm so close, I can't—"

"Say my name," he ground out.

"Cole, please."

"Don't hold back tonight." He pulled out, just a touch. "Let me have everything." He ended the sentence with a forceful thrust and she came apart around him.

"Ah, little one, you test my own self-control," he said, and she knew he was doing his best to hold back and not take her with the intensity he wanted.

"Do it." She wrapped her legs around his waist. "Let go of your control for once."

"I wanted to be gentle tonight." He rocked his hips in a lazy rhythm.

She loved the gentleness he'd been showing, but she had to admit, she went wild for the rough and hard Cole, too. "Forget gentle." She bit his earlobe. "Take me completely. Make me forget everything except you."

"You sure about that?" he asked, and for just a second she questioned the intelligence of what she was asking.

She swallowed. "Yes, Sir."

"Take hold of your knees and pull them to your chest."

She hesitated. In that position, he'd go so deep. And he wasn't exactly small.

"Unless you've changed your mind," he said. "But if you want me to take you the way I want to right now, you need to know that I'm going to fuck you so deep, you'll think I've become a permanent part of your body."

She shivered at his words but hooked her arms under her knees and pulled them toward her, giving him greater access to her body.

"That's my girl," he said. "You'll take me any way I want, won't you?"

"Yes, Sir." God help her, she would. After all, why would she not, when doing so only gave her more pleasure, more passion, and more happiness than she'd ever thought possible?

Her body trembled at the sight of him kneeling before her, taking himself in hand and moving toward her. He caught her looking and gave her a lazy smile. Making sure she kept her eyes on him, he slowly stroked his erection.

"I think you were right with what you said earlier. I don't know if I can go to sleep without fucking you first." Still he kept stroking.

"Please, Sir."

"I think I could stay here and look at you forever, spread wide and waiting for me to claim you, your body given to me to use however I want." He started to stroke himself faster. "Just the anticipation of how good you're going to feel when I push inside that first time."

He tipped his head back, and she couldn't take her eyes off him. He was magnificent to watch. Hard male muscle. The way he took his cock in hand and worked it. Fuck. If she didn't want him inside her so badly, she'd be happy to watch him pleasure himself.

His jaw clenched and he opened his eyes and looked down at her. "It's too late for gentle."

"Yes," she said, in either understanding or agreement—she didn't know.

He didn't say anything else; he simply placed himself at her entrance and drove into her with one powerful thrust. Normally, he'd go slowly to allow her time to take him, and her breath caught in her throat at the sensation of him filling her all at once.

He held still and looked down at her with a silent question in his eyes. *Are you okay?*

She nodded. *Please don't stop.*

He must have felt the same way because he only moaned, "Oh, God. Sasha," before starting a relentless rhythm that had her on the edge within a few thrusts.

She didn't even try to stop her climax. He'd told her to come whenever, and since that wasn't something he often allowed, she was going to take advantage of it while she could. She wiggled herself to take him easier and bit the inside of her cheek as the first orgasm swept through her body.

He slowed down after her slight tremors stopped, but only so he could work her with long intentional thrusts that lifted her lower body from the bed.

"Holy fuck, Sir."

He didn't stop, but took it for the encouragement it was, this time alternating between long and deep and shallow and fast. When her second orgasm hit, he held still.

"I love the feeling of your climax pulsating around me," he said as the tremors subsided. "I love knowing what I do to you." He pressed deeper into her. "Feel what you do to me?"

His body shook, betraying the amount of self-control he was using to remain still.

"Yes, Sir. But let me feel it more." She lifted her hips. "Let me feel you finish."

With a low groan from his throat, he drove into her again, and this time, he let himself go.

"Bloody hell, Sasha," he panted, but he gathered her to his chest. She sighed in blissful contentment. Being in his arms, lying on his chest, was hands down her favorite place to be. She knew in a few minutes he would get up so he could clean her. When he'd collared her, they'd stopped using condoms. She loved the feel of him bare within her, but it was a bit messier. Even so, once he'd cleaned them both, she knew he'd come back to bed again and hold her.

Yes, if this were a dream, she never wanted to wake up.

Cole smiled when he saw the e-mail he'd been waiting for had arrived in his in-box. He'd been waiting to show Sasha his childhood home for quite a while. But after their conversation the previous night, he'd decided he wanted to do that and more.

In the months since they'd been together, Sasha continued to grow stronger and more self-assured. He loved watching her become the fierce woman he'd known she was when he'd first seen her. But it bothered him that she didn't know exactly what she did to him. He'd told her so in words, and he'd thought he'd shown her with actions. Apparently, though, he hadn't been as clear as he'd thought.

That was going to change with the UK trip.

But in order to pull it off, he needed some help, and that's where their friends came into play. The idea had hit him the night before. Now he had to contact Nathaniel and Daniel to get them involved.

It would be tricky; everyone was going to have to keep the main reason for the UK trip a secret. He knew both Nathaniel's wife, Abby, and Daniel's submissive, Julie, hated keeping secrets from Sasha. He could only hope that in this case they wouldn't mind so much and would follow along.

He pushed back from his desk and went into the guest bedroom. The safe inside the closet held what he was looking for. Sasha didn't even know of the safe's existence and, since she was at work at the floral shop she owned with Julie, he could open it without her finding out.

He opened the safe and carefully took out the small case he'd come for. Perfect. He'd get the contents adjusted and ready. He couldn't wait to see the expression on Sasha's face when she realized what it was.

Now he just had a few phone calls to make and everything would be set in motion.

Chapter Two

"Sasha," Julie said a few days later when Sasha entered the store after having lunch with Cole. "What's the deal with this UK trip? Is it really going to be a house party? Abby and Nathaniel are coming, too?"

Sasha put her purse under the counter with a smile. "Did Cole send you and Daniel the details?"

He'd expanded on the idea behind the trip to the UK, invited their friends, and talked about adding some role-play scenarios to it. He'd planned on being the lord of the manor, and Sasha was to be his head servant. Abby and Nathaniel, along with Julie and Daniel, were to be houseguests. She'd have loved for Dena and Jeff to go as well, but Dena was pregnant and, with her history of late-term miscarriage, there was no way she was going to travel out of the country. Fortunately, Julie and Sasha had a relationship with a company that provided temporary employees, so it wouldn't be a problem for them both to be out at the same time.

Julie was smiling. "Yes, and it sounds like so much fun. I can't wait."

"I think it'll be fun, too. I mean, when was the last time you and I went anywhere? And I've always wanted to go to the UK."

"Seriously." Julie's eyes grew big. "Ohh, we need to go shopping!"

"Definitely. And you know, I think this trip will be a good chance for you to get to know Cole."

Sasha always got the impression Julie merely put up with Cole because he was part of her life. Her best friend had never been one to keep her feelings about him secret. Especially in the early days of their relationship.

Julie twirled a rose stem. "True, but I'm coming around to you guys being a thing. I just never in my wildest dreams thought you'd be with anyone like him."

"You're coming around, or Daniel's told you to zip it where we're concerned?"

Cole and Daniel, Julie's Dom, were old friends, and Daniel had not taken kindly to the way Julie questioned the budding relationship.

Julie grinned. "Maybe a little of both. I have to admit, even though I know it's none of my business, I'm still insanely curious about the rules Kate mentioned when she stopped by that one day."

Kate, Cole's ex, had shown up unexpectedly at Cole's place the morning after Sasha had first slept over. While she was there, she'd alluded to certain rules Cole had given her about his punishments. Rules he had seemingly not given Sasha.

"Oh, that." Sasha decided to tease Julie a bit.

"You know?"

"Yeah, I asked him about it. Damn stupid on my part, because he decided to make it a rule for me, too."

"Do tell."

"It's nothing really. Just that I'm not allowed an orgasm for twenty-four hours following a discipline session." Sasha rolled her eyes. "He put it in the protocol and everything."

Julie nodded. "I get that. Daniel hasn't so much made it a rule, but he may as well have."

"Last time I'm asking anything having to do with a rule, though." She leaned close to her friend. "That morning Kate came over, following the first time he used a cane on me? I came four times the night before."

"Four?"

"Yes, which is why that rule utterly and completely sucks."

"I agree."

"Are canes still a hard limit for you?" Sasha asked.

"Yes, and I don't see that coming off the list anytime soon."

Julie had been dating Daniel for more than a year and she had been wearing his collar for nearly that long. It was still considered relatively early in her submissive journey, though, and Daniel was her first Dom.

"You know they're not all about pain, right?" Sasha asked Julie. "When they're used certain ways, they can feel really good."

"I know. I talked to Abby. She can actually orgasm when Nathaniel uses one on her."

Sasha shook her head. "I don't see that happening. Ever."

"Me neither. But it does give me hope that one day we can play with them."

Sasha stilled the hand Julie had been twirling the flower

with. "I don't say it often enough, but I want you to know how proud I am of you. Could you have even imagined a year ago that you would be the collared submissive of one of the most highly regarded Doms in the area?"

Julie laughed. "No, never."

"Funny how time changes us, isn't it?"

Her words echoed in her head several weeks later as Cole drove them toward his childhood home. If someone had told her six months ago that she would be here today with Cole, she'd have called them a liar to their face. Nor would she have thought it possible that she would feel so content, at peace, and in love.

"It's so beautiful here," she said. "So green and lush."

"Only because it rains so much."

"It's not raining now."

In fact, not only was it not raining, but it was a gorgeous summer day. She wished they had rented a convertible so she could feel the wind in her hair. Cole said it wasn't much farther to the estate, but she didn't care. She could ride for hours looking at the beautiful scenery.

"Here's the drive," Cole said, turning off onto an unpaved road.

She twisted around, trying to find the house, but she couldn't see it. "Where's the house?"

"Just a ways up."

She sat forward in her seat, anxious for the first look at Cole's childhood home. "Seeing this," she said, "I understand why you didn't want a penthouse in the city. All the space. You don't even have very many neighbors."

There were a few small houses scattered here and there, but

nothing particularly close to the estate they were pulling up to. Cole turned a curve, and a massive dwelling came into view.

"Oh, wow." She had no other words. Nothing to describe her amazement at what she saw. "House" didn't do the structure justice. It was much larger than anything she had imagined.

"I remember it being much bigger," Cole said.

"Are you serious? Bigger than that?"

"I was a child the last time I saw it and looked at it with a child's point of view."

"I guess that makes sense." She observed him, watching for any emotion. He never spoke much about his childhood. She'd only heard bits and pieces from him.

He caught her staring. "Why are you looking at me like that, little one?"

"I'm not sure if you're happy or sad to be here."

They'd made it to the front of the house, and even though she couldn't wait to get out and explore the house and grounds, at the moment she was concerned only with the man at her side.

He parked the car, turned in his seat, and took her hand. "You're with me, which automatically means I'm happy. The location doesn't matter."

"Just wanting to know if I should be prepared to slay dragons for you this week."

"Little one. Don't you know?" He brought her hand to his lips for a quick kiss. "You already have."

Chapter Three

The next afternoon, Sasha stared out the window in the morning room. She thought that was a silly name, "morning room." Did that mean you couldn't use it after lunch? Why wasn't there an afternoon room or an evening room? English people were funny.

"What's the smile for, little one?"

She jumped at the sound of Cole's voice. He strolled into the room, hands in his pockets, looking at her with *that* look. The one that said without words that he wanted to tie her up and do wicked, wicked things to her.

She dropped to her knees. "I was thinking about how impractical it is to have a room you use only in the morning."

He dug his fingers into her hair, and she moaned at how good his touch felt. "I suppose it is a bit impractical. Stand up and walk with me outside."

She scurried to her feet. She'd been looking forward to exploring the grounds of his childhood home. He held out a hand and, with their fingers entwined, they made their way out the door.

They'd explored the inside yesterday, and everyone else was scheduled to arrive tomorrow. Even though she was excited to see her friends, she was glad to have a couple days alone with Cole.

They made their way past the rose garden and maze to a large expanse of open field.

"When I was a boy, there were sheep here," he said. "I was a bloody terror, running around, playing Viking warrior."

Sasha looked over the field, and in her mind's eye, she could picture it: a four- or five-year-old Cole. He would have run across the grassy meadow, short, stocky legs pumping as hard as they could while he charged at the sheep. And in her mind, he held a stick as a sword. The image made her smile.

"Looking back now, it's easy to see why my parents only had me. I was a handful and a half."

"I can picture bits of it in my head, but honestly, I have a hard time seeing you as a child."

He grinned at her and put his arm around her shoulders. "I'll have to see if Mum has pictures."

"Is she coming?" She'd yet to meet his mother. Of course, he hadn't met her parents, either, but they had invited her brother over for dinner once.

"Here? No, I think she's in Italy now."

She nodded. From all accounts, it didn't sound like his mother stayed in one place for very long.

"She's never been very content." He frowned. "With anything."

His expression made her sad. She wanted to ask his mother what the hell her problem was. How could she not be content?

She remembered his statement about people trying to change him. Was his mother one of the people who had always tried to change him? If that was the case, it was no wonder he never felt as if he could satisfy anyone.

"That's a sad life. Never being content. Always traveling and never setting down roots." She brushed his hand. "For what it's worth, I think I'll be content as long as I'm with you. No matter where we are."

"There's no one else I want to set down roots with," he whispered. "But I want to do it in Wilmington. I'm glad I was able to purchase this place, but just being here has proven to me that home is in the States."

"I'd move here if you wanted to."

"Thank you, little one. You don't know how much that means to me."

She turned and put her arms around him, just wanting to show support. To simply be there for him. He sighed and kissed the top of her head.

They stayed wrapped in each other's arms for several long minutes. He gave her a squeeze and pulled back. "Right, so enough of melancholy. Why don't I show you where I had my first kiss?"

Cole couldn't hold back his grin at Sasha's dropped jaw.

"What?" she asked.

"I had my first kiss right down there." He pointed to the old barn. "Come on, I'll show you."

She took his hand and they walked down the gently sloping hill to reach the small weathered barn. The building hadn't been maintained very well. He was going to have to hire some-

one to keep the house and yard up. This place was too important to him to let it fall into ruin, even if he had no desire to live
here full-time.

He let go of Sasha's hand only long enough to open the iron
gate and push aside the overgrown weeds.

"Ugh." She followed behind, swatting at the tall grasses. "You
have your work cut out for you here."

"I'm going to hire some people to help me clean it up."

She waved away a fly. "I certainly hope it wasn't like this
when you brought your girlfriend here to seduce her."

"What makes you think I seduced her? Maybe it was the
other way around." He held open the barn door so she could join
him inside.

"Really?"

He pulled her deeper into the barn, a place he hadn't been
for more than twenty years. Back then, it had smelled of grain
and hay and sheep. Now it was all musty and dirty. "I was thir-
teen and she was fifteen."

"Ohh, an older woman?" She pushed his shoulder. "Look at you."

"Right? Mary Catherine was the vicar's daughter. She had
strawberry blond hair that had these perfect ringlet curls."

"At fifteen?" Sasha's nose wrinkled. "Ringlets?"

"It was natural and she hated it. Threatened to cut it all off."

"Smart."

"I liked it. I thought it'd be fun to pull. But she came over
one day with her father for a visit. I was in here, helping with a
pregnant sheep that was having some trouble. Mary Catherine
strolled in like she owned the place and said, 'I've decided I'm
going to kiss you today.' I was in shock. She was so pretty and
all the guys wanted her."

The look on Sasha's face was a combination of disbelief and fascination. He laughed and pulled her to his chest.

"Come here. I just looked at her with my jaw hitting the floor, much like yours is now. She gave me a smirk and walked over and kissed me." He lowered his lips to hers for a quick kiss. "We snogged for a bit that day, and I fell even harder. Followed her around school for days until she broke my heart."

"What happened?"

"She was only using me to get at my stepbrother."

"The asshole kid who lived to get you in trouble?"

"That very one. I was devastated. Told my mum I was over girls for good."

Sasha brushed some hay off her shoulder. "Hmm, that didn't work out very well, did it?"

"No. It lasted about two weeks."

Her grin was infectious. "A whole two weeks? Wow. She must have been something to make you forget Mary Catherine."

"Oh, she was, but I wasn't able to forget Mary Catherine."

"You liked her that much?"

"Nah. The girl I went with after two weeks was Mary Catherine's little sister."

Her hand flew to her mouth, but she lowered it and gave him a stern look. "Cole Johnson, that was a horrible thing to do."

"I disagree. Emily Anne was twelve and totally smitten with me." Sasha rolled her eyes. "Twelve?"

"Don't give me that look. She was only a year younger than me."

"And you were using her to make her sister jealous."

"Yeah, and it worked, too."

"Mary Catherine left your stepbrother?"

"Not exactly. The next time she came over, she attempted to give me a blow job in the barn."

"Are you serious? The vicar's daughter?"

He nodded. "It's always the ones you least expect. Unfortunately, asshole kid caught her trying to unzip my pants. I told him it was all her, but I was sent off to boarding school within the month anyway." Damn, so much for not being melancholy.

Sasha stroked his arm. "Cole, I'm so sorry."

He shrugged. "It made me who I am today. I can't find it in me to regret it." He didn't want to dwell on the past; he hadn't even meant to bring it all up. He just wanted her to know something about him.

She must have picked up on his thoughts. "I wonder where she is now. Do you ever think about that?"

"Oh yes. She's actually in that far house over there." He pointed to the cozy cottage-looking home across the valley. "She got pregnant at seventeen. Married the guy. I hear they're still together."

But it appeared Sasha's mind was no longer on his past. She palmed his cock and asked in a low whisper, "Did you ever get blown in the barn?"

"No, but, Sasha, you don't——"

"Please, Sir. Let me." She was already moving to her knees.

What man alive could resist that? No one. Not a single man. He fisted her hair with a nod of his head.

With victory surging in her eyes, she made quick work of his trousers. Within seconds, they were around his ankles and his cock was freed. "Poor Mary Catherine," she said. "So close. But so far away. Girl never knew what she was missing."

She parted her lips and licked him, dragging her tongue around the slit, which was already glistening with precome at the thought of her hot mouth. But Sasha was in the mood to play. Instead of taking him deep in her mouth, like she normally did, she licked her own lips.

"Fuck, Sir. I love your cock." She licked the very tip a few more times, and he thought he'd lose his mind.

"Then suck it. Open your mouth, take me inside, and suck me down like I know you can."

"But it's so much fun to do this." She licked it again, and he knew if she kept it up, he was going to lose his shit.

He tightened the fist in her hair. "Suck it. Fucking *now*, sub."

Recognizing his "This is no longer a game" voice, she dropped all pretense of play and took him deep into her mouth. Even so, he gave a solid thrust and drove deeper. He fisted her hair with both hands, keeping her still and not letting her move her head.

"That's it." Fuck, she felt good. "Keep it right there. Let my cock fill your throat. Breathe through your nose as best you can."

He let go of her hair just for a minute, allowing her to take a deep breath. He lightly scratched her head, knowing she liked it. But she knew what it meant when his grip tightened once again.

"Again," he said.

She once again opened her mouth wide and took him to the back of her throat.

"Very nice," he said. "Now swallow."

Her nails dug into his upper thigh. They didn't do this often, but it was something he wanted her to work on. She obeyed, and it took all his control not to release down her throat.

"Breathe when I pull out," he instructed her. He kept his hands in her hair, holding her still while he guided them both. He knew he wouldn't be able to keep his current movements up for very long. Her nails scratched him deeper, and he welcomed the pain.

He pushed into her throat again. "Yes, that's it. So good."

He pulled out, and this time he didn't have to tell her to breathe. "You love my cock filling your throat, don't you?"

Of course she couldn't answer. But she didn't have to; he knew her so well. "Get ready. I'm going to come down your throat. Take it all. Every last drop."

He shoved his cock deep inside one last time, holding her head still as he released. Afterward, he felt completely spent. He'd come so hard, he didn't want to move for hours. Hell, he wasn't sure he could move. But he forced himself to remain upright, holding out his hand and helping Sasha up.

"Was it worth waiting for?" she asked.

He led her to a pile of hay. "Yes, little one." He sat down and pulled her into his lap. "It was worth every minute of the wait. In fact, it was so good, I think you deserve a reward."

Cole scanned the inside of the barn. There was precious little to be found, but he did spy some coils of rope in the far corner.

"I'll be right back." He went to retrieve the rope, making sure it would work. Worst-case scenario, she would have a few rope burns on her wrists.

He made it back to where she was resting on the hay and noticed how her eyes widened with excitement when she saw the rope. "Excited?"

"When you said 'reward,' Sir, I didn't know rope would be involved."

"Is the rope a problem?" he asked, even though he was fairly certain he knew the answer.

"No, Sir. Everything is always better with rope."

"I agree. Now, the question is, where do I string you up?" He looked around, trying to find a place that was safe and not too dirty. His eyes landed on something.

He walked over to a wooden block against the back wall. "Come here, little one."

She walked toward him with just a hint of trepidation, but mostly excitement.

"Stand up here on the block." Once she was in place, he bound her wrists together and pulled them above her head, attaching the other end of the rope to a hook in the wall.

"How does that feel? Not too tight or uncomfortable?"

She gave the rope a good tug. "No, Sir. Everything's good."

"Everything is about to get much, much better." He stroked her ass and unzipped her pants, pushing them down her legs and exposing her from the waist down. "What a good girl."

"Oh no. Fuck. Red!" Sasha jerked her arms, as if trying to get away.

He shot straight up, heart racing, and worked to untie her. He blocked everything out, unable to focus on anything other than getting her loose. She wasn't trembling, which meant if it was a panic attack, it wasn't presenting the way they had before. Her demeanor didn't look like it did before one, either.

"What's wrong?" He gave the rope a hard jerk, finally pulling it free. Bloody hell, he was an idiot. He'd tied her up without scissors nearby. That was a rookie mistake, and not only did he know better, but Sasha deserved better.

"Outside," she sputtered out. The second her hands were free, she bent down to pull up her pants, moving quickly and straightening her appearance as best she could.

"What?" She wasn't hurt. That was all he really cared about.

"There's someone outside, walking this way. I don't know how much they saw."

His mind finally registered that nothing was wrong with Sasha, and what she'd been saying worked its way into his brain.

Someone was outside? He couldn't fathom who would stop by to visit, but then again, word had gotten out that he'd bought the place. It could be anyone. Probably there were a good number of people living nearby who remembered him.

Damn stupid, rotten timing. He wanted nothing more than to finish what he'd started with Sasha. He'd just send whoever it was away.

But from outside the barn came a familiar "Yoo-hoo!" that made him moan.

"What?" Sasha asked. "Do you recognize that voice?"

"Cole?" asked the lady outside. "Are you down here? I thought I saw something."

"Who is it?" Sasha sounded pissed. And he couldn't blame her. After all, he'd been minutes away from making her come so hard, she'd forget her name. Not to mention, the knees of her jeans were dirty, telling anyone who cared to look exactly what she'd been doing not too long ago.

He sighed heavily. "Mary Catherine."

Chapter Four

*W*hat the fuck?

Sasha knew she shouldn't be angry at Cole; there was no way he could have known Mary Catherine was going to show up and ruin what would have been an earth-shattering orgasm. But the fact was, she *was* angry, and he was the closest person to her.

She put her hands on her hips. Sasha had been too hesitant and unsure to say anything when Cole's ex had unexpectedly dropped by the morning after she and Cole had slept together for the first time. But that was then and this was now. And now she was not hesitant or unsure. "Is it like a game your ex-girlfriends have? Trying to see how many times they can cock-block us? Do they get bonus points if they see me naked?"

"Sasha," Cole said.

"Hello!" the perky voice from outside said. "I hear voices."

Sasha rolled her eyes.

Seconds later, a petite woman with gray-streaked strawberry

blond hair appeared in the doorway. "I thought I saw someone in here."

But the blonde didn't pay Sasha any attention. She had eyes only for Cole.

"Cole Johnson," she said, obviously not caring about her cold reception. "I heard you'd bought this place, and then I saw the strange car yesterday. I put two and two together and decided to come say hi."

"Hi," Sasha said, but Mary Catherine didn't even look her way.

"I tried the house and no one answered, but the car was still outside, so I took a chance you'd be down here." She threw her hands up. "And here you are!"

"How are you, Mary Catherine?" Cole asked.

The blonde looked entirely too pleased to be the focus of his attention. Her cheeks actually flushed. "Good. I'm good. How are you?"

"I'm well, thank you."

"I can't believe you're back. Are you here for good?"

He moved to stand by Sasha's side and slipped an arm around her shoulders. "No, actually. We're just here for a week or so. This is my Sasha. Sasha, this is Mary Catherine. We grew up together; she was the vicar's daughter."

He spoke it all very calmly, giving no indication that he'd ever breathed a word about Mary Catherine before this introduction.

The woman still didn't look her way. "Married?"

Cole shook his head. "Not in so many words."

She frowned at that. "In any words?"

"In the ones that matter." Cole stroked Sasha's collar, perhaps to see if the other woman noticed and would have a clue to its meaning.

From all appearances, she didn't seem to. "I was married. We divorced last year."

"I'm sorry to hear that."

Mary Catherine laughed. "I'm sure as hell not. He was an arse and a bore. I was glad to get rid of him. Do you have any kids? I have three."

"No. No children."

Now she looked at Sasha. "That's too bad. Infertility?"

"Nothing of the sort. Just not ready to give up the hot-as-hell sex. Plus, I hear your boobs get flabby. And you have to deal with diapers and colic and driving and college. And did I mention I'm not ready to give up the hot-as-hell sex?"

Cole coughed, obviously trying to cover up his laugh. But in front of them, Mary Catherine's eyes blazed.

"I think that's just selfish," she said.

Sasha shrugged. "That's because you've never had sex so good it lasts for days and an orgasm so intense you black out." Her work here was done. She patted Cole's chest. "I'll leave you two old friends to catch up. I'll be waiting for you in the dining room, naked. We still have to christen the table."

"She's lovely," Mary Catherine said, sarcasm dripping from her voice.

"She's incredible." Cole watched Sasha's retreating backside with a combination of pride and desire. Holy hell, she'd been sexy as fuck when she put Mary Catherine in her place.

"Is that really what you look for in a woman?"

Cole bit back his angry reply and asked calmly, "Why are you here, Mary Catherine?"

"I told you, to welcome you back home."

"This is not home. This is an investment property. Home is in the States, where I'll be returning in less than a week."

She didn't appear to give his remark any thought. Instead, she walked around the barn, looking over everything. "Lots of memories here. Do you remember?"

"Of course." He needed her to leave; he had a hot date waiting in the dining room. "Come on. Let me walk you to your car."

"Don't I even get a hug? For old times' sake?"

"No, I'm afraid not." He started walking to the barn door.

"She doesn't let you touch other women? Is she afraid she'll lose you?"

That was enough. He stopped dead in his tracks, turned around, and gave her the look that had earned him the nickname "Badass Brit." Mary Catherine's eyes grew wide with shock.

He spoke slowly. "If you were a bloke, you'd already be knocked out on the floor for being so disrespectful toward Sasha. She is the best thing that ever happened to me, and no one—I repeat, *no one*—will disrespect her. The best thing you can do is go back to your house and your children and leave her alone. Now, if you'll excuse me, I'm needed in my dining room."

He left her standing there, and didn't look back to see if she stayed or left. Good Lord, he could have slapped his thirteen-year-old self. He used to fancy *that*? With a renewed purpose, he quickened his stride and made his way to the house. Once inside, he made a beeline to the dining room, only to find it empty.

What the hell?

"Sasha?" he called. Where was she? He went to the morning room, where he'd found her earlier, but she wasn't there. Nor was she in their bedroom. He stood near the window, trying to think of where she might be. A movement outside caught his attention.

The greenhouse.

He made it there in record time, and she gasped when he pushed the door open. She caught herself on her hands before she fell over into the pot of dirt she was mixing.

"You're back sooner than I anticipated," she finally said.

"Yes, and you're not in the dining room and you're not naked." He crossed his arms and gave her the same look he'd given Mary Catherine moments before.

"I thought—"

He held up his hand to stop her. "I don't care what you thought. I'm going to be in the dining room in three minutes and you'd better be in there, completely naked."

She opened her mouth as if she was going to say something, but apparently thought better of it. She stood up, brushed her knees off, and hurried out the door.

He waited for thirty seconds and then followed. He had a table to christen.

Chapter Five

C ole waited outside the front doors as the car holding their guests for the week pulled up. Sasha watched him from her place off to the side of the door. She brushed her hands over the uniform Cole had set out for her, and they trembled just a bit in excitement.

The week Cole had planned for them all was so unlike anything she'd ever done, and she couldn't imagine any of the players had done anything similar, either. He hadn't told her much, just to expect a little bit of role play. She rather liked being dressed up in the servant's outfit Cole had selected specifically for everyone's arrival today, especially wearing Cole's collar. It wasn't exactly like when he trained her in slave service for two weeks, but it was close enough.

Since that time, she'd done everything she could to get to the root of why she liked being Cole's so much. In fact, she'd filled half a notebook with thoughts. On one hand, she felt like she shouldn't like it. After all, she was a small-business owner. She was intelligent and self-sufficient. So why did she get off on serving Cole?

She'd never questioned her submissive nature before, but once she'd experimented as his slave, she couldn't help but question the way that experience made her feel. She'd found everything about serving him twenty-four/seven made her feel at peace and content. Even though he'd told her that they weren't going to be in a Master/slave relationship at this point in time, her belly still quivered with excitement simply thinking about it.

Maybe that was why she had so looked forward to this week. No, it wasn't exactly like being a slave, but it was pretty close. Already she could see Cole's eyes grow dark with lust and wanting when he looked at her in the uniform, even though it was only for role play. Of course, he probably also liked the fact that she didn't have anything on underneath her short skirt.

"When you least expect it, I'm going to push you against a wall, lift your skirt, and fuck you good and hard," he'd told her when he'd set out the uniform.

"Yes, Sir. Please and thank you and can you do it now?" she'd asked, but he'd just laughed, given her backside a swat, and told her to be patient.

Cole opened the car door and let Abby and Julie out. The two women had their heads together, looking over the huge house. The driver of the car let Daniel and Nathaniel out and then got the bags from the back. Cole motioned Sasha forward.

Game on.

She scurried down the stairs to where Cole stood, talking with the foursome. "Ah," he said when he saw her. "Here's my servant girl, Ms. Blake. Ms. Blake, will you take the ladies up to their quarters? I'm sure they would like to refresh themselves after such a long journey. The gentlemen and I would like drinks in the library in thirty minutes."

Thirty minutes. She hid her smile. Even though it was a role play, he was giving her time to chat with her friends. "Yes, my lord." She curtsied and didn't miss his wink as she stood. "Mrs. West, Ms. Masterson, if you don't mind following me."

Both ladies bade the men good-bye and walked behind Sasha as they all made their way to the entrance. They kept the roles up until they crossed the threshold and the heavy wooden doors closed behind them.

"Girl, look at you," Julie said. "You look hot dressed like a maid."

Abby nodded. "I have got to get me one of those uniforms. Nathaniel would die."

"It has definitely fueled a few fantasies," Sasha said, tugging at the short skirt. "I'd be lying if I said otherwise."

"And look at this house." Julie walked around the foyer. "It's huge. How old is it, anyway?"

"I think Cole said at least a couple hundred years. It's been renovated a few times." Sasha motioned the women to follow her. "Come on upstairs. Let me show you your rooms."

"Definitely won't find anything like this Stateside," Abby said. "It's stunning."

"Wait until you see the gardens. I think we're doing something out there tomorrow. Cole won't tell me all of his plans."

Was it her imagination, or did a look pass between Julie and Abby?

They didn't say anything else, so she led them upstairs to the massive bedrooms. She stopped at the first one on the right. "Abby, you and Nathaniel will be in here." She pointed across the hall. "Julie, you and Daniel are in there."

Julie's eyes danced with merriment. "And where do you sleep?"

"Servants' quarters are up another flight of stairs."

"Avoiding the question?" Abby asked.

The front door opened downstairs and the sound of masculine laughter filled the air.

"Master Johnson sometimes requests assistance in the night, so he's asked me to sleep in his chamber," she said, trying to keep a straight face as she fell back into her role. "But he wouldn't want such scandalous information to get out. So you will keep that to yourself, yes?"

"Of course," Abby said.

"So if you hear anyone walking the halls in the middle of the night, it's probably me. No need to check." Sasha tapped her lips as if in thought. "And if you hear any screams, or moans, or anything like that, it's just me providing the assistance Master Johnson requires. He told me I have to try to be quieter, but sometimes I can't help it."

Julie didn't even try to contain her laughter. "Deal. As long as you ignore it if there are any strange noises coming from our room."

They shook on it.

Abby trailed her finger along the doorframe to her room. "I don't feel like refreshing myself in my room. I want to see more of this place. Can you show us around a bit?"

Shit. Shit. Shit. Sasha ran down the hall to the library. Or as quickly as she could move while carrying a tray of drinks. The tour she gave the women had taken longer than she'd planned, and she was ten minutes late bringing the drinks to the men.

Coming to a stop outside the door, she took a deep breath and knocked.

"Enter," Cole said from inside.

She pushed the door open just a crack. Cole stood near the fireplace. She couldn't see the other two men.

"Today, if you please, Ms. Blake. I believe you've kept us waiting long enough."

Shit.

She pushed the door all the way open and stepped inside.

"Put the tray on the table to your right and then come kneel before me," Cole said in a voice so chilling she shivered.

She hurried to do as he asked, still uttering curses in her head as she went to her knees in front of him.

"When did I tell you to have drinks here?" he asked.

"Thirty minutes after you bade me take the ladies to their quarters."

"I see. So you did understand?"

"Yes, Sir."

"And was I not being generous in allowing you time to talk with the ladies?"

"Yes, Sir. Very generous."

"And yet you thank me by disrespecting my guests here in the library."

"I meant no disrespect, Sir."

"Whether you meant it or not is inconsequential to this discussion. You were given a command, you did not follow it, and now there will be consequences."

Dammit all to hell. This was not how she'd pictured the first day going.

"I asked Master West and Master Covington if they would

like to assist in your correction. However, due to the relationships they have with the ladies upstairs, they have passed."

She allowed herself a sigh of relief. How embarrassing would that have been? Bad enough for Cole to punish her, but for someone else as well?

"Herr Brose arrived twenty minutes ago, though, and he has no issue with helping me."

Suddenly, there weren't enough curse words to mutter in her head. Herr Brose was the man who had mentored Cole years ago. People thought Cole was a hard-ass, but that was only because they'd never met Herr Brose.

"I've decided that since you were ten minutes late, you will get ten strokes. Five from me with my cane and five from Herr Brose with his belt. You will then apologize for being late. Do you have any questions?"

"No, Sir."

"Tell me why you're being punished."

"Because I failed to obey your command to serve drinks in the library within thirty minutes."

"Very good. Come lean against the mantel and get ready. I'm not requiring you to be naked since there are others present."

Wasn't that strange? For the first time since she could remember, other people seeing her scars had not entered her mind. That was very interesting. She wondered if it meant she was almost one hundred percent better.

She stood up and walked to the mantel. It was rather low, so she could rest her head on her arms on top of it. She didn't look to see if Daniel and Nathaniel remained in the room. She assumed they did, since she was to apologize to them later.

There was some faint murmuring behind her. She realized that this would be the first time a Dom other than Cole touched her. She waited for the panic to set in. Looked for signs of the terror clawing her throat or the sweats that she remembered so well. But there was nothing.

She didn't have time to rejoice in the newfound knowledge, however, because someone stepped up behind her. A familiar hand lifted the hem of her skirt and tucked it in her waistband.

"Hard and fast," Cole said. "No need to count."

She only had time to nod before the first one fell. She sucked in a deep breath and braced herself for the second. True to his word, the next four fell swiftly. When he was finished, though, he didn't move away. Instead, he moved up to stand near her shoulder. To be close to her in case she needed him, she supposed.

She jerked briefly when Fritz ran a hand over her backside. But Cole placed a hand on her shoulder, and she knew she'd be okay.

"Okay to continue?" Cole asked.

She felt Fritz step away, probably waiting for Cole to indicate he could proceed. She could lie. It would be easy and Cole would never know. No one would. But it was more than deceiving Cole that stopped her from doing so. She wanted to prove that she could have another man touch her. That she had grown even further in her healing process with Cole. And she couldn't do that if she lied now.

"Yes, Sir."

The air behind her moved as Fritz got back in place. "Counting is not necessary."

Like Cole, his strokes were hard and fast. And though she didn't cry, a few tears escaped her eyes. She had the feeling Fritz went a bit light on her.

Cole pulled her dress back into place. "Go say your apologies and serve the drinks to the men."

Sniffling just a bit, she moved gingerly to the table in front of where the men sat. Oh so carefully, she moved to her knees and bowed her head. "Please forgive me for my tardiness. I meant no disrespect."

"All is forgiven," Daniel said.

Nathaniel added, "Agreed. Think of it no more."

She rose to her feet and served each man a drink. It was crazy, but she didn't feel self-conscious at all. When everyone was served, she put the tray back down. Cole hadn't sat down yet, and he'd shaken his head when she'd offered him a drink. It actually worked out better that way, because she was able to give his glass to Fritz.

Before she could wonder what to do next, Cole came up beside her and scooped her into his arms. "Gentlemen," he said. "If you'll excuse us."

She didn't hear if the men answered. Her attention was on how good it felt to be in his arms, his smell, the movement of his chest as he spoke, the beating of his heart, just him in general. They left the library and he carried her into a small sitting room nearby, where he sat on a couch with her in his lap.

"Are you okay?" he asked, stroking her hair and pressing a kiss against her forehead.

"Yes, Sir." She could stay in his arms forever; there was nowhere else she'd rather be. She always felt so protected and secure in his embrace. And not just physically, but emotionally as well, for she knew she could bare her soul and he would guard it with his life.

"I wasn't sure how you'd feel about Fritz being involved."

"It wasn't until he stepped behind me that I realized it would be another Dom for the first time since you."

"That thought did cross my mind." She heard the smile in his voice.

Which was why he'd stood by her shoulder, she realized.

"Any signs of panic?" he asked.

She took her time in responding. Mentally, she checked for signs that she knew would be a precursor to a panic attack. But there was nothing. She almost felt giddy at the thought. She pulled back and looked at him. "There's nothing, Sir. It's almost as if the panic was never there to begin with."

"But we both know it was," he said. "So you'll forgive me if I remain rather close by your side today. Just in case."

He had just caned her. And in addition, he had asked another Dom to use a belt on her. Though her backside was sore, her heart was full. Because he had just proven how diligent he was in his care of her.

She snuggled deeper into his embrace. "Thank you, Sir."

"Did Abby and Julie get settled?" he asked.

"I believe so. When I left them, they were planning to go outside." She turned a bit so she could face him. "And I *am* sorry I was late."

"Hush." He pressed a finger over her lips. "It has been dealt with. There is no need to bring it back up."

Sometimes she had a hard time understanding how he could wipe it away so quickly. After all, she still remembered. But she knew she shouldn't dwell on it. Instead, she should remember it only for the lesson it taught her. A very interesting topic. Perhaps that would be the subject for tonight's journal session.

"Damn," Cole said. "There's no water or ointment in here."

"I'm fine to sit here by myself."

"Perhaps you're fine with it, but I'm not." He was silent for a couple seconds. "I'll carry you up to our room. I believe every-thing I need is in there."

And though they had a house full of newly arrived guests, for the next hour Cole and Sasha focused only on each other. She knew he wouldn't let her climax for the next twenty-four hours, but that was okay. She had him.

And that was all she needed.

Chapter Six

Sasha peeked out the kitchen into the dining room the following afternoon. Everyone was sitting down; Cole, of course, was at the head of the table. She took a deep breath, ran her palms over the uniform, and squared her shoulders. Though she had served tea for the Dominants in the group before, this was the first time she would also be serving the submissives. Not only that, but Julie and Abby were her friends, and she wanted everything to be perfect.

Since the table was set, she could start on the tea. The water on the stove appeared to be almost ready, so she took the tray she was going to use and placed it beside the stove.

"Good Lord, woman, are you wearing that?"

She jumped at the sound of Cole's voice, spinning around and placing a hand on her chest. "Sir, you frightened me."

"Be that as it may, I asked you a question."

"Yes, Sir. This is what I'm wearing." Which he'd known, because he was the one who'd set it out this morning. She didn't remind him of that, though.

He was frowning, and she didn't like that, but she didn't know what to do. He walked closer to her, and she resisted the urge to kneel before him. His hands went to her upper thigh.

"The skirt is entirely too short." His hands inched their way up, and before long, he was teasing her sex. "And what is this? No bloomers? Someone is a dirty, naughty girl."

"I'm sorry, Sir. I'll do better in the future." She couldn't think of anything else to say. After all, he was the one to pick out the outfit.

"I'm sure you will. And I'm sure the thrashing I'm about to give your backside will also help you to remember."

He was going to spank her? Here? Now? "But, Sir. The water. And your guests are right outside the door."

"Yes, they are. I reckon they'll hear just how naughty you've been. Because I'm going to spank you loud enough so they hear."

Shit. He was completely serious. "The water," she tried again.

"Will be fine. Trying to get out of your spanking, however, only earns you more strokes."

She wisely kept her mouth shut.

"Go stand in front of the counter. I want your hands on the edge, legs spread, and your backside raised up."

She didn't move immediately. Instead, she watched as he opened drawers, searching for something. But before she could see what he was looking for, he glanced up and saw her watching.

"You're only adding to your spanking," he said, and went back to searching in the drawers.

Fuck. She left him to his hunt and crossed the floor to the spot he'd indicated. It wasn't until she moved into position that she heard the drawer close.

He was quiet as he made his way to her, and when he was behind her, he placed a wooden spoon with holes on the countertop to her right.

"Do you know why I picked the one with holes?"

"Less wind resistance, Sir?"

"Yes, which also means it'll hurt more. Perfect for a naughty servant, I think. Lift your skirt and show me your arse."

She did as he commanded and quickly got back into position.

"Very nice. I'm not going to have you count, but I don't want you to hold back. Cry, scream, curse my name. I want my guests to hear how I handle servant girls who dress inappropriately."

She told herself it was part of the role play. He wasn't really going to give her a punishment spanking. Not like yesterday. But that didn't stop her from clenching her ass in anticipation of the first strike.

"Oh dear," he said, running a hand over her flesh. "We can't have that. I guess I'll have to resort to drastic measures."

She groaned because she knew exactly what he meant by "drastic measures." He'd done something similar weeks ago.

Sure enough, she felt the cool wetness of lube being applied to her anus. And she muffled a cry as he pushed a plug in.

"There we go. I like it so much, I'm going to have you wear it while you do the tea service. As a reminder of who owns this arse." He gave it a light swat and then bent low to whisper, "And who's going to fuck it later."

With that, he started spanking her with his hand. Lightly. And soon she found her arousal spiking regardless of the people sitting in the dining room, waiting.

Jesus. There are people waiting for me to serve tea.

Slap. "You're not with me."

"Sorry, Sir. Just thinking—"

Slap. "Did I tell you to think?"

"No, Sir."

Slap. Slap. Slap. He was spanking harder now. She couldn't stop the moan that escaped her throat. If he'd just *touch* her.

"That's it, you naughty girl. Let it out." He spanked her again. Then he ran his fingers between her legs. "*Tsk, tsk, tsk.* Look at this. Spankings make you horny."

She jerked as his next swat landed on her clit. "Yes, Sir." He stopped, and she whined. "Please, please, Sir."

A hard and swift pop on her flesh told her he'd picked up the spoon. "How's that?" he asked, giving her another.

She sucked in a breath as the next one landed. "So good, Sir."

He gave a grunt of satisfaction and continued between spanking her and bringing her to the very edge of her climax and then letting her hang there. After a while, she was no longer aware of making noises, but she was pretty certain she was. And it seemed like forever until it felt like he wasn't putting as much strength behind his strokes.

"Want more, Sir," she muttered.

He chuckled low in this throat. "Not right now. Maybe later. After tea."

Tea. Damn. She'd forgotten.

How was she supposed to serve tea while wearing an anal plug and being horny as hell?

"If you're good, I'll let you come after." His breath tickled her ear and sent shivers down her spine.

"Thank you, Sir."

He straightened her clothes and kissed her forehead. "You're welcome. Go get everything ready. I'll see to my guests."

She nodded and headed back to the stove to redo the water.

Cole walked into the dining room and all conversation stopped. He took his seat at the head of the table. "Tea will be served shortly."

"Damn, did you have to do that now?" Daniel asked. "I'm not looking forward to having tea with all the blood in my body congregating in my dick."

"There's nothing to hide here." Cole tipped his head toward Julie. "Seems to me your relief is sitting by your side when she'd be more useful on her knees. We have time."

Julie didn't say anything, but her cheeks flushed just a bit. Cole didn't think she'd have a problem serving Daniel in the dining room. They'd played in public before. His phone buzzed with an incoming text, and when he looked back up, Julie had slipped under the table.

By the time Sasha entered, Julie was back in her seat, this time with a soft smile on her face. Sasha picked up on it immediately, which Cole thought he was able to notice only because he knew her so well.

He'd given her instructions on how he wanted the service to go, and she did exactly as he'd requested. She started by serving Nathaniel first and then going around the table to end with Cole. He couldn't stop himself from running a hand up her naked thigh and pinching her butt as she poured his water.

"You're doing great," he whispered, and his heart melted at the look of love and happiness that seemed to wash over her. But she only nodded in acknowledgment of his praise before she headed back into the kitchen.

"Did you ever get our tea service back from Sasha?" Nathaniel asked Abby.

"No, Master," his wife replied.

"Make a note to do it when we get home."

The rest of the service passed without incident. Sasha was flawless, as Cole had known she would be. He didn't have anything planned for after, but no one seemed to mind. Nathaniel announced that he and Abby were going to explore the nearby village. Daniel said he and Julie were still recovering from the time difference and were going to their room "to rest."

"If that's what you want to call it," he told his old friend. "I'm going to grab Sasha and shag her into next week."

Daniel shook his head, following Julie up the stairs to their room.

When everyone had left, he went into the kitchen, where Sasha waited. At his entrance, she dropped to her knees. It was a sight that never failed to leave him breathless.

He rested his hand on top of her head. "I don't recall ever witnessing a more perfect tea service, little one. You were exceptional."

"Thank you, Sir."

"You did everything brilliantly, and watching you in that role was one of the hottest things I've ever witnessed."

"I'm glad I pleased you, Sir."

"Never doubt it." He lowered his hand to help her up. "Come here."

She moved with such grace and poise, so far removed from the wounded submissive he'd first met her as. When she made it to her feet, he pulled her tight to his chest, grinding his erection against her.

"I'm hard as hell and ready to make good on my promise to fuck your arse."

He didn't miss the tremor of excitement that ran through her body. When they first met, she'd hated anal sex. Now she couldn't get enough of it.

"I want you naked and bent over our bed, so when I walk in the room, I see your greedy arse just begging to be filled and fucked." He gave her backside a slap. "Go."

"With pleasure, Sir," she murmured in that sexy *fuck-me* voice. But instead of leaving, she pulled her dress over her head, unsnapped her bra, and dropped them both to the floor. "You know where to find me."

And find her he did, moments later, waiting for him exactly the way he asked. Without a word, he came up behind her, went to his knees, and gave her wet slit a long lick. He'd caught her off guard; she jumped and gave a cute little yelp.

"Couldn't wait to taste this pussy," he said against her skin. "Been thinking about it all day. How wet it'd be for me." He gave it another lick. "How sweet it'd taste. Tell me, little one, do you like it better when I eat you out or fuck your arse?"

She gasped for breath as he licked her again, because this time he wiggled his tongue part of the way inside. "I don't know how you think I can decide between the two, Sir."

"Try anyway."

He didn't let up. He kept licking her and licking her, and when he licked her clit, she screamed, "Oh my God."

He slapped her backside. "Tell me."

"I'll go with anal sex, Sir." She squealed and rose on her toes at the slap he gave her clit.

"Why?"

"Dammit all, are you serious? How am I supposed to think with you doing that?"

"Do it or I stop." He didn't start again until she took a deep breath and spoke.

"Because when you take me that way—"

"Say it, Sasha."

"Because when you fuck my ass, it's raw and primal and taboo and it's somehow more intimate." She shuddered as he resumed tasting her. "It's like you're claiming me over and over. I never feel more submissive than I do then."

She was right on the edge of climax, exactly where he wanted her. He pulled back and rubbed her backside. "Very good. See how easy that was?"

"Yes, Sir," she replied in an almost whine.

"I think it's time I took this plug out so I can claim you again. Don't you agree?"

"Yes, Sir."

He gently pulled the plug out and set it aside to clean later. He was so hard after spanking her and watching her at tea, he knew he wouldn't last long. He prepared her with the lube he had waiting and stroked some on his cock.

He started the long, sweet push inside her. "You may come when you wish."

"Thank you, Sir," she said in a tight voice.

She knew what to do in order to make taking him easier, and he felt her body relax and the slight push back as she took him inside. He watched as his cock worked its way in.

"Fuck, I wish you could see this." He reached between her legs and rubbed her clit. "Your hot arse swallowing my dick whole. It's all I can do not to pound you into that bed."

Her breathing grew choppy, and he kept up the wicked whispers while he worked her clit with one hand and worked his cock up her ass with the other. She came hard, pushing back toward him, as if she was desperate to have more of him inside her.

He couldn't hold back anymore, and he grabbed her hips

hard, holding her still as he released into her. It was only when he looked down that he realized exactly how hard he'd been holding her.

He pulled out and lifted her all the way onto the bed to rest while he went into the bathroom for a warm rag. She hadn't moved when he returned, so he cleaned them both and then joined her, pulling her into his embrace.

"I was a bit rough," he said as she snuggled closer. "You may have bruises on your hips."

Her voice was heavy with sleep when she answered. "That's good."

"It is?"

"Mmm, I like having your marks on me."

He couldn't ask her anything else because within seconds she was snoring softly. He kissed her forehead and decided to rest a bit himself. His eyes closed and he drifted into sleep with the feel of her breath hot against his chest and her fingers entwined with his.

Chapter Seven

The following morning, the men went off together to the town pub, leaving the ladies time to talk. The three of them discussed going somewhere, but they eventually decided they'd rather stay at the estate and do some exploring.

Though they planned to hit the attic, they ended up lingering over the breakfast Daniel had made.

Sasha took a bite of the eggs Benedict and hummed in pleasure. "I love, love, love eggs Benedict. This is delicious. I'll have to thank Daniel again. It's almost good enough to make me want to cook."

The only thing she ever made in the kitchen was coffee. Fortunately, due to the time he spent in remote locations for work, Cole handled meals just fine.

"You know," Abby said, "if you're ever interested in learning to cook, I have a few easy recipes I could show you."

"I did the *easy* thing once before on Julie's recommendation. I spent three hours peeling and dicing carrots." She shot her best friend an evil look. "I almost lost a thumb and my fingers were orange for days."

Julie rolled her eyes. "Oh my God. Drama much? Maybe next time it would be a good idea to read the recipe before ordering the meal kit online?"

"I did. It said 'Easy to prepare. Ready to eat in thirty minutes.'"

"Obviously they meant for someone who knew how to boil water."

"I know how to boil water: in the microwave."

"You're worthless."

"Only when it comes to cooking. I'm brilliant at everything else."

"You also have a big head."

"As one who is brilliant at everything other than cooking rightfully would."

Julie flipped her off.

Abby shook her head. "Your shop must never be boring with you two in it."

"It's boring as hell. Julie put a no-kinky-sex-talk rule in place."

"For all the good it does." Julie huffed.

"I'll make you a deal," Sasha said. "I'll never mention sex in the shop again if you can tell me, honestly, that you and Daniel have never had a quickie there."

"Honey. Trust me." Julie placed her hand on top of Sasha's. "There was nothing quick about it."

They were still laughing when the doorbell rang minutes later.

Abby looked over to Sasha. "Are you expecting someone?"

"No, and Cole didn't mention anything, either." She pushed back from the table. "I'll go see who it is."

Julie and Abby followed her to the front door. This was something she didn't like about the house, she decided. There wasn't a way to see who was at the door unless you went upstairs or into another room.

She pulled the door open and found a smiling Mary Catherine on the other side.

Or course, that smile disappeared quickly once she saw Sasha. "Oh," she said. "It's you. Is Cole around?" She craned her neck as if Sasha were hiding him behind her back.

"No. He's stepped out for a bit, but I'll be sure to tell him you stopped by." She moved to close the door, but Mary Catherine stuck her foot out.

"I'll just wait here for him."

Dammit all. She really didn't want Mary Catherine in the house, but to put her out would reflect badly upon Cole and there was no way she'd do that. Besides, the woman really hadn't done anything to Sasha, if you didn't count cock-blocking her, ignoring her, and telling her she was selfish for not wanting kids.

She gave Mary Catherine a curt nod and opened the door wider to let her pass. "Suit yourself."

The other woman came to a stop when she saw Julie and Abby standing nearby.

"Abby. Julie," Sasha said. "This is Mary Catherine. She knows Cole from when he was a kid."

"Delighted," Mary Catherine said, but she didn't make a move to shake their hands or anything. "Though it was a little more serious than that. Why, we were practically engaged!"

"Engaged, my ass," Sasha mumbled.

Across the massive foyer, Abby had a peculiar look on her face. "Really? That's interesting."

Though Abby was as friendly and down-to-earth as one could be, she was Nathaniel West's wife and she had a certain *presence* about her. It wasn't always obvious, but now, as she stood and carefully observed Mary Catherine, she looked almost regal.

Mary Catherine certainly noticed. She flushed and started wringing her hands. "Yes, but he went off to university in the States and, well, things happen."

Abby raised an eyebrow.

"I met my ex-husband, and by the time Cole came back and enrolled at Oxford, I was married. I wish I had waited for him. That we could have had the large family he always wanted." Mary Catherine shot Sasha an evil look.

"Cole wants a large family?" Abby asked, somehow managing to keep her expression neutral. Sasha was impressed. She noticed Julie had to cough into the crook of her elbow to cover her laugh.

"Yes." Mary Catherine nodded. "It's his fondest dream."

"And yet he doesn't have a single child," Abby said. "What a travesty."

She walked to a love seat in a nearby nook and sat down. "Come, sit down with me."

Mary Catherine, looking as if she'd just found her new best friend, hurried over to do just that.

Abby smiled at her and patted Mary Catherine's knee. "How many children do you have?"

"Three."

"Three? Wow, I have two of my own, a girl and a boy. They're wonderful, but they're a handful."

Sasha had no idea where Abby was going with her current topic of discussion, but it was almost like a train wreck; she had to keep watching.

"In fact," Abby continued, "we have another friend who couldn't come this week because she's pregnant with their first. It's a wonderful thing to be a mother, but not everyone wants kids."

"I can't imagine not wanting kids."

Abby continued as if Mary Catherine hadn't said anything. "I don't know if it's my experience as a mother, or because I'm a writer and I notice things, or if it's because I married a man whose attention to detail is as frightening as it is impressive. Odds are, it's probably a little bit of all three."

"I'm with you on Nathaniel's attention to detail," Julie chimed in. "That man is scary observant."

"It's served him well," Abby said before turning back to Mary Catherine. "Now, I'm not saying you aren't a mother to three children. I'm just saying I would expect a woman who has three kids would be a little bit better at trying to bullshit someone."

Mary Catherine gasped and stood up.

"Sit back down," Abby said in a tone she must have picked up from Nathaniel. Surprisingly, the other woman did just that. "Now, I haven't figured out your game, but I know your type, and let me tell you this: You stand a better chance of marrying into the royal family than you do of ever being with Cole Johnson. And I know this because even if he weren't completely committed to Sasha, which he is, and even if he wanted kids, which he has emphatically denied on multiple occasions, he still won't be with you. Because he hates liars. And you, my dear, have done nothing but lie from the minute you walked into this house."

Mary Catherine stood back up. "I don't have to sit here and listen to you talk down to me. I'm going."

"We won't stop you," Abby said.

Mary Catherine threw her shoulders back and marched out the door Sasha held open for her. It closed behind her with a loud *click*.

For several seconds, no one said anything.

Julie broke the silence first. "Damn, Abby. Remind me to never get on your bad side."

"Who? Me?" Abby asked, and they all dissolved into laughter.

That night, everyone gathered in the downstairs sitting room. Sasha wasn't sure what Cole had planned, but based upon the grin he currently wore, she could tell he was up to something.

"I thought we'd do something a little different tonight," he said when everyone was seated. "There's some jewelry in my family that's been passed down from generation to generation. I knew it had been hidden at some point, but I didn't know the entire story until I came across some documents in the attic."

He went over to a small table beside the antique couch and picked up a pile of papers. "I summarized everything here, and I thought it'd be fun to act it out." He gave each person a sheet. "Daniel, you'll be the stable hand. Julie, you're the housekeeper. Nathaniel and Abby, you're visiting gentry. I'm the earl, and Sasha's the servant girl."

Everyone spent the next few minutes reading the sheets he had prepared. The only sounds were the occasional giggle.

"It's supposed to be fun," Cole assured them. "There's no right or wrong. Don't worry about being historically accurate. And there's no script, just a general story line. Dig into your character and have fun." He glanced at his watch. "We'll start in fifteen in the dining room. Everyone good with that?"

After the other two couples left, Cole walked up to Sasha and held out his hand to help her off the couch. "Know why you're always the servant girl?" he asked when she was on her feet and pressed tight against him.

"Because the earl's single?" she guessed.

"No, because your ass is so spankable."

"You know if you want to spank my ass, you can just do it. You don't have to do an entire role play," she teased.

"I'm well aware of that." He gave her a swat on the backside as if to prove the point. "But this is fun. And I get to see you in that hot maid costume."

"I'm guessing I'm not supposed to wear anything under the costume?"

"That's entirely up to you. You should go get dressed, though. I purposely didn't give a lot of time before we started."

She stepped away to get dressed, but turned back before leaving the room. "One request, Sir?"

"Anything."

"Will you wear your three-piece suit? It does crazy, wild things to my libido."

He laughed, but followed up with "Yes, of course."

Ten minutes later, Sasha stood in the hallway while Nathaniel, Abby, and Cole sat in the dining room. Abby had pulled her hair up in an elaborate-looking style. As she passed Sasha on the way in, she whispered, "It's really easy, and I love it when Master pulls the pins out one by one."

Nathaniel coughed. "I have to thank you for inviting us to your estate, Earl Johnson. We've had a delightful time."

"Yes, my lord," Abby said. "Such a nice change from being in the city. I detest London this time of year."

"You are both most certainly welcome to visit anytime you'd like to get away. Consider it a standing invitation." Cole raised his glass.

"Lot of trouble brewing with the king, wouldn't you say?" Nathaniel asked.

"I try not to say." Cole shook his head. "I fear I'm in enough trouble as it is over what I've already said."

"Is that so?"

"Yes. Why, just the other day I was telling someone that Henry   "

"My lord! My lord!" Julie dashed into the dining room.

Cole stood up. "Ms. Masterson, what is the meaning of this ruckus?"

Julie had found a white apron somewhere and she was twisting it as she answered. "It's awful, Lord Johnson. Just awful."

Abby rose to her feet and put her arms around Julie. "There, there. It's quite all right, child. Come have a seat and tell us what troubles you so."

"Probably knowing she's going to have to pick up all those hairpins in the morning," Nathaniel said, which earned him a nasty look from his wife.

Julie took several deep breaths and faced Cole. "I was in your mother's chamber, cleaning it up since she's coming next week."

Cole nodded. "Go on."

"And I went into the chest to make sure everything was there, just the way she likes it. You know, my lord, how particular she is about everything being just so. There was that one time, the—"

"Yes, yes, I know exactly how the countess is. What happened?" Cole asked.

"It's missing, my lord. All of it."

"All of what?"

"All the jewelry."

"The jewelry is missing? Impossible." Cole slammed his fist on the table. "Jewelry does not vanish. Someone took it."

"Have you had any visitors from the king?" Nathaniel asked. "Maybe someone who would try to steal it?"

"I can't imagine anyone being so bold as to steal from me after I welcomed them into my home."

"Perhaps one of the servants?" Abby asked.

"Surely not one of my servants. Why, my servants have been with me for years. Not a one of them would stoop so low as to steal from me."

Daniel appeared beside Sasha and winked.

"I think Julie missed her calling," Sasha replied, nodding toward her friend. Daniel's submissive sat in a chair with her arm dramatically thrown over her eyes, murmuring, "Gone. All gone," while Abby tried to calm her down.

"That's my girl." Daniel laughed, and after listening to the group in the other room, said, "Looks like we're up."

Sasha nodded, and he took her by the wrist, dragging her into the dining room.

"Look what I found out in the stables, trying to get away." Daniel pushed her toward Cole.

"Who are you?" Cole asked.

"I was just looking for somewhere to spend the night, my lord," Sasha said. "And I thought to use your stables."

"A likely story." Cole glanced at Daniel. "Did she have anything in her possession?"

"No, my lord."

Cole slowly walked around her. "Where did you come from, girl?"

"Please don't ask me that, my lord."

"You are found on my estate, shortly after some very valuable items go missing, and I'm not supposed to ask where you're from?"

Sasha nodded. "That's right. And I'd be ever so thankful if you didn't ask what I was doing."

"What are you doing?" he asked.

"I requested that you not ask me that."

"Yes, which is precisely why I asked."

Sasha clamped her mouth shut and crossed her arms over her chest.

Cole turned back to Daniel. "How thoroughly did you check to make sure she wasn't carrying anything?"

"I only checked her hands, my lord."

"That's what I thought. Strip her."

"My lord, there are ladies present," Nathaniel said.

"Then nothing they'll see will come as a shock. Now, Covington "

Daniel walked behind Sasha and lifted the dress over her head. She'd slipped a black tank top under the outfit to cover her back, so she was exposed only from the waist down. Like the day before, when she was late bringing the drinks, she wasn't uncomfortable. She felt only excitement.

"Hmm." Cole took his time looking over her body. "Very nice, and she doesn't seem to be hiding anything. Search the pockets of her dress. Look for hidden ones."

"Aha!" Daniel said, holding up a sheet of paper. "A summons from the king."

Cole jerked it out of his hand and held it up to Sasha. "You come from the king's court?"

"It's not what you think."

"Then what is it?" He narrowed his eyes. "And what does it have to do with my family's jewelry?"

Sasha said the first thing that came to her head. "I plead the Fifth."

Cole's eyes danced with amusement. "There is no Fifth Amendment yet. You can't plead the Fifth."

"Then I invent it."

"Wrong country."

"Damn."

"Out with it."

"I'm just looking for a place to sleep, I promise. That's all."

Cole cupped her chin and held her face so she had no choice but to look at him. "I have ways to get you to talk."

"Please, Sir," she said. "I'll do anything. Just don't send me back to the king."

He cocked an eyebrow. "What happens if I send you back to the king?"

"He'll see me as a traitor. I'll be killed."

"Why would you be a traitor?" Cole began to run his finger over her cotton-covered nipple.

She sucked in a breath. "Because I didn't follow his instructions."

"Do you have trouble following instructions?" His hand dipped lower, danced across her belly.

"Sometimes, my lord."

"What instructions were you given by the king that you didn't follow?"

"I'm supposed to gather information about you and report back to him."

"And how did you think to go about doing that?" His fingers brushed her upper thigh.

"There are rumors about you in . . . bed."

"Ah, now we are getting somewhere. What sort of rumors?"

"They say you have peculiar tastes."

"My lord," Julie interrupted, "must we sit and listen to these lies about you and your character?"

"I assure you, Ms. Masterson," Cole said, "they are not lies."

Julie gave a dramatic gasp.

"Covington?" Cole asked Daniel. "Kindly take Ms. Masterson over your knee and show her what happens when people interrupt me."

Daniel crooked a finger at a surprised Julie.

"Now," Cole said, turning his attention back to Sasha. "The jewelry. Where is it?"

"The king is going to take it. I hid it."

"And why should I believe you? How do I know you didn't stash it away to use it as a trap?"

"Can I do something to prove it to you?"

"What did you have in mind?" he asked, pressing his erection against her as his finger slid along the wetness between her legs.

"Anything. I'll do anything."

"Anything?" He took a step back, and she looked around the room.

Daniel was sitting in a chair with Julie over his lap and was working on getting her underwear down. She was doing her part to stay in role, twisting and turning and trying to get away. Abby was sitting on Nathaniel's lap, but Sasha couldn't see where his hands were.

"Show me what you heard about my tastes. What I like my bed partners to do," Cole said.

Sasha dropped to her knees and unbuttoned his fly as quickly as she could. Above her, Cole hissed in pleasure as she freed his cock. He fisted her hair.

"That's it. Now take it in your mouth like the naughty servant you are." He groaned as she did just that, taking him deep and sucking the way she knew he liked it. "Fuck, yes."

He started working his hips, thrusting in and out of her mouth. Being with him when he let go of some of his firmly held control always turned her on. She squirmed, trying to find her own relief.

"Getting off on having my cock in your mouth?" he asked, taking a firmer grasp on her hair. "You'd better not come. You'll wait for me to give you permission or else I'll spank your ass so hard, you'll be begging to go back to the king."

She made herself keep still and focused on him. He wasn't trying too hard to hold his release back. It wasn't long until he pushed into her and held her head in place while he climaxed.

Sasha quickly pulled his pants back up and set them to rights the best she could.

"I think that's all I can take of role play for one night," Cole said. "If you'll excuse me, I'm going to take this little hideaway servant and inflict my peculiar tastes upon her."

From what she could tell, the other couples felt the same way. Daniel had finished spanking Julie, but she was still wiggling in his lap. Abby was sitting as still as a statue, though it sounded like she was muttering something in German.

"But, my lord," Sasha said, as Cole lifted her into his arms, "I never told you where the jewels were."

"That's okay," he said, not even breaking stride. "I have something far more valuable."

Chapter Eight

"I don't get it." Sasha looked in the mirror and pulled at the hem of the dress Cole had laid out for her to wear today. "I thought I was going to be a servant this week."

He came up behind her and stilled her hands. "Do I not have the right and authority to change my mind?"

His stare was piercing, and she couldn't look away. "You just rarely do, Sir." To be honest, she really couldn't think of any time he'd changed his mind, but she thought it best to err on the side of caution.

"That doesn't mean I can't. The fact of the matter is, we need six people to play croquet, and Fritz had to leave."

Not to mention, she thought, but didn't say, with the other four people being couples, Fritz and Cole would look odd. Of course, she didn't suppose either man cared very much what other people thought.

And she also supposed it didn't matter that she'd never played croquet before because she was fairly certain Cole was the only one in the group who had. He'd also provided croquet outfits for everyone. The women were all wearing skirts, while the men wore what looked like golf outfits.

Cole lowered his lips to her neck. "We'll pretend that Lord Johnson is completely taken by his servant, and since he can't get enough of her, he asked her to join him for an afternoon of croquet."

"If he really wanted to make an impression, he'd know croquet wasn't the way to her heart."

"That's only because she's never played his way before."

"She's never played, period. And why would your way be any different?"

"Because my way is Dom Rules Croquet," he whispered in her ear, and then he gave her earlobe a sharp bite.

His words sent shivers down her spine, and a combination of arousal and excitement coiled in her belly.

"Leave it to you to find a way to make croquet kinky." She tilted her head, giving him better access to her neck.

"It's a gift."

"Thank God."

He laughed, and doing so, his lips tickled her.

"Mmm." She hummed. "We could stay here and be kinky inside."

"Tempting, but we'll save inside kink for later."

"Promise?"

"Most assuredly."

They were late meeting everyone outside. Though the white collared shirts and long shorts weren't their normal style of dress, she had to admit the men looked pretty good. Abby and Julie must have just recently been told about Dom Rules Croquet, because they were both looking over the course with trepidation.

"I still don't see how you can make it anything other than croquet," Julie told Abby.

Abby raised an eyebrow. "Really? I'm more shocked it took them this long to do it."

"Okay. True."

"Sorry to keep you waiting," Cole said, and then winked at Sasha. "My servant girl needed some extra encouragement."

Her heart did the little extra skip thing it normally did when he looked at her that way.

He walked toward the playing area and stopped near a wooden box. "I set everything up this morning. Now, in regular rules, the purpose is to get your ball around the course in the proper order of wicket and stake."

It sounded boring as hell to Sasha. Sort of like pool, but outside.

"But then I thought," Cole continued to speak, "anyone can play croquet. Let's do something completely different. I actually had plans to do more activities outside today, but in light of a particular neighbor who can't take no for an answer, I decided we'll just do this outside and move everything else inside."

He had been less than delighted to hear about Mary Catherine's unexpected visit the day before. But even he had to admit Abby had handled it brilliantly.

"For today," he said, "we're going to take turns. Every time you properly get a ball through a wicket, you get to pick something from this box. Fair warning: everything has been wrapped, so you won't know what you get until you've already picked it."

From the expressions on the men's faces, Sasha suddenly had a good idea of where the men had gone the day before.

"It's just the women picking? Right?" Daniel asked. "I don't think it'll be fair otherwise since we know what's in the boxes."

"Good point," Cole said. "Nathaniel?"

"Sounds good to me."

"Let's get started," Cole said.

Everyone agreed he should go first since he was the only one who'd ever played before.

"Not that it really matters," Sasha said. "He's not picking a box."

He gave her a knowing wink and the game started. Abby was the first woman to get a ball through a wicket. She groaned and asked Nathaniel, "Do I have to?"

"No." He crossed his arms. "But if you don't pick, I will— and I helped wrap."

With a resolute sigh that sounded completely fake, she walked to the box, reached in, and pulled out a brown paper package.

"Do I open now or wait?" She balanced it in her hands, then held it up to her ear and shook it.

"I think now," Nathaniel said.

With an excitement that dispelled any notion she wasn't looking forward to seeing what she'd picked, Abby tore through the paper and pulled out a blindfold.

"A blindfold." She held it up. "Kind of boring. You had all morning yesterday and the best you could come up with was a blindfold?"

"Really?" Nathaniel asked.

"Yes," Abby kept on, much to everyone's surprise. "You'd think someone with all your experience could do better than that."

"Is that a challenge?" Nathaniel asked. "For me to come up with a not-boring way to put the blindfold to use through all my years of experience?"

Abby realized what she'd said and started stammering, "No, uh, I didn't mean boring. Did I say boring? What I meant was, uh, oh crap . . . bewitching. Yes! A blindfold. How bewitching."

"Bewitching?" Nathaniel was obviously having fun at his wife's discomfort. "I'm not sure I've ever heard you use that word before."

"It was on my word-of-the-day calendar."

"Now you're just digging yourself a deeper hole. You don't have a word-of-the-day calendar."

But Abby was undeterred. "It could be on my phone."

"Is it?"

Finally caught, Abby took a deep breath and admitted defeat. "No."

Her husband didn't move, didn't say anything; he simply waited.

"No, Master," Abby eventually said.

"Yes," Nathaniel said. "I'll definitely have to think up a very nonboring but utterly bewitching way to use the blindfold tonight. Especially since there was very little usage of the word 'Master' in your entire exchange."

Abby wisely didn't say anything else.

Julie was the next to pick from the box. She wasn't quite as enthusiastic as Abby had been and the fact that she pulled out a pair of nipple clamps didn't help.

"I hate these things," she said.

Daniel was the exact opposite. "I was hoping you'd pick those."

Julie crossed her arms over her chest. "I don't feel so good. I think I'm coming down with the stomach flu."

"You forget, I'm the one who came up with that ruse."

It must have been an inside joke, because Julie broke out into giggles. "Shh. You're giving away our secrets."

"Me?" Daniel asked. "You're the one who brought it up."

Cole looked over at Sasha, who'd yet to draw anything from the box. "I think we should add a penalty if you don't get the ball through the wicket within a certain number of strokes."

"But that's not in the rules," Sasha said, irritated Cole had picked up on her strategy so quickly.

"It's Dom Rules Croquet, and as I'm a Dom, I'm adding the rule."

"I can't help it that I'm athletically challenged."

"Too bad. Get the ball through on your next turn or you'll pick two items from the box."

"You know, girls." Abby tapped her lips. She was thinking hard about something, and from the look in her eyes, it was going to be epic. "There are three of us and three of them. I say we overthrow this dictatorship and do our own thing."

"You're right," Julie said. "This game blows. I'm not playing, and I'm not wearing nipple clamps."

"Yes, you are," Daniel said, moving toward her.

"You have to catch me first." And with that, Julie took off running toward the maze. Abby motioned for Sasha to join her and sprinted to catch up.

Sasha watched her departing friends and took a quick glance back at the three men. She shrugged. "Sorry, Sir. Girls have to stick together." Before she could question her actions, she broke off into a run. "Hey, guys, wait for me."

She caught up with them at the entrance to the maze.

"Oh shit." Julie was half laughing while trying to catch her breath. "Did we just do that?"

"I think they were going to end it early anyway," Abby said. "There really wasn't much in the box to begin with."

"Shh, I hear them." Sasha could barely make out the sound of the three men. "Let's go into the maze."

She'd been through the maze only once. The day after they arrived, Cole had walked through it with her. At the time, she'd been captivated by the different types of plants she saw. Now she wished she'd paid closer attention to the path they needed to take.

"There's a back entrance to the house somewhere around here." Sasha tried to picture an aerial view of the maze. "Ugh, I should've been listening when Cole was going over the pattern of the pathways."

"I don't hear them anymore." Julie looked over her shoulder. "Do you think they gave up?"

Abby snorted and then whispered, "Have you known them to give up on anything, ever?"

"I don't think 'give up' is in Cole's vocabulary," Sasha said.

"I know Nathaniel's never heard of it."

"Then why can't we hear them?" Julie asked.

Sasha thumped her friend's shoulder. "Because they don't want us to hear them."

"Or maybe because they're planning what to do to us when we get back."

They were all quiet as they thought about that. But really, how bad could it be? Sasha thought. There were three of them, after all.

"Okay," Sasha said. "Here's the plan. We find the exit in the maze that leads to the back of the house. We go in through the old servants' entrance. That'll put us in the kitchen. From there, we sneak through the pantry because it leads to the ballroom. We go through the ballroom out to the back stairs and up to our bedrooms. It's foolproof!"

Julie bit her bottom lip. "I don't know. It sounds too easy."

"Easy?" Abby asked. "With all that sneaking around? We'll be lucky if we make it to the house, much less all the way upstairs. Hell, they're probably on the other side of this hedge, listening to everything we're saying."

"I know," Julie said. "One of us could call them. That way if they're close enough, we'll hear their phone ring."

Abby shook her head. "Won't work. I'm pretty sure they're smart enough to turn their phones off if they're going into stealth mode."

"So what do you suggest?" Sasha asked.

"We have to go with your idea." Abby shrugged. "It's either that or sleep out here tonight, and you guys know I love you, but I don't do camping."

Julie agreed. "Okay, first thing, then, is to find our way out of here. Sasha, do you have any idea which way?"

With renewed determination, Sasha retraced their footsteps, and though it took longer than she would have liked, they finally made it out of the maze.

"I'll go first," Sasha said, "and make sure the path and kitchen are clear. Then I'll come back for you."

"And if you don't come back?" Julie asked.

"Then you know one of them found me and you're on your own."

"Fair enough. Let's do this thing." Abby nodded. "Good luck."

Sasha wasn't sure why her heart pounded the way it did. Seriously, she told herself, the worst she could do was run into Cole. But that didn't exactly help matters. She peeked out the exit of the maze and scanned the short distance to the house. It looked clear.

She gave Julie and Abby a thumbs-up and darted to the kitchen door. Too late, she wondered what they were going to do if the door was locked, but it opened to an empty kitchen.

Certain at least the first part of the escape plan was clear, she ran back to the maze.

"All good," she said. "Let's go."

They all three ran together, and she didn't think any one of them took a breath until they were safely in the kitchen.

"I don't like it," Julie said. "It's too quiet. They have to be somewhere."

"Maybe they decided to finish the game," Sasha said.

"Right." Abby stuck her head out into the hallway. "And they just decided to ignore the fact that we ruined their fun. No, I agree with Julie. Something's going on." She looked back over her shoulder. "Looks clear. Do we go through the pantry or down the hall?"

"Pantry leads directly to the ballroom. Hallway's more exposed." Sasha checked to make sure the pantry was empty.

"I vote we stay in the kitchen and bake something to say we're sorry." Julie pointed to her left. "Sasha, I think those are carrots over there. Why don't you get started on them and we'll make a carrot cake?"

"You're lucky I don't throw one at you. Pantry, you think?" Sasha asked.

"Pantry," Abby and Julie said together.

They stepped into the pantry. It was only a short walk to the back entrance of the ballroom. But as soon as they stepped into the large room, Sasha knew something was off. The room was pitch-black, which didn't seem right. Normally, the front double doors were open to let in light.

"Uh-oh," she said, right at the exact moment the room suddenly lit up.

When her eyes finally adjusted, all she could focus on were the three men in the middle of the room. She froze, trying to decide if she should turn back and run into the pantry or stay where she was.

"You know," Cole said, and she couldn't hear any emotion in his voice, "if you look out from the upstairs office, you can see directly down into the maze."

"Dammit," Abby muttered behind her. "I didn't think about looking up."

"Rookie mistake," Sasha agreed. "We'd suck as spies."

"The hallway's exposed. Go through the pantry." Julie glared at Sasha. "Brilliant plan."

"Yeah, well, I didn't hear you come up with anything other than a carrot cake," Sasha reminded her.

Daniel was trying to hide his grin. "Carrot cake sounds pretty good."

Julie perked up. "I'll go make one!"

"No," Cole said. "You ran off together; you can deal with the consequences together. Besides, Sasha doesn't cook. Especially with carrots."

"Damn," Julie said.

"You brought it on yourself." Nathaniel crooked a finger at Abby. "Come here, Abigail."

Abby didn't hesitate. "Yes, Master."

She seemed to almost glide as she crossed the floor to where her husband stood, holding up the blindfold she'd unwrapped earlier. She knelt down before him, and he wasted no time covering her eyes.

He stood back. "You look very . . . What's the word? *Bewitching.* Yes, you look very bewitching like this."

"So bewitching," Cole said. "I think Sasha and Julie need blindfolds, too."

Julie and Sasha exchanged an uh-oh look.

Cole lowered his voice. "Now."

They both hurried to their respective Doms and knelt.

Cole's hands were quick and efficient as he blindfolded Sasha. "Now, my naughty girl, you won't be able to see what's happening or who's doing it."

Her mouth grew dry. *Who?* Did that mean either Nathaniel or Daniel might touch her? She wasn't sure she liked that, and even though playing with others wasn't a hard limit, she thought it was for the other two women.

"Stand up and undress," Cole said. "I have a tank top I'm going to put on you to cover your back."

Everything was quiet. Sasha assumed the other guys were preparing Julie and Abby the same way Cole was preparing her. She heard a small yelp from Julie and then Daniel saying, "I knew they'd look good on you."

"Use your safe word at any time." Cole's voice was thick in her ear. "Unfortunately for you, you didn't pull anything out of the box. Fortunately for me, I get to pick. But first . . ."

Something covered her ears and all she could hear was rain. Had he put headphones on her? She shook her head. That's what it felt like. Because she couldn't hear, for a minute she panicked, thinking Cole couldn't hear, either.

"Yellow," she said.

The headphones came off. "Sasha, are you okay? What's wrong?" His gentle voice was back, tinged with worry.

"I panicked, Sir. Thinking you couldn't hear me. Which makes no sense because I said yellow. It's okay. I'm fine to continue."

"Are you sure?"

"Definitely, Sir."

He ran his hands over her, and her body relaxed into his touch. "Are you okay for me to put the headphones back on, or should I leave them off?"

"I'd like to wear them, please, Sir."

He pressed a kiss against her shoulder. "My strong, fierce Sasha."

It was almost as if her body hummed with pleasure at his compliment, and this time when he put the headphones on, she felt only calm. She had no idea what to expect or what or who was going to touch her. The waiting about drove her wild.

When something finally touched her shoulder, she jumped. It wasn't a paddle or a flogger or a cane or anything that she'd anticipated. It was soft. It came again, longer this time, and she knew what it was.

A paintbrush. He was painting her. Or, more to the point, painting *on* her.

It was the simplest thing, but it made her crazy. What was he painting her with? What color was it? She couldn't tell anything because he switched brushes frequently. Some were very fine and seemed as if he was writing. But others were wider and covered more area.

She moved once, and he smacked her backside in a sharp reminder to be still. She wondered if Abby and Julie were also being painted and, if so, what they looked like. The rhythmic cadence of rainfall combined with the gentle sweeps of the brushes and she felt herself start to drift. She swayed, and two arms came around her and carried her somewhere soft so she could lie down.

She jerked awake to complete quiet and blackness. In fact, the silence was so vast it was deafening. She tried to lift her hand to her eyes to see if the blindfold was still on, but her hands were tied down. Where was she? And, more to the point, where was everyone else?

She repeated to herself that Cole wouldn't leave her unattended. She knew he was nearby, watching. If she focused, she might be able to sense him. Taking a deep breath, she tried to hear something, anything, but it was pointless.

Just when she thought she'd go crazy at the absolute nothingness, there was movement around her head and her ears were uncovered. Everything seemed so loud until she heard the voice she wanted to hear the most.

"Back with us, little one? You were the last to wake up. Too bad you were all such naughty submissives; we had something really special planned for after the game." His voice was calm and gentle, and any remaining tension in her body fled at its sound. "Let's get you up so you can see my masterpiece. Though I'll admit, painting was fun and not really a punishment. Even if my game was boring."

He had her unbound within seconds, and since she was still blindfolded, he kept hold of her hand as she stood. They walked a few steps forward before he pulled them to a halt.

"Ready?" he asked.

"Yes, Sir." She was almost giddy with excitement to see how he'd painted her.

The blindfold fell away and she gasped. Her body was painted in vibrant reds and yellows and greens. Swirls here and figure eights there. She twisted, and it was as if the lines on her body were alive.

"It's beautiful, Sir. I had no idea you were a painter." She couldn't stop staring at herself.

He held up a mirror. "Look at the back. I did it before you fell asleep."

She looked at her back. In his magnificent script, he'd written COLE's on the tank top across the area on her back where her scars were. The sight made her eyes tear.

"I wish I could keep it on forever," she said.

"Look at me," he said, and when she did, his eyes blazed with a fiery promise. "Never doubt it. Whether it's written or not. Whether you can see it or not. Hell, whether you feel it or not. I love every part of you, and I'll say it and write it and prove it over and over, until you're as sure of it as you are of your next breath."

Chapter Nine

On Saturday evening, Sasha paced Cole's bedroom, trying to decide what was going on. When she entered, the first thing she'd noticed was the dressing gown someone had placed on the bed. Curious as to what that meant, she walked to the large picture window to see if she could find Cole. It was early evening, and he typically went for a walk at this time of day.

She peeked out, and her breath caught when she saw him dressed in a dark three-piece suit, talking with Nathaniel. Most of the time, he only wore a three-piece suit for discipline sessions. Is that what he had planned today?

She went over the entire week in her mind, trying to pinpoint something, *anything*, unresolved that would have led to a discipline session. Not only could she not find anything, but she knew Cole, and she knew he wasn't the type to let an issue hang out there. If he thought she needed correction, he would have brought it up when the incident happened.

Satisfied that whatever was going on didn't involve her being bent over a chair, waiting for him to cane her, she undressed and slipped into the dressing gown. No sooner had she folded the clothes she'd been wearing than someone knocked on the door.

She scurried over and opened the door.

"Hello, little one."

Cole looked so unbelievably handsome she didn't move for several seconds. At his raised eyebrow, she realized he'd called her *little one*, and as such, she needed to be kneeling.

She dropped to her knees. "Hello, Sir."

"Stand up for me, Sasha."

His voice sounded serious, nothing at all what she expected. Worry started to tickle her brain as she made her way back to her feet.

"Sir."

"Our friends are waiting for us, but I have to talk to you privately first."

"Is something wrong?"

He gently brushed his knuckles across her cheekbones. "No, little one. Nothing is wrong. I just thought it might be time to let you in on the real reason we all came to the UK."

She thought back to the week they'd just spent: enjoying the area with their friends, laughing and having fun, growing even closer to Cole as she learned about his past. That wasn't the real reason?

"I don't understand, Sir."

He rubbed her eyebrows with his thumbs. "Don't frown, little one. I much prefer it when you smile."

She leaned into his touch; everything always seemed so much better when he touched her. It was almost frightening, the effect he had on her. "Tell me what our real reason for being here is. That's why I'm frowning."

"Do you remember the conversation we had the night I brought up the trip?"

She couldn't help the smile that crept across her face. "Parts of the conversation. More than that, I remember what happened *after* the conversation."

He gave a short laugh. "Indeed? Yes, I remember that as well." He took her hand and led her to a nearby couch. She knelt beside him and sighed when he ran his fingers through her hair. "You told me you sometimes felt like you were living in a dream and sometimes had a hard time conceiving what you meant to me."

"Yes, Sir. I remember." She leaned her head against his knee, wanting to feel more of him.

"The thing is, I collared you rather quickly, and we didn't have anyone with us to witness it. I know you've never worn anyone's collar before mine, and I've collared only one other woman."

She was glad he couldn't see her face because she knew her frown had come back. Why was he talking about that, and why the hell would he be mentioning Kate?

"You see, Sasha, everyone is here in the UK because I invited them to our collaring ceremony."

Her jaw dropped, and she looked up to see his face. He had such an expression of love and adoration, it made her heart hurt. "Sir?" was all she managed to get out.

"I know you wear my collar daily, but I'd like for us to make it official. In front of those we love and those who will support us in our lifestyle choices." He slid off the couch and came to his knees before her. "Sasha, my beloved little one, will you wear my collar?"

"Cole." She threw her arms around him. "How did you know I wanted a ceremony?"

"I wish I could take the credit for knowing, but I didn't. I thought it might be a way to show you how much you mean to me."

"I didn't stay to watch when Daniel collared Julie and I've always regretted that. And then I thought, maybe it's better that way because then I won't know what I'm missing."

He gathered her into his arms and pulled them both to standing. "I wish you had told me sooner. I want to meet all your needs, even the unspoken desires you don't feel comfortable sharing with anyone."

She nodded against his chest.

"But, Sasha, you have to tell me. You have to share them with me." He pulled back and made sure she was looking in his eyes. "Understand?"

"Yes, Sir."

"I think to make sure we keep communication open, I'll have you pick back up your journaling. I want you to write every day. Even if it's only a few lines. That way if there's something you want me to know, but maybe don't feel comfortable talking about, you can write it first."

"I like that idea."

"You do?" His eyes danced with mischief. "Even if I still count off for grammar?"

"Yes, especially if you count off for grammar. Maybe you're rubbing off on me. I actually don't mind writing now."

"I'm glad." He kissed her. "Before we start the ceremony, I'm going to need to take your collar off."

Her hands flew up to her neck. "I know you're going to put it back on me, but just the thought makes me sad."

"I'm actually not going to put this one back on you."

"You're not?"

"There you go with the frowning again."

She sighed. "You keep saying things that make me sigh."

"I suppose I do." He reached behind her neck and undid the clasp. "I think we'll have this made into a bracelet or something."

"It's my first collar," she said. "I'd like to keep it."

"Of course." He took a long slender box from the drawer beside the couch they'd been sitting on. "Would you like to see your new collar?"

She nodded even though she couldn't imagine liking any collar better than the one he'd just taken off her.

"Remember when Kate came by that first morning?"

Seriously? Kate again? Sasha didn't consider herself jealous, but seriously? "Yes," she said, when what she wanted to say was *Kinda hard to forget your ex-slave coming by the morning after the best sex of my life.*

"She stopped by to drop off a box I inadvertently left when I moved out."

Ah, yes, she remembered. He'd asked her to take the box to his bedroom, and while she'd been off doing that, he'd had a few words with Kate in the living room. "I remember," she told him.

"The box contained the jewelry that my family hid when we fell out of favor with Henry the Eighth."

"It still boggles my mind that you can sit there and be all 'Well, you know Henry the Eighth had it out for my family.' I mean, that's like me tracing my ancestors back to George Washington."

He laughed. He did that a lot lately, according to Daniel,

who'd said so at dinner the other night. He'd smiled when he said it. Then he added that Cole had rarely laughed around Kate. She was glad he felt more jovial around her.

"I'm glad we were able to hide the family jewelry. Or else I wouldn't be able to give you this." He opened the box and revealed a gorgeous choker collar. It was double-stranded pearls, and every so often distributed among the strands there was a gem that looked like an emerald. But surely it couldn't be.

He lifted it out of the box. "The technical name for it is a carcanet, but it looks so much like a collar, I can't help but think my family was getting kinky five hundred years ago. Sasha?"

She couldn't speak. She could barely breathe. Matter of fact, she wasn't even able to think very much.

"Sasha?"

"You're giving me a piece of your family jewelry? That's five hundred years old? I can't even . . ."

"I want you to have it. I want you to wear it."

"But, Sir. It's priceless."

"As are you."

She shook her head, unable to wrap her mind around the idea. "Sir," she started, but was unable to finish.

"Sasha, I'm not going to argue with you about this. But it would mean a considerable amount to me if you would wear my collar. You've been doing so. I'm just changing the collar."

"To priceless jewels."

He held up the necklace. "This is nothing but metal, some rocks, and some pieces of sand that got stuck in an oyster. Believe me when I tell you, it is nothing. It means nothing to me compared with you."

Tears filled her eyes, but she nodded, accepting the gift of his collar. "Thank you, Sir. I would be honored to wear your collar."

Joy washed over his face, and it wasn't until that moment that she knew how much it meant to him, too. "It is I who am honored," he whispered.

He leaned forward and his lips gently brushed hers. She tried to pull him closer, but he pulled back. "Abby and Julie will be here in a few minutes to help you get ready."

"But I'm ready now," she said. "Why do Abby and Julie have to help me get ready?"

"Damned if I know. But it was the condition they asked for in exchange for keeping quiet about the ceremony."

She rolled her eyes. "I love those two, but seriously?"

He stood up. "I don't get it, either, but they seem excited about it. I'd better get out and let them come in."

Sasha leaned back in the couch. "Oh, all right. Send them in."

He left, chuckling, and when he opened the door she heard mumbles from outside. Within seconds, Abby and Julie rushed in. As soon as she saw the excitement in her friends' eyes, she knew exactly why Cole had agreed to their request. She didn't think it was possible to be more excited, but seeing the two of them proved her wrong.

Julie actually had tears in her eyes. "Do you remember when you helped me get ready for my collaring ceremony with Daniel?"

"I remember." Even though she'd helped her get ready, Sasha hadn't been able to stay for the ceremony. It had been too soon after the incident with Peter. She was still too injured, both physically and mentally, to offer support for Julie in her BDSM journey. And in her heart of hearts, she'd thought Julie was taking things too fast with Daniel. But she had still wanted to support her friend, so she'd helped her get ready.

Sasha looked behind Julie to where Abby was standing. Abby held something in her hands. She smiled. "It's a dress. That's why Cole set out the dressing gown. Julie and I thought you should have something a little formal."

"Yeah," Julie said. "Of course, we were afraid you'd think something was up when you saw that on the bed."

"Well, I definitely knew something was going on. The only outfits he's set out this week were the servant's uniform and the croquet dress. Besides, usually when he wears a three-piece suit, he also has a cane in his hand."

"We didn't show him this dress," Abby said. She placed a long white garment bag on the bed and motioned Sasha to come forward. "It's Scottish lace. Julie and I thought that would be appropriate."

Abby glanced quickly over her shoulder to make sure she had Sasha's attention, and then she unzipped the bag. Sasha gasped as Abby took out the gorgeous gown. It was white and covered in fine delicate lace.

"Oh my. It's exquisite." Sasha ran a tentative hand over the lace. "It sort of looks like a wedding gown."

Julie came up behind her and looked over her shoulder. "This designer does make some gorgeous wedding gowns, and I'm sure this particular one has been used as a wedding gown before. But we thought it was perfect for your collaring ceremony."

"Besides," said Abby. "A collaring ceremony is a lot like a wedding ceremony."

Sasha looked at the dress, certain she had never seen anything more gorgeous. "I love it."

"I knew you would." Julie gave her a hug. "I remember think-ing the night of my ceremony that I hoped you'd one day find your own happily-ever-after. Never in two million and a half years would I have thought that someone would be Cole Johnson."

"That would have been two of us," Sasha agreed. "And now I can't imagine being with anyone else."

Abby stood to the side, watching them both with a knowing smile. "Just you both wait. It only gets better from here."

Julie sniffled. "I knew I wouldn't make it through this day without crying. Where are the tissues?"

Sasha's phone rang right as Abby passed a box to Julie.

"I'll let it go to voice mail." She couldn't imagine talking to anyone right now anyway.

"You might want to check that," Julie said. "It might be Dena."

Sasha found her phone where she'd left it on the couch and, sure enough, it was Dena.

"Hey there," she said.

"Hey, girl," Dena said. "I so wish I could be there for you today."

"You're on bed rest. I know you'd be here if you could."

"I don't know why Cole had to take you all the way to England to collar you. But I'll give him points for originality."

Sasha laughed. She couldn't wait to show Dena her new col-lar. "I can't believe you guys kept it a secret from me."

"You have met your Dom, right?" Dena asked with a laugh. "When he tells you to keep something secret, you keep it secret."

"Don't tell anyone, but he's really a softie."

"I've seen him in action. Trust me, he may have a soft side, but he's no softie."

Sasha muttered an agreement, but deep inside she was pleased that Cole showed his soft side only to her. It was like they had a secret they shared only with each other.

"I'd better let you go," Dena said. "I'm sure Abby and Julie are champing at the bit to get you ready."

They said their good-byes, and Sasha turned back to her friends. "What else do I have to do to get ready?"

In hindsight, that wasn't the best question to ask. Another hour later, they'd discussed how they wanted to do her hair, how much makeup she should wear, and if she needed shoes. Sasha didn't quite understand the shoe thing, but Abby was busy texting, and when she looked up, she said no to the shoes.

When they finally let her look in a mirror, Sasha couldn't believe the transformation. The combination of the dress and the light makeup made her look different than usual. But she could see this excitement in her eyes that absolutely transformed her. Hell, she *felt* different.

"Cole is going to die when he sees you." Julie stood behind Sasha in the mirror. "You look beautiful. And you know what else?"

Sasha shook her head.

"I don't even have to ask how you're doing; it's written all over your face."

Sasha laughed at Julie's mention of the phrase she told her she wanted someone to use one day. "Thank you."

Julie gave her a quick hug. "Are you ready? Because I think there's a certain Dom waiting for you."

Abby and Julie led the way with Sasha following close behind. She had assumed the ceremony would be held indoors, perhaps in the library. But her two friends led her outside, where she could see what looked like hundreds of candles burning in the garden.

Abby squeezed her hand. "We're going to have a seat. Cole will let you know what to do next."

Sasha jumped when somebody touched her shoulder.

"It's just me, little one."

"Sir, you startled me."

"Forgive me. That was not my intent. But I wanted us to walk out together."

"Is there anything I need to do or prepare myself for?" she asked.

"No, little one. I would have told you."

He knew her so well. Knew her struggles. What caused her stress. And likewise, he knew how to alleviate those stresses and struggles.

She nodded, and he cupped her face, softly stroking her cheek.

"You look incredible," he whispered. "In fact, incredible doesn't begin to touch it. I need more adjectives."

"Thank you, Sir."

He held out his hand. "Are you ready?"

"It seems odd, walking in together hand in hand."

He put his hand down and looked at her with a raised eyebrow. "Because you're a submissive?"

Duh, she wanted to say, but nodded instead.

"I'm sure there are a lot of people who would agree with you, and I'm not saying they're wrong. Just that for *us*, you and me, I think it works better to show that we're each equal in the relationship. More important, I want you to know that I don't view you as lesser than me. Quite the opposite, in fact. As a Dominant, I hold you and your well-being so far above my own. It's quite humbling to have you trust me so much."

He never stopped amazing her. Just when she thought she couldn't love him any more, he'd say something like what he just did and her heart would swell. She held her hand out. "I'm ready now, Sir."

He lifted her hand to his lips for a quick kiss and then led the way outside.

Chapter Ten

The candles that lit the garden looked amazing, like something out of a dream. They gave just enough light for Sasha to see the path and the smiling faces of their friends. She felt as if she were walking on air the entire way down the stone pathway to where Cole had set up a small table. Something was on it, but it was covered up by a white tablecloth.

Most shocking was Fritz, standing beside the table. She looked up at Cole, but he only winked at her.

"Cole and Sasha," Fritz started, when they came to a stop before him. "Is it your intent to enter into a Dominant/submissive relationship?"

Cole gave her hand a squeeze. "It is."

"Yes, Sir," she replied.

Fritz stepped to the side and waved Cole to the table. She felt his absence when he dropped her hand to lift the white cloth. Underneath was a bowl. She couldn't figure out what that was for. She'd been to a few collaring ceremonies and she'd never seen a bowl used before.

Cole took the bowl and handed it to her. She looked down into it as she took it. *Water?*

What was she going to do with water? Was she supposed to drink it?

Before her, Cole simply gave her the smile that always lifted her mood and eased her fears. She was being crazy. Cole knew what he was doing. He had the entire ceremony under control. She needed to relax and enjoy it.

"Sasha, my dearest little one, when you came to me, you were frightened and unsure. There were issues in your past that clouded your vision of the future." He took a sponge from the table and put it in the bowl. He squeezed some water out of the sponge so it was only the slightest bit damp. "You are mine now and I am the one who will carry your fears and worries, letting there be only light for your journey forward. With this water, I wash all the pains of yesterday away."

With the gentlest touch, he ran the sponge across the bare skin of her neck and down her arms.

"The nightmares that have haunted you are gone, washed away." He knelt down and dribbled water across her feet. "The doubts you had, the fear, and all the secret things you kept hidden in your soul. They are all gone. There is only you and you are mine."

He stood up and took the bowl, but she could barely see him for the tears gathering in her eyes. His words healed the remaining dark spaces inside her, and she knew the past wouldn't bother her anymore. She had a feeling her panic attacks were gone forever, too.

He put the bowl back on the table and took both her hands.

"I vow to you today, in front of our friends, that I will protect you, love you, cherish you, and pamper you." The corner of his mouth lifted with just a hint of a smile. "I also promise to correct you when needed, push you when called for, and to ensure you never have trouble falling asleep. Knowing this, do you consent to be my submissive and to wear my collar as a symbol of my dominance?"

"Yes, Sir," she managed to get out.

Cole nodded to Fritz, and the German Dom took a pillow from under the table and placed it on the ground beside Cole.

"Though I once told you about why I would ask my submissive to kneel on rocks," he said so low she knew no one else could hear, "tonight it would please me more for you to use a pillow."

When she knelt before him, it felt right. Sure, she'd enjoyed walking in beside him and standing face-to-face, holding hands, but it was when she knelt for him that her world felt like everything was in its place.

He briefly touched her hair, the small act filling her with even more peace. But it wasn't until she felt the collar being placed around her neck that she understood exactly what peace was. Though less than an hour had passed since he'd taken off her old collar, the feel of her new one caused her entire body to relax. And when he fastened it into place, she muttered a soft "Yes."

His chuckle told her she hadn't been as quiet as she thought she had.

"I'll admit," he said, "I feel better with it around your neck as well."

She wasn't sure if she was supposed to say anything or quote her own vows. Obviously, Cole had been planning this and would have had time to come up with something. She didn't have a way with words like he did, and she didn't think she could come up with anything meaningful on the fly. She hoped he didn't ask her to say anything.

But, of course, he knew her better than she knew herself, it seemed.

He held his hand out to her. "Come stand by my side, little one."

She rose slowly to her feet and found herself facing Cole, once more in front of Fritz. For some reason, the big German Dom didn't seem as scary when he was smiling.

"Cole," he said, "I've known you for a long time. Probably longer than anyone here. I was with you as you discovered and defined your Dominant nature. You probably don't remember, and you'll probably punch me for bringing it up, but there was a certain night when you were just starting out. We'd just finished a training session. It had been awkward. The chemistry wasn't working, the sub had left, and we were talking. You looked at me and said, 'Fritz, one day I'm going to find the One. And everything's going to click. She won't be perfect, and we know I'm certainly not. But together we're going to be pretty damn close, and when we're together, sparks will fly.'"

Cole didn't move his gaze from her as he answered. "You're right. As soon as we finish, I'm busting your nose."

Around them, their friends laughed.

"Hold on," Fritz said. "I'm not finished. You've had some rough times. You never quite seemed settled. I think that's why you were always off traveling the world. You thought you had what you wanted, but deep inside, your heart was still searching."

Cole squeezed Sasha's hands.

"Sasha," Fritz said to her, "I don't know you as well, but I know you've had some obstacles to overcome. And I know what

I see before me now is a strong, independent woman who knows with her head and trusts with her heart. It's a beautiful and precious thing that you offer to my friend, and I thank you for not being perfect, because he's certainly not. But together you two are pretty damn close.

"So, Cole and Sasha, I don't have any earth-shattering words of advice. I can't promise you that life will be smooth. I can't even promise that you're going to *like* each other all the time. But I can tell you this—those sparks? They're so bright, they're blinding. And you have a circle of friends who are delighted and honored to share in this moment with you."

Sasha wiped a tear from her eye, and she heard either Julie or Abby sniffle.

"Oh, right," Fritz said. "You can kiss now."

Cole's lips came over hers, and she no longer heard sniffles and she was no longer aware of Fritz or the candles or anything other than Cole. He filled her, and in those seconds when he held her, she knew she filled him, too.

"I love you, my Sasha." His voice was rough and hoarse.

"I love you, Cole."

It was only Fritz's cough that finally pulled them apart. She found herself surrounded by Julie and Abby, both of them *ooh*-ing and *ahh*ing over her collar. Nathaniel and Fritz brought out food that seemed to have appeared from nowhere. Daniel passed out champagne flutes, and everyone toasted them.

It was the happiest day of Sasha's life.

She took Cole's hand and was about to tell him that very thing when suddenly everyone got quiet. She looked around, trying to find out what happened. Her gaze wandered up the path she'd walked down with Cole not long ago to find it wasn't a what, but a who.

"Dammit all to fucking hell and back." Cole knew he should have stopped by Mary Catherine's house after her interaction with the women. But he'd put it off because he didn't want to see her, and he knew if he went by her house, she'd get the wrong idea.

All that would have been preferable to the look on Sasha's face when she saw Mary Catherine standing at her collaring ceremony.

"Get her out of here," Sasha said. "I won't have her spoiling my perfect day."

But he was already walking that way. He'd pick the woman up and physically throw her out if he had to.

"I've been about as patient as I'm going to be," he said. "But this is a private event on private property and you need to—"

She held up her hand, but that wasn't what stopped him. It was the look on her face. She looked like her world had just fallen apart.

"Let me," she said. "Just one quick word and I'll leave you alone forever."

He shook his head. "No, you've been nothing but rude to—"

"Let her have her say." Sasha came up behind him and slipped her hand in his. "Go on, Mary Catherine."

For once Mary Catherine looked uncertain of herself. Her eyes darted from him to Sasha to their friends behind them. "I don't . . . I mean . . ." She took a deep breath. "I don't know exactly what I just witnessed. That is, I think I know, but I'm not sure. But whatever. I know enough to know that my husband never looked at me the way you look at her. And it hit me. I can't have that with you, but I can have it with someone. I want someone to look at me that way." She wiped away a tear. "That's all. And I'm sorry I was mean to you, Sasha. You're obviously a very special woman."

Cole could count on one hand the number of times he'd been surprised. Interestingly enough, they'd all involved Sasha. But nothing surprised him more than when she dropped his hand, walked to Mary Catherine, and hugged her.

"It's okay," he heard Sasha say. "Come have some refreshments."

And though Mary Catherine tried to refuse, his little one was very persuasive. Within minutes, she had Mary Catherine drinking champagne and had introduced her to everyone.

By the time Sasha made it back to his side, the night had grown chilly. He took his jacket off and draped it over her shoulders. "You leave me speechless," he told her.

She smiled and looked across the lawn to where Julie was talking with Mary Catherine. "I felt bad for her. She lost out on you."

He chuckled, his heart bursting with love and pride for the woman at his side. "It's true what Fritz said earlier."

"That you're going to punch him?"

"No." He took her hand and kissed it. Then he slowly entwined their fingers. "What he said about me being unsettled. He was right, and I never realized it. I was always looking for something. Do you know that I haven't once looked into a job overseas since we've been together?"

Her eyebrows furrowed. "You haven't?"

He shook his head. "No."

It was amazing he'd never noticed it. But he no longer felt the need to travel the world. He was content—*settled*, to use Fritz's word—with his life in Delaware. Writing what he felt like, when he felt like it.

Sasha frowned. "I don't want to keep you from working."

"It's not that, little one. It's that there is no need for me to look anymore. I found what I was searching for." He traced her collar. The collar that represented who he was and where he came from. The one that had been handed down for hundreds of years. Perhaps because the universe knew this was the woman it was truly meant for. "You may wear my collar, but make no mistake about it. You're the one who's claimed me."

The collaring ceremony was long over. Mary Catherine had left for her house hours ago, waving and telling everyone to keep in touch and come back soon. Fritz left shortly after, saying he'd see everyone in Delaware in a few months. Abby and Nathaniel were flying to Switzerland in the morning to spend a few days at their chalet and had turned in early. Julie and Daniel had stayed up with Cole and Sasha the longest, but even they eventually turned in, knowing Cole and Sasha wanted some alone time.

It was early in the morning, and though they were flying home in a few hours, neither Cole nor Sasha could pull themselves away from the other long enough to sleep.

"I don't even know if it's worth it to try to get any sleep now." Sasha was as content as she could be, lying on Cole's chest, his heart beating in her ear.

"I don't, either. Though I must say I'm envious of Nathaniel and Abby's private jet."

"You don't think you'll be able to sleep on the flight home?" Sasha asked.

"It's not that. I won't be able to strip you down and do wicked things to your body."

She laughed. "It may do us good to take a breather."

"Isn't that what we're doing now?"

"I mean, a longer breather."

His arms tightened around her. "I'm never going to get enough of you."

"I certainly hope not."

"It was a perfect day, wasn't it?" His fingers lightly brushed her collar.

"Yes." She propped herself up on one elbow and looked down on him. "Know what surprised me, though?"

"Mary Catherine?"

Mary Catherine showing up had definitely been a surprise. Not to mention the way she'd looked when she was confessing how her ex-husband had never looked at her like Cole had looked at Sasha and how lonely she was. The pain in her eyes was obvious, but even more so because Sasha knew exactly how she felt. Before she'd gotten together with Cole, how many times had she seen the way Daniel looked at Julie and wanted to be on the receiving end of a look like that?

The pain of those memories had been what had moved her forward and caused her to wrap her arms around the hurting woman. But as surprising as that entire scene had been, that wasn't what had surprised her the most.

"No, not her," Sasha said. "I was thinking about Fritz."

"I still owe him a punch in the gut." Cole appeared to be in deep thought. "But I might let him get away with it since everything he said was true. What was surprising about him?"

"I didn't expect for him to be so poetic."

"Fritz? Poetic? I'm not sure he'd think that was a compliment."

"That's why what he said was so surprising. It didn't fit the image I had of him. It came as a shock to hear him talk about love the way he did. Is he with someone?"

Cole's expression clouded over briefly. "No. He's never been serious about anyone, as far as I know."

Which seemed odd to her. "The way he talked, it would seem otherwise."

"Let me rephrase," Cole said. "He hasn't been serious about anyone he's been with. I do think he has feelings for someone."

"Unrequited love sucks." She kissed him just because she could. "I feel bad for him."

"I wouldn't say it's unrequited. As far as I know, he's never told her."

Something lurked behind his eyes; she was sure of it now. "You know her, don't you?"

He nodded. "I've known for years how he feels. I thought he would have done something by now; Kate and I split up ages ago."

Two hundred questions ran through her brain, but she only asked one. "Your ex, Kate?"

"Yes."

"Wow."

"Ball's in his court, so to speak. If he wants her, he can man up and do something about it." He shifted so he was on his side, facing her. "No more talk of Kate, or Fritz, or Mary Catherine. We have a few more hours before we have to get out of bed. . . ." He trailed off and ran a hand down her side, cupping a breast.

Sasha arched her back in pleasure as he drew her nipple into his mouth. "I take it our breather is over?"

But Cole's mouth was too busy to reply, and by the time he could speak, taking a breather was the farthest thing from her mind.

Also available from
New York Times bestselling author

TARA SUE ME

TARA SUE ME

THE
SUBMISSIVE

THE WORLDWIDE PHENOMENON
Before there was **Fifty Shades of Grey...**

Abby King yearns to experience a world of pleasure
beyond her simple life as a librarian—and the brilliant and
handsome CEO Nathaniel West is the key to making her
dark desires a reality. But as Abby falls deep into
Nathaniel's tantalizing world of power and passion, she
fears his heart may be beyond her reach—and that her
own might be beyond saving...

HEADLINE
ETERNAL

TARA SUE ME

THE DOMINANT

THE WORLDWIDE PHENOMENON
Before there was **Fifty Shades of Grey…**

Nathaniel West doesn't lose control. But then he meets Abby King. Her innocence and willingness is intoxicating, and he's determined to make Abby his. But when Nathaniel begins falling for Abby on a deeper level, he realizes that trust must go both ways—and he has secrets which could bring the foundations of their relationship crashing down…

HEADLINE
ETERNAL

TARA SUE ME

THE
TRAINING

THE WORLDWIDE PHENOMENON
Before there was **Fifty Shades of Grey**...

It started with desire. Now a weekend arrangement
of pleasure has become a passionate romance.
Still, there remains a wall between Nathaniel West and
Abby King. Abby knows the only way to lead Nathaniel
on a path to greater intimacy is to let him deeper into
her world than anyone has ever gone before...

HEADLINE
ETERNAL

TARA
SUE ME

The *New York Times* bestseller

THE
Enticement

A SUBMISSIVE NOVEL

Abby West has everything she wanted: a family,
a skyrocketing new career, and a sexy, Dominant husband
who fulfills her every need. Only, as her life outside the
bedroom becomes hectic, her Master's sexual requirements
inside become more extreme. As the underlying tension
and desire between them heats up, so does the struggle
to keep everything they value from falling apart...

HEADLINE
ETERNAL

TARA SUE ME

The *New York Times* bestseller

AUTHOR OF THE SUBMISSIVE

THE Collar

A SUBMISSIVE NOVEL

Desperate to escape the pressures of her carefully controlled life, Dena Jenkins joined a BDSM club as a submissive. There she met brooding Dominant, Jeff, and they couldn't stay away from each other. But their blazing connection has proven difficult to maintain and resulted in a history they'd rather forget. To save their passion, Dena and Jeff will have to rediscover what it means to trust—and give themselves to each other completely...

HEADLINE
ETERNAL

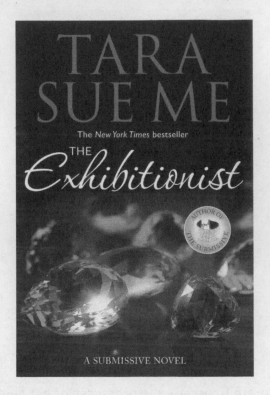

TARA SUE ME

The *New York Times* bestseller

THE Exhibitionist

A SUBMISSIVE NOVEL

She's ready for even more... When Abby West discovered her submissive desires, she felt like she was born anew. But lately, her Dominant husband hasn't been the demanding Master who once fulfilled her every passion. Their new BDSM group has invited Nathaniel to guide them to a new level, and he's promised to show them the way. Only this time, uncovering their sexual limits may also expose their relationship to more conflict than it can withstand...

HEADLINE ETERNAL

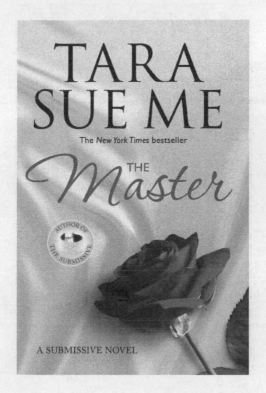

TARA
SUE ME

The *New York Times* bestseller

THE
Master

A SUBMISSIVE NOVEL

She's ready to try again... Sasha Blake is scarred from a
BDSM session gone wrong, but she can't deny how drawn
she is to a strong Master. Cole Johnson knows how to push
all of Sasha's buttons, but he's convinced she's not the
submissive he needs. When forbidden desires turn into
scorching action, Sasha and Cole come face-to-face with
their demons—and realize their deepening relationship
might be too dangerous to last...

HEADLINE
ETERNAL

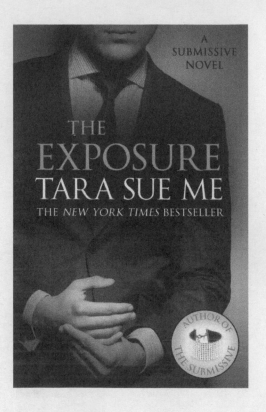

A
SUBMISSIVE
NOVEL

THE
EXPOSURE
TARA SUE ME
THE *NEW YORK TIMES* BESTSELLER

AUTHOR OF
THE SUBMISSIVE

She's ready for her close up... Meagan Bishop gave up modelling after an ill-fated tryst left her career and heart in shambles. When the sexy photographer responsible reappears with an offer to pose for a BDSM spread, she's determined to refuse—until an anonymous blackmailer entices her to accept. Now her body is again at the whim of the man who broke her heart, and she's finding his strong direction undeniably intriguing...

HEADLINE
ETERNAL

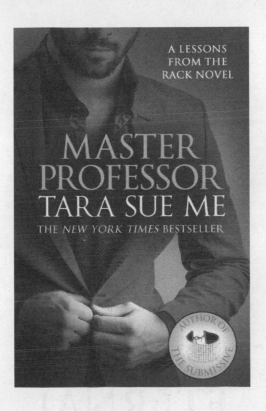

A LESSONS FROM THE RACK NOVEL

MASTER PROFESSOR

TARA SUE ME

THE *NEW YORK TIMES* BESTSELLER

AUTHOR OF THE SUBMISSIVE

Students are begging to be held after class...
Andie Lincoln is madly in love with Terrence Knight—her
childhood friend-turned-Hollywood's newest golden
boy. But he's a Dominant and wants her trained as a
submissive before he'll consider a relationship with
her. He enrolls her at the RACK Academy with strict
instructions for her teachers: do whatever you
need to, but *don't* take her virginity...

HEADLINE
ETERNAL

HEADLINE
ETERNAL

FIND YOUR HEART'S DESIRE...

VISIT OUR WEBSITE: www.headlineeternal.com
FIND US ON FACEBOOK: facebook.com/eternalromance
CONNECT WITH US ON TWITTER: @eternal_books
FOLLOW US ON INSTAGRAM: @headlineeternal
EMAIL US: eternalromance@headline.co.uk